ISLAND OF FOG BOOK II

Labyrinth
of Fire

Labyrinth of Fire

By Keith Robinson
Printed in the United States of America
First Edition: November 2009
This Edition: April 2013
ISBN-13 978-0-9843906-1-8

Visit www.UnearthlyTales.com

ISLAND OF FOG BOOK II

Labyrinth
of Fire

Keith Robinson

MEET THE SHAPESHIFTERS

In this story there are nine twelve-year-old children, each able to transform into a creature of myth and legend . . .

Hal Franklin *(dragon)* – His transformation began as a strange itchy rash on his arm. Then he developed green reptilian scales and accidentally breathed fire. Although terrifying in his dragon form, he has yet to master flight.

Robbie Strickland *(ogre)* – Odd bursts of strength led to a full-blown ogre transformation, with long powerful arms and a dimwitted toothy grin. Robbie's ogre form is three times his normal height, a mass of shaggy hair and muscle.

Abigail Porter *(faerie)* – She was among the first to demonstrate newfound shapeshifting abilities when she sprouted insect-like wings and buzzed around in Hal's garage one dark night. She has keen night vision.

Dewey Morgan *(centaur)* – This small, shy boy impressed everyone when he transformed into a sleek centaur. He restlessly clip-clops around in circles as though he can't control his hoofs.

Lauren Hunter *(harpy)* – With enormous owl-like wings, yellow eyes, and powerful talons for feet, this beautiful white-feathered human-creature soars and swoops like a bird of prey. (And Robbie has a crush on her.)

Fenton Bridges *(rare, unnamed lizard monster)* – He was considered a gargoyle when he clung to the side of the lighthouse and spat endless streams of water. In fact he's a rarity, black and reptilian with an impossibly long tail.

Darcy O'Tanner *(dryad)* – When she vanished during an attack in the woods, it turned out she had simply turned invisible, blending perfectly into the background. Dryads are only seen when they choose to be.

Emily Stanton *(naga)* – The last to change, and not a moment too soon, Emily became an underwater serpentine creature with no arms or legs, just a human head on a snake-like body. She can communicate with all serpents.

Thomas Patten *(manticore)* – The redheaded boy showed up on the island six years after his supposed death, having spent half his life in the form of a vicious, red-furred, blue-eyed lion creature with a scorpion's tail.

THE STORY SO FAR...

Hal and his friends grew up on a perpetually foggy island. Their parents had always been vague about what lay Out There, that unseen place beyond the fog, saying only that there was nothing left and that the island was their home. But the children, now twelve years old, were bored with life on the island . . . and more determined than ever to discover the truth.

So when Hal and Robbie ventured into Black Woods one Wednesday afternoon after school, they discovered that the fog came out of a hole in the ground. No wonder the woods were off-limits! The boys attempted to block the hole with branches and leaves, hoping to stop the fog and see a blue sky for the first time ever. But their efforts were thwarted by the appearance of a terrifying red-faced beast. Blocking the fog-hole would have to wait.

At school the next day, that annoying Abigail Porter insisted she had something important to tell Hal. He wasn't interested, but her passing comment about building a raft filled Hal with excitement. He and Robbie built the raft down by the docks and set out to sea, hoping to leave the fog behind and reach the mainland. They were astonished to find that the stories of a gigantic sea serpent were true, and again their attempts to discover the truth were thwarted.

Not surprisingly, Abigail had been spying on them and witnessed their failed attempt. Again she mentioned her Big Secret, and later that night she tapped on Hal's bedroom window and urged him to meet her in his garage. There she grew insect-like wings and buzzed around the garage. This, she told Hal, was what the adults were trying to keep under wraps. The children were freaks of nature, some kind of experiment, locked away on the island where they could be studied in private.

Abigail then asked Hal was *his* Big Secret was.

But Hal didn't believe any of it—didn't *want* to believe any of it. What scared him the most was that Abigail was right: he did indeed have something to hide, and it terrified him. A strange green rash on his arm had been itching like crazy and was now turning into a hard scaly skin. What on earth was happening to him? Abigail's theory was pure nonsense . . . wasn't it?

Yet some of his other friends were acting a little strange as well. Robbie, for example, had displayed sudden bursts of strength. Just for a second, Hal had even seen him grow tall and broad. He had put it down to his imagination at the time, but now he wasn't so sure.

And Fenton. On Sunday morning, Hal spotted the big boy leaning over the bridge and spitting a long, long stream of water from his mouth. Twice, and without stopping to refill. And why were Fenton's teeth growing into fangs, and his eyes glowing red? Something was definitely amiss.

Stranger still was the announcement that a stranger was arriving to take over class on Monday morning. A stranger? On the island? How could that be, if the world Out There was in ruins and everyone was long dead? Where was this stranger coming from?

Miss Simone swept into class on Monday morning, a striking blonde with blue eyes. She wore a long silk cloak over an oddly quaint, simple frock. She was barefoot, and smelled of the ocean. She started out fairly pleasant, telling the children of a disaster that had occurred Out There—a virus that had killed almost everyone on the planet. The fog, she said, kept the virus at bay, filtered the air. But the children didn't believe her. They witnessed her quick temper and saw through her fibs. Abigail was right: there *was* some sort of conspiracy, and the parents were in on it. Nobody was to be trusted.

When Miss Simone asked the children about any physical changes that might be occurring, such as Fenton's odd fangs, the children kept quiet. Hal was sure that some of them, himself included, had such secrets. But what about the others? What about Emily, Darcy, Lauren and Dewey? Were they *all* involved in this? Were they *all* freaks of nature?

Following Miss Simone when she left class seemed like a no-brainer. Hal, Robbie and Abigail trailed her through the fog all the way to the cliffs. Then she jumped off and was lost in the swirling water below. So the three children went to check out the fog-hole in nearby Black Woods, hoping the red-furred creature was not still around. But it was, and Robbie, who had gone on ahead, came across it first; he became an ogre and got in a few punches before blundering away. The red-furred creature turned out to be Thomas Patten, a boy thought to have been killed six years earlier when he fell from the cliff . . . and yet here he was, large as life, in the form of a lion-monster known as a manticore, with a deadly scorpion tail. It was at this point that Hal underwent his first full transformation—into a dragon.

With Abigail buzzing around like a faerie, Robbie shuffling home in ogre form, and Hal uncertain how to control his new dragon body, it was clear that they were more than just freaks. They were full-fledged *shapeshifters*, able to transform at will. At least, so Abigail said. Hal found it difficult to change at will, and certainly couldn't fly. He was a fire-breathing, flightless dragon.

What was Fenton turning into? And what about the others?

When Miss Simone returned the next day to question them further, the children clammed up and put on a united front. They would discover the truth once and for all, and that meant breaking into the lighthouse grounds, the one place on the island they had never explored.

But they had to be quick, because Fenton was leaving. His transformation had been witnessed by the adults, and now he and his parents were going on to "a better place" . . . or so Miss Simone said. The children, Fenton included, had better find out the truth before he was gone forever. Yet Fenton failed to meet them at the lighthouse, and the others proceeded without him.

With Robbie's ogre strength, breaking into the lighthouse was easy. They rushed up the winding stairs to the top of the structure . . . and emerged above the fog under a clear, blue sky, with the ocean spreading to the horizon in one direction and the mainland just a mile or two away in the other. The air was clear and fresh. The virus was a myth.

Lauren demonstrated her own transformation into a harpy. Although she could soar and swoop, her flight was somehow limited in altitude, perhaps dampened by the fog. Then the children found crates of magical clothing that altered in shape during transformations. After donning their new *smart clothes*, Dewey startled them all by turning into an impressive centaur. By now everyone had successfully changed except Emily and Darcy, both of whom remained genuinely confused and unaware of any physical abnormalities of their own.

Fenton reappeared, somehow clinging to the side of the lighthouse—a giant black lizard creature with an impossibly long tail and glowing red eyes. He spat water on them, and the children assumed he was a gargoyle.

The children now had one purpose in mind: to block the fog-hole. With their fearsome transformations the group was more than a match for Thomas the manticore! They set off immediately for Black Woods. There they ran into the red-furred monster once more, and during the altercation Darcy disappeared. When she finally reappeared, she did so literally. All the time they had been looking for her, she had lain unconscious on the ground before them, blending in so perfectly with the woods that she was completely invisible. She was, Abigail suggested, a forest-dwelling dryad.

After blocking the fog-hole, the children returned home to confront their parents and Miss Simone. One by one they demonstrated their shapeshifting abilities . . . all except Emily, who remained "ordinary." As the fog slowly lifted, Hal began to worry when Miss Simone mentioned that the young shapeshifters were immune to the virus. Did this mean the virus *was* still present in the air, and that the adults were at risk? When Hal admitted that the fog-hole had been blocked, the parents and Miss Simone began to panic. They had to get off the island! They had to cross into Miss Simone's world, *now!*

A mad rush to the lighthouse ensued, and the virus struck just as they got there. With adults collapsing on the rocks with swollen, blistering skin, choking for breath, it was up to Hal to do something. Miss Simone had mentioned a 'hole' to her world—a portal that lay just under the water a short distance out to sea. Hal had to find it.

But how would he get the unconscious adults to it?

Miss Simone, between gasping breaths, told him that Emily was the key. She could talk to the sea serpent!

Hal knew that simply urging Emily to transform would be useless, so he threw her into the ocean and dragged her underwater, hoping that her natural instincts would kick in. They did, and Emily became a human-headed snake. As one of the naga folk, she went off to find the giant serpent . . . and a ride to Miss Simone's world was assured.

* * *

Emerging by the side of a lake in a strange new world, goblins tended to the recovering adults while Miss Simone took the children to see the fog-machine. It had been running almost non-stop for thirteen years, clicking and whirring and rattling outside a cave. Halfway up the tunnel, she explained, was another of those holes; the fog belched through this hole into Black Woods.

One last task was required before the night was out. Hal was sent up the tunnel, back to the island, to capture Thomas the manticore. Once more he confronted the vicious monster, and managed to contain him.

Weary, the children returned to the banks of the lake and collapsed, sleeping under blankets beneath the clear moon and starry sky. When Hal awoke, it was morning.

And the sky was blue.

The journey continues . . .

66"There was a time," the teacher said, "when a fellow could easily cross from our Earth to the *other* Earth no matter where he was. Our twin worlds were riddled with holes, hundreds and thousands of them."

A boy of seven yelled, "You're making this up!"

Several other children, sitting cross-legged in the grass and basking in the sun, tittered and rolled their eyes.

The teacher smiled and absently stroked his beard. "Children, I'm not here to tell tall tales. I'm here to educate you. It's true—holes were commonplace. Once upon a time, our people stepped back and forth between the worlds with hardly a thought. Creatures too. In days gone by, you might have found a hole in the side of a mountain, and if you stepped through you'd find yourself in the middle of a forest. Many holes were underwater, useful only to fish and other sea creatures. Nobody knows how or why they opened, but make no mistake, children—our worlds were literally full of holes."

The children stared at each other in amazement.

"But . . . where are they all now?" asked a freckle-faced girl.

The teacher shrugged. "They closed, one by one. Today there are but a handful left. The holes have a limited lifespan, anywhere between a decade and a century, so it's just a matter of time before the few remaining holes close and we're forever sealed off from our twin Earth."

"Is that good or bad?" one of the children asked.

"That depends how you look at it," the teacher said. He looked carefully around his group. "You're aware of the arrival of the new shapeshifters, yes?"

There was a chorus of indignant cries. "Of *course* we are!" a yellow-haired boy shouted. "I saw them this morning!"

"Me too!" yelled another.

The teacher held up his hand. "All right, then. And you know how important these young people are, don't you?"

He paused, listening to the murmured responses.

The teacher sighed. "I see I need to clarify this. Like myself and my good friend Lady Simone, these young shapeshifters were brought across from the other world to fulfill their destinies as emissaries, to smooth relations between humans and all the other creatures of this world. Shapeshifters can communicate more directly with dragons, harpies, naga, centaurs, and so on."

The teacher plucked a long blade of grass from the soil and studied it absently. The sun moved behind a solitary cloud and a shadow passed over the group. "It's becoming increasingly difficult to live with certain other species. The nearby centaurs, for example, repeatedly complain that our mining operations are damaging the environment. Pah!" The teacher threw down the blade of grass with disgust. "Meanwhile, some time ago, certain dragons in the north started attacking the village of Louis and eating people. For some reason a wildebeest diet isn't good enough for them anymore."

There were several gasps.

"But creatures like centaurs and harpies speak the same language as humans," a bright-eyed boy at the front said. "Why do we need a shapeshifter to translate for *them*?"

The teacher gazed at the boy, pleased. "A very good question, my boy."

The boy glowed with pleasure.

"It's not just a case of understanding the language," the teacher said. "Using a shapeshifter to talk to dragons is one thing; dragons talk in grunts and roars, and we need a shapeshifter just to understand their words. Their translated language is rudimentary at best. But talking to a harpy, or a centaur, or an elf . . . Even though we understand their words perfectly, we don't fully understand their feelings or thought processes. Why do centaurs always seem so grumpy and uptight to us? Why do elves refuse to have anything to do with us, even though we try so hard to be friends? How is it that the naga always get the wrong end of the stick when we try to explain something to them?"

Nobody answered.

The teacher spread his hands. "The truth is, even though we understand their *words*, we don't understand their *hearts*. And why should we? After all, we're human and they're not. There's a world of difference between all the various species and cultures. Our shapeshifters help to bridge that gap. A shapeshifter can talk to the centaurs and get inside their heads and hearts, fully understand them, find out why they're so grumpy and uptight, actually *feel* that grumpiness and understand it . . . and then explain it to humans in a way we can relate to."

"So . . . it makes it easier to get along and be friends," the bright-eyed boy said. "But is it true that these new shapeshifters are the last of their kind?"

The teacher heaved a long sigh. "It does seem that way. Our air is different to that of the other world, the oxygen much richer, and shapeshifters cannot be bred here—at least not successfully. They must be born and raised in the other world. Only when the time is right can these young shapeshifters come across to our world."

A movement caught the teacher's eye. The sun moved out from behind the cloud, and he squinted. The silhouette of an unknown person was watching him from the shade of an enormous oak tree a few hundred feet away. He frowned, wondering who it was.

"I myself grew up in the other world," he continued after a moment, "in a private school, separated from normal society. My classmates and I led normal lives until we turned eight; then, one by one, we started to show signs of change. I wasn't the first, but I was the first to be brought into *this* world—too early, as it turned out, for my transformation wasn't complete. The scientists were impatient for me to start work, you see, and they felt that my transformation was as complete as possible. But I hadn't yet learned to fly."

The teacher pointed at a daisy growing in the grass. "You see the flower? Imagine it in its early stages, a closed bud, ready to open. As long as you leave it alone, it will open and show its colors. But if you pluck the flower and take it home, perhaps to watch it bud from the comfort of your bedroom, well . . . it will never happen. The flower will die."

"But *you* didn't die," a girl protested.

"No, but I might as well have," the teacher mumbled. "Having wings is not the same as actually *using* them. And simply flapping them up and down doesn't enable me to fly. Children, I'm a flightless winged creature—and yet others who look exactly the same as me can fly without effort. There's more to flying than just flapping wings, you see; perhaps even a touch of *magic*. Unfortunately, I doubt we'll ever fully understand."

The man sighed and climbed to his feet. He took a couple of steps backward, away from the children, and gave a tired smile. "I'm afraid the lesson is over for today, children. Run along back to the village, and I'll see you next week."

And, in a flash, the teacher transformed into a winged horse—huge and powerful, shiny black flanks, with equally black feathered wings that stretched and pumped up and down, causing strong drafts with each beat. His simple garments somehow rearranged themselves around his torso, becoming a single flowing cloak tied low around his neck and draping across his back. The horse reared onto its hind legs, whinnied long and hard, then galloped away, kicking up clods of grass and dirt as it went.

The wings, although impressive when spread, were now folded uselessly across its back.

Chapter One
A new world

For the first time in his life, Hal Franklin woke to a blue sky. He lay perfectly still, staring in wonder and soaking up the warmth of the morning sun. Finally he threw off his blanket and sat up.

The campfires had died out, leaving six small piles of ash and charred logs in a large, neat circle. Within this circle, bundled under thick blankets, lay sleeping men, women and children. Some of Hal's friends were missing. He saw Dewey, Darcy, Lauren, and Abigail, but Robbie was already up and about, along with Emily. Fenton was missing too, but then, he'd gone missing the previous evening, before any of them had settled down to sleep. Hal vaguely remembered waking in the night and seeing the big boy's glowing red eyes and giant black lizard body.

All the parents were present except Lauren's dad. Staring at his own parents, snoozing peacefully, Hal shuddered when he remembered the events of the previous evening, back on the island. He and his friends had been foolish enough to block the fog-hole in the middle of Black Woods. For the first time in thirteen years, the fog had stopped belching through. The air had gradually cleared and stars had begun to twinkle in the sky.

It had seemed like a brilliant idea at the time. No more fog across the island! Confused by years of secrecy, angry that nobody had told them why they were turning into monsters, the children had refused to believe that the fog was there to protect them from a deadly virus. "It filters the air," the mysterious Miss Simone had told them. It had seemed like just another of her lies.

By the time the adults found out that the precious fog-hole had been blocked, and the children realized their mistake, it was too late to do anything about it. What followed was a frantic nighttime rush to the lighthouse, led by Miss Simone, the stranger from another world. Being shapeshifters, the children were immune to the virus—but their parents were not. They had succumbed quickly with bloated, blotchy, sensitive skin, puffy lips, and swollen tongues, a massive allergic reaction that caused severe headaches, dizziness, restricted airways, unconsciousness . . .

Hal shuddered. It was hard to believe that he and his friends had nearly got the adults killed! Even Miss Simone, herself a shapeshifter, had passed out; being older, her immune system was not as strong as the children's.

The fog-hole was one of a few remaining portals that led to another world. The artificial fog had been pumping through nonstop for roughly thirteen years, a makeshift means to protect the inhabitants of the island. Another portal lay just off the coast of the lighthouse, below the surface of the ocean. It was through this portal, this hole, that Hal and his friends had arrived in Miss Simone's world—a place they called *Elsewhere*.

Hal struggled to his feet. He turned in a slow circle, taking in the breathtaking scenery of this new world. Sitting by the lakeside was Wrangler, Emily's faithful border collie, looking like he was about to jump in and swim. The lake certainly looked inviting. It was perfectly calm, dazzling in the sunlight, reflecting the mountains as though the surface of the water was a giant mirror. Having lived his life on a perpetually foggy island, Hal had never seen a horizon before.

A disturbance in the middle of the lake caused gentle waves and ripples. The hump of an enormous water beast appeared, a flash of white before it sank below the surface. The sea serpent that had dutifully guarded the island for so long now had a new home. Or perhaps this was where it had come from in the first place!

In the nearby forest, Hal saw no signs of life. He knew there were strange, short people living there—goblins—but the outpost, a small village of sorts, was set too far back into the woods to see from this distance.

"We're really here," a sleepy voice said.

Abigail Porter stared at Hal through half-closed eyes. Her cheeks looked even more freckled than usual in the sunlight. She sat up, pulled the red scrunchy from her hair, and absently began smoothing her dark brown tangles. Like Hal, she wore the strange, simple green garments that he liked to call *smart clothes*.

"We're really here," Hal agreed. "The sun is so bright! And look at the sky— not a cloud anywhere, and not a patch of fog. Can you smell the air? It's so . . . so *sweet*, somehow." He breathed in deeply, savoring it. But then he felt giddy and almost staggered.

Abigail laughed. "I'm sure that's probably the richer oxygen content that Miss Simone was going on about." She finished pulling her hair into a much tidier ponytail and secured it with the scrunchy. "Where is she?"

Hal shrugged.

Abigail jumped to her feet and went around kicking the other children awake, being careful to leave the adults alone. Hal checked on his mom and dad, and found them snoozing so soundly that he smiled and crept away. Their faces were still a little puffy, but the goblins had done a good job of treating them, and the fiery redness and swelling had eased.

Miss Simone returned shortly afterward, with Mr. Hunter, from the direction of the forest. Mr. Hunter made a beeline for his wife. He pulled back the blanket and peered at her arms and neck.

Miss Simone tossed her long, blond hair, then rolled her eyes at Hal as if she'd just been on the receiving end of a rebuttal. Hal opened his mouth to ask what was up, but Miss Simone shook her head. She sighed and went to check on the other adults, her long silky green cloak flowing.

Robbie Strickland came bounding around the lake just then, his face red. "The bugs!" he yelled. "They're *amazing*! The *size* of them—I've never seen anything like—"

"Shh!" Darcy O'Tanner looked cross as she climbed out from under her blanket. She pointed at the sleeping parents and put a finger to her lips.

Robbie reluctantly shut up. He was tall and skinny, and his smart clothes hung on his frame as though they were three sizes too big. Like Hal and all his other friends, Robbie appeared at first glance to be barefoot—but his smart clothes included flexible soles made from some kind of soft plastic that molded to fit the bottoms of his feet like melted wax.

Robbie hurried over to Hal and held aloft a loosely curled fist, as though he was about to bop Hal on the nose. He turned his palm upward and opened his fingers. In his hand was a plain old ladybug—but it was a giant, about half the size of his palm. Hal stared in amazement.

"This is nothing," Robbie said, awestruck. "I've seen—"

"It's not nothing," Abigail interrupted, peering closely. "It's a ladybug."

"No, I mean it's nothing compared to—"

"It's *not* nothing," Abigail said again. "I just said it's a ladybug. Don't you ever listen?"

"Yes, but it's nothing compared—"

"Robbie, I've told you twice already and I'll tell you again. Stop calling it *nothing*. It's clearly a very large ladybug, and if you think it's *nothing* then you must have a screw loose somewhere. *This* is nothing." Abigail held up the empty palm of her hand.

Robbie almost squashed the ladybug flat as he fought to control his temper. His face grew red. "Let me finish! I'm trying to tell you that—"

"She's teasing you, Robbie," Hal said, laughing. "Calm down before you turn into an ogre again, or that ladybug really will be nothing—just a squished mess."

"Children," Miss Simone said quietly, ushering them closer. She glanced around, and frowned. "Where's Emily? And Fenton?"

"No idea," Darcy said, brushing herself down.

"Nor me," Dewey said sleepily, still under his blanket.

"I think Emily said she was going for a swim," Lauren murmured, sitting up. She yawned. Lauren Hunter had a cute snub nose, and when she smiled tiny dimples appeared in her cheeks. Her brown, wavy hair was even messier than Abigail's, and she had dark circles under her eyes. Still, Robbie paid rapt attention when she spoke.

"Oh—that explains why Wrangler's sitting by the water," Hal said.

"And Fenton?" Miss Simone asked, her sharp blue eyes flicking from one child to another. "Did he ever revert to his human form?"

Nobody had seen him since last night, when the big boy had snuck off along the bank of the lake.

"That boy worries me," Miss Simone said, and sighed. "All right. Just so you know, I've arranged for—"

But just then a splash diverted her attention and she glanced toward the lake. Her eyebrows shot up. "Ah."

Emily emerged. At first glance she looked perfectly ordinary, as only her head showed above the surface. Her almost-black hair was plastered against her milk-white face as though someone had poured a pot of ink on her head. But as she rose out of the water, her pale neck kept on going until it was clear that she had no human shoulders or arms—just a long, flesh-colored, scaly body the thickness of what should have been her waist. She eased out of the water and fifteen feet of snake-body twisted through the grass, glistening in the sun.

Wrangler, her dog, whined and sank low in the grass, watching her warily.

As Emily coiled around the legs of the watching group, weaving in and out, Hal felt a slight bump as her cold, wet, scaly skin touched his ankle. Then Emily rose to eye level. "What's up, guys?" she said, grinning.

Hal had seen her change into this form the previous evening, when he'd dragged her underwater and practically drowned her. He still felt bad about that, but his tactic had worked—she'd changed into one of the *naga* folk and saved the day by communicating with the gigantic sea serpent, effectively hitching a lift into Elsewhere. Still, Hal had been a little preoccupied at the time, and failed to notice how her smart clothes had turned into a layer of skin. Hal's own clothes became a kind of belt around his throat when he transformed, but Emily's dress turned transparent and wrapped around her snake-body with only a few wrinkles here and there to give it away. It reminded Hal of an empty snakeskin he'd found once, where the snake had literally shucked it off and slithered away.

In one quick motion, Emily changed. Her second skin turned into a green, knee-length dress of thin, silky material. Her shoulders bulged, and arms peeled away from the trunk of her body. The single, thick mass where her legs should be shortened and split into two, shaping into proper human legs with the fluidity of melting butter. Emily Stanton smiled and snapped her heels together as if she'd just performed a magic conjuring trick.

Now Wrangler jumped up. Tail wagging, he ran to her and sat on her feet, looking up with doleful eyes.

"Poor boy," Emily said, stroking his head. "You just can't understand what's happening, can you? Yesterday we were all living on the island as normal human people—and now look at us. Monsters in a strange land!"

"I'm hungry," Darcy said. "Is there anywhere we can eat, Miss Simone?"

"As I was saying," Miss Simone said, "I've arranged for some wagons to take us to Carter."

"Who's Carter?" Dewey piped up. All the children were twelve years old, but Dewey was slight in build and low on self-esteem, and often seemed years younger. However, in recent days his alternate centaur form had boosted his confidence no end, somehow made him seem like a grown-up.

Miss Simone smiled. "Carter's not a *who*. Well, he was two hundred years ago—the first human settler in this region. Carter is the village that was named after him, about an hour's ride away from here. It's where you'll be living for the time being."

* * *

There wasn't much to do for the next half hour except sit by the lake and munch on leftover bread. Fenton still hadn't appeared, and they all called for him over and over. During this time, the adults began to wake, groaning. But despite their aches and pains, and sensitive skin, they seemed pleasantly surprised at how much better they felt. Whatever creams the goblins had given them to smear on their skin, and whatever curious medicines they'd administered, had done a good job.

The children watched with some amusement as Wrangler jumped as if bitten. He peered closely at something in the grass, then jumped again as something nipped his nose. When Emily went to see what it was, she squealed and ran away. Intrigued, Robbie went to look—and, with a broad grin, informed them that it was a millipede about a foot long. The other girls squealed and ran away too, even Abigail, who normally didn't care much about bugs.

Three wagons arrived at last, drawn by perfectly ordinary horses and not, as Hal half expected, unicorns or something equally fabulous. Grumpy goblins drove the wagons, and Hal recognized one of them—Gristletooth?—from the previous evening.

They all shouted one last time for Fenton, then gave up. But, as they were collecting blankets and tidying the makeshift camping area, the boy appeared suddenly. He rose from the long grass some way off and headed toward them. One by one, Hal and his friends, then Miss Simone, and then all the adults, turned to watch him.

Fenton Bridges was human again. Well, almost. His teeth were stuck in some kind of animal form—fangs that his lips had trouble concealing. Also, his eyes glowed red. But what caused everyone to stare was the fact that he wore only a discarded shirt tied around his midriff. He looked self-conscious, but also had a defiant look that said, "Yeah? What of it?"

Hal remembered that Fenton had been in his black lizard form since—well, since *before* they had discovered the smart clothes tucked away in crates at the lighthouse. Fenton had never grabbed any for himself, and must have left his normal clothes somewhere back on the island. Normal clothes didn't magically reappear, so now he had nothing to wear. Maybe that explained why he had not changed back until now!

"Whose shirt is that?" Fenton's mom asked, breaking the silence as her son approached. Her voice sounded hoarse.

"It's mine," Mr. Morgan, Dewey's dad, announced gruffly, absently brushing bits of grass off his white vest. "I lost it last night as we came through that . . . that underwater hole. It got ripped off as something big picked me up."

Robbie looked away, his face reddening. Hal remembered how his friend, in his huge ogre form, had plucked people out of the water and thrown them ashore. He also remembered the shirt he'd seen floating near the bank afterward, just after they'd all collapsed on the grass. Fenton must have grabbed it in the night.

"Good to see you back," Hal said, as the boy approached.

Fenton gave a shrug and nodded toward the wagons. "So we're off, then?"

Miss Simone patted him on the shoulder. "We'll find you some clothes when we get to the village. In the meantime, there are plenty of blankets. Climb aboard, everyone."

They set off for the village of Carter. All the children rode with Miss Simone, while the parents, climbing unsteadily to their feet, divided themselves between the other two wagons. It was a slow ride across long grass at first, but then they joined a dusty track and picked up speed. It was still bumpy in places, though, and the constant swaying and jolting began to get on Hal's nerves. If only they'd brought their bikes!

The thought of his bike, left behind on the island, gave Hal a stab of regret. Would he ever see it again? What about all the things he'd left in his room? He supposed there was no reason he couldn't go back to the island and fetch a few things; after all, the cows, horses, pigs, sheep and chickens would need to be brought into Elsewhere at some point, so why not a few odds and ends too?

When he mentioned this out loud, Miss Simone—seated at the front alongside Gristletooth—turned and spoke quietly so that her voice didn't carry to the other two wagons following behind.

"Mr. Hunter woke me early this morning and said he'd lain awake all night worrying. He demanded that we return to the island and bring the livestock across. Not in a few days as I'd planned, but *now*. He said the cows wouldn't milk themselves." Miss Simone shrugged. "Actually I didn't think the livestock was all that necessary. We have everything we need right here; why bring more animals across?"

"We can't just let them starve to death!" Lauren said, appalled. "And my poor cat, Biscuit, is still on the island too. I need him!"

Miss Simone raised her hands. "I know, I know. It's okay. The fog-machine is running again, at full speed, belching fog back up the tunnel to the island. I told Mr. Hunter that it may be a few days or a week before the air is safe again—the fog needs time to work, you see. But he insisted that he take a party of men and goblins to the island *today*, to begin the task of bringing the animals through the tunnel." She rolled her eyes. "So I need to dig out some biochemical suits. And find some fields to put all the animals in. My work is never done."

"Ugh!" Emily suddenly exclaimed. "Fenton! Close your mouth! You're dribbling water all over my foot."

Fenton's eyes glowed eerily red. He pulled a blanket around his chubby frame and opened his mouth to retort, but more water gushed out. It soaked the front of his blanket in seconds. He scowled and turned away.

It was a long journey, but the children couldn't get enough of the spectacular scenery, all rolling hills and mountains in the distance. The dirt track cut across fields and through occasional thickets, a well-traveled route even though Hal saw not a single soul all the way to the village.

They saw a flock of gigantic eagle-like birds that flew over a nearby forest, their wings beating in what appeared to be slow motion. "Rocs," Miss Simone said, hardly giving them a glance.

"Just how big *are* they?" Robbie asked, sounding awestruck.

"Big enough to carry this cart away," Miss Simone said airily.

A short time after, as they passed through a thick clump of woods on a steep hill, Darcy leaned forward and strained her eyes. A brilliant smile lit her face. "I think I saw a wood nymph! A shadow under the trees."

"I doubt that," Miss Simone said, with a laugh. "You don't see wood nymphs unless they want you to."

"This one wanted me to," Darcy said quietly, still smiling. "She waved."

Miss Simone gave her a curious look.

Hal wondered how a wood nymph could possibly know that Darcy was one of them, especially from a distance, when she was in normal human form. Maybe they had some kind of psychic connection.

"Carter is straight ahead," Miss Simone said eventually, gesturing to thin columns of smoke rising over the hill. Once they crested the hill and started down the other side, the village sprawled before them: hundreds of stone cottages with straw-thatched roofs, in the center of a bowl-shaped part of the countryside. It was another ten minutes before they arrived at the main gate. A lightweight fence of posts and thin horizontal branches surrounded the village, the suggestion of a perimeter rather than actual fortification. The gate was a large archway with a sign nailed across the top, with the word CARTER carved neatly into it. Goblin sentries sat at a nearby table playing some kind of crude board game. They rose and nodded as the wagons passed by.

Word had already spread that the newcomers—*the shapeshifters*—were arriving, and preparations had been made. The best empty cottages had been hurriedly dusted and cleaned, and sheets laundered. Shelves had been filled with food given by many willing neighbors. As the newcomers trundled into the village, the streets were lined with eager, cheering people. The welcome was tremendous, and Hal had never felt happier than at that moment—not to mention overwhelmed by the sheer number of people. Having been raised on an island with only a small handful of friends, he felt as though he were in a dream when he saw dozens of new children, together with their folks.

Hal and his friends jumped off the wagon and tore around the village in delight. Most of the people they met were friendly and welcoming, but a few had suspicious looks, some even surly. Hal shrugged it off; he guessed there would always be a few bad-tempered sourpusses even in a bright, cheerful, sunny place like Elsewhere.

Emily, Darcy and Lauren headed off in one direction, while Dewey stopped in amazement to talk to a centaur that had appeared. Hal would have liked to overhear the conversation, to see how Dewey got along with the enormous adult centaur, but Abigail got impatient and dragged him away. Robbie couldn't help exclaiming every time he saw a bug, and finally Hal and Abigail left him ogling a spider hanging in a giant web—a spider that was bigger than his hand.

Fenton remained in the wagon, huddled in his blanket, and was still there when Hal glanced back one last time before rounding a corner.

There was a lot to see. The dusty lanes between endless stone cottages were trampled as flat and hard as the paved roads back on the island. They curved around and branched off in so many directions that the village was like a maze. Hal and Abigail quickly got lost, but didn't care. The cottages fascinated them, with their stone walls, overhanging thatch, stout oak doors, and thick chimneys. The windows were small, with lead-lined glass panes; some stood open, and Hal smelled food cooking from within. Immediately he was hungry.

Hal stopped in an alleyway to stare up at the back of a cottage. A square metal tank was securely fixed to the roof, and a pipe ran down through the thatch. It was ugly, but only visible from the back. Other cottages had similar tanks. "See that?" he said. "Dad kept promising he'd install one of those, to collect rainwater. Would have saved my mom a lot of trouble, carrying buckets of water back from the stream every day."

"It would have been handy," Abigail agreed, nodding. "And it would have been nice to have the outhouse plumbed in too."

Hal looked around. "Speaking of outhouses . . . where *are* they?"

"Just go in the gutter," Abigail said, pointing to a channel by the roadside. "I'll turn my back and shield you, if you like."

"I don't need to *go*. I just wondered where they were."

They walked together, sticking mainly to the streets but peering down all the tight little alleys. People nodded to them as they passed, and others stopped in mid-conversation and turned to stare. As the morning wore on, the temperature soared and the sun's powerful rays began to irritate Hal's sensitive white skin. Abigail complained too, and they ended up seeking shade wherever they could, usually on doorsteps. A group of boys, two older than Hal and two younger, spotted them and started whispering to each other.

"You're the new people!" one of the older boys said, a tall thin person with a shock of curly black hair.

"That's us," Hal agreed.

"So what's it like, being freaks?" the boy said rudely.

The others tittered and nudged one another.

This sudden attack surprised Hal, and he felt hurt. But Abigail never missed a beat. "We wouldn't know," she retorted. "Please enlighten us."

Hal and Abigail moved on, ignoring the hoots and jeers that followed them. Hal's happiness ebbed. Now, wherever he looked, he thought he saw suspicion or scorn hidden behind the welcoming smiles. The old man clipping the hedge nodded and winked, but there was a hardness in his eyes. The woman standing on her doorstep beating a rug smiled and waved, but Hal was sure he spotted a look that said, "Go back to where you came from, freaks."

Chapter Two
Indoor plumbing

Tiring of their exploration, Hal and Abigail returned to the wagons, where they found goblins waiting. One gestured and pointed at Abigail, and she finally said, "Oh, you want me to *follow* you! Why didn't you say so? See you later, Hal!" and off she went with the goblin. Another approached Hal and nodded vaguely over his shoulder, then stomped away, glancing back to make sure Hal was following.

The goblin led Hal to his new home. It was a cottage like any other in this new world, but this was the first he had seen the inside of. It was cool and dark and he was grateful for the shade, though it took a moment for his eyes to adjust.

His parents were already there, and his mom greeted him with excitement. "They have indoor plumbing!" she exclaimed, her face red. "Toilets that actually flush! I can't believe it. I just can't believe it."

The cottage wasn't the grandest in the village, but it wasn't too shabby either. "It will do for now," Miss Simone had apparently assured his parents earlier. "We have some bigger, better houses for you all outside the village, surrounded by countryside . . . but they need to be cleaned up. For now, these empty cottages should be fine."

"And there's really a cottage for each of us?" Hal's dad had asked, amazed. "We're not putting anyone out?"

"They're spare," Miss Simone had assured him again.

Hal's mom relayed all this to him as she showed him around. "And look, here's the bathroom." Hal's eyes grew round at the sight of a large shiny bowl with a wooden seat. Above it hung a metal tank with a pull-chain. "You pull the chain when you're done, and all the waste is flushed away." She squeezed his arm. "Oh, Hal, it's just like the old days."

Hal chuckled. She appeared to have recovered from her virus attack the night before! Who would have guessed that a toilet would cheer her up so much?

He tried the toilet for the first time and jumped back in alarm when he pulled the chain and water gushed noisily down a pipe into the bowl. He looked, blinked, and smiled. The bowl was clean once more, and water was somehow trickling *up* another pipe into the metal water tank, refilling it as if by magic.

"Indoor plumbing," he mumbled with awe, twiddling one of the two small faucets that allowed water to splash into a sink. The water was clean and fresh, and he gratefully washed his hot face. Then, curious, he twiddled the other faucet. Why have two? More cold water gushed out—but then it suddenly turned warm. Hal's mouth dropped open. A second or two later he snatched his hand away as the water went from warm to hot.

He turned the faucet off and stared at it. Then he opened the cupboard doors under the sink, half expecting to find a small fire raging. But there was nothing to see except a couple of innocent-looking pipes.

He asked his mom about it, and she showed him the narrow door of a tiny closet. In the closet was a roughly welded cylindrical metal tank about Hal's height. The tank sat on a low wooden platform, and underneath was a single blackened rock that glowed orange from within. Peering at it closely, Hal found a couple of short, thin metal rods sticking out, and attached to the rods were wires that led into the base of the water tank.

Hal wanted to know how it worked, but his mom had already wandered off. Shaking his head, he gently closed the closet door and went to inspect his new bedroom.

It was small but cozy. In the wall directly opposite the door was the tiniest window he had ever seen, no more than a foot square. It had no curtains, but he guessed he wouldn't need any as the room was shrouded in darkness even in the bright sun. Lanterns hung everywhere, the bed was springy and soft, there was a small chest of drawers, and he had a small ornate desk and chair tucked into a corner. A fur-skin rug of some strange creature he didn't recognize sprawled on the bare floorboards. He knew that he would be perfectly happy with his new bedroom, and the smallness of the square window was oddly comforting; at least no one would be able to crawl in and attack him in his sleep!

He wasn't sure why these dark thoughts crept into his head, but he put it down to the ugly remarks those boys had made. Or perhaps the heat of the sun was working him over. He lay down on his bed for a while.

Then Miss Simone arrived. After a quick chat in the kitchen with Mr. and Mrs. Franklin, she knocked on Hal's open door and sidled into the bedroom. She'd discarded her cloak, as the day was warm. "Hal, I think it would be a good idea for you to go and see Orson. He's talking to the children at this very moment, in the meadow outside the north gate. He likes to roam free, so the children have to go out and see him for their weekly history lesson."

"Who's Orson?"

"My friend, the winged horse," Miss Simone said. She perched on the corner of the bed. "You remember I told you about him?"

Hal stared at her feet. Until now he'd thought she walked around barefoot all the time, but now he realized she wore the same smart shoes that he did. The waxy layer was coated with dust from the streets.

"Hal?"

He blinked. "Sorry. Uh . . . yeah, the winged horse. Right." He frowned. "Oh, you mean the one who can't fly."

"The one who can't fly," Miss Simone repeated. "I think you and he should talk. You share the same problem, and perhaps you can help each other. Orson is not the most cheerful person in the world. He's rather depressed, actually. Ashamed of himself. That's why he avoids the village."

Hal immediately thought of the scornful looks he saw—or imagined—on the faces of the villagers.

"So you'll go and see him?" Miss Simone asked, inclining her head to one side.

"Sure," Hal said, sitting up. "But do you have anything to keep the sun off?"

Miss Simone's eyebrows shot up. "Oh, you poor boy! I forgot. Yes, I'll get some sunblock for you. For *all* of you."

* * *

Hal stood in the shade of a huge oak tree, leaning against its trunk, watching from a distance as the teacher plucked a long blade of grass. The children watching him—about fifteen of them, all aged seven or eight—sat cross-legged in the long grass, their backs to Hal, listening with obvious fascination. Hal wished he could hear too, but was too far away and caught only tiny snatches of sentences here and there: ". . . increasingly difficult to live with certain other species . . . complain that our mining operations are damaging the environment . . ." Then there came a loud "Pah!" and the man's face creased with annoyance.

Hal watched the man, intrigued. So this was Miss Simone's friend, Orson, the winged horse. The one who couldn't fly. He was heavily bearded, and clothed in a long robe. He looked like a grumpy wizard, except that he was probably only about Miss Simone's age.

Exactly Simone's age, Hal corrected himself. Orson and Miss Simone had grown up together, gone to school together, transformed together.

Miss Simone had made it clear that a transformation wasn't complete until all aspects of the new body had been thoroughly explored, practiced, and experienced *before* crossing over into Elsewhere—and that included flight. Simply growing wings wasn't enough; they had to be *used*, and full flight obtained, before the transformation could be considered successful.

Unfortunately for Hal—and for Orson—flight had never been mastered, and now it was too late. Orson had been brought up in Hal's world too, raised from infancy to childhood in a secluded spot within a small tight-knit community. Orson and his eleven friends had begun to change around age eight, becoming all

16

manner of creatures including an elf, a mermaid, a gorgon, and others. Orson had become a winged horse. But whereas Miss Simone, as a mermaid, had practiced her swimming and learned how to breathe underwater, and the gorgon had used her vicious stare to turn rodents into stone, Orson had been too afraid—or perhaps too doubtful—to learn how to fly. He'd needed more time. So when he was brought across to Elsewhere, it was rather like taking bread out of the oven too early: the dough collapses, solidifies, and refuses to rise again no matter how many times it's put back in the kiln. Like half-baked bread, Orson was *unfinished*.

And so was Hal. He and his friends had arrived twenty years after Orson and Miss Simone had come to live in Elsewhere as shapeshifters. Hal's best friend Robbie, the ogre; little Dewey, the centaur; Darcy, the wood nymph; Emily, the human-headed, snake-bodied naga; Lauren, the snowy-white, yellow-eyed harpy; Fenton, the monstrous lizard-serpent that was so rare it had no name; Abigail, the faerie; and Hal, the fire-breathing dragon who was *supposed* to be able to fly.

Abigail should come and visit Orson too, Hal thought. *She can fly, but she can't shrink to the size of a real faerie, and her ears aren't pointed! She's like half-baked bread as well.*

Orson finished his talk and got up. He looked thoroughly miserable as he stepped back and glanced around at the young audience one last time. Then, in the blink of an eye, he transformed into a sleek black horse with shiny black wings. But instead of soaring into the air, he simply galloped away across the meadow, wings folded across his back.

Hal sighed. Was he destined to the same fate? To spend his life in Elsewhere as a fabulous winged creature that couldn't fly?

Too bad I didn't get to speak to the man, Hal thought. *Then again, what are we going to talk about? How we're both failures at being freaks?*

He watched the children run off back to the nearby village, then trudged after them, hunching his shoulders and keeping his face down. He could stand the heat, but direct sunshine on his bare white skin was uncomfortable. Even with a layer of moisturizing sunblock cream that Miss Simone had given him, his skin felt tingly and sore. His old island home in the other world already seemed like a distant memory. A lifetime of fog, and now blistering heat . . . It was a dramatic change for he and his pale-faced friends.

An enormous bug flew by, a dragonfly longer than his forearm. Its purple body glinted in the sun as it buzzed an erratic flight across the field. Hal had often put bits of cardboard in the spokes of his bike and ridden at speed along the road, and the dragonfly sounded much like that—only louder.

Dragonfly. A flying dragon of sorts. The irony wasn't wasted on him.

He returned home feeling a little dejected. He helped his dad move a table in the kitchen, then a chest of drawers, then waited while his mom pondered over the new arrangement. Then she ordered them to move the chest of drawers and table back again. "Make up your mind," his dad grumbled.

Despite the sun, Hal couldn't help venturing back outside after devouring a thick sandwich of cheese and crisp lettuce. It was mid-afternoon by now, and he wondered what his friends were doing. He suddenly felt very alone, even though people milled around and said hello to him. He needed Robbie and Abigail.

Instead he bumped into Lauren and her dad. "Lauren!" he said, barely able to contain his happiness at seeing a familiar face.

"Hi, Hal," she said, looking breathless. "Dad's arranging to bring the livestock and Biscuit to Elsewhere."

"The cows won't milk themselves," Mr. Hunter said grimly. He was looking much healthier than he had earlier that morning, although he still had several red patches on his face. "I've got Simone rustling up a whole load of those goblin fellows to help herd them back here."

"But—the virus—" Hal said. "You can't go back there until—"

"Got biosuits," Mr. Hunter said. "And the fog has been belching out onto the island since this morning. If we don't do something soon, those animals will start fighting for food."

Hal doubted that very much, but had to laugh at the image of cows and pigs getting into a fight, with chickens pecking on their heads, and sheep cheering them on, and horses standing by rolling their eyes with disgust.

"And you're really going to bring them through the fog-hole?" Hal asked doubtfully. He clearly remembered his own journey through the narrow tunnels when he'd gone to fetch Thomas the manticore, and couldn't imagine cows and horses making the same journey. Would the horses and cows fit?

"The alternative is to make them swim underwater," Mr. Hunter said. "Or leave them to die."

Hal watched Lauren and her dad go. It occurred to him that any of his friends could revisit the island without harm from the virus, and perhaps deal with the livestock—but they'd probably get trampled on by cows, or the horses would run off somewhere. Probably best to leave it to biosuited adults!

He spotted Dewey being picked on by the same four boys he'd run across earlier. They were trailing him, taunting him, and the tall thin boy occasionally stuck out his foot and caused Dewey to stumble.

Suddenly angry, Hal stormed over. "You'd better watch it," he said evenly, glaring at each of them in turn, "or you'll get kicked. Have you ever been kicked by a centaur before?"

The boys stopped dead, then glanced at each other and started crying "Oooh" in mock terror. "You're *so* scary," one of the smaller boys piped up. "Bet you wouldn't last a second in a fight with my brother." He looked proudly at the tall thin one with the mop of curly black hair. "Carl once punched an elf in the face and made him *bleed*."

Dewey pulled at Hal's sleeve. "Don't do anything rash," he whispered. "They're trying to provoke us into transforming. They're hoping we'll be seen as bullies—cowards who only fight when we're bigger and meaner than them."

Hal's annoyance died away as he realized Dewey was right. Of course Dewey couldn't just turn into a centaur and rear-kick them, any more than Hal could turn into a dragon and roast them alive! It was best to ignore the boys.

Still, he couldn't resist stepping up to the tall boy, Carl, and turning on his fiercest stare. The boy was taller and older, but Hal was unafraid. He put his face inches away, so they were nose to nose—or rather Hal's forehead to Carl's chin.

"I don't know what your problem is," he said quietly, "but get over it. We don't want any trouble."

Carl raised his eyebrows and grinned. "I don't have a problem. *You* do. You're one of those freak show *shapeshifters*. You're not even human. Nobody wants you here. Most people are just too scared to say so, so they *pretend* to like you. But you'll never be welcome here."

Hal stared at him, disconcerted by the hatred and scorn he heard in the boy's voice. Before he could think of a reply, Carl deliberately turned his back and strode away, followed closely by his entourage.

"Nice," Dewey muttered, watching them go. "If it's not Fenton picking on me, it's someone else."

Aware of several surreptitious looks from passers-by, Hal nudged his friend and suggested they move on. Dewey was headed toward the east side of the village, where his new home stood, and Hal, having nothing better to do, walked with him.

"How was your chat with the centaur?" Hal asked.

"It was all right," Dewey said with a shrug. "The centaur's name is Mack— well, something like that anyway. He said it using the back of his throat, like he was coughing up some spit, but I couldn't pronounce it that way, so I called him Mack instead. He fumed for a bit, then kind of accepted it. He's a bit grumpy."

"Did you change into a centaur?"

Dewey shook his head. "No, I didn't feel like I should, for some reason. I don't know why. People were looking, and . . . well, another time, maybe. But Mack knows who I am. He didn't *ask* me to change either, but kept looking at me through narrowed eyes as if wondering something."

Hal nodded. "I'm starting to get the impression that we're not as welcome as Miss Simone says we are. Maybe it's my imagination, though."

They cut through an alley so narrow that they almost had to turn sideways to squeeze between the cottages. Then they emerged onto the street again, a busy lane where carts were being pushed back and forth. Little clouds of dust kicked up as a red-faced man, sweating profusely, pushed a rickety, wooden wheelbarrow filled with what looked like rocks—but under the blackened sooty coating, they glowed orange from deep within. Hal stared, recognizing the rocks immediately; there was one under the water tank at his new home. He wondered if they were hot. They *looked* hot, like they'd been pulled straight from a fire.

"Dewey!" a woman's voice called. It was Mrs. Morgan, Dewey's mom, waving from a doorway a couple of cottages down. Dewey darted across the street, and Hal followed, weaving in and out of the milling people.

Miss Simone emerged in the doorway behind Mrs. Morgan. "Ah, there you are, Dewey. Come on in."

Mrs. Morgan waved both Dewey and Hal inside, and closed the door. The noise from the street cut off abruptly, and the darkness and silence of the cottage felt wonderful to Hal, who was beginning to get a headache from the heat and glare. He sank into a rocking chair in the combined living and dining room, and mopped his brow.

Miss Simone asked Dewey to sit, and Mrs. Morgan sat with him on the sofa. Mr. Morgan was out. *Probably helping Mr. Hunter and the others retrieve animals from the island*, Hal thought.

"Dewey," Miss Simone said, her hands clasped together, "I believe you're going to be the first to put your shapeshifting abilities to good use. There's a certain matter that the centaurs and humans cannot agree on."

"What matter?" Dewey asked, looking nervous.

"All will be explained," Miss Simone said grimly, "when I take you to meet the centaurs later this afternoon."

Chapter Three
The trouble with centaurs

Dewey looked nervous. Hal nudged him and whispered, "You'll be fine," but his words felt empty. The truth was that he didn't know anything of the sort, and felt equally nervous.

Hal had insisted he come along for moral support, and Miss Simone had agreed, saying it would be good experience. She had further suggested that all their other friends come along too. So it was a large group that left the village that late afternoon: Hal, Robbie, Abigail, Lauren, Darcy, Emily, Fenton, and of course Dewey, accompanied by Miss Simone and three of her trusty goblins. Leading the way was the dour centaur *Macq-kh* (as Miss Simone carefully spelled his name)— or simply Mack, which was a lot simpler. Speaking in gutturals was not easy, and it seemed that centaurs had a strange language of their own as well as stilted English.

Miss Simone had assured the children and their parents that this was not a dangerous mission by any means, just a discussion, however heated it might get. The goblins were coming along not for protection, as Hal had first assumed, but because they had a common interest in this important matter. Goblins and humans suited each other so well that they tended to agree on just about anything when it came to intertribal politics.

Mack was an imposing figure. Hal had never been comfortable around horses, but this one was half human and had an attitude, which somehow made him worse. He was very tall, towering over them exactly as a horse rider would. His hair was long and flowing, but not particularly clean; his upper torso seemed to be one big slab of sharply defined muscle, as if carved out of stone, and his teeth were fanged. Dewey had fangs too when in centaur form, only his were very slight in comparison. Centaurs seemed to attract flies, and they buzzed around Mack with a vengeance, causing him to absently swish his tail. The flies were extra large too, and Hal made sure to walk at a safe distance.

The group followed a well-beaten trail through a field into the nearby forest. Unlike the island's Black Woods, which was a tangled mess, this forest was spread out and oddly *tidy*, as though it was tended to on a regular basis. The grass was lush, and large random clumps of bluebells grew all over. The trees were taller than Hal had ever seen, and had bluish-gray leaves—but they shed a lot of loose bark and seeds, making the trail slippery. Still, with the sun's rays slanting through the leafy canopy and a strong sweet scent in the air, the forest seemed almost enchanted.

"I love forests," Emily said happily.

They came upon a series of small shelters made from stout tree limbs and thick straw thatch. It seemed that the centaurs didn't have homes as humans did; instead they used communal shelters and slept wherever they wanted, sharing almost everything they had.

Then the group entered an enormous shelter that seemed to go on forever, a massive framework of horizontal logs resting on the boughs of living trees, secured with rope and packed with thousands of smaller branches. Completely covered over with thatch, the roof was thick and impenetrable, but the framework allowed for large openings around the tree trunks. "For air circulation and light," Miss Simone explained, "as well as irrigation for the trees' roots."

Stunned by the scale of the construction, Hal and his friends walked slowly, open-mouthed, under the fifteen-foot-high roof. It was dry underfoot, and so trampled that no grass grew. Instead, the dirt floor was covered with scatterings of straw, rotting tree bark, and sawdust. "They cut a lot of wood," Miss Simone explained, winking. "They're very industrious, always building walls, adding smaller shelters here and there. As the trees grow, occasionally the framework needs adjustments, so that involves more sawing and trimming."

"How big *is* this place?" Emily whispered, awed.

Miss Simone shrugged. "It takes about fifteen minutes to walk from one end to the other. A few months ago, one of the trees in the middle fell in a storm. It demolished a good portion of the shelter, as you can imagine. But the centaurs simply rebuilt, using every scrap of the fallen tree and any other dead trees they could find. They try their best to use deadwood rather than cut down living trees, even if it means hauling logs across long distances. They pride themselves on being environmentally friendly wherever possible."

Fifteen minutes, Hal thought, staring ahead into the increasing darkness of the shelter. However, pools of light shone down here and there, and it didn't seem dark at all once inside. Deeper into the shelter, walls began to appear, as well as designated paths. It became like a small town, with centaurs clip-clopping around everywhere, going about their business.

And their business appeared to be chemistry. The full-height walls, made from woven branches and twigs and stuffed with straw, created private and semi-private sections. In some of these open-fronted rooms stood high benches, covered with small glass bottles containing liquid that bubbled and smoked.

"Who makes the bottles?" Robbie asked, fascinated, as Mack led them past.

"Why, the centaurs," Miss Simone said, sounding surprised. "Glass is easy to make. Blowing glass into the shape of bottles is child's play. They're also excellent metallurgists and blacksmiths, except that they don't have a great desire for armor and weaponry as our friends the goblins do." She winked at one of the goblins, who Hal again recognized as Gristletooth.

The goblin simply grunted.

"But centaurs are mostly interested in chemistry," Miss Simone continued, gesturing to the endless array of bottled potions. "It was the centaurs who developed the fog that protected your island against the virus for so long."

Hal developed a new respect for the surly looking centaurs.

Some of the centaurs wore clothes. Most of the males were bare-chested, but others wore light tunics or long, flowing robes. One or two wore bulky over-the-shoulder sashes of fur and leather. Hal was absently running these observations through his mind when he came across a female centaur—the first so far—and was taken aback by the difference in stature: slighter in build, fairer skin, far less hirsute, and much pointier ears. Hal saw other female centaurs shortly afterward, and he came to the conclusion that they were all a little fierce-looking and surly, as intimidating as the males. They tended to drape themselves with what looked like leftover patches of animal fur, stitched together into the rough shape of clothing but with large gaps around the sides. *Centaur fashion*, Hal guessed.

Mack finally stopped in what seemed to be a central meeting arena—a clearly defined circle about thirty feet across, with posts around its perimeter, each hung with an oil lantern. Hal glanced at the little flames, then up at the straw ceiling.

"Hence the buckets," Miss Simone said, pointing at many tin buckets dotted around the place. Each bucket was filled with water, which evidently dripped from gullies in the roof when it rained. "They're for emergencies. Occasionally a lamp falls and breaks, a fire starts . . . It doesn't happen often, but the centaurs are prepared. It wouldn't do for a fire to take hold here."

Hal stared at her. How on earth did she always seem to know what he was thinking? She couldn't *possibly* be a mind reader!

Miss Simone grinned at him. "I don't read minds, if that's what you're thinking. But I *can* read expressions quite well. It's obvious what you're thinking when you glance at the lanterns and then up at the thatch with a worried look on your face."

Abigail tittered quietly, and Hal scowled.

Centaurs began to appear, and a silence fell. Mack stood to one side of the arena and gestured for Dewey to step up. As he did so, a dozen or more centaurs moved forward, standing just beyond the perimeter until there was a wall of stern faces glaring down at the humans and goblins.

Dewey shuffled forward.

There was a silence. Finally Dewey turned to Miss Simone. "Should I—?"

"Do not speak yet," Mack snapped.

Miss Simone put her hand on Dewey's shoulder and winked at him. She leaned forward to whisper something in his ear, and he gave a slight nod.

Then there was the thud of centaur hoofs and the audience dutifully moved aside to allow passage for three majestic beasts. These were clearly centaur leaders, each adorned with shiny gold buckles and red velvet cloaks. The two in front stopped before Dewey, then parted, stepping sideways to allow the third a central position. The third centaur was old, with long, flowing gray hair and an equally gray beard that hung down to his navel. All centaurs had pointed ears, but this one had such *long* pointed ears that they drooped. He walked gingerly as if in some discomfort.

"All hail *Grah-tkh*," Mack said loudly, and Hal jumped as the shelter echoed with a booming "HAIL!" from every centaur present.

The leader—governor, king, emperor, or whatever his title might be—gave a long, deep bow, which the other centaurs respectfully mimicked. Then he spoke in a light, quavering voice. "Lady Simone, it is kind of you to make the journey here. My legs are not what they once were."

"The honor is ours, Khan," Miss Simone said, dipping her head.

The centaur then turned to the trio of goblins. "Chief Gristletooth, we are, as always, honored by your presence."

As the goblin made some grunting sounds, Hal glanced sideways at Robbie, who stood with feet and hands together, head bowed, as he did when being yelled at by his father. Hal couldn't help smirking; his friend was thoroughly cowed. Then again, so were all the others. Emily and Lauren were gripping each other's arms, and Darcy was huddled behind them. Fenton, not surprisingly, looked defiant—but even he had a cautious, darting glance that gave away his anxiety.

Poor Dewey must be quaking in his smart shoes! Hal thought.

Abigail seemed more curious than anything. Hal had the distinct feeling she was about to ask a rude question.

The centaur leader, the one with a name that sounded like Grahtik, looked Dewey up and down. "So *this* is the one who will liaise?" he asked, sounding doubtful. "Boy, perhaps now would be a good time to, *ahem* . . ."

Dewey shuffled his feet and glanced at Miss Simone. She nodded.

Then Dewey changed. In about one second flat he was a centaur, rearing up on hind legs while his front legs sprouted and kicked. His smart clothes vanished and became a light cape tied around his throat. He came down on all fours and spun around restlessly. Unlike all the other centaurs, Dewey was small and seemed to have trouble standing still. He clip-clopped in a small circle, as if his feet belonged to a real horse that he had no control over.

The centaurs merely stared at him, their faces impassive. But after a while, Grahtik gave a nod. "Very well, then. Let us discuss the situation at hand."

He cleared his throat and spoke directly to Dewey, earnestly and quietly, as if Miss Simone and Hal and all the others were no longer present.

"The mining has long been an issue for us. It is not the safety of your miners we are concerned about, nor the noise, nor even the fact that they are tunneling right beneath our feet. What concerns us—what has *always* concerned us—is the increasing injury to Mother Earth." He placed a hand on Dewey's young shoulder. "It is bad karma, my friend. We centaurs have long believed in respect for nature—and nature includes the rock below our feet. Keep digging, keep ripping out the guts of the earth, and we will surely be punished."

The leader raised his hands dramatically and looked skyward, although there was nothing to see but a thatched ceiling.

"Judgment is nigh upon us. We have not only felt the murmurs of discontent below the surface, but have heard the angry rumblings in the distant mountains, been touched by unnaturally warm midnight winds, and have tasted the bitterness in the water."

There was a grumble of agreement and several centaurs nodded.

"Oh, puh-*lease*," Miss Simone murmured through unmoving lips, so quietly that only Hal and his friends could have heard.

"It is only a matter of time before Mother Earth responds with *fury*," Grahtik continued, clenching his fists in a show of anguish, "as she has already done in the north." He glanced at Miss Simone, and then around at Hal and his friends. Hal felt a chill as the leader's sharp eyes bore into him for a second. "And so I, as khan of the centaurs, offer a suggestion."

Suggestion, Hal thought. *More like ultimatum, or even warning . . .*

Grahtik again placed his hand on Dewey's shoulder, as if the boy were his own son. "You, my boy, must convey to your human friends that the mining cease immediately."

Miss Simone almost exploded. "*What?*" She quickly grew red in the face, but after a deep breath said quietly, "Do you have *any idea* how much we rely on—"

"I know *exactly* how much," Grahtik interrupted quietly, giving Miss Simone a steely stare. "You humans abjectly refuse to give yourselves over to nature. Everything must be in haste; everything must be bigger and better. You are unable to deliver a message to neighboring human villages *by hand*—oh no, you have to use the power of Mother Earth to send *holograms*. You cannot rely on fire alone to heat your palaces—no, you have to go one better and install underfloor heating using the power of Mother Earth. You have heated water in even the humblest of abodes. Furthermore, it has come to my attention that some of your homes are now using Mother Earth for *lighting*!" Grahtik spat rudely on the floor. "There's *no need* for you to use these rocks, Lady Simone. There's *no need* for all these self-powered machines and technological devices. I implore you—go back to the old ways. Use *fire* for heat and light, *boil* your water in a pot, and for heaven's sake send messages via carrier pigeon as you used to! Return to the simpler life and stop gouging the lifeblood out of Mother Earth."

Gristletooth the goblin stamped a foot and stepped forward. "You're surely not suggesting," he said, in a deep, growling voice, "that we halt all progress and take a step backward!"

The goblin's fists were clenched and the muscles in his forearms bunched up tightly. For a moment Hal wondered if the goblin might lose his temper and punch the centaur on the snout—if he could reach up that high.

Miss Simone was red-faced. "We respect your views, Khan, but we cannot comply. The rocks in the earth are part of our lifestyle now. Besides, we're not the only village to use them, and you can't seriously be suggesting that—"

"No," Grahtik acknowledged, holding up a hand of gnarled fingers. "Unfortunately I have no jurisdiction or say in matters pertaining to other regions of the land, and neither do you, Lady Simone. I would, however, remind you that the village in the north has proved my point. The earthquakes and volcanic activity began right after the mining started—"

"Oh, please," Miss Simone said, shaking her head. "The village of Louis was founded in that region *because* of the volcanic activity and its natural hot springs, not the other way around."

Grahtik bristled with anger. "Activity *increased*, then. Nevertheless, we do have a treaty, my Lady, and I trust you will honor it."

Miss Simone bowed deeply, although Hal suspected it was not so much out of respect but because she was counting to ten.

"Our treaty is very clear," she agreed stiffly, "and after fighting so hard, for so long, to bring shapeshifters into our world, it would be madness for me not to act in compliance with it." She paused. "As per the treaty, we will allow our resident shapeshifter, Dewey Morgan, to ponder your, uh, *suggestion*, for a number of days. He shall give us the benefit of his wisdom after that time."

"And he will spend time as a centaur, yes?" the khan urged. "He cannot be expected to think on our behalf while in human form, mixing with humans."

Dewey's head shot around to Miss Simone. He looked wide-eyed.

Miss Simone nodded. "Of course. I will see to it."

The centaur grunted. "We have our disagreements, Lady Simone, but I do trust you. And so you will honor his decision if he agrees that it is best for the miners to cease their work?" The leader centaur's long beard positively quivered with anticipation.

"I will," Miss Simone said heavily. "But *you* will honor his decision if he decides that mining is to continue. Your argument about harming nature is, after all, entirely unfounded. It is simply your superstitions getting in the way here."

Grahtik bristled again, growing red in the face. "The way I see it, it is your human *greed* that's in question here. Why should you be allowed to plunder from nature simply to make your lives a little more *luxurious*?" He spat out the last word with disgust. "Where does it end? First the rocks—and when you've drained the last vestiges of energy from the rocks, and the earth has responded with fury and pulled many of us into its depths—what then?"

Miss Simone shook her head. Hal could see her grinding her teeth. "I do believe you're a hypocrite, *Grah-tkh*," she said, clicking the back of her throat and pronouncing his name perfectly. "All of us, centaurs too, make use of the earth's resources. Humans just like to reach a little farther. We're more ambitious. We—"

"And one day, Lady Simone, your ambition will be your downfall," the centaur growled. "We all know about the *other world*." For a moment, the centaur glared at Hal and his friends. "The human race, left alone to its ambition . . . Inevitably they will cause their own destruction sooner or later. By forbidding the mining of precious energy from the earth, I'm not only saving our land, but *saving you from yourselves*."

A long silence fell. Hal could see that Miss Simone and the centaur leader were on the very edge of restraint, and all around the circle, centaurs stood with stone-faced determination. Yet despite the tension, it was nothing more than a heated debate—exactly as Miss Simone had forewarned.

Abruptly, the meeting ended. Grahtik bowed, and even managed a tight smile. "Always a pleasure to see you, Lady Simone. May the gods favor you."

With that he turned, pulled his velvet cloak around him, and hobbled away, followed closely by his consorts. His departure eased the tension immediately, and the shelter was suddenly filled with murmurs, rising quickly in volume and then fading as many of the centaurs left to go about their business.

The centaur named Mack looked bemused as he trotted over to Dewey. "I expect you're feeling a little pressure, son."

"A little pressure!" Dewey exploded. His restlessness increased. "Miss Simone, I can't decide something like this! I'm just a twelve-year-old boy—I only arrived here yesterday—I haven't even finished school—"

"Calm yourself," Miss Simone said soothingly. "You're the only person who can clearly see the same situation from both sides. You may not think it just now, but you'll see. We ask only for your honest appraisal."

"But whatever I say—" Dewey protested. "I mean, I'll be responsible for—"

"The only responsibility you hold, son," Mack said, "is to ensure that your opinions are honest and unbiased. You've lived as a human all your life, so it could be argued that you're already biased. However, studies have shown that shapeshifters do tend to become very quickly immersed in their alter-forms. We have confidence in you to make your decision objectively."

Abigail suddenly nudged Hal's arm and whispered, "Come with me."

"What? Where to?"

But Abigail was pulling at his arm, so he made a face at Robbie and gestured for him to come too. Robbie looked back at Miss Simone and the centaur Mack, but they were engrossed in conversation with Dewey.

"At least *that* centaur seems a bit more talkative now," Robbie muttered. "They're a sour lot, aren't they?"

They headed back the way they had come. "I just wanted to see one of those potions they were working on," Abigail said. "It looked like fog."

"Well, they did invent the stuff," Robbie muttered. "What's the big deal?"

"I'm just curious, that's all."

They came to one of the sectioned areas where a centaur was working at a bench. The bench was way too high for use by humans; Hal felt like a dwarf when stood next to it. But even from their low angle they could see that the bench was filled with bubbling potions. One in particular was a large glass pot filled halfway with a colorless liquid. Rising from the surface of the liquid was a smoky substance—*fog*. It wisped out of the bottle's neck and flowed slowly down the side, spreading across the bench.

A centaur wearing a protective apron over a somewhat raggedy tunic, and skintight gloves that came almost up to his elbows, was bent over what looked like a crude microscope. He seemed unaware that he was being watched. There was a gentle murmuring of voices throughout the shelter, together with the constant sound of heavy footfalls, so it wasn't surprising the centaur hadn't heard Hal and his friends approach.

"What are we *doing* here?" Hal whispered to Abigail.

"Just looking," she whispered back. "For all their talk about not harming the land and keeping life simple, they sure do a lot of messing around with potions. I'm surprised the centaurs bothered developing the fog for our island, considering how distasteful they are of us."

"That's cool," Robbie said. "A bottle of fog! What do you suppose they're doing with it?"

The centaur straightened up, dipped a feathered pen in a pot of ink, and made a note on a thick sheet of paper—or, more correctly, a paper-thin slice of wood that looked as though it had been cut straight from a log and trimmed to a rough square shape. He slowly turned, writing on the stiff tablet with a look of intense concentration.

Then he saw Hal, Robbie and Abigail staring at him and jumped back with a start, dropping the tablet with a soft *phut!* sound on the straw-covered floor.

"What are you doing here?" the centaur said, glancing beyond them over their shoulders. "Where's Lady Simone?"

"She's just coming," Abigail said, smiling. "We were just *fascinated* with your work and had to get a closer look. Is that fog?"

The centaur looked at the bottle of fog, and for a moment seemed unsure how to answer. He had a gentle face, and his forehead was furrowed in thoughtfulness rather than typical centaur surliness. He gave a shrug and nodded. "It is fog, yes. And this—" He pointed at something on the bench the children couldn't see from where they stood. "This is a sample of the virus. It's just a few particles locked inside a liquid agent."

Hal suddenly felt nervous. "You have a sample of the virus? Here?"

"Of course. How do you think we developed the fog without having samples of the virus to work with?" The centaur's eyes suddenly gleamed, and Hal recognized the same geeky expression that Robbie often wore when discovering new bugs. "It doesn't start out as a virus, you know. Viruses die within hours without hosts. This one begins as tiny spores, lighter than air, blowing around on the wind, landing, settling like a fine coat of dust, then blowing around again, waiting for something living that sweats, thus beginning a chemical reaction that—" He broke off. "Well, perhaps you don't want to know the details."

"Sweats like a human, you mean?" Hal said.

"Sweats like *any* mammal," the centaur said, with a shrug. "But only humans are adversely affected by the spores. What's particularly interesting is that when the spores are activated and the victim develops symptoms—most notably in the form of multiple and severe allergic reactions—sometimes the victim's immune system is strong enough to overcome it. But then a mutation occurs and a true viral infection is born, one that passes from human to human, and sometimes to other mammals. Meanwhile, the original spores continue to blow around the world. It's fascinating."

"So what are you trying to do now?" Abigail asked, gesturing toward the unseen virus sample on the bench.

The centaur looked uncertain again. "Didn't you say Lady Simone was supposed to be here? I'm really not at liberty to discuss—"

"Are you trying to find a cure?" Abigail persisted.

The centaur thought for a moment. "Each virus is unique, although with similar symptoms, rather like a common cold—so there really is no such thing as a one-for-all cure. The best we can do is neutralize the spores by using the fog to prevent the initial chemical reaction from occurring. But it doesn't *kill* the spores." The centaur pointed to the floor. "Like the wood chips and straw under our hoofs. During hot, dry periods there's always a danger that a torch or lantern might fall and start a fire, so we regularly moisten the floor to make it less combustible. But in the absence of moisture, the wood chips and straw dry out and the threat of fire returns. Similarly, remove the fog and the dormant spores become viable again."

"What's your name?" Hal asked, suddenly curious. "You're the first centaur that hasn't treated us like we're something nasty."

"*Fle-khk*," the centaur said from the back of his throat, and Hal felt sure he felt a gob of spit land on his cheek.

"Fleck?" Robbie repeated.

"No, *Fle-khk*."

Robbie nodded sagely. "Fleck, right."

"Nice to meet you, Fleck," Abigail said, holding out her hand.

The centaur looked at her hand as though it was something poisonous, but after a moment reached out and grasped it gently.

Then Miss Simone's voice carried through the shelter. "*There* you are. You shouldn't run off on your own like that." She marched toward them with three goblins and five children in tow. Dewey was back in his human form, looking thoroughly relieved.

"We didn't run," Abigail said. "Just sort of ambled."

"We were talking to Fleck," Hal said.

"You mean *Fle-khk*," Miss Simone retorted sharply. She took the centaur aside and spoke quietly to him, out of earshot, and Hal sensed she was making apologies for the disturbance. Then she turned and clapped her hands. "Come along, children. Let's leave the centaurs to their work."

Chapter Four
Meeting in the village hall

Dewey was the center of attention when the group returned to Carter. But Miss Simone steered him off for some private words about his mission. "I'll need to talk to all of you later," she warned, before they drifted away. "After dark, head for the village hall when you hear the bells ringing."

The children parted, heading off to their new homes. "See you later," Abigail said, waving madly at Hal and Robbie before vanishing around a corner.

"Like your new house?" Hal asked Robbie.

"It's okay," Robbie said, shrugging. "Pretty nice. My room's small, though. I don't have room for any bug jars, especially as the bugs here are so big."

Hal laughed. "You don't want to take *these* bugs home, do you?"

Robbie suddenly seemed animated. His face glowed and his eyes shone, just like Fleck's had earlier. "Hal, this place is *awesome*. That spider we saw—it was massive. I swear I could see my reflection in its ocelli, and the fangs are—"

"In its *what* now?" Hal said, already lost.

"Central eyes," Robbie said impatiently. "Oh, and that foot-long millipede. Hal, this place—"

But Hal only half listened to his friend rambling on. He would have been happier if Elsewhere had normal-sized bugs.

The evening descended, and the village began to wind down. The heat of the day lifted and a cool breeze crept in. *The temperature changes quickly around here*, Hal thought with a sudden shiver, fingering his thin clothing. As the sun sank lower on the horizon, Hal and Robbie decided that it was probably time to head home.

"When are these bells supposed to ring?" Hal wondered aloud. Something bit him on the neck, and he slapped at it. When he looked, he was disgusted to find a squashed butterfly in his hand.

Robbie looked carefully at it. "That's the same one I saw back on the island!"

"The *exact* same one?" Hal teased.

But Robbie missed the joke. "No, but the same kind. Remember? Near the fog-hole? It's a blood-sucking butterfly. I *wondered* where it had come from—and now I know. Through the fog-hole, just like Thomas."

The reminder of Thomas made Hal wonder where Miss Simone and the goblins had taken the boy. Like Hal and his friends, Thomas had grown up on the island. But unlike them, he had transformed much earlier in life, at age six, and the change had been a tremendous shock. He'd run blindly through Black Woods and ended up falling off the cliff, supposedly to his death on vicious rocks. His parents had of course been devastated, and left the island shortly afterward. But instead of returning to the mainland as the children had thought, Miss Simone had secreted them through one of the holes to Elsewhere, explaining that Thomas was not dead after all, but on the run in his alter-form, a manticore.

Hal shuddered at the thought of the manticore, a large, lion-like creature with red fur, human face, blue eyes, and three rows of teeth. Worse, the manticore's giant scorpion tail ended with a ball of poison-tipped quills, and a large, deadly black stinger.

Capturing him alive had been risky, but now that he was under lock and key somewhere, Miss Simone could work to undo his natural manticore urges and bring him back to humanity. Thomas's parents would be happy to see him again, but not if their son remained a snarling, cold-blooded killer.

Hal decided that he'd had his fill of manticores. The problem was that Thomas was just *one* of them; there were many more across the land.

"Well, I'm starving," Hal said to Robbie, shaking himself back to the present, "so I suppose we'd better get home for dinner before we're due at the village hall—wherever that is."

They separated, and Hal wondered then exactly where his friend lived. They had grown up on the island just across the street from one another, but this village was crowded and unfamiliar. It was going to be difficult remembering routes and directions in such a busy place.

Hal took a wrong turn but soon ended up where he was supposed to be. The village was confusing, but small. His new home had a rust-colored door with a large wrought-iron knocker shaped like a goblin's head. Hal smiled. Did goblin homes have *human* head door knockers? For that matter, where *did* the goblins live? Presumably somewhere in the village, but somehow Hal couldn't imagine them in quaint, cozy cottages with thatched roofs.

He pondered this as he walked into his new kitchen, where his mom was preparing some dinner. She was sniffing at an iron pot containing some kind of stew. After a moment she returned the pot to the griddle that stood over the fire in the hearth. "Just in time," she said, giving Hal a smile. Like her son, Mrs. Franklin was sandy-haired and short, with green eyes. She had gray around her temples, and worry lines across her forehead.

"Dad not back yet?"

Hal's mom shook her head. "He won't be until the morning," she said quietly. "I do hope he doesn't get his biosuit snagged on a rock or branch. But maybe the fog is doing its job already . . ."

"And they're really bringing the animals through the fog-hole?" Hal asked.

His mom nodded. "They're going to try. All the men have gone, along with a bunch of those goblins. It'll take all night to organize things and herd all those cows, sheep, horses, pigs—"

She broke off and went to sit down at the table.

"Are you okay?" Hal asked, sitting down with her.

"I just worry. There's always *something* to worry about." Mrs. Franklin closed her eyes. "First we couldn't have children, all those years ago. Then we met Miss Simone and everything seemed like it was going to work out—a life on a private island with everything taken care of. Then the virus came and everyone we knew on the mainland was lost. When the fog made the air safe over the island, it wasn't exactly a relief—more like a punishment. I remember that many of us half hoped the virus would work its way through the fog and put us out of our misery."

"Mom," Hal said awkwardly.

She patted his hand and forced a smile. "Once we realized we were here to stay, the next six years were fine. But then—"

"Thomas," Hal said quietly.

"Thomas, yes. That was awful. It made us realize something, too. We all knew that you children were special. We knew you'd change eventually, become these fantastic creatures . . . but I don't think we truly believed it would happen until it happened to Thomas. Despite what Miss Simone had shown us of her world, things that just astounded us, we couldn't bring ourselves to believe that our children would *actually become shapeshifters*. And once we knew what had happened to Thomas, we realized just how real it all was, and that one day . . ."

"One day?" Hal prompted, getting a bad feeling.

"One day, our children would have to go off on dangerous missions."

Hal felt a moment of relief. "Oh, *that*! Mom, the centaurs were okay. A bit grouchy, but there was never any danger."

His mom looked at him for a long moment. "Dewey is fortunate," she said at last. "He's a centaur. Robbie's an ogre; ogres are harmless and stupid, not exactly a threat. Abigail is a faerie—hardly any danger from *her* kind either. Darcy's the same. I don't even know why they need a wood nymph shapeshifter, but I'm told there's a good reason." She patted Hal's hand. "But some of you are not so fortunate. Poor Lauren has to deal with the harpies, who are spiteful and vicious. Emily has to deal with the naga, who are irritable and contemptuous—a bit like the centaurs, only worse."

Hal was impressed by his mom's knowledge of Elsewhere's inhabitants.

"Fenton is a rare beast," she continued, "but I hear he's not likely to be in any danger with others of his kind. You, on the other hand . . . Hal, you're a *dragon.*

33

I've never seen one, of course—apart from you—but I hear they're terrible creatures, perhaps the most dangerous threat to the land. And . . . and it's *my son* that has to deal with them."

Hal nodded. "I know, Mom. It sucks. But hey, maybe it'll be years before I meet one. Maybe—"

He stopped, seeing his mom's expression. She was shaking her head slowly. "Mom?"

"Miss Simone wants to see you in the village hall tonight."

"I know."

"She's sending you on a mission. *All* of you, but you in particular, Hal. It's a mission that involves dragons. You'll be gone for a few days or more."

Hal's mouth dropped open. "When?"

"You're leaving tomorrow afternoon," Mrs. Franklin said, licking her lips. She swallowed. "You're supposed to go to the village in the north, where the dragons have been causing a lot of trouble. By trouble, I mean . . . well, they've been attacking the village and . . . *eating* people."

* * *

When the bells rang, Hal set off for the village hall with a feeling of dread. His mom had told him where to find it, and he followed her directions closely. He was amazed he hadn't found the village hall earlier, but when he arrived he realized why—it was jammed between a bunch of cottages, and the entrance was a narrow alley that opened out into a courtyard of neatly cropped grass. The hall stood in the center of the clearing, surrounded on all sides by the backs of cottages.

It was a simple stone building with a thatched roof and a short tower at the back. It was from this tower that the bells had chimed; Hal saw a teenage boy emerge from a small door at the base of the tower and head off home.

Inside the hall was room for perhaps a hundred people. Hal understood there were more than three hundred human residents in the village, but the hall was very old and perhaps had been built with a smaller population in mind.

Chairs lined the hall, facing the front where a raised platform reminded Hal of the school plays they'd held from time to time in days gone by—not in the old schoolhouse, but in a community hall on the island. They hadn't used that in years, though. Probably never would again either!

Gristletooth was already present, sitting in a chair at the front. Alongside him sat Emily, trying to strike up conversation but not getting very far; with every question she asked, the goblin sank deeper into the chair.

Darcy and Lauren were also present. As Hal wandered over, Robbie came rushing in, looking breathless. "Have you heard?"

Hal nodded.

Robbie stared at him. "Aren't you worried?"

"What's to worry about? A bunch of dragons?" Hal tried to laugh, but his throat felt dry.

Abigail arrived soon after wearing a heavy cloak over her thin smart clothes. It was only then Hal realized he was shivering. His smart clothes had some kind of built-in warming magic, but still, it was cold outside! Robbie, as usual, seemed unaffected by the cold, but Emily, Darcy and Lauren also wore cloaks. Perhaps there was some secret village cloak closet that only girls knew about.

Then Dewey and Fenton arrived. Hal was surprised to see them together. For years Fenton had bullied Dewey, even in the last few days on the island—and now here they were, seemingly the best of friends.

Miss Simone swept into the hall as everyone was getting seated. Her cloak billowed as she threw it over a chair. Then she dragged another chair out of the first row and turned it to face Gristletooth and the children.

"You're going on a mission," she said without preamble. "Tomorrow afternoon. Your fathers should be back before you leave, so you can say goodbye. I've made arrangements for travel—one of Gristletooth's soldiers will be taking you on his wagon. It's a long way to Louis, the village in the north. It'll take about eleven hours to get there, so if you leave by noon tomorrow you should be there sometime before midnight."

"We can have picnics on the way!" Emily said brightly.

Miss Simone ignored her. "Hal and Lauren, this primarily concerns you both, but your friends will be going for moral support, and also because it will be extremely useful for them to meet their own kind."

"*Our* kind?" Emily asked, leaning forward. "Oh, how exciting!"

"This is *not* exciting, Emily," Miss Simone said. "It's very dangerous, at least for some of you. But, nevertheless, a few of you will be able to meet your own kind along the way. For instance, there are ogres everywhere so Robbie's bound to spot some. Abigail may come across a patch of faeries. That sort of thing."

"And me?" Emily persisted, barely able to contain her excitement.

"Possibly," Miss Simone said. "Unfortunately, Lauren will have to meet the harpies, and I would consider hers a secondary mission, since it's not just dragons attacking the village, but harpies too."

Hal looked sideways at Lauren. She looked grim.

Fenton's chair creaked as he leaned forward. "What about me?"

Miss Simone shook her head. "I doubt very much that you'll meet your kind, Fenton. There are only two others like you, and we *know* where they are—and they're not on your route." Then she looked long and hard at Dewey. "It's very important that *you* go on this journey, Dewey, as it was the village of Louis that discovered the rocks we're mining. We call them geo-rocks, but it's a bit of a misnomer; they just happened to be discovered at a geothermal mining site . . ."

Miss Simone looked around at all the puzzled faces.

"Well, never mind about that for now," she said, with a sigh. "The point is, Dewey, that you'll see how useful the rocks are to us—but you'll also see why the centaurs are so concerned. Understood?"

Dewey nodded and murmured, "Understood."

Miss Simone looked at Hal. "It would be beneficial if, along the way, you managed to learn how to fly. I fear the dragons will not take you very seriously if you turn up on foot. Lack of flight would be seen as a great weakness."

Abigail, seated next to Hal, nudged his arm. "Don't worry—I can ride on your back. I'll hold on to your reins and do all the flying myself."

Incredulous, Hal turned to argue that she was barely able to lift him off the ground in his *human* form, never mind his dragon form. But then he saw the twinkle in her eye. "Yeah, maybe we can fool them," he said with a grin. "You fly for us both, and I'll make a lot of roaring noises."

Abigail giggled.

But Miss Simone frowned. "I doubt that will work. In fact—"

"They're *kidding*," Robbie said. "Miss Simone, tell us about the dragons. Where do they live? What's Hal supposed to do when he finds them?"

Miss Simone got up and began pacing with her hands behind her back. She did that a lot, Hal thought, remembering how she had paced back and forth the first time she had arrived in the classroom on the island. It was hard to believe that had been only a few days ago . . . and now here he was, barely settling into his new home and the woman already had a dangerous mission for him.

"The dragons," Miss Simone said slowly, "live in various parts of the land. There are some up in the mountains, and some in forests. But the ones we're concerned with are those that live in the Labyrinth of Fire."

"The Labyrinth of Fire!" Darcy and Emily echoed at the same time.

"There's a chasm that stretches north-south, next to a volcano. The volcano's been there forever, oozing lava and rumbling from time to time, occasionally blowing its top. There are endless tunnels around the volcano. The whole area is nothing but layers of cooled lava tube formations."

"What are those?" Lauren asked.

Miss Simone waved her hand dismissively. "You'll find out more when you get there. Anyway, the lava runs down these tunnels. The dragons love it."

"They love the *lava*?" Hal said, puzzled. "Surely the lava would—"

"Burn them, yes," Miss Simone agreed. "Obviously they avoid the *active* tunnels. But there are many more tunnels that are safe, where lava no longer runs. Those are warm and dry. It's like one big heating system under the ground."

She took a seat once more.

"Several years ago an earthquake caused the ground to split apart, creating a chasm two hundred feet wide. It almost cut the labyrinth in half. Many of the tunnels now open on the new cliff face, looking down into the chasm. Since that happened, the dragon population has increased. It's like the chasm is the ideal dragon home."

"Oh, it sounds *wonderful*," Darcy said dryly.

"Anyway," Miss Simone said, "now the volcano spills its lava into the chasm, mostly by way of the tunnels and lava tubes. So don't try and walk along the bottom of the chasm; if the dragons don't get you, the lava will."

Hal sighed. "How many dragons are there?"

"Hundreds. Far too many to fight. That's why we need you, Hal."

Hal blanched. "And . . . and I'm supposed to *talk* to them?"

"Most of the dragons eat wildebeest. There's a never-ending herd not too far from the village. Dragons eat a lot in one go, but then don't need to eat again for a week or two. When they do, they fly directly over the village and return home shortly afterward dangling dead animals. It's rather disgusting and frightening. Of course, everyone hides when the dragons fly over. It's usually late at night, and sometimes so late that everyone is in bed, already asleep. But up until six months ago the dragons were content to feed on wildebeest and leave people alone. Now there's a small group of dragons that detaches from the pack and attacks."

Everyone shuddered.

Miss Simone nodded. "Exactly. Now, like many pack animals, the dragons have a leader. So you'll deal with the leader, Hal. Perhaps you can persuade the leader of the pack to show restraint."

Yeah, right, Hal thought.

Chapter Five
The farmers return

It was the day of the journey. Last night's brief meeting at the village hall had left Hal's mind buzzing and his stomach knotted with anxiety. It had taken him a long time to fall asleep.

It didn't help that he was in unfamiliar surroundings. The village was quiet, but not as quiet as the island. The slightest noise was unusual to him. Hal had woken every ten minutes or so, listening hard to late-night activity in the streets outside: muted voices, doors closing, and an occasional laugh. His small bedroom window allowed a tiny smudge of moonlight into the room, but Hal didn't like the idea that someone—a stranger, *anyone*—might peer in at him while he slept, so he had hung a sheet over the frame. In total darkness he had finally drifted off to sleep, trying not to think too hard about all the dragons he was supposed to face over the next few days.

Hal climbed out of bed. Since he had no pajamas, or even any underwear, he'd slept in his smart clothes. Now they were badly wrinkled. They *looked* clean enough, and didn't smell much, so were probably good for another day . . . Still, his mom would probably kick up a fuss if he didn't change into something else. But into what? All his old clothes were back on the island.

On impulse, he searched the small chest of drawers and, to his surprise, discovered fresh clothes. They were smart clothes, similar to the ones he wore but with subtle differences in pattern or texture. There were also extra pairs of the eerie plastic smart shoes. They were stiff and lifeless at present, like thin bits of plastic cut into the shape of feet. But there was something else in the drawer: underpants! They were a little baggy, but cut from the same mysterious cloth as the outer garments. And there was a cloak too, neatly folded. Obviously Miss Simone had been busy organizing new wardrobes for her shapeshifters! Now Hal understood where Abigail and the other girls had gotten their cloaks the previous evening.

He stared into the drawer for a while, suddenly missing his familiar T-shirts, jeans and sneakers. Was all that in the past? Was he now expected to wear smart clothes for the rest of his life? He didn't *have* to wear them, but if he changed into a dragon in an emergency, then ordinary clothes would be ripped to shreds and he'd be in a bit of a pickle. Maybe he could get into the habit of taking a spare set of clothes around with him . . .

He dressed and shuddered at the way the smart shoes rippled and clung to his feet as he left his bedroom. He used the indoor toilet, washed with heated water, and brushed his teeth with a nice fresh bowl of mint-flavored powder that turned to a gritty sludge when wet. Then he joined his mom in the kitchen for a somewhat brooding breakfast. His dad's place at the table was disturbingly empty. Even though it was a new table in a new kitchen, his mom had arranged it in the same way as the old house, so that at least *something* was vaguely familiar . . . and yet one chair was empty. Hal couldn't remember the last time his dad had skipped breakfast. Even when he rose extra early and snuck off to the farm hours before dawn, there was always a *feeling* that he'd been there, some small clue like an unwashed plate, crumbs on the table . . . but this morning he was just *missing*.

"The men will be back shortly," his mom said. She'd hardly touched her eggs and was pushing them idly around her plate with her fork. Finally she got up and threw her breakfast in the trash. "I'll eat when they're back," she said stiffly. "You go on out, now. Head down to the gate where we arrived yesterday. I'll be along in a minute."

Hal stepped outside, marveling at how bright the sun was, and how fresh the air smelled. It was a cool morning, and he felt better as he ambled around the village. Eventually he ran into Dewey and Darcy. It turned out that Dewey had somehow memorized where everyone lived, so they banged on doors as they went. Lauren still seemed sleepy, and a little grumpy. Emily had already been out, having taken Wrangler for a walk earlier, but she was happy to join them anyway.

When they arrived at Robbie's, they found him outside the front door, poking a stick under a stone. "Look at this!" he exclaimed, as the group approached.

"No thanks," Darcy said. "Whatever kind of bug that is, leave it alone or we'll go on without you."

Fenton looked surprised to see them when they knocked on his door. For a moment, suspicion crossed his face. But when Darcy urged him to join them, he shrugged and tagged along. At least he was human again—no glowing red eyes, no dribbling, just an ordinary boy.

Still, there was something different about him. Finally Hal realized what it was. The boy was wearing smart clothes at last! He chuckled to himself as they wandered through the streets. These magical clothes were smart enough to change their shape, to stretch and adapt to suit different physical forms, whether it was a centaur or an ogre or a winged creature—but they seemed unwilling to take into account Robbie's bony frame or Fenton's plumpness.

"Morning," Abigail said cheerfully, as she emerged from her new home. She called back over her shoulder, "See you later, Mom."

Hal and his friends chatted idly, commenting on toilets that flushed and heated water that flowed from faucets, before moving on to more serious topics.

"I hope our dads are all right," Dewey murmured.

Darcy clapped him on the back. "They'll be fine. They have biosuits, and the fog is pumping through. If there was any sign of trouble, they would have turned back last night and came home. Or they'd camp out near the hole."

"Assuming the virus didn't—" Fenton started. But even the big bully felt it best to hold his tongue on this occasion.

"I hope Biscuit's all right," Lauren said wistfully.

"He's a *cat*, Lauren," Abigail said, shaking her head. "Cats know how to survive on their own. I'm more interested in the livestock."

Emily sighed. "I'm going to miss Wrangler. Mom said he'd be better off staying home when we go off on our journey today."

The morning market was already underway, and villagers were hurrying along with baskets of fruit and vegetables. Once more Hal saw a man pushing a cart filled with those curious black rocks that glowed orange from within, that he now knew were called geo-rocks. He *must* ask Miss Simone about them. All he knew was that they were being mined from the heart of the earth and were somehow used for power.

Hal again caught strange glances from people. When he tried to make eye contact, the villagers looked away hurriedly. Were they afraid? Suspicious? Perhaps even scornful of the new freaks in town? The surreptitious glances bothered Hal, but he couldn't figure out what was behind them.

"I wonder where I can get some jars," Robbie said thoughtfully.

"What for?" Abigail asked. Then she rolled her eyes. "Not for keeping bugs, surely? They're *huge*, Robbie! Study them outside—don't take them home to your poor mother!"

Hal grinned. "That's what I said."

"But everything is so different here," Robbie said. He had that gleam in his eye again. "It's not just the bugs that are big. Have you seen the rats? I saw one scurrying around last night, and—"

"Oh, man," Hal said, shaking his head. "Rats too? You gonna put one of those in a jar as well?"

"No, but—I'm telling you, these things are huge!"

Abigail glanced over her shoulder, then gave Hal a nudge. She spoke loudly. "Fenton, I have to say I'm surprised you came out with us. It's not like you to be so, well, *friendly*. Are you ill?"

Fenton scowled, and his eyes glowed red.

"It's true," Robbie said. "Have you turned over a new leaf or something?"

"I'll turn *you* over, beanpole, if you keep going on about it."

Abigail giggled. "I think Fenton's realized that we're actually the only friends he has in this place. He either sticks with us, or he's on his own. And being on his own in a place with lots of people is worse than being on his own in a place with *no* people."

"Go and boil your head," Fenton growled, and promptly dribbled down his shirt. He angrily wiped his chin.

"What I think," Hal said, "is that he's being all buddy-buddy with us because we know how to control our transformations. He wants to know how to walk around without red glowing eyes and fangs."

"And drool on his shirt," Abigail added.

"How would you like your heads banged together?" Fenton snapped.

Despite the ribbing, Hal was amazed that Fenton hadn't lashed out. A week ago he would have by now. By rights, Robbie should have been on the ground holding a bleeding nose. But Fenton seemed to be putting up with them—not in the most gracious way, as clearly his insults were still flowing freely, but at least his fists were under control.

"I'm just glad we're all friends," Dewey mumbled in a small voice.

They arrived at the gate on the far side of the village. This was where they had arrived in Carter the day before, and it was where the men and goblin folk would return shortly. A crowd had already begun to form; several villagers stood in groups, mostly women but a small number of men too, and plenty of children. Hal spotted the bully Carl and his pals, and groaned inwardly. Luckily they hadn't spotted *him* yet.

Miss Simone was there too, talking to the goblin sentries. After a few minutes someone yelled, "They're here!" and everyone surged toward the gate. Hal tried to hurry to the front but people were jammed so tightly together he could barely breathe. Abigail sprouted wings and rose into the air, shooting straight up about a hundred feet, where she hovered effortlessly.

Hal wondered if she was aware how high she was. Was this the highest she'd flown before? The fog back on the island had dampened all flight, so Abigail and Lauren—and presumably Hal, if he'd been able to fly at all—had been restricted to a relatively low altitude. Here in Elsewhere there was no such restriction.

Abigail drew a number of surprised looks. Robbie nudged Hal and shouted up to her. "I can see your panties!"

Giggles ran through the crowd. Hal punched Robbie hard on the arm and glared at him. "You can be such an idiot sometimes," he said through gritted teeth.

Robbie rubbed his arm and said nothing. He looked hurt. After a while he drifted away, squeezing between people to get to the front.

Hal sighed. "What can you see, Abi?" he called up to her.

Abigail buzzed lower and hovered just clear of the crowd, self-consciously pulling her dress tight around her legs. "They're back," she said. "Cows, horses, pigs, goblins, sheep, and our dads."

41

"Are you kidding?" Hal gasped. "They brought all the animals through in one go? All together?"

"I'd lift you up and show you if you weren't so fat and heavy," she replied. "You'll have to push through the crowds. Why don't you change into a dragon and burn yourself a path?"

"I'll just push," Hal said. He jostled and shouldered his way through, for a moment feeling an uneasy sense of claustrophobia as the adults around him surged and nearly squashed him. Finally he ended up in a flower bed near the rickety perimeter fence.

Up on the hill, an amazing sight greeted him. At the front, Mr. Morgan's horse pulled a cart loaded with supplies, probably all types of food and essentials. Then, just as Abigail had said, the entire herd of cows ambled along behind, followed by grunting pigs and bleating sheep. A number of goblins scurried back and forth, using thin sticks to discourage any straying from the path. Other goblins, and the men—one of them his dad, Hal thought proudly—rode horses and trotted calmly alongside. As the odd, and very long, procession headed down the hill toward the village, the tail end came into view over the rise, and Hal laughed. Were those *chickens* running along? How on earth—

A goat ran off into the trees, and a goblin on horseback galloped off to retrieve it. Hal began to hear the incessant clucking of chickens. Horses snorted, and men constantly called out. At the rear, a goblin occasionally reached into a bag and flicked chicken food onto the trail.

Hal couldn't imagine how this entourage had been brought through the tunnel. The cart had been loaned by the goblins, but the cows, the horses . . . how traumatic had it been for them, coming through that pitch-black, confined space?

He rushed to greet his dad. Then his mom launched from the crowds as though shot from a cannon. They both jumped on Mr. Franklin almost before he had time to dismount. "Whoa!" he said. "Steady on there."

There was a great deal of commotion as Hal's friends, and their mothers, rushed out to greet the men. Cows reared back in alarm and began to amble off into the nearby fields. Sheep scattered, and pigs tumbled gratefully down into a ditch. The goblins rushed around, but soon gave up. The livestock was *here*, and that was all that mattered.

When Hal disentangled himself from his mom and dad, he spotted Abigail and her mom, Dr. Porter, standing aside, huge grins on their faces. Of all the eight children, Abigail was the only one without a father to greet. Mr. Porter had been killed when she was just a baby, when he and a couple of other men had left the safety of the foggy island to investigate the state of the virus-stricken mainland. Their biosuits had protected them from the virus, but not from a group of half-crazy, scavenging survivors.

Wrangler rushed around barking, happy to see his sheep again. He tore off to round them up. The border collie should have gone with the farmers to the island and saved the goblins a lot of work!

Then Hal heard a squeal of delight. Lauren was holding aloft an old plastic cage, and inside hunkered a scared white cat with light brown patches. Lauren hugged the cage and whispered through the bars, "You are *so* handsome."

The next couple of hours were chaotic for the villagers. It transpired that there was already a field of sheep just over the hill, so local farmers began shepherding the new flock over the rise to join them. Likewise, the cows were taken off to a nearby farm. However, the pigs were a curiosity. No one had seen tame pigs before; villagers simply hunted wild boar in the woods. It seemed laughable to the local farmers that anyone would breed pigs in captivity.

Hal heard his dad arguing about it with a group of locals. "It makes perfect sense," Mr. Franklin said. "Set a bunch of pigs loose in a fresh, green field and they'll munch their way through grass, weeds, and even tree roots. The trees will eventually fall and you can use the deadwood for fuel. Within a year you'll have the darkest, richest soil you've ever seen, ready for crops. We call pigs *hog tractors* for good reason. When you're done with one field, move the pigs to another. Meanwhile, twice a year the sows will give birth to a litter of ten . . ."

Hal could see that his dad was beginning to convince the local farmers. Perhaps the locals would benefit from the presence of the islanders in other ways, besides the shapeshifting talents of the children.

The chickens were allowed to run amok, as were the goats—at least for now. The horses were met with approving eyes. "This one looks strong," a villager said gruffly, admiring Mr. Morgan's enormous gray stallion.

"He's a shire," Dewey's dad replied proudly.

"How'd yer fit him down the tunnel?"

"With difficulty. We had to coax him in, ended up bribing him with treats. Once he got started, the others followed—cows too. Once in the tunnel, they couldn't turn around and go back." Mr. Morgan looked a little grim, and Hal got the feeling it hadn't all gone swimmingly.

Miss Simone appeared, red-faced. She finally caught sight of Hal through the crowds and hurried over, her blond hair bouncing and her cloak flapping. "Hal! Time is marching on. We need to round up the others so you can get moving."

Mr. Franklin overheard this and gave Miss Simone a long, hard stare behind her back. Unaware, she placed her hands firmly on Hal's shoulders.

"Go get yourself a few changes of clothes in a bag and meet at the north gate as soon as possible. You can say your goodbyes there. Hurry now."

Hal nodded and set off, glancing back one more time to find his dad moving toward Miss Simone with a scowl on his face. *What's that all about?*

On the way home Hal bumped into Lauren, who was cradling her cat basket. She looked happy, despite the mission ahead. Or maybe she had just put it out of her mind because the idea of dealing with other harpies was too frightening to think about.

His mom beat him home. He found her in the kitchen, filling a large floppy pouch with water. "Keep it with you," she fussed. "You're not used to this heat."

"Thanks, Mom," he said. The pouch had a leather strap, so he hung it around his neck. Then he noticed that his mom was wringing her hands. "What's wrong?"

"This *journey*," she said, turning away to stare out the kitchen window at the busy street outside. "I don't think I can let you go, Hal. It's not right."

"What isn't?"

She sighed. "It's not right that a young boy of twelve should be sent into the dragons' lair. That's a *man's* job. Heck, it's the job of many men together, an army of men—not one single boy."

"You know why it has to be me, Mom," Hal murmured.

"Yes," she said, sounding bitter now. "Because you're a shapeshifter. Because you're the only one who can *talk* to these beasts, to make them *see reason*." She slammed a fist down on the well-worn oak counter. "But that doesn't make it right. You're *my son!*"

The front door burst open at that moment, then slammed shut. Quick, heavy footsteps brought Hal's dad storming into the kitchen. His face was red. "He's not going," he growled. "Hal, you're not going. You hear?"

Mrs. Franklin's face lit up. "You talked her out of it?"

"No—she's insistent. She said he *is* going and that's final. She said it's his job and we need to remember the pact." Mr. Franklin's fists clenched and unclenched a few times. "Easy for her to say."

"I know," Hal's mom agreed, moving closer to take his arm. "It's one thing agreeing to everything before the baby is even conceived—but Hal is all grown up now, and he's our son, and no one has the right to use him like this. I don't care if we move back to the island. Give me the fog any day—at least we're safe there."

"But, Mom—" Hal started.

"They'd probably shut the fog-machine off if we went back to the island," Hal's dad said grimly. "But we can stay here, in this world. We'll run away, the three of us—we'll take off somewhere, just grab a couple of horses and go."

"Yes," Mrs. Franklin said, nodding. "Let's do it. They're not using our son. I'll pack a few things quickly, while you go and—"

"Stop!" Hal yelled.

His parents stared at him in surprise.

Hal shook his head. "We're not running away," he said firmly. "How far do you think we'll get on our own in this place? There are monsters everywhere!

Even if Miss Simone doesn't send soldiers after us, how will we survive on the run? We'll starve—or worse, we'll be eaten alive by something in the woods, like a manticore. And what about my friends? What about *your* friends? We can't live in some secret place forever, on our own, scraping around for food, trying to stay hidden for *the rest of our lives*."

Tears welled up in Mrs. Franklin's eyes.

"Hal," his dad said, "you don't know what you're facing—"

"I probably have a better idea than you do," Hal argued. "And anyway, we have no choice. I don't want to run away. I'm scared, but . . ." He swallowed. "I'd rather face the dragons and die, than be a coward and run away."

His mom let out a sob.

Mr. Franklin slowly rubbed his thick beard, staring at the floor.

"Dad," Hal said, "this isn't up to you. I'm going to do this whether you let me or not. There are people dying in that other village, because of the dragons."

"I know, I know," his dad said quietly. "But you're *twelve*—"

"Think of all those people being *eaten alive*," Hal went on. "Think of the children who don't have parents anymore. Think of the parents who don't have *children* anymore! I might be able to do something to stop the dragon attacks."

"We could just slaughter the lot of 'em," his dad mumbled.

"What, every last dragon?" Hal argued. "What if the villagers attacked and all they managed to kill was a few? What would the other dragons do then? They'd be angry! There would be no stopping them after that. They'd attack the village every night until every last person was—"

"Stop!" his mom cried. She pulled Hal toward her and hugged him. "He's right, George. I hate this, but he's right."

"I know," Mr. Franklin said softly.

Chapter Six
The journey begins

The children had been told to meet at the northern gate, where their carriage awaited. Hal imagined it would be a long, boring journey in a horse-drawn cart similar to the one they'd arrived in. Eleven hours on the road!

But it was neither the mode of transport, nor the duration of the journey, that bothered him. It was the thought of those dragons. His sense of foreboding for what lay ahead was so powerful that he felt as though he was going to a public execution. *His* execution. He imagined the stage, and the wooden block where he would place his neck, and the executioner with his shining ax . . .

Shaking off such morbid thoughts, Hal steadied the sloshing pouch of water around his neck as he walked with his mom and dad to the village gate. The streets were crowded. Hal guessed half the village had turned out to see them off on their journey. People jostled in the narrow streets, craning their necks to catch a glimpse of the shapeshifters as they set off on their mission, while numerous kids darted down side streets to see if they could find a better vantage point.

A middle-aged woman glanced in his direction. Her eyes opened wide when she saw Hal. She nudged the man next to her, who turned. Then the couple sent word through the crowd, and heads began to swivel. The crowd slowly opened up ahead, allowing passage for Hal and his parents.

He felt his dad's gentle hand on his back, and realized he'd stopped in the street. Moving once more, he found it disconcerting to see, and *feel*, so many eyes tracking him. Villagers watched in almost total silence as Hal trudged toward them, but began whispering as he passed. Hal recognized the same expressions he'd seen yesterday, the same shifty glances, and suddenly realized what they meant. It wasn't suspicion he saw in their eyes, or scorn, or disgust—it was *pity*. It was a collective voice that spoke volumes once identified. It said, "Sorry you have to do this, but we're glad it's *you* and not us." It was a look of pity, gratitude and shame all rolled into one.

By the time Hal had processed this realization, he was outside the gate where most of his friends, and all their parents, waited alongside Miss Simone. His mouth dropped open when he saw the carriage that would take them to Louis. It wasn't a horse-drawn cart at all, but something else entirely—a giant of a thing that towered above the crowd. The vehicle was twenty feet long and ten feet wide, open-topped, with a heavy steel or iron framework covered with rusted panels.

46

The monstrous machine stood on six gigantic cast-iron wheels, each taller than a man, and each with deep treads formed by welded metal blocks. The axles and suspension system raised the vehicle so high off the ground that a thin ladder had been fixed between the front and middle wheels on one side.

Goblins were underneath, tinkering away at the front end where an oily engine lurked. Various pipes ran back and forth, as well as steel rods and chains.

"Climb aboard," Miss Simone urged, and clambered quickly up the ladder.

Fenton was next. His parents tried to hug him before he left, but he shook them off, looking embarrassed. They didn't seem to mind too much though, and actually laughed as he hurried up the ladder.

Because their son isn't in any danger, Hal thought.

As Hal's friends headed for the ladder, his mom and dad hugged and squeezed him tightly, and he felt his mom's tears on his shoulder. They whispered in his ear, and he felt a bag pressed into his hand—spare sets of clothes.

Then he, too, clambered up the ladder. He stepped over the short metallic wall and found himself on a flat platform with sturdy sides all around and seats everywhere.

A goblin sat in what was obviously the driver's seat. Levers and switches surrounded him. Behind him were five rows of passenger seats. An aisle ran down the middle of the vehicle, with three seats on either side. Five rows, with six seats per row . . . that was thirty people! This wasn't so much a car as a *bus*—although it looked more like a giant-sized off-road buggy than anything Hal had ever seen.

Giant buggy, Hal thought, the pun suddenly registering. *Another giant bug for Robbie's collection! It even has six wheels, the way an insect has six legs.*

"This thing actually moves?" Robbie said aloud. "It looks so heavy, with the steel framework and metal panels, and those gigantic wheels—"

"Naw," Fenton said, giving him a sarcastic glare with a tinge of glowing red. "This thing doesn't *move*, skinny boy. It's just something to *sit* in. It serves no purpose at all, it's just a big garden ornament to have a picnic in from time to time." He rolled his eyes. "Of *course* it moves, moron."

"Ugh!" Emily said. "These seats are filthy."

"Why don't you wash them, then?" Fenton said with a sneer. He shook his head and went to sit near the front, behind the driver's seat.

When Darcy climbed aboard, she immediately looked like she wanted to climb back down the ladder again. She tugged absently at her blond hair as she gazed with obvious trepidation around the contraption.

All the children claimed a set of three seats each, and either sprawled or lay down flat on them. Miss Simone stood at the front, facing them. "This vehicle is not the smoothest of rides, but it's faster and more comfortable than horse-drawn wagons, and there's plenty of room to spread out." She touched the goblin driver on the shoulder. "All you need to do is sit back and let Blacknail here drive you. He'll take you all the way to Louis, and bring you back."

"Wait," Abigail said, frowning. "You're not coming with us?"

"Me?" Miss Simone looked surprised. "Good heavens, no, I have too much to do here. Blacknail will be in charge, and when you get to Louis a man named Charlie Duggan will meet you. He'll tell you everything you need to know." She turned to Blacknail. "All set?"

"All set," the goblin agreed, his voice deep and growling. Immediately in front of him was a small glass panel that stuck upright, a solitary window that no doubt protected him from the wind as he drove.

"Buckle up," Miss Simone said loudly, looking around.

There came the sound of clunks and clacks as Hal and his friends fiddled with the seatbelts—then a terrific roar that made everyone jump as the buggy's engine bellowed into life. It was deafening for a moment, but then it died away and became a constant, rhythmic puttering as the buggy idled. The vibrations were strong, and Hal felt his teeth chattering.

"How fast does this go?" he asked Miss Simone.

She shrugged. "Almost as fast as a galloping horse," she said. "But half the speed of a unicorn." She moved to the ladder and began to climb down. She paused before disappearing from sight. "Remember—when you get to Louis, Charlie Duggan will meet you. He's a good friend of mine."

She looked across at Dewey. "Look and learn. Your opinion about mining is considered extremely valuable, so make sure to see the situation from both sides."

Dewey visibly quailed.

Miss Simone turned to Lauren. "Good luck, my dear. Harpies are not easy to deal with, so you'll have to be inventive."

Finally she gazed at Hal. "Don't bluff dragons unless you can get away with it. If they call your bluff, then you're done for. Be respectful, firm, and strong, but don't be rude—and don't insult them. Remember this: humans cannot take on dragons in all-out battle. There are hundreds of the creatures in the labyrinth. We have no leverage over them, and they know it. We *could* fight them, but the losses on both sides would be horrible. I wish I could tell you what to say to them, to persuade them to leave the humans alone, but . . ."

The engine roared again; Blacknail was getting impatient.

"Goodbye for now," Miss Simone called, and climbed down the ladder.

Pure white steam belched up the outside of the vehicle, to the sound of huffing that came from somewhere down below. The goblin struggled with a handle and there was a terrible grating, groaning sound. Then the buggy lurched forward and Hal felt his head snap back. Moments later the buggy jolted to a stop, and everyone jerked forward.

Grasping a pair of levers, the goblin pushed on the left-hand side while pulling on the other. The buggy turned to the right, spinning easily, turning almost ninety degrees without moving forward. Hal imagined those six great wheels churning up the dirt, and he leaned over the side to watch. Sure enough, the dirt was being plowed up. The wheels on the left were turning forward, while the wheels on the right were turning *back*ward, resulting in a tight turning circle. This thing could maneuver!

It was only then, looking down over the side of the buggy at the cheering crowd, that Hal realized he might never see his parents again. Maybe he was being melodramatic, but the possibility was there, and it scared him. He peered down, finding his mom and dad easily in the crowd. His mom blew him a kiss, and he smiled feebly in return.

With a clear run ahead, the buggy picked up speed.

All things considered, he and Lauren had the raw deal here. They'd drawn the short straws. Sure, the others might be in danger just because they were coming along—but only he and Lauren were *obliged* to face the enemy. Somehow this made him feel a little bitter toward the others.

Abigail sat quietly, looking across at Hal. When he became aware of her, she got up and came to sit next to him. "Everything's going to be fine," she said softly.

In that moment, Hal knew she was the best friend he could ever have.

The crowds were soon left behind. The buggy trundled along the dirt trail, kicking up dust and huge clods of dirt. Some of that dirt came flying up into the buggy, and Hal realized the folly of sitting by the side.

"It's like going on a field trip," Abigail said over the noise of the engine. She had a little gleam in her eye. "Just think—picnics, walks, monsters . . ."

"I hate field trips," Hal said. "Bugs crawling all over my lunch . . . where's the fun in that?"

"Well, at least you can *see* the bugs here. The ants are about four inches long and the mosquitoes are the size of my big toe."

The buggy left the road and cut across the long grass. Looking back, Hal grimaced at the sight of the deep trenches left by the wheels in the soft grassy soil. They were ruining the landscape!

The buggy swayed gently from side to side as it rode effortlessly over rises in the terrain. Blacknail seemed to know exactly where he was going, and he cut straight across the country no matter what was ahead, veering only to avoid trees. Slopes and bumps were of no consequence—Blacknail simply plowed over them. Bushes were obliterated, and sometimes prickly branches were flung up over the wheels and into the buggy. Pretty soon the floor was scattered with earth and leaves, and Hal continually brushed himself down.

"How do you know the way?" Robbie asked the driver.

Blacknail turned his head briefly, scowled, and turned to the front again. "Compass," he said shortly.

That explained the need for going in a straight line, Hal thought, although he couldn't imagine the entire journey being this way.

Darcy held on grimly to her seat. Hal had stopped holding on so tightly a little while back, finding that his seatbelt held him in check pretty well. But Darcy was clearly unhappy, and all conversation with Emily had ceased.

Hal pointed her out to Abigail. Abigail stared for a moment, then called, "Hey, Darcy—how are you doing?"

Darcy made a gagging motion with her fingers in her mouth. "This thing's making me sick. The motion . . . and the height. I don't like heights."

"You don't?" Hal said. "I didn't know that."

"Neither did I," Darcy admitted. "I first realized it when we went to the top of the lighthouse on the island. Didn't like those stairs much, but figured it was worth it to see the view. And it was. But . . . I don't like heights."

"We're not *that* high up," Emily said, sounding a little exasperated. "Anyway, you'd better get used to it. We've got a long way to go."

Fenton unbuckled his seatbelt, got up, and leaned out over the side. "These wheels are huge! If I fell out now, I'd fall right under the middle wheel and get squashed into the dirt."

"Fenton, don't be an idiot!" Darcy snapped.

As if to prove her point, a sudden bump jolted the entire buggy and Hal lifted off the seat. Fenton stumbled and fell forward. For a horrible moment Hal imagined him plunging over the side, being squashed flat, with red blood and bones matting the wheels and bits of gore flying through the air—

But Fenton's fall was checked. In a flash he grew an impossibly long black tail, slick and reptilian, which whipped around one of the seat supports. One second it wasn't there, the next it was. Suspended over the edge, Fenton waved his arms momentarily before hauling himself back on board. He stared at his tail, and then a huge gush of water poured from his mouth and drenched his shirt.

Everyone stared in amazement as Fenton slowly uncoiled his tail and struggled sideways into his seat. He fumbled with the seatbelt.

"Are you stuck with a tail now?" Dewey asked.

"Shut up, small fry," Fenton growled.

Robbie began to laugh. "He can't get rid of his tail! *That's* going to be interesting to watch."

Everyone laughed except Abigail. "Fenton—seriously, you can't change back properly? I can understand that you grew your tail instinctively just then, but can you still not will yourself back to normal?"

Fenton didn't answer for a moment, but finally turned to look at her. "The first time, back on the island—when I had that toothache?—I changed into this lizard thing and don't know how or why it happened. It just happened, out of the blue."

"Was this when you went to see my mom?" Abigail asked.

"Yeah," Fenton said, rubbing his jaw. His fangs stuck out at odd angles unless he was careful to conceal them with his lips. "I went to see Dr. Porter, and she was examining me, and—well, maybe she prodded me or something, and I yelled, and *changed*, and she screamed, and before I knew it I was out of the window running home. I couldn't get my head around it. I was an animal—a long, black reptile-lizard-monster, and my legs were short, and I was low to the ground, and was running funny . . ."

"I know how that is," Hal agreed.

The buggy went over another large bump, and everyone grimaced.

"But I went home anyway," Fenton continued, "and scared my mom half to death. Took me a while to convince her that I was *me*."

"How did you do *that*?" Dewey piped up.

Fenton sighed and squirmed in his seat, trying to get comfortable with his long, lizard tail in the way. The tip moved restlessly, swaying this way and that as though it had a mind of its own. "I slipped in through the front door, went down the hallway, and sort of trapped my mom in the living room. She couldn't get away. She was screaming, but I just stayed put until she calmed down. Finally she realized it must be me, and then she was sorry. It was okay after that."

There was a pause. The afternoon sun beat down on Hal's head, and he realized his skin was starting to feel sensitive again. The rushing wind felt good, but he had a feeling he was going to start burning if he didn't use some more sunblock. He fished in his pocket for it.

"How did you change back?" Abigail persisted.

"I didn't," Fenton said. "I stayed like that all evening. Dad came home and freaked out. Mom went out, and came back later. She said she went to see your mom, Abi, but your mom already knew about me—because I'd changed in front of her earlier."

"Yes, my mom went to call Miss Simone straight after you left," Abigail said, nodding. "She used the ivory horn in the drawer. When you blow into it, you hear nothing—but Miss Simone heard it. It's a mermaid thing, apparently."

Everyone stared at Abigail, puzzled.

"So I've been told, anyway," Abigail said, shrugging. "She blew the horn and waited. Miss Simone turned up eventually, and they talked. Mom said that Fenton had turned, and Miss Simone practically threw a fit, she was so excited. She said she'd make arrangements and then come to school on Monday to see us."

"Arrangements?" Emily asked.

"Homes to live in," Abigail said. "Anyway—Fenton, what happened next?"

"Nothing much," Fenton said. "I couldn't go to bed, so I just hung around in the living room. Mom and Dad were there, talking about this and that, telling me it was going to be okay . . . and then at some point I fell asleep. It was way after midnight by then." Fenton looked mildly embarrassed and looked away. "I woke up for some reason. Dad was covering me up with a blanket, saying I was back to normal. Then I was asleep again, and I awoke next morning. I was human again."

"Oh!" Darcy exclaimed. "You changed back in your *sleep*."

"Naked," Abigail said, grinning.

"Thing is," Fenton continued, "I thought I'd had a bad dream or something. Sunday was a bit of a blur, like I'd had a knock on the head."

"Yeah, you did seem confused," Hal agreed, remembering his brief encounter with Fenton that morning.

"Mom and Dad kept looking at me funny, but they said nothing. I think they were glad I didn't ask them anything. They decided to let Miss Simone explain everything on Monday morning."

"So on Monday morning you heard the story like the rest of us," Abigail said, "and Miss Simone said you were leaving in a day or two."

"Yeah. My parents had already started packing."

"Why didn't you tell us you'd transformed?" Hal asked.

Fenton shrugged. "Something like that is kind of hard to explain."

They listened to the grumbles and groan of the engine as the buggy continued its dead straight course across endless fields. Up ahead, on the horizon, lay a forest. They wouldn't be able to cut through *that* in a straight line.

"So how did you manage to change again?" Hal asked. "What caused it the second time?"

After a couple of eventful days at school, they had all decided to hold a farewell party for Fenton. It was just a front, of course, while they dug into the secrets of the island and invaded the lighthouse grounds. Hal and Robbie had last seen Fenton, in human form, at his home; the next time was at the lighthouse, a lizard creature clinging to the smooth curved wall.

"I went to meet you," Fenton said, with a scowl. "But I was early, and no one was there. I waited outside the gate for a while, and then wondered if you were inside already. So I tried climbing the fence."

"With the barbed wire on top?" Emily exclaimed, horrified.

"Barbed wire isn't a problem if you use a jacket," Fenton said, hardly able to contain his scorn. "So I found a good place to climb. There's a big old tree—"

"I know the one," Hal said, nodding. "But it's still awkward."

Fenton shrugged. "Well, it *looked* easy. I climbed the tree, threw my jacket

52

over the wire, and kind of jumped across from the overhanging branch."

"And you didn't get scratched up?" Robbie asked, amazed. "I wish I'd tried that years ago now."

"I *did* get scratched up," Fenton said. "It cut me bad. All across my chest and face. Really bad. Blood everywhere. And I fell off the fence, too, into the lighthouse grounds, so I knew I was going to be stuck there."

"Oh, Fenton!" Darcy looked horrified.

Fenton shrugged.

Then Abigail snapped her fingers. "And *that's* what caused you to change! Some personal trauma or injury—you instinctively changed, right?"

"I don't know exactly why," Fenton said, "but yeah, I changed. When I got over the shock of it, I realized I wasn't hurting anymore."

"The injuries healed when you changed," Hal said, nodding.

"After that I just kind of hung around until you all showed up."

"*Literally* hung around," Robbie said, remembering. "Up on the lighthouse wall. You soaked me with dribble."

"It was either that or bash your head in," Fenton growled. "You called me a big fat tub of lard with no brains—remember?"

Robbie evidently did, because he reddened and sank lower in his seat.

They rode in silence for a while. The forest loomed ahead. Every so often a huge belch of white steam erupted from the front, blowing over them like fog, only warmer. Somewhere beneath the rattles and clanks, a faint huffing and puffing could be heard.

Hal was dabbing sunblock on his face when he realized Abigail was grinning at him. "What?" he asked, pausing with a glob of the cream on his finger.

"I just think it's funny how poor sensitive Hal needs to protect his poor sensitive skin against the horrible hot sun."

"Get lost, Abi," Hal said shortly. He wiped his finger clean and stuffed the tiny slim tin box back into his pocket.

Abigail laughed. "You won't need that stuff anyway. I found that out when I flew earlier this morning." She raised her voice so that everyone could hear. "Remember when I buzzed above the crowd and Robbie shouted something really childish about my panties? Well, my sunburn went away."

Emily looked puzzled. "Because you flew, or because of your panties?"

"Because I *changed*, idiot!" She looked around. "See? Transforming heals our blistering skin as well as injuries like Fenton's cuts from the barbed wire."

Darcy nodded. "It's true. You know when I scraped my foot on the rocks, and Hal carried me the rest of the way to Black Woods on his dragon back? Well, sometime after that I changed into a dryad—and when I changed back, my foot was better."

It was well after midday by this point, and Blacknail leaned sideways and opened a compartment under the dash. A fine mist rose. Somehow the buggy had a built-in cooler or refrigeration system. Blacknail pulled out a sack, rummaged inside, and pulled out a loaf of bread. He bit into it, then tossed the bag to Emily.

Amazed, she started pulling out all sorts of food: more bread, hunks of ham and cheese wrapped carefully in clean cloths, tomatoes, even a couple of apple pies. The children tucked in, and nothing more was said until the sack was empty and everyone was belching.

As the forest loomed ahead, Lauren unbuckled her seatbelt and stood, holding onto the seatback for support. The buggy chose that moment to lurch violently, and she nearly fell down. After a moment she stepped out to the aisle.

"What are you doing?" Emily asked. "Sit down before you go overboard!"

"I need a break from this bumpy ride," she said. "Before we get into the forest, I'm going to have a stretch."

And with that, she changed. White feathers erupted from her skin all over, shaggy in places, fine in others. Her eyes turned bright yellow. Her dress remained intact, but altered its shape in subtle ways, becoming wider at the shoulders and slimmer at the waist—and opening at the back to allow an enormous pair of white and gray feathered wings to erupt with a *whump!* sound, like an umbrella opening.

Then she bent her knees and launched into the air, beating her wings as hard as she could. For a second it seemed as though she was going nowhere, but then she was off and away over their heads.

She rocketed upward into the sky. Wings beating strongly, she went straight up until she was a speck. Gasping, Hal and his friends could only watch with envy as she finally stopped flapping and began to turn in circles like a buzzard waiting for an injured animal to die. She looped around in ever-widening arcs, slowly descending, until she began a long, slow, straight dive. She screamed, but Hal could tell from the way she broke into laughter that she was excited and happy rather than in distress. She soared downward, wings out straight, coming in from the front end of the buggy. Blacknail suddenly noticed her and yanked on a lever, making the buggy swerve sharply.

"Harpy!" the goblin yelled over his shoulder. He pulled hard on the two levers and jammed his foot down on a pedal, and the great buggy lumbered to a halt. He reached for a long leather bag and delved inside.

Then he stood up, wielding a crossbow. He fitted a short arrow and took aim.

Chapter Seven
Faeries and ogres

Hal struggled out of his seatbelt and leapt to his feet. "No!" he yelled, as the goblin grimly followed the path of the swooping harpy, his fat finger on the trigger. "Don't shoot!"

There was sudden chaos as everyone aboard began yelling at the goblin driver. "That's Lauren!"—"Don't shoot her!"—"Leave her alone!"

The goblin paused, his crossbow unwavering. He glanced around, frowning. Then he began counting the passengers. Finally he let out a long sigh, removed the arrow from the bow, and sat heavily in his seat. The buggy continued to tick over, rumbling and clanking quietly.

"Not smart, kids," Blacknail said after a while. "If yer gonna do stupid stuff like this, make sure I know about it first."

"We assumed you knew," Emily said, her voice sounding a little whiny. "We just . . . forgot that you can't see backward."

"I can't hear nothing, neither," Blacknail snapped. "Unless you yell at me, I can't hear what any of you are saying—and I don't care, neither, unless yer asking me something. So when I see a harpy coming at me out of the blue—"

"We get it," Hal said. "Sorry."

"But since Lauren's stretching her wings," Robbie said, getting up, "I think I'm going to run for a bit. Is that okay?"

He directed this question at Blacknail and waited for an answer. The goblin glowered, his pig-like face darkening. Then he nodded. "Whatever. But we'll never get there at this rate."

"Oh, I don't expect you to wait," Robbie said. "I thought I'd run alongside, see how fast I can go. If I get tired, I'll jump back on board."

Dewey looked concerned. "You'll never keep up."

But Robbie climbed onto the side of the buggy and stared at the ground. Suddenly he changed. Thick fur sprouted from his head and neck, and he grew, quickly and silently. The buggy began to tip to one side as the ogre's weight increased. The goblin shouted, "Gerroff!" just before Robbie jumped.

Hal expected to see his friend disappear from sight—but Robbie was already three times his normal height, a mass of hair and muscle, with long arms and boulder-sized shoulders, and at full height he stood taller than the buggy. He turned and gave a goofy grin.

"Anyone else?" the goblin asked sourly.

Abigail jumped up and sprouted her wings. They glimmered in the sunlight. Her dress seemed to come alive, the patterns shifting and glowing faintly. She hovered into the air with a constant buzzing, and then shot away.

Then Dewey, looking meek, got up and hurried across to the ladder. Moments later he was a centaur, galloping merrily ahead.

Blacknail looked around at the rest of them. "That it?" he said sarcastically. "Can we press on now?"

Without waiting for an answer he buckled himself back into his seat, then pushed forward on the two levers. Instantly the buggy lurched again, kicking up clods of dirt behind.

Hal watched Robbie. The ogre stupidly waved goodbye, and then seemed to remember he needed to run alongside and not be left behind. He began a shambling run. He was a huge creature, impossibly clumsy, and there was no way he was going to keep up with the buggy. He tried, though, and made a pretty good attempt—but he was already falling behind.

"Um, Blacknail," Hal called. "I think we're going to have to slow down so Robbie can catch up."

"I ain't slowing down," the goblin retorted. "Serves him right."

"But—" Emily started.

"I ain't slowing down," the goblin repeated. He pointed toward the forest up ahead. "I'll stop when we get close. He can catch up then, before we go in."

Abigail was a tiny speck somewhere off to one side. Lauren was another speck high in the sky. Hal envied both of them. If *only* he could fly . . .

Hal considered jumping off the buggy to practice. He'd never learn to fly if he sat around in human form! But he knew he wouldn't easily keep up with the buggy on foot, and if he couldn't fly, he'd quickly be left behind. He chewed his lip for a while, before deciding he'd better stay put and try some other time.

Eventually Blacknail stopped just outside the forest, as promised. This time he turned off the engine, and the buggy shuddered before going quiet. Steam huffed for a long time afterward, and rose gently on all sides, while the hot engine and surrounding framework ticked and creaked.

"Peace," Emily said, her voice loud in the silence. "How far have we come, Blacknail?"

"We've only been driving a couple of hours," the goblin said gruffly. "You just had lunch, remember? We won't be there until just before midnight."

"Oh." Emily sounded disappointed.

Blacknail twisted around, looking annoyed. "Where are the others?"

The others he referred to approached at different speeds. Lauren arrived first, swooping down on the buggy as if it were prey. She landed neatly in the aisle.

Neat trick, Hal thought.

Abigail arrived next, buzzing loudly. Her face was red as she collapsed into the seat next to Hal.

Dewey trotted up, looking happy. He barely seemed out of breath, but his face was ruddy. He changed back to his human form the moment he grasped the rungs of the ladder and started climbing.

It was about ten minutes before Robbie lumbered up. He didn't appear to be out of breath either. As he climbed over the side of the buggy, it tilted alarmingly and everyone yelled—but then it tilted back again as Robbie became human and took his seat.

"You'll break the suspension if you do that again," Blacknail complained. He sighed. "What a waste of valuable time. From now on we stay together."

He started the engine and threw the levers forward. The buggy crawled into the forest, fitting neatly between the first pair of trees, but scraping the bark off another as it maneuvered toward a clearer spot. The terrain was lumpy and squishy. The giant wheels flattened everything, and sank a quarter of the way into boggy ground beneath the ferns. But there seemed to be no danger of getting stuck; the vehicle just kept on moving without a stutter.

A thin sapling bravely stood its ground until the buggy reached it. Then the tree lay down flat, uprooted, as the buggy bounced over. Branches snapped and scraped at the iron underbelly. Hal looked back; the tree was no more.

But larger trees had to be avoided, and this made the route through the forest awkward. Still, Blacknail was an expert driver, and he steered the buggy cleanly through numerous gaps that Hal felt sure were far too small. Often the buggy navigated a gap, stopped, turned almost ninety degrees, moved forward a few yards, turned back on course, and continued on its way through another gap Hal had not even noticed.

Brambles and ferns vanished, pulverized under the six iron wheels. A rotten log that lay across their path exploded into a shower of bark and earth. A stream was momentarily interrupted as the buggy cut through it; then the water pooled into the deep ruts left by the wheels before continuing on its way.

Movement on the forest floor alerted Hal, and he swung to focus on it. It was a mass exodus of giant black ants, each about the size of Hal's hand. He shuddered. There were so many that it was like a river of oil running quickly through the forest. Hal imagined that the buggy's weight and noise sent vibrations through the forest floor, disturbing the ants' nest. As the buggy thundered on, Hal saw ants crushed under the wheels. To his horror, some flicked up into the air and landed in the buggy. The girls started screaming.

There were also giant millipedes. They were as long as cats, shiny and black, with tan-colored legs. They scuttled along with the stream of ants.

The journey through the forest continued, a slow, awkward trek under low-hanging branches that threatened to drop all manner of ghastly creatures on them. As the buggy scraped and bumped trees, leaves and occasional birds' nests fell.

The buggy was a mess, its deck piled up with leaves, twigs, acorns, gigantic dead ants, now a birds' nest or two, and spattered with a healthy dose of mud. The seats were plastered with the boggy mess, but it crawled relentlessly onward with Blacknail hunched over the levers. After a while the trees thinned and the sun's rays shone down through the leafy canopy above. The grass here was long and lush, filled with patches of bluebells.

"How pretty!" Emily exclaimed.

Something buzzed nearby and Hal flinched, thinking it was a giant mosquito or something equally nasty. Robbie spun in his seat, trying to focus on it.

Then another buzzing creature appeared. The two of them zipped around with high-pitched whines, too fast to see. When one got close to Darcy, she gave a cry and ducked, waving her hands around.

Abigail rose out of her seat. She had a strange look on her face, a wide-eyed anticipation. She sprouted her wings and buzzed off the deck, keeping pace with the moving buggy.

The two buzzing creatures immediately came to her with little *zzzip!* sounds and hovered just in front of her face.

Hal gasped. They were miniature people about the size of his hand, both female, with strawberry-blond hair and pointed ears. They wore raggedy frocks and had wings just like Abigail's.

"Faeries!" Abigail exclaimed, her eyes shining. "Hello! Can you understand me?"

One of the faeries zipped closer and whispered in Abigail's ear. Or, more likely, it was yelling in her ear over the noise of the engine. In any case, Abigail broke into a huge grin and nodded. She waved at Hal and called, "I'll catch up!"

Then she was off, following the tiny faeries into the forest.

Blacknail, suddenly glimpsing Abigail as she took off, turned angrily in his seat. "Where's *she* going?"

"She'll catch up," Hal said. "She's met some friends."

Blacknail's reply was unintelligible, but Hal doubted it was something he wanted to hear anyway. He grinned, pleased that Abigail had met her own kind. Maybe they'd teach her how to shrink down to their size and grow pointy ears, things that Abigail hadn't yet learned.

The edge of the forest drew near. Blacknail steered the buggy out between the trees and emerged onto a dusty plain with patches of dry grass here and there. The landscape ahead was dismal and ugly, littered with rocks. The buggy picked up speed, and the iron wheels began throwing up debris. Hal sighed. If it wasn't twigs and leaves raining down on them, it was dust and stones. The buggy was an efficient means of transport, but had the goblins never considered adding a roof?

Hal glanced back once or twice, searching for Abigail. Eventually she appeared, buzzing across the plain. She dropped onto the buggy and sat next to him, beaming.

"They showed me their home," she said proudly. "But it's private. They don't want humans to know where they live, so they swore me to secrecy. And they gave me this."

She held up a tiny glass ball. It was only the size of a fingernail, but probably quite a hefty object in the hands of a faerie.

"What is it?" Hal asked.

"No idea," Abigail said. "They had a huddled discussion and went to fetch it, so I guess it's quite important somehow. They handed it to me like it was worth a fortune. I'm flattered, but I wish they'd told me what it was for."

"You didn't ask?"

"Of course I asked!" Abigail said indignantly. "But they just said to keep it with me and wait until I had a quiet moment on my own." She squinted at the ball. "I swear there's something inside, but I'm not sure."

She slipped it into a little pocket on the front of her dress.

"Can we stop for a moment?" Emily called to the driver.

Blacknail glared at her. "Why?"

"I need to . . . you know, pay a visit."

The goblin looked bewildered. "What are you talking about?"

"She needs to pee!" Robbie yelled.

Blushing, Emily nodded.

Blacknail looked as though this was the most inconsiderate, inconvenient thing he had ever been asked. His face turned red with annoyance, but he ground his teeth together and made no comment. The buggy jerked to a sudden stop and the engine died, leaving only the sounds of hissing from below.

"Make it quick," Blacknail snapped, his gruff voice suddenly loud and clear in the silence. "*All* of you. I ain't stopping again any time soon."

The children hastened down the ladder, glad for the respite. The buggy was noisy and rough, and very messy. Hal stood back and looked up at the monstrous vehicle. It was caked with mud and dust.

Emily hurried over to a large boulder and disappeared. Hal didn't feel the urge to go himself, and besides, he figured he could probably slip off the side of the buggy even while it was moving—at least while in his dragon form, and assuming he could catch up again.

His friends hung around in the shade of the buggy, stretching their legs. "It's too hot to pee," Fenton complained. "I'm sweating it out."

"You should drink some water," Darcy said. "We're not used to this heat, you know, or direct sunlight. My mom said we should drink lots of water."

"Drank it already," Fenton said. His tail curled around his feet, and he watched it with a curious expression.

"Have some of mine, then," Darcy said, handing her pouch to the boy.

"What time is it?" Robbie asked. "Anyone know?"

Nobody did. The problem with being shapeshifters was that they had to wear smart clothes—so wristwatches had to be left at home, or be lost the moment a transformation occurred.

Abigail looked up at the sun, shielding her eyes. "I'd say it's . . . let's see, probably two thirty-three."

Everyone laughed.

Hal decided that now would be a good moment to practice flying. He transformed, suddenly filling the space with his bulk and almost making Lauren jump out of her skin when she turned to find his snout inches from her face.

"Sorry," Hal said—but he only succeeded in roaring. His friends scuttled back to give him room. Hal swung around, careful not to club anyone with his tail, and stretched his wings. It was funny how they moved so easily, as if they had been part of him all his life. It took no effort to twist and angle and stretch them; he had perfect control of every single muscle. He flapped them hard, *whump whump whump*, up and down, causing a small dust storm that forced his friends to leap back, choking and covering their eyes.

He pumped harder, concentrating. He could do this. He just had to *flap*, catch the air in a certain way by angling his wings . . . He stood on tiptoes, willing himself to lift off, wings beating faster and faster. Any second now, he could feel it . . . any second now and he would be airborne.

Any second now.

He flapped harder. This *had* to work. His great leathery wings were catching the air, he could feel his body lifting with every down-beat, was standing on tip-toes, barely touching the ground—

Any second now.

Why was this so difficult? He let out a frustrated roar and beat his tail on the ground, wings still pumping. He didn't feel tired at all, but was aware of his friends standing by, watching. How stupid he must look! How *humiliating* . . . !

He gave up, trying to ignore the disappointed expressions of his friends as he became human again. When Emily returned, they climbed aboard the buggy. Blacknail started the engine and unwelcome noise filled the air. Blacknail pushed forward on the levers and the buggy lurched forward.

Nobody said anything about Hal's failed attempt to fly. He'd try again sometime, when he was alone. He felt so *close* . . .

The journey continued. The sun beat down on them, and Hal wished again that the buggy had a roof. After a while he crawled behind the seats, where it was shaded as long as the buggy was facing a certain direction. Lying flat on his back, he decided he could probably go to sleep for a while.

The others took his cue, and before long all eight of them had taken up residence on the floor, either between or under the rows of bench seats. The space under the seats was extremely tight, but Hal found it was fine once he'd gotten situated. At least now he was shaded no matter which way the buggy turned. The floor was filthy, but so were the children, so that hardly mattered.

The vibrations of the buggy were worse than ever, but the shade was wonderful and after a while Hal drifted off.

* * *

The rain woke him.

Surprised, Hal watched heavy fat drops of water spatter the floor of the buggy. He was sheltered, but only for a while; soon the rain was coming down hard and running in pools under the seats.

Hal crawled out and sat up. The sun was dipping behind the horizon under a clear sky, while above them loomed ominous gray rain clouds. A rainbow had appeared, and Hal stared in wonder.

He looked back the way they had come and found absolutely nothing of interest. The forest was now so far behind that it was beyond the horizon. "Man, that was some sleep," he murmured, stretching.

Fenton sat on his own at the front. Dewey and Robbie were sitting together, but staring off into space, lost in their own thoughts. Darcy, Lauren and Emily remained stretched out on the floor, but were now waking.

Abigail sat staring into her small glass ball, ignoring the pattering rain. She had a look of intense concentration on her face.

"See anything?" Hal asked.

Abigail shook her head slowly. "Well . . . *something*, maybe. But I don't know what. I'm too big to see it. I guess you have to be faerie-sized to see into this thing." She sighed and slipped it back into her pocket. "You're a wreck," she said, looking him up and down.

"Almost as bad as you," Hal said.

Abigail grinned. Her hair was a tangled mess, her face and dress wet and dirty, but her smile remained as bright and cheeky as ever.

"Are we nearly there?" Emily called, sitting up.

Blacknail glanced at her. "We'll eat soon. Then travel some more. We'll be there when the sky turns orange."

Hal, Robbie and Abigail exchanged glances. When the sky turns orange? Was the goblin trying to be funny?

The landscape changed in subtle ways as they traveled. In the far distance, to the north, mountains rose over the horizon. The dusty, rocky plains grew even dustier and rockier, and enormous cracks began to appear in the ground. Blacknail navigated carefully, referring to a map. He had draped it over the metal panel in front of the levers, and stuck it in place with heavy magnets. From his seat, Hal could see faint marks on the worn sheet of paper that probably indicated the more substantial chasms that were impossible to drive over, so Blacknail was making sure to plot his route and avoid dead ends.

The buggy detoured around one such chasm. It was roughly fifty feet across at its center point, but as they drove alongside, heading east, the chasm narrowed to twenty feet, then ten, then five . . . and finally petered out. Blacknail navigated around the end of the chasm and headed directly north once more. As they passed by, Hal peered down into the chasm and wondered how deep it was.

"Quakes," Blacknail shouted over his shoulder. Everyone jumped, and looked at him in surprise. "That's what caused the cracks."

Was Blacknail actually making voluntary conversation? Hal shouted back, "You mean earthquakes? How often do they happen?"

The goblin shrugged. "Last one was two years ago. Big one too. Had to work out new routes." He pointed at his crumpled, sodden map.

"How often do you come up this way?" Robbie asked.

Blacknail shrugged again. "Once in a while." Then he lapsed into silence.

The rain persisted, but it felt good—nice and cool, far better than the hot sun. And the rain dampened the ground too, so that dust no longer flew. As the mountains in the north loomed closer, they left the rain clouds behind. But now the sun was sinking low in the west, and its rays were weak.

"The sky's turning orange," Hal called. "Does that mean we're nearly there?"

Blacknail shook his head. "It'll get dark first, and *then* turn orange."

Hal was puzzled, but he let it go.

Shortly after, the goblin eased up on the controls and allowed the buggy to slow and stop. He switched off the engine, heaved a sigh, climbed to his feet, and stretched. Then he kicked open the compartment under the dash. Once again a fine mist rose from the darkness, cool air mixing with the heat of the day. Blacknail pulled out another food sack. "Eat," he said, tossing the sack to Emily. "Walk around. Go potty. We'll set off in half an hour."

Whoever had filled these food sacks must have thought they were feeding a party of twenty. The children had felt full to the gills after lunch earlier, but this new sack set their stomachs rumbling again. Small roasted chickens, lettuces, carrots, apples, oranges, bananas . . .

"Oh, *man*," Robbie said thirty minutes later, holding his stomach. "I didn't realize how hungry I was."

Blacknail belched loudly. "Finished with the food?" As he stuffed the sack back into the compartment, Robbie nudged Hal. "Look," he murmured.

Following his gaze, Hal squinted—and rubbed his eyes. Shambling along in the distance were three ogres. They had noticed the buggy and its occupants, but didn't appear concerned. They came from the direction of a jagged outcrop of rock, where a huge slab of ground had broken free and tilted, so that one end stuck up in the air and the other poked down into a crack. It was large enough to hide a small village behind.

Where the ogres were headed was anybody's guess. There was nothing ahead of them but open land, except for the mountains on the horizon. Still, they strode purposefully, huge arms swinging, bodies hunched. Fascinated, Hal, Robbie, and all the others watched them as they stopped at the edge of a chasm.

"What are they doing?" Robbie asked, puzzled.

"Go and ask," Abigail said. She leaned over and poked Robbie hard on the arm. "Go on—those are your people. Ask them what they're doing."

Robbie looked doubtful, but climbed down the ladder and headed slowly in the direction of the ogres.

One of the ogres was crouched low, reaching into the chasm with a long arm. It rummaged around and finally drew back a hand caked with some kind of white substance. Whatever it was, the ogre considered it food; it licked its hand hungrily while a second ogre crouched and reached into the chasm.

The third, evidently bored, glanced over and spotted Robbie. For a moment it didn't react . . . but then it casually backhanded the first ogre as if to say, "Eyup—lookee here."

The three ogres stared at Robbie.

Robbie, clearly nervous, faltered and stopped. Then he changed. It was a swift transformation—from boy to ogre in the blink of an eye. Now Hal had a sense of scale, and he realized that Robbie was a mere youngster compared to the other three ogres. So age did matter, then. Robbie was a boy, so he was a younger, smaller ogre. Likewise, Hal was a boy and would probably be dwarfed by the dragons he was supposed to face.

Robbie approached the ogres. They seemed puzzled, but unafraid, watching with deep frowns. "Hurrgnnn," Robbie said, waving a hand. No more than twenty feet away now, it was frightening how small he appeared next to the adults. If Robbie was three times taller than Hal, these brutes were twice as tall again!

One of the ogres shambled closer, closing the distance in two or three quick steps. It towered over Robbie and bent to peer at him. Then it mumbled something and pointed back toward the nearby hill of rock.

Robbie shook his head and said something in reply. Then he jabbed a meaty finger over his shoulder. The adult ogre glanced up, and for a moment Hal had the distinct impression the ogre was staring right at *him*.

The ogre shrugged and turned away, returning to the chasm. It stuck its huge arm over the edge, reaching down. Robbie shuffled closer.

Once again the ogre scraped around, and finally drew up its hand, covered with something Hal couldn't make out—something white and lumpy and sticky. The ogre sucked on its hand, licking it clean.

Robbie peered into the chasm for a long moment, then backed away. He waved goodbye and headed back toward the buggy. The three adult ogres barely noticed him go.

When Robbie transformed and climbed back into the buggy, everyone clamored for an explanation. Robbie looked disgusted. "I guess it's a sort of treat," he said, grimacing. "Like bears finding honey, or dogs finding an old bone."

"But what *was* that?" Emily pleaded. "That sticky white stuff?"

"I guess insects like the shade of the chasms," Robbie said. "You know how big the insects are in this place? Well, they lay big, sticky eggs too."

Lauren and Darcy squealed together, while Fenton guffawed. "Ogres eat *insect eggs?*" he said. "Oh man, that's gross."

"*Some* ogres," Robbie snapped. "And not all the time. Eggs are just . . ." He trailed off, looking sheepish.

"Just a treat?" Abigail finished. "You know, I always knew you were an egg-head when it came to bugs, Robbie, but I never realized how egg-centric you were. What an egg-citing diet you have! I guess the yolk is on you, though—"

"Oh, shut up," Robbie mumbled, and returned to his seat, red-faced.

Hal thought he saw the faintest of smiles on Blacknail's gnarled face as the goblin turned away and started up the engine.

Chapter Eight
The village of Louis

The sun sank behind the mountains in the west, and the sky darkened. The moon emerged and stars began to twinkle.

Except in the northeast. There, an orange hue had started to show on the horizon. As the sky turned black, the arc of orange grew brighter. It was similar to the earliest signs of sunrise—only it couldn't be the sun, because it had just dropped behind the mountains in the west.

As visibility dwindled, Blacknail stopped, climbed down the ladder, and fiddled with something on the front of the buggy. A sharp hiss was followed by a hum of power, and suddenly the way ahead was illuminated with bright yellow light. Having never seen artificial light before, the passengers badgered the goblin until he gave in and explained how it was done.

"Geo-rocks," he said, waving a hand dismissively. "Connected to tungsten filaments inside sealed glass containers with reflective cones. The air is sucked out and the filaments are superheated." The goblin hunched over his levers.

"Oh, you mean light bulbs," Hal said. He'd seen a few, though never lit up.

Blacknail glared. "If you know about light bulbs, then why'd you ask?"

Tired from the constant bumping and shaking, Hal wished the journey would end. Surely the village was close now? There was the orange sky, just as Blacknail had promised—so where was the village of Louis?

He wasn't the only one craning his neck trying to spot the village. "Are we there yet?" Emily called, sounding bored.

"Does it *look* like we're there?" Blacknail retorted.

After navigating more treacherous chasms, the buggy started up a gentle incline. This went on for a while until, finally, they crested the hill and started down the other side.

Hal gasped. Now he could see the village. It lay at the foot of the hills, huge and sprawling, five times larger than Carter and with taller buildings, some with four or five floors. This wasn't a village but a town—or even a *city*. Hundreds of tiny windows were lit up, either with the light from fireplaces, candles and lamps, or from artificial lights like those on the front of the buggy. Some of the lights were unusually bright, and there were even some out in the streets, high on posts. Awed by the sight, Hal wondered if this was what cities had looked like back in his own world, across on the mainland—Out There.

The orange glow in the sky was not directly over the village as Hal half expected, but off in the distance to the east. As the buggy rumbled down the hill into a strange mist, Hal saw endless cracks and crevices all around, many filled with water—natural pools in the rock. The mist rose from these pools as if they were hot. To his amazement, as they passed close, Hal felt intense heat coming off the water.

Blacknail confirmed that the pools were indeed hot. He pointed out mechanical contraptions around the sides of some of the pools—machines with thick metal pipes and cylinders that ran from the water along the ground toward the village. "Geothermal power," he grunted.

Hal looked around at his friends, wondering if any of them had any idea what the goblin was talking about. Judging by the blank expressions, he guessed not.

They trundled away from the pools, following endless pipes. The sky was black and starry, but the strange orange glow seemed brighter than ever now, illuminating the eastern hills. He asked Blacknail what was causing it.

"Lava," the goblin said simply.

Stunned, Hal's mouth dropped open. He glanced at Abigail next to him. Her eyebrows had shot up. Robbie twisted in his seat to face them both.

"Lava," he repeated. "He means the stuff that comes out of volcanoes."

Abigail clicked her tongue. "Yes, thanks, we *know* that, Robbie. We're not morons, you know."

"The Labyrinth of Fire," Hal murmured. But no one heard him. The noise of the engine drowned him out.

At last the buggy arrived in Louis. There wasn't a gate as such, just a small wooden sentry box, where a goblin peered out. Blacknail gave him a curt nod and the sentry promptly lost interest.

Buildings loomed. Not houses but places of work, most of them closed for the night but some with doors wide open, brightly lit inside, with people—men, women and goblins—laughing and drinking from tankards.

"Shops, warehouses, pubs," Blacknail said airily. He had slowed the buggy and the noise of its engines was reduced, though still loud in the night. "The business end of town. We need to park."

He steered carefully down a narrow street, the great iron wheels churning up the dirt, then turned sharply into an alley and slowed to a stop. The engine died, the bright light went out, and suddenly the passengers were plunged into darkness and the air was filled with hissing. Steam poured up the sides and escaped up the walls of the surrounding buildings. Finally the buggy sighed and was quiet.

Faint sounds came to Hal's ears as they sat in silence for a moment: laughter and yelling from the pub, and somewhere a dog barking. The alley was pitch-dark.

Blacknail dug out a lantern. Its sudden glow in the darkness, and its dancing shadows, made the goblin's face even uglier than usual. "We walk from here," he grumbled. "Not far. Grab your bags."

The children wearily followed the goblin down the ladder and stepped out of the alley into the street. Yawning, Hal trudged alongside his friends, dragging his bag of clothes, wishing for bed. The air was cool now, and it was late.

They passed more shop fronts, all dark. The street wound round and they came to a large building marked DOG & BONE INN. Blacknail waved them inside.

After the cool night air, the warmth inside the inn felt wonderful. A huge fireplace crackled in a large room filled with tables and chairs. At the far end, a polished counter spanned the width of the room. Behind it were more bottles than Hal had ever seen in his life. The firelight danced off the glass, making that entire end of the room seem alive.

A very tall man appeared. He was burly and round-faced, with curly red hair and thick sideburns that came all the way around to the corners of his mouth—but he had no beard or moustache. He beamed and thumped Blacknail on the back. The goblin, as solid as he was, flinched.

"Good to see you, Blacknail," the man bellowed. He came over and towered over Hal and his friends. "And these are the kids at last! Welcome, welcome." He glanced at Fenton and raised a bushy eyebrow. "Nice tail." Then he grinned. "You look tired. There are beds made up for you, but if you're hungry or thirsty, why, just say so. Need some food? Bread, soup?"

"I just want to go to bed," Emily complained, rubbing her eyes.

"My back's killing me," Darcy mumbled.

The man laughed. "Quite a journey, eh?" His voice bounced off the walls and echoed through Hal's head. "I'm Charlie Duggan. You call me Charlie. Go to bed, the lot of you, and come down for breakfast when I shout."

Hal didn't need to be told twice. When Charlie pointed the way up the stairs and to the right, Hal found himself jostling with his friends on the staircase. Upstairs they found exactly eight bedroom doors standing wide open. The rest were closed. Hal didn't know whether the other rooms were occupied, and he didn't care—he picked a room at random, mumbled goodnight, and closed the door behind him. He pulled his filthy clothes off, kicked them into a corner, and crawled into bed. He was asleep in less than a minute.

* * *

"Breakfast!" a man's voice bellowed up the stairs.

Hal woke on his back, staring at the ceiling from a warm, soft bed. Sunlight streamed in through the window. Hadn't he fallen asleep just a moment ago?

He yawned, stretched, and propped himself up on his elbows. His room had a small sink in one corner. Amazed, he climbed out of bed and turned one of the faucets. Cold water rushed out. The other was a hot faucet. He would never get over the idea of running water, especially *hot* running water.

There was a big dirty smudge on his pillow; his hair was still filthy from the journey in the buggy. He rinsed his hair thoroughly, then scrubbed it dry on a clean white towel, leaving a faint dirty stain. Pulling some fresh smart clothes from his bag, he dressed quickly and wondered what to do with his dirty laundry. Shrugging, he left the pile on the floor and sauntered downstairs.

The dining room was empty apart from Fenton and Darcy, who were seated at a large table. Charlie Duggan cheerfully delivered a huge plate of scrambled eggs and ham and set it down with a bang. Fenton tucked in immediately, while Darcy continued chewing on some bread. Fenton, now tail-less, wore the same clothes as the day before, and his hair stuck up on end. He looked a mess. In contrast, Darcy had obviously had a good wash and put on some clean clothes. She must have been up before Charlie had called for breakfast, considering how carefully she had brushed her golden hair and tied it back in a ponytail.

Hal joined them, scooping a dollop of egg onto his plate. Shortly after, Abigail arrived and sat next to him. Like Darcy, she was clean and freshly dressed, her dark brown hair pulled back in a ponytail. She seemed to have developed a few new freckles in the night, Hal thought, studying her as she reached for the ham. She smelled good.

"Isn't she pretty, Hal?" Darcy said quietly.

Hal found Darcy staring at him with a grin. His face immediately heated up.

"He was *gazing* at you, Abigail," Darcy said, giving her a wink.

Abigail grinned. "Well, Hal declared his love for me yesterday, on the way here. I was quite surprised, but—"

Hal spluttered and egg shot across the table. "I did NOT!" he said indignantly. "What—where did you—?"

Both girls laughed, and Fenton snorted and thumped the table. "No use denying it, squirt," he said, grinning, waving a fork in Hal's direction.

Robbie, Emily and Dewey showed up just then. Robbie was a mess. Like Fenton, he wore the same dirty clothes and his hair was all over the place. Knowing Robbie, he probably hadn't even brought any fresh clothes! Hal sighed inwardly, a little embarrassed for his friend. Emily was clean and tidy, and even Dewey looked neatly combed, so why couldn't Robbie make an effort?

They scraped their chairs and bumped the table as they sat, and Robbie immediately tucked in. Emily looked from Darcy to Abigail, her eyes narrowed. "What were you saying just then? No use denying what?"

Darcy patted Emily's arm. "It's so sweet, Em. Yesterday, on the buggy, Hal told Abigail that he loved her."

"Awwwww," Emily said.

Once again, Hal nearly choked on an enormous mouthful of ham. He chewed furiously, words of denial on his tongue.

Robbie's fork was poised. Hal assumed his friend was staring at him with shock and horror, and he frantically swallowed his mouthful. "She's *kidding*."

But Robbie wasn't paying attention. He was staring over Hal's shoulder.

Then Lauren came into view and sat down in the spare chair to Hal's right side, directly opposite Robbie. She smiled around the table, the dimples in her cheeks a little more pronounced than usual. "I slept like a log," she said, and everyone agreed. "This place is amazing! Running water in our rooms, heated flooring—"

Hal hadn't noticed the heated flooring, but he agreed that the inn had far more conveniences than any house he had ever lived in.

He was pleased that the conversation had turned away from imagined declarations of love, but nevertheless he couldn't help thinking that Robbie was the one who should be declaring his love—for Lauren. Robbie nodded once in a while, only half listening, but his attention was fixated on Lauren by way of sneaky glances in her direction. Hal wondered why he didn't just *tell* her he liked her. Then again, he was such a mess this morning that surely Lauren—who was clean and washed—wouldn't give the mop-haired, scruffy boy a second glance.

Fenton burped loudly and shoved his plate back with a sigh. "Now *that* was some breakfast." He stared at Dewey's plate, then at Dewey, who was nibbling on a piece of ham. Fenton picked up the bowl of scrambled eggs and dumped a huge pile on Dewey's plate. "Come on, pal—eat up. You'll never grow to be big and strong like me if you peck like a bird."

Other guests started showing up. They gave the children curious stares, and whispered to each other, but otherwise kept to themselves. After a while, Charlie gave instructions to a young lady wearing an apron, then brushed his hands and came over to the table. When he removed his own apron, Hal noticed he wore smart clothes. "Right, kids," the man boomed. "Young Mirabelle here is taking over for me, so I can give you a tour and tell you what's what. Come on."

"Where's Blacknail?" Emily asked. "Doesn't he eat breakfast?"

"He doesn't eat breakfast with *kids*," Charlie corrected her with a wink. "Grumpy old thing."

Charlie led them outside. The morning was already warm, and people filled the streets. For a moment everything looked exactly like the village of Carter, except that here, in Louis, tall buildings loomed over the houses. They came across a four-story square wooden structure with windows everywhere, and two chimneys poking through a slanted slate roof. Through the windows, Hal could see several white-coated people.

"That's the lab," Charlie said, as they passed. "All the scientific stuff goes on there. It's where most of the cool things are invented, like your magic clothes. And,"—he stopped and grinned—"there's a hole on the top floor."

"A hole?" Dewey repeated. "Someone fell through?"

Charlie laughed until his eyes watered. Finally he shook his head. "No, I mean a *hole*. To your old world. It's suspended in mid-air. We built the building around it long ago. Some of the scientists—me included—pop through from time to time, for research purposes. It comes out high above a gigantic lake. I built a pier there—I'll have to show you sometime."

Hal immediately wanted to see it, but Charlie shook his head. "Later, maybe. Right now I want to show you something else." He moved on, turning to talk over his shoulder. "Our village is about five times the size of yours, and it's the most advanced human settlement on the planet—that we know of anyway. We have powered lighting, heating, refrigeration, plumbing, remote communication—"

"Carter has plumbing too," Hal said.

Charlie nodded enthusiastically. "An up-and-coming place, that. If Simone has her way, Carter will become like Louis. But those centaurs . . . well, they object to the mining. Come and look at this."

He led them around the corner and stopped by another large building, just a story high, but very long. It had no windows and was connected at one end to the research building. Surrounding it on three sides was a hot, bubbling pool, covered with a stiff wire mesh.

"The village," Charlie said happily, "was founded in this area because of its hot spots. Earth's outer layer is the crust—you know that, right?" Everyone nodded. "Well, below that layer is magma, which is incredibly hot, molten rock. The heat from that magma is tremendous. It provides more than enough energy to power every city in the world—if we can only harness that energy." Charlie grinned. "Well, we can. Hot pools like this one start off as ordinary rainwater that trickles down through the earth's crust, between gaps in the plates, to where magma flows. The magma heats the rainwater, and boiling water is forced back to the surface under pressure, where it bubbles away happily near the surface in natural springs. The water cools on its way up; sometimes it's toasty warm, good enough for a swim in the middle of winter. But this particular pool, and many others like it, remain at near-boiling point—hence the wire mesh, to prevent idiots from scalding themselves. In some places the water is so intensely hot that it escapes the earth in the form of steam."

Hal was fascinated. He had read about magma in the past. When volcanoes erupted, lava spewed out. There was almost no difference between magma and lava except that it was called magma when underground and lava when erupting or flowing above the surface. He seemed to remember that lava released all its gas into the air and cooled differently, forming a harder rock, whereas cooled magma contained air pockets—a bit like the difference between the smooth, dry crust on a loaf of bread and the soft, moist inner texture. But in any case, he had not heard of hot water springs.

"What's really fascinating," Charlie said, dropping his booming voice a couple of decibels, "is how long it takes rainwater to trickle down to the magma and return as hot water. How long do *you* think it takes for rainwater to reach the magma?"

"A few months?" Emily guessed.

"At least a year," Robbie said, sounding scornful.

Charlie smiled. "Try a few *thousand* years."

Everyone gasped.

"Once boiled, the water returns very quickly, within a year. But think about that for a moment. When you see an ordinary pool or puddle, you're looking at water that has just recently rained down. The water *here*—" Charlie jabbed a finger toward the hot pool. "—has already been underground and *returned*, and is perhaps four or five thousand years old, maybe older still."

Charlie waved his hands expansively at the curious building standing over the pool. "Inside is an enormous generator. It uses steam to drive it. To generate steam from the hot water in this pool, the water must first be heated a little more, through a method known as flashing. As it heats, it generates steam, and in turn the steam drives the generator—which gives us power for lighting and so on. Of course, we also pump hot water from all these springs to homes around the village, through pipes in the walls and under the floors. Continuous heating as well as hot running water."

He beamed. "That's geothermal energy, my friends. Natural energy at work, and completely safe to the environment."

Now Charlie frowned. He urged Hal and his friends to huddle closer.

"The centaurs don't see it this way. They're a funny lot. They're okay with the geothermal energy—everyone knows the earth is heated down below, and there's nothing wrong with using some of the escaping heat. But . . ."

The big man leaned closer still, until his broad nose was less than a foot away from the circle of young faces.

"Years ago, geothermal scientists discovered some strange rocks. We called them geo-rocks. You've seen them, I'm sure—small boulders that glow from within. They form on their own. We don't break 'em off or anything like that, they just form on their own. It's like the ground splinters, and each splintered section shrinks and shrinks, becoming more compact and dense, like it's imploding. And as it shrinks, it starts glowing inside, like energy is trapped in there. We don't know how it happens, but we often find these rocks littering the tunnels around

71

here, still a little too large and dull to use. If they're not glowing, they're worthless. Leave them long enough and they'll continue shrinking and then start glowing. *Then* they're usable. But leave them alone and they'll continue to shrink to the size of marbles, getting brighter and brighter until they turn into little white specks and vanish. So we get 'em at just the right moment, when they're *ripe*, so to speak—and as we use them, as we suck out the energy, the rocks gradually dull and die. They last about six months, depending on use. When they're fresh and ripe, they look hot enough to burn your hands, but they're not at all—at least not on the surface. All that energy inside . . . it's like it's *trapped*, held in by some incredible force, like a miniature version of the earth's crust."

"And you stick *rods* in them?" Hal said, remembering the one he'd seen in his home, heating the water tank. "Isn't that, uh, dangerous?"

"Extremely," Charlie said, nodding. "The rods are only inserted a little way, just enough for the energy to start flowing. Any farther and—"

He made a silent *boom!* gesture with his hands.

"The centaurs think that mining for these geo-rocks is causing earthquakes," Dewey said quietly. He looked very serious and grown-up.

Charlie looked down at the boy and nodded. "There aren't many centaurs in these parts, so we have no trouble from them. But they're a thorn in Simone's side, I know that much." Charlie sighed. "The founders of this village settled here because of the hot spots, and because there were already cracks in the ground from volcanic activity and earthquakes. It's also true that there have been a number of earthquakes since we started removing geo-rocks from the ground, but it's just coincidence—superstitious nonsense. These rocks vanish anyway, all on their own. What difference does it make whether we let them vanish, or remove them and use them *before* they vanish?"

Dewey chewed his lip, looking thoughtful.

Charlie clapped his hands together. "All right. Now that I've explained all that to young Dewey here, he can mull it over and conclude that harnessing all this energy is a *good* thing." He raised an eyebrow. "Don't forget that I come from your world too. I grew up with Simone, went to school with her, became a shapeshifter. I *saw* the old world before I came here. It wasn't pretty. Power plants belching smoke into the air, crude oil escaping into the sea, poisonous vehicle emissions . . . Let me tell you, girls and boys—geothermal energy, *and* the geo-rock system, is efficient, plentiful, and safe to the environment."

"What kind of shapeshifter are you?" Emily asked, changing the subject.

Charlie grinned. Without a word, he transformed. Everyone jumped back as a huge winged creature exploded into being before them. It had the head, shoulders, and front legs of a gigantic predatory bird like an eagle, and its enormous wings spread high and wide. Yet its powerful hindquarters and tail were distinctly lion-like. It was a shimmering golden color all over, feathery at the front and furry toward the back.

"A griffin!" Abigail exclaimed, awed.

The griffin beat its wings hard and lifted off the ground. Hal watched, envious, as the creature—*Charlie*—rose directly upward, leaving the children bathed in a giant shadow.

"I wish I could fly like that," Hal murmured.

Abigail nudged him gently. "You will. Maybe Charlie can help you."

* * *

Hal asked Charlie about flying as the big man walked them through the village. "How do you do it?" he asked. "On the way here, I beat my wings forever and I just couldn't take off. And Orson can't fly either."

Charlie sighed. "I know. Orson was my best buddy back in school. He was one of the first to transform. But they brought him across too soon and he never learned." The man looked sideways at Hal. "I don't envy you, being a dragon."

There was a long silence. A shadow passed over them, and Hal glanced up. Clouds were rolling in. He watched them for a moment, convinced they were coming together right above the village.

Charlie glanced up too, and frowned. "That's not a good sign."

"So how can I learn to fly?" Hal persisted. "There *must* be a way."

"I don't know the answer, Hal," Charlie said. "Do you know how to whistle?"

Hal shook his head, then reconsidered and nodded. "A little. Not the really loud whistle that Fenton can do with two fingers in his mouth, but, you know, I can whistle between my teeth . . ."

Charlie nodded. "You either know how or you don't. You can learn, but some people just never get it. You can ride a bike too, but before you learn it seems like the most impossible thing in the world to balance on two wheels. Same with swimming—trying to stay afloat and all that."

"But everything else came easily," Hal said. "I can move my wings just fine. I can twist them around and angle them as if they've always been there. How did I learn that? And my tail—I never had a tail before, and now I have, and I can make it swing and curl and all sorts. If I can learn *that*, why can't I learn how to fly?"

"If you figure it out, let old Orson know too," Charlie said. "The guy feels like a failure—and he *is*, to all intents and purposes. The trouble with flying horses is that they tend to fly a lot, and the only way to mingle with them is to fly halfway up a mountain to where they graze in some unreachable pasture. Orson should have been conversing with the flying horses by now, requesting their services for payment. Can you imagine how cool it would be for humans to travel the countryside on flying horseback?" Charlie shook his head ruefully. "A missed opportunity, that."

The group grew weary of the tour. The village seemed to go on forever. Hal asked why it was called a village when it had obviously outgrown that status and become a town, but Charlie just laughed and said that some things never change.

"Lauren, what's wrong?"

Hal and Charlie stopped and turned. Robbie was peering anxiously at Lauren, who had turned as white as a sheet.

"I . . . I feel something," she said. She sniffed the air. "I smell it too."

Everybody started sniffing.

"I don't smell anything," Emily said. "I mean, apart from the donkey manure in the road."

"And Fenton's armpits," Abigail said with disdain.

"No, I *smell* something," Lauren said again. She sniffed hard again, her eyes widening. Then they turned yellow and Robbie stepped back in alarm.

Lauren transformed. In a flash she was a harpy, spreading her white feathered wings and crouching, ready to launch. She beat her wings once, twice, took a few steps, and leapt into the air. She was off, beating hard, soaring above the rooftops.

"What's got into her?" Darcy said, chewing her lip.

Charlie looked worried. "I have a bad feeling about this."

Before he could go on, Lauren returned. She landed heavily, her knees buckling. She folded her wings and straightened, glaring around. In harpy form she had none of her usual cute features—the sweet smile, the dimples in her cheeks—but instead looked savage and wild. Still, it was Lauren who spoke. Her voice trembled. "Harpies. Hundreds of them, from the west. Coming to attack."

Chapter Nine
Harpies

Charlie was already running for the nearest sentry tower as Hal digested the news. In the distance, Charlie shouted, "Sound the alarm! Harpies!"

Then the alarms blared, a series of short bursts from an amplified horn that echoed across the village. Immediately people dropped what they were doing and ran for cover, diving into the nearest house they could find. Homeowners waved them inside, strangers or otherwise. There were no words, just a hurried shuffling, scuffling sound up and down the streets. While the faces of many wore panicked expressions, it was clear this was a regular occurrence.

Hal stood with his friends in the middle of the street. Charlie came hurrying toward them. "Lauren, you've bought us time we don't normally have. Harpies usually come down on us from the clouds, and we rarely have time to get inside. This time we have an early warning."

Lauren nodded, her wings flexing anxiously. "Should I go and—"

"No," Charlie said emphatically. "You can't reason with harpies at the best of times, much less while they're on the attack. We'll have to take cover as usual."

"Can't we fight?" Hal asked. "I mean, I'm a dragon, and you're a griffin, and Robbie's an ogre, and Fenton's—"

"You're more than a match for harpies," Charlie said, placing his big hands on Hal's shoulders. "But there are just too many. It would be like picking off a swarm of wasps one by one. No, let's take cover. They'll find nobody in the streets this time, and will go away disappointed."

A neighbor waved them inside her house. It was crowded in the kitchen. The house owner, a rather large woman, took up much of the window as she peered out. Charlie stood behind, hands on her shoulders, while Fenton, Emily, Darcy, Dewey and Lauren crowded on each side, each vying for a spare inch to peer out.

Hal, Robbie and Abigail, who had been last to enter the house, headed for the living room to find another window.

"I see 'em," Robbie said.

Craning their necks, Hal and Abigail looked skyward. A dark stain spread across the low cloud cover as hundreds of winged creatures poured downward. Though they were white-feathered, they appeared gray and dull against the bright white clouds. Hal thought he saw hundreds of blazing yellow eyes, but then realized he must be imagining it.

The harpies plummeted, then abruptly fanned outward, going in all directions. They were silent, bent on their mission—whatever that mission might be. But after a brief silence, a terrible ruckus began.

The harpies were screeching with anger. Hal heard bangs and thuds and breaking glass, and shouts from men and women, as well as cries from children. Above the noise came curious *thwack!* sounds, one after the other, and then Hal spotted three centaurs trotting down the street, letting loose arrow after arrow from enormous, slender bows. Each arrow hit home, and several harpies squealed and lurched off into the sky. A few tumbled to the ground, mortally wounded.

A harpy landed in the street immediately outside the living room window, and Hal, Robbie and Abigail jumped back in alarm. Unlike Lauren, this harpy was slick with a disgusting greasy substance, its feathers dull and sticky, and wearing filthy rags. It had rage in its eyes as it looked around, wings spread. This creature was a male adult, scarred from previous attacks, looking for a fight.

It looked their way and snarled, then launched itself at them. Hal leapt back, dragging Abigail and Robbie with him. He assumed the harpy would bounce off the glass, but he was taking no chances—and a good job too because it came straight into the living room in an explosion of glass fragments. Hal felt stinging pain on his face as shards tore past.

The harpy wasted no time and reached for Abigail, a wicked gleam in its eyes. It was already half turned away, as if it fully expected to grab Abigail's wrist and yank her through the window. But Hal shoved her aside, and the harpy's grasping claws missed her arm by inches. As the creature turned back, Hal transformed into a dragon, knocking Abigail even farther sideways with his sudden huge bulk, and Robbie backward with his tail. The harpy's eyes widened, and Hal let out the loudest, most savage roar he could muster.

Hal's breath was filled with hot steam and the harpy fell backward with a screech, its feathers blackening. It scrambled for the window, launched itself over the sill, and took the remaining glass with it. Then it was gone.

Before his sudden anger could evaporate, Hal scrambled out of the window too, crunching flat a chest of drawers and splintering a chair on his way. Outside, he tore into the street and launched himself into a group of the winged creatures. They had a sack full of food that they were hungrily fighting over, and didn't see Hal until he was mere feet away. He blew fire, and the harpies screamed and tore off into the sky, leaving the food behind.

Hal didn't break step. He hurtled around the corner and found more harpies trying to fight their way into a house. The owner, a frightened young man, was bashing at them with a chair, but two harpies ganged up on a third and pushed their unfortunate, battered colleague ahead of them. The trio tumbled into the house and began to claw at the man, who started yelling in terror and pain.

There was no easy way for a dragon to climb through a window, so Hal simply threw himself at it. His reptilian hide seemed impervious to broken glass and splintered wood. He felt invincible!

He fell inside and landed on top of the battered harpy. Balancing on his hind legs, he grabbed a harpy in each outstretched clawed hand and threw them so hard that they bounced off the walls, stunned. Then he knocked the third around the head with his club-ended tail. One at a time, he unceremoniously picked them up in his jaws and tossed them out of the window—one, two, three. He didn't care how much he hurt them.

Glancing back at the terrified man, he wanted to say, "It's okay," but knew he wouldn't be understood. So he toppled out of the window into the street and stood over the limp, feathered heaps.

A rush of air over his head caught his attention. But it was a griffin. Charlie! Whether Charlie saw Hal or not was unclear, but it didn't matter as long as he was out fighting these cowardly creatures.

He hoped someone—Robbie, or Fenton—had stayed behind in the house to look after Abigail and the others.

A woman's scream chilled his blood. It was close, perhaps a few houses down. Hal hurried along the street, his ears pricked and his nostrils twitching. The harpies smelled bad. Their pungent odor was everywhere, so strong that he couldn't rely on it to locate any particular one of them. So he listened instead.

The scream came again, but was cut off with a vicious slap. Furious, Hal stampeded over to a doorway and tore right through it without stopping. The door flew down the hall as Hal squeezed himself through the frame. He kept his wings tight against his back to avoid damaging them.

He peered into a small bedroom. There, a woman had been cornered by a couple of harpies. One was male, the other female, and they were laughing and trying to grab a bundle from the woman's grip. "Hand it over," the male said in a horrible, rasping voice.

The female harpy made a lunge, and the woman screamed once more, cradling the—

Hal gasped. It was a baby!

He saw red. He tore through the doorway, dimly aware that he also dislodged the doorframe and some of the wall, and leapt on top of the nearest harpy—the female. It squirmed under him, trying unsuccessfully to disentangle itself from his long claws, while Hal let loose with a ball of flame directly into the male's face. It screeched and spun, and somehow managed to crash through the bedroom window to the street outside. Hal moved his feet, reached down, and gripped the filthy female in his jaws. He swung his head hard, and the creature flew out the same window, catching the frame with a *thunk!*

Gasping from anger rather than physical exertion, Hal stood for a moment and waited for the pounding in his head to ebb. He had never felt like this before. It was like the angriest day of his human life multiplied by twenty and backed up with fearsome dragon power.

He realized for the first time how dangerous he could be when provoked. But worse, he realized how dangerous *other* dragons could be—especially those that were larger and stronger than him, which was probably most of them.

"Thank you," the woman said, trembling, still cradling her baby. It was crying. Maybe it had been crying all along and Hal just hadn't noticed.

Hal blinked. The woman had thanked him! She appeared apprehensive, but certainly not terrified of him. She probably knew he was a shapeshifter.

Hal nodded, and slowly turned to leave through the bedroom window. Windows were easier than tight doorways and passages. He glanced with dismay around the room before he left, appalled at the mess he had made: scorch marks on the wall, doorframe ripped out, a collapsed bed where he'd put his weight on it, not to mention the window itself. Still, the woman and her infant were safe.

Outside once more, he found that the harpies were leaving. With screams of rage they flocked into the sky and circled like vultures before disappearing for good, taking with them sacks of food, clothing, sheets, and other objects Hal couldn't make out. He understood them now. They didn't work or grow their own crops or bake their own bread—they just came along and stole whenever their supplies ran low. Hal was full of contempt for them.

The clouds drifted apart and the sun broke through. As the streets brightened, people emerged from doorways. Hal returned to the house in which he'd left Abigail and his friends. He got some curious stares on the way, but one man—the frightened young man Hal had helped earlier—was excitedly pointing at him and telling his neighbors about his experience.

Hal changed back into his human form, and now people smiled and nodded. A wave of pride swept over him. He was no longer a freak, but a trusted protector. People *liked* him.

Abigail burst out of a doorway and flung her arms around his neck.

Startled, Hal waited until she let go, then took a step back and cleared his throat. "Uh . . . are you all right?"

"Fine," she said, grinning. "Thanks to you. Why are you blushing?"

Robbie emerged from the doorway. "I was itching to go out and bash some harpies with you, but Abigail told me I should stay," he said, looking distraught. "Fenton went off, and I was stuck here. Sorry, Hal."

Hal punched him lightly on the shoulder. "If you'd left the others alone, I'd have roasted you alive. *I'm* the one who should be sorry. I didn't even *think* about leaving you all unprotected . . ."

The kitchen was a mess. Glass littered the place from a smashed window, and the kitchen table, along with one of the four chairs, lay on its side. In the middle of the floor, three harpies struggled angrily to free themselves from a thick, sticky substance that bound their bird-feet to the stone tiles. The same glue had got caught up in the harpies' filthy feathers and wings, and they looked pitiful.

The red-faced house owner brandished a broom. Every now and then she whacked a harpy around the head.

Dewey, Emily and Darcy stood in the hallway, just out of range. They told Hal that Fenton wasn't back yet. "It was amazing," Darcy said, sounding awed. "We heard the commotion you were making in the living room and went to see what was going on—but then these three monsters bashed their way in through the kitchen window. Charlie was knocked senseless for a moment—"

"Banged his head on the table," Emily added.

"—but then Fenton changed into his lizard form and spat all over the harpies," Darcy finished.

"Where is he now?" Hal asked, looking around.

"He went hunting," Dewey said.

"And Lauren?"

Robbie gestured down the hallway. "She's in the bedroom, feeling sorry for herself. I think she's ashamed of . . . of what she is."

Charlie popped his head into the kitchen to say he would be back as soon as he'd gathered a report of injuries, deaths, and missing babies. The children watched through the broken window as he transformed into a griffin and flew off. Hal and his friends turned and stared at each other, appalled.

Missing babies?

Somehow that was far more shocking than the prospect of deaths. And the village had to deal with this sort of thing *on a regular basis?*

The harpies started screeching again, and the house owner battered them angrily with the broom while Emily grabbed a small pot plant and lobbed it. It broke on a harpy skull with a *crock!* sound and scattered soil everywhere. Darcy and Dewey held back, not quite so eager to get involved.

Hal gave Robbie a push. "Go see Lauren," he said, keeping his voice low. "Emily and Darcy are busy."

"But, she's *crying*," Robbie said, looking horrified.

"So go and comfort her," Hal urged.

As the three harpies in the kitchen spat curses, Emily's temper flared and her neck began to stretch. "Keep your voices down," she warned, "or you'll be sorry."

The harpies stared at her, amazed. Emily's neck had stretched to nearly three feet long, and her face had taken on a distinctly menacing quality—large black eyes, a forked tongue that slipped out for a brief instant, and a subtle bony ridge on her forehead. The skin on her long, bare neck had toughened and become scaly. When Emily opened her mouth wide, fangs stuck out—wickedly sharp.

The harpies sank to the floor, subdued.

Abigail pulled at Hal's sleeve and pointed. Robbie had tiptoed down the hallway to the bedroom at the back of the house and was leaning in through the doorway. From inside the room, Lauren snapped, "Yes, I *am!*"

They crept closer. Now they could hear Robbie murmuring to her. "You are not. You're *nothing* like them," he said. "You can *become* a harpy, yes, but you're nothing like them. You're human. Would you ever consider breaking into someone's home and stealing? No, you wouldn't. What about kidnapping? No? Of course not. Because you're *not like them*. You're . . . you're a nice, human girl, worth more than a hundred harpies put together."

"They're awful," she cried from behind her hands. "I'm so ashamed." Her sobs came harder and her shoulders shook.

Robbie shuffled closer, turned around, and knelt on the floor next to her. He reached around her shoulder . . . but his hand hovered there, not quite touching.

For a moment he stayed that way, his face creased with indecision, his fingers flexing as if getting ready to touch something scalding hot. Lauren continued sobbing. Then Robbie tentatively allowed his arm to drop onto her shoulder.

Instead of pulling away in disgust, Lauren turned toward him and sobbed openly onto his shoulder. Robbie's eyebrows shot up.

Hal sighed. "Go Robbie," he murmured.

"For heaven's sake!" Abigail said, amazed, as they backed away from the door. "Was that so difficult? What's wrong with a simple hug anyway? Boys are hopeless. It's not like she's going to *bite*."

She paused.

"On the other hand," she said, thoughtfully, "she's a harpy, so I guess she might."

* * *

The harpies in the kitchen were cut free and hauled roughly by villagers to a warehouse several blocks away. Charlie led the way, looking extremely grim. The children followed at a distance, trying to stay out of the way.

Fenton had not returned, but Hal and the others guessed he would be around somewhere, probably wondering how to change back into his human form.

A crowd had gathered outside the warehouse. Other harpies were transported inside. One was unconscious, dragged by its feet through the dirt.

"Kids!" Charlie boomed over the crowd. His red hair bobbed into sight. "Boys! Girls! In here. You too, Lauren."

Feeling a little self-conscious, Hal and his friends picked their way through the crowds and into the warehouse. It wasn't a very big warehouse, more of a large shed with gigantic doors. It was dark inside, and smelled of rotten garbage. As Hal's eyes adjusted to the gloom, he saw men milling around a huge cage in the center. Inside the cage, he counted thirteen harpies including the unconscious one lying in a heap. Two were arguing over a stubby green shoot from some plant or other; its few leaves had been all but nibbled off. In the end, one of the ugly creatures gently tore off part of a leaf and handed it to the other, who grabbed it eagerly and began gnawing on it. Then another harpy started pestering them in a whiny, scratchy voice.

"Quiet!" Charlie roared, and the commotion ceased immediately, both inside the cage and out. Men and women dutifully stepped back to allow Charlie space. "Right," he said, looking at a sheet of paper. "No deaths. Thank goodness."

A huge sigh went up.

Charlie held up his hand, glaring at the sheet of paper as if it were something nasty. "Twenty-two reported injuries, mostly superficial cuts from flying glass, a few bites here and there." He kicked the cage with a heavy boot and the harpies within hissed. "A few more serious injuries though—two unconscious ladies, one badly bruised boy of seven—and old Gilligan had a heart attack."

The crowd moaned angrily.

Charlie once more held up his hand for quiet. A silence fell.

"And . . . a baby was taken."

Chapter Ten
Lauren's idea

Charlie's announcement caused a few in the crowd to swear loudly. A woman screamed, "Kill them all!" But Hal sensed a ripple of surprise too, as though the news was expected to have been much worse. He couldn't understand it. How could the kidnap of a baby be considered 'not as bad as expected'?

Charlie stepped over to Lauren and grasped her shoulder. "Folks, this dear young lady is Lauren. She's a shapeshifter—a harpy."

Mouths dropped open and suspicion flickered across several pairs of eyes. A rough-looking man pulled his jacket back and reached for the hilt of a knife.

"Ladies, gentlemen," Charlie said, his voice rumbling softly. "Lauren was able to give us advance warning of the harpy attack. She gave the alert several minutes before the sentries saw the harpies coming out of the sky." He looked around. "I think you understand the significance of that. The extra couple of minutes gave us time to get inside. Last week, fourteen babies and toddlers were snatched. Before that, seventeen. This time—one."

A murmur carried throughout the warehouse. Whispered voices continued on outside the building to the street.

"What happens to them?" Emily suddenly cried out. "Are you saying—surely you're not saying that—that the babies—"

"They're fine," Charlie reassured her. "Well, as fine as they can be in the hands of these foul creatures." He jerked his thumb back toward the cage, where several harpies hissed again. "Dead kids are no good to them. In fact, a single death would destroy all their bargaining power."

"Bargaining power . . ." Hal murmured. Then he said loudly, "Are you saying the harpies take babies to *bargain* with?"

"They can only carry so much food away," Lauren said. Her voice was flat and emotionless. She had a hard stare in her eyes, and her lips were curling. "So they take infants, sometimes older children. Light, easy to carry, defenseless . . . and worth more than anything else in the world."

Charlie patted her shoulder. "That's right, my dear." He looked around at Hal and his friends. "The first time they took a baby, the entire village turned out to lynch every last one of those harpies. We went up the hill—farmers, innkeepers, metal workers, carpenters, shop owners, cobblers—you name it. A thousand strong, we were, and I led the way, as a griffin. The harpies met us halfway, and told us they'd kill the baby unless we gave them food. Well, we attacked—and they just flew off. The whole lot of 'em, taking to the sky, laughing at us. With the poor little mite dangling."

Emily gasped.

Lauren closed her eyes. "Somehow I *knew* this. It's what I would do, if . . ."

"We had no choice on that occasion," Charlie went on. A murmur of agreement went through the crowd. "We gave 'em food—they wanted a lot—and they returned the baby, unharmed."

"Then we attacked the filthy beasts," a woman shouted.

The harpies in the cage jeered and laughed.

Charlie kicked the cage again. "It's true," he said heavily. "Once the little one was safe and sound in his mother's arms, we attacked the harpies. Again they flew into the sky. We trashed their nest, but it hardly made a difference. And while we were gone from the village, they attacked again and made off with even more than usual, including several more babies. People were badly injured. We were back to square one, only worse."

"We should have poisoned the lot of 'em," a man yelled, "like we used to do in the old days."

There were several cheers.

"Sneak in there," the man continued, "put poison in their water, and let 'em die in their sleep."

Charlie sighed. He turned to Lauren. "It may come to that unless you can somehow convince the harpies to change their ways. They're lazy, greedy, and treacherous, but they're cunning and will do anything for a bit of food. They don't bother to grow their own crops, you see, and they're far too lazy to hunt. It's much easier for them to steal from us. And the easiest way to steal is to take our babies and children and then bargain for whatever we can spare." He stared at his sheet of paper for a moment. "One baby is worth a cartload of food. That's a lot of food. They took seventeen last week, so that was seventeen carts of food. They release a baby when each cart is delivered. And if the cart is not filled to their liking, they send it back. And if we try to attack, or—"

He broke off and closed his eyes. He was grinding his teeth so much that Hal could see the muscles in his cheeks flexing and bulging.

Hal was too horrified to speak. But Robbie suddenly swung around—and *changed*. In half a second he was an ogre, and Hal jumped back to avoid being stepped on. The crowd gasped and there was sudden panic as the ogre, enormous within the confines of the warehouse, stomped toward the cage.

Robbie wrenched the door open and reached inside. The harpies made a terrible ruckus and fell over themselves to get clear, but the ogre's huge hand gripped a harpy by the shoulder and yanked it out of the cage. The harpy's wings flapped as Robbie turned and held the creature high off the ground. A green shoot fell from its hands.

"Whaahh yunn darrrr!" the ogre roared, and Hal had no idea what that meant.

Robbie grabbed one of the harpy's wings with one hand, then quickly grabbed the other. The harpy must have been in pain, dangling by the wings like that, but it was *laughing*, a hideous cackle that sent a chill down Hal's spine.

The ogre slowly began to pull on the wings, stretching them outward . . .

All the harpies were screeching by now, most of them terrified, huddled in a corner of the cage. The villagers were yelling too, but with eagerness, baying for blood. Still the dangling harpy was cackling, as if drunk with giddiness.

A wing broke with a sharp *snap!* The creature immediately stopped laughing and began squealing instead.

"No!" Charlie shouted. "That's not the way!" He looked around desperately, first at Lauren, then at Hal. "Do something! Stop him!"

Hal rushed forward and kicked Robbie hard in the leg. The ogre barely flinched, but the kick got his attention. "Stop that," Hal said sternly, as if talking to Emily's dog. "Put it down. Bad ogre."

Robbie blinked at him, looking puzzled. Then he sighed and dropped the harpy in a heap on the ground.

There were several cries of disappointment from the crowd, but Charlie looked angry. "Everyone outside! Now!"

With much ushering, the crowd filtered outside to the street. Charlie ordered a few men to stand guard and fix the cage door. Lauren picked up the green shoot and stared at it thoughtfully while being propelled outside by Charlie's strong hands. Then, as the last to leave the warehouse, he pulled the enormous doors shut with a bang and the clamor of harpies was cut off.

Charlie planted his hands on his hips and stood glaring at the crowd, and at Robbie, who hunkered under the overhanging roof of a shop front. "This is *not* how we behave," Charlie growled. "As bad as things get, we will *not* start torturing creatures—even harpies. No, no, no. People, we will fix this problem. But not like this."

"Then how?" yelled a tall, skinny woman. "You've been telling us for months that it will get better, that we'll find a way. *How?*"

"The only way is to *fight* them," a man at the back shouted. "We've got shapeshifters everywhere now. Let's use them! We've already got a griffin, and now we've got an ogre, a dragon, a—a giant black lizard thing—"

"And a gorgon down at Carter," the skinny woman agreed.

"The gorgon is only effective if the harpies actually *look* at her," Charlie started to argue—but his words were drowned out by a chant that began with a few and quickly spread throughout the crowd.

"Fight! Fight! Fight!"

Charlie closed his eyes. Then he glared at Robbie, who finally shrank back to his human form. "See what you've done?" he boomed, raising his voice to be heard. "Inciting the crowd like that. What were you thinking?"

"I wasn't," Robbie mumbled.

Charlie placed his hands on Lauren's shoulders, bent down, and peered into her eyes. "My dear—is there anything you can think of that will help settle this peacefully? And by peacefully, I don't necessarily mean nicely." He shot the warehouse doors a wicked glare. "Any form of blackmail will do. Just something to end this *without bloodshed*."

Lauren looked faint.

Abigail, who had been silent until now, suddenly yelled, "Quiet!"

A few people trailed off immediately, but the chant went on for quite a while longer. Finally it was silenced by a bellow from Charlie.

Abigail sprouted wings and hovered in the air where she could be seen and heard by all. She buzzed around slowly in front of the crowd, and spoke loudly. "My friends and I will go up the hill to see the harpies. Lauren has a plan. We'll get the baby back safely *and* we'll force the harpies to stop these attacks."

"So *you* say," a man snapped.

Hal changed. His friends jumped back as his huge reptilian body burst into existence. He coiled his tail around, stretched his neck, and let loose a terrible roar along with a burst of fire.

The crowd cowered.

Abigail, appearing unfazed by the display, smiled. "Trust us, people. Lauren's plan is good. Now go home and let us work out the details. We'll bring the baby back safe and sound, and the harpies won't bother you again."

There was little to be said after that. The crowd slowly dispersed. When the children were alone outside the warehouse, Lauren turned to Abigail.

"I *really* hope you have some ideas, Abigail," she said, sounding cross. "You've dropped me right in it."

Abigail looked grim. "Then you'd better get your thinking cap on, Lauren. Think *harpy*. Think about what would hurt them, or persuade them to stop attacking the village. You need to try and think like a harpy."

Lauren stood there with her bottom lip quivering. Hal felt sorry for her, but knew that she was probably their best bet.

Charlie stood aside, silent. The streets were almost empty now, apart from a few stragglers and shop owners, who looked on with sad expressions.

Fenton appeared. He was on the warehouse roof, scrabbling for a hold on the tiles. With his long tail coiled around a stubby vent pipe, he lowered himself down the slanted roof until he reached the gutter. He released his tail—and then the gutter gave way with a clang and Fenton promptly fell to the ground below. He landed awkwardly, sending up a cloud of dust.

"Fenton's back," Emily said in the silence that followed.

Dewey grinned nervously. "I suppose he'll be stuck like that until we go to sleep tonight."

"*If* we go to sleep tonight," Darcy said. She nudged Lauren. "How's it going, sister? Got that harpy brain working yet?"

Lauren frowned. She stared at the harpy's mangled green shoot in her hand. "Maybe." She gestured to Charlie, who took a couple of strides closer. "I *think* I have an idea. But . . . it means play-acting."

"I can act," Charlie rumbled. "What's the deal?"

Lauren gathered everyone around her and tentatively outlined her idea. At first she was nervous, almost red-faced with embarrassment, certain that her idea was ridiculous. But as she spoke, and heads began to nod thoughtfully, she grew bolder and took charge. The innocent green shoot became the focus of attention for a moment as she waved it around, then tore off a tiny piece of leaf and touched it to her tongue. She spat it out immediately, but explained how the shoot would come into play.

Hal was proud of her, and he could tell from Robbie's glazed expression that he was too. By the time Lauren finished, Emily and Darcy were grinning broadly, and Abigail had a wicked gleam in her eye.

Only Dewey looked doubtful. "But . . . it's a *horrible* lie," he mumbled. "Even though it's a lie, it's just . . ."

"I know," Lauren agreed. "But I think it's necessary."

Charlie thought so too, but he had doubts of his own. "If this goes wrong, we could lose that child." He sighed. "But we'll run the same risk no matter when we take a stand, and we have to take a stand sooner or later."

"Then let's get started," Lauren said. "Charlie, go and pull that door open and keep talking as you do so, so the harpies can overhear you. Darcy—will you go and rustle up a nice big chunk of ham or something?"

"Will do," Darcy said, and hurried off.

"And Robbie—bring us a cart."

Robbie grinned. "Aye, captain."

Hal watched, fascinated, as Charlie began to open one of the huge warehouse doors. As he did so, he turned back to face the children, his voice echoing up the street. "So it's agreed, then. A sacrifice it is."

The harpies began screeching from within the warehouse.

* * *

Robbie the ogre shuffled slowly up the hill, pulling an old, four-wheeled cart ahead of the group. On the back of the cart, thirteen harpies sat back to back in a line, tightly trussed with rope. One of them whined in pain, its wing broken. Another had a mass of blood on its forehead and had only recently woken.

Hal and the others hung back a little way so that the harpies couldn't eavesdrop. Fenton followed close behind, low to the ground, his long black body leaving a smooth trail in the dirt.

"It's like catnip," Lauren said. "Biscuit *loves* catnip. I sprinkle some on the floor and he rolls on it and licks it and goes crazy." She held up the green shoot. "This is like harpy catnip. Are you sure you can't taste anything?"

Abigail shook her head and spat with disgust. "It tastes like a leaf."

Lauren shrugged. "Well, when I tasted it, I felt tingly all over. Just the tiniest piece and it made me feel relaxed and comfortable—just for a moment. I felt like nothing could annoy or worry me. It was like . . . nothing mattered, you know?"

"And that harpy didn't care about his wing being broken," Hal said. "Until Robbie actually broke it, that is."

"Yes," Lauren said. "This little plant took away the harpy's worries, made him giggle like an idiot . . . but I guess it didn't take away his pain." She frowned. "But there's more to it than that. When I felt the buzz . . . I also felt as though the wind changed. It was like my senses were heightened for a moment, and I could make the breeze move whichever direction I wanted."

"The *breeze?*" Emily repeated.

Lauren smiled. "It sounds silly, I know. But I have a feeling these little green shoots provide more than just a happy buzz. It's like they tap into some strange power that only harpies possess."

They walked in silence. Then Hal remembered something. "It got cloudy just before the harpies came down on the village."

Lauren gave him a strange look. "I heard some villagers saying that they should have paid attention to the weather and gotten inside earlier."

"Charlie said the clouds weren't a good sign," Hal agreed. "On a clear day, harpies would be seen in the sky, but with clouds everywhere . . ."

"So the harpies only come on cloudy days," Abigail said, sounding puzzled. "It sounds perfectly logical to me. So what?"

Hal shook his head. "I think it's a little more than that. Right, Lauren?"

But Lauren said nothing more.

The hill wore on. The village, large and sprawling, didn't seem all that far behind, yet they had been walking for an hour now, steadily climbing toward a sheer cliff face that formed one side of a towering mountain. According to Charlie, the children had only to follow the well-worn tracks as far as the craggy rocks; there, in the shadow of the mountain, they would come across a foul stench.

Hal was already getting a whiff of something nasty in the air. "Do you think they can see us?" he asked, worried.

"It's possible," Abigail agreed. "Darcy, maybe you should do your thing. Let's cover the harpies."

Together, while the cart trundled onward, the children unfolded a large sheet and flipped it over the surprised harpies so that it completely covered them all. Then Dewey weighted down the corners with stones so it wouldn't blow away.

"That's better already," Emily said, satisfied. "All right—shh!"

Silently, Darcy reached under the back end of the cart and unfastened a bag. As soon as she had it loose, she stopped and allowed the cart to go on ahead. The children crowded around the bag.

Inside was a large slab of roasted boar. It was an entire thigh, browned and seasoned and delicious. Hal was tempted to take a bite . . . but he decided that would be a little distasteful, considering what they intended to do with it.

Uncaring about messing up her dress, Darcy held the joint tightly to her chest and clamped her arms around it. Then she turned invisible.

As a wood nymph, her camouflage was extremely subtle and clever. She wasn't exactly transparent, but her skin—and her smart clothes too—took on the color and texture of the background, so that she appeared invisible. When she moved, she was like a blur, a smudge in reality that no one could focus on. The moment she stood still, it was very difficult to see her at all.

The really clever thing about her camouflage was that each onlooker saw different colors and textures, depending on where that person stood. Hal saw the cart behind her, *through* her, while Emily, standing to one side, saw the hill or the nearby boulder.

Blinking furiously, Hal adjusted his eyes. It was like looking out of a window at the lawn, only to find a spider walking across the glass an inch from his nose. Without moving he could adjust his focus and the spider would become sharply defined while the lawn fuzzed out. As soon as he was able to track Darcy's whereabouts, she moved again and was lost. However, the joint of meat she held was partially visible between her arms, so he kept his eyes on that instead.

"Is the meat hidden?" Darcy asked quietly, sounding anxious.

"Good enough," Abigail said. "Go."

"Good luck!" Lauren said. "See you up there."

The remaining children caught up with the cart as a blurry figure hurried up the hill in a small cloud of dust. In moments she was gone. Hal wasn't worried about the harpies spotting her; the nest was still a fifteen-minute walk ahead, and Darcy was hard to see from just a few feet away!

The trussed prisoners were complaining about the sheet, but Fenton leapt onto the cart and hissed at them. There was a sudden silence.

Hal and the others hurried around to the front of the cart, where Robbie tirelessly pulled it along. "She's away," Hal said quietly.

Robbie grunted.

Sometimes Hal wondered if Robbie understood what was being said. He guessed he did, but got the impression that Robbie's mind clouded when he was in ogre form. Yet Hal's dragon mind seemed sharp. If turning into a somewhat stupid ogre dulled Robbie's mind, but turning into a dragon had no effect on Hal's, did that indicate dragons were as smart as humans?

Likewise, Fenton failed to interact when he was in his lizard form, merely following and sometimes protecting them like a faithful dog. He understood what was going on, but seemed incapable of contributing in any useful way.

Hal made a point to ask Robbie about this sometime. The idea of losing clarity of mind when transforming . . . Hal shuddered. But perhaps it explained how it was that Thomas Patten had considered *eating* them, back in the woods on the island. His manticore mind had clouded his human judgment, especially since the boy had spent the last six years in that hideous form.

What if Hal, or one of his friends, had been chosen to turn into a *really* dumb creature, and then lacked the wit to turn back into a human? What about Orson? Just how smart were horses, anyway?

"The smell is overpowering," Emily said. "I think we're getting close."

In fact they had another ten minutes' walk ahead. But soon the craggy rocks rose before them, pointed and vicious. The mountain that towered above threw them into shadow, so that the area beyond the jagged rocks appeared dark and foreboding. Harpies came into view as they approached.

"Stop!" one ordered. It was a male, scrawny and dirty, yellow eyes blazing. He wore torn pants only, no doubt stolen from the village. "Leave the cart there. I'll check it, and then you can have your baby—"

"We don't want the baby," Hal said shortly, and kept moving.

The harpy was speechless. Hal, Robbie, and all his friends crested the hill between the rocks before the harpy could find its tongue. "You—what do you mean, you don't—"

"We don't want the baby," Lauren snapped. Hal could hear the tremor in her voice, and hoped the harpies couldn't.

More harpies appeared—five of them. They appeared skittish, except for one, who strode forward with her wings outstretched. This grimy, smelly female wore a tattered, filth-encrusted dress that hung loosely off her shoulders. She shoved the male aside and stopped in front of Hal, sniffing at him. Then she sniffed at Lauren. "You seem . . . familiar, somehow."

"I have a familiar face," Lauren said. "Anyway, we've come to tell you that we're not here to trade."

The scowling harpy glanced at the sheet-covered cart and the creature that guarded it. Her eyes widened. "What—what is *that?*"

Lauren glanced back at Fenton. "Oh, he's my friend."

Abigail sprouted wings and buzzed up to the cart. She moved the stones aside so that the sheet could fall back. Beneath, the hapless prisoners cowered under Fenton's red-eyed stare.

"And those are *your* friends," Lauren went on, waving toward them. "You can have them back. We don't want them."

Boldly, she continued walking into the nest, and Robbie stomped after her, dragging the cart. Hal and the others matched them step for step.

"Stop!" the filthy vixen snapped. But as the ogre loomed over her, she fell back, then hurried to catch up as the group marched past.

"They're going to sacrifice one of us!" a male harpy screamed from the back of the cart. "I heard them talking about it back in the village!"

Hal was listening intently, but his gaze was focused on the harpy nest. It was the most disgusting thing he'd ever seen. The circle of jagged rocks, tucked under the base of the mountain, formed a huge mouth, like a shallow cave. Within this cave, hundreds of harpies lounged around, lying in or on top of piles of filth—bones from stolen roasts that had been picked clean long ago, discarded, blackening skins from large fruits and vegetables, dirt-encrusted blankets, torn and bloody clothing . . . The trash was everywhere, strewn across the rocks and in the spaces between. And the stench—

Hal gagged.

The feathered layabouts started pointing and jeering. Many were giggling, almost helpless with mirth. They were chewing on the little green shoots, drunk with happiness. Little dust clouds whirled eerily around their bird feet, as though somehow conjured for idle entertainment.

But the harpies on the back of the cart had no such shoots and were anything but relaxed. They yelled and screeched to be heard, angry and scared. "Get us out of here! Kill 'em! Save us!"

The harpy queen, as Hal suddenly thought of her, flew overhead and landed with a thump before them. She crouched and spread her arms wide, showing them her dirty claws. "Come one step closer and the baby gets it."

Lauren smiled, but stopped. "You're assuming we care."

Hal spotted what he was looking for. To one side, against the face of the mountain, a cage had been constructed. Clearly it was for prisoners, but right now the door stood open. Inside were five or six makeshift cribs, each big enough to hold several infants. In one, a tiny white blanket moved as an infant squirmed.

An angry burning sensation began deep down in Hal's stomach, rising slowly to his chest. That poor frightened baby!

"Of *course* you care," the queen said, her eyes darting from Lauren to Hal and then to Abigail and Dewey. She gave Robbie a sideways glance, keeping the ogre in her sight and out of reach. "Now, where's our offering? You know the rules—one kid for one cart of food. All I see is a cart full of prisoners."

Hundreds of harpies around the cave watched in silence as their queen negotiated. Most were lying around or sitting, a few standing, but they all stared with yellow eyes at Hal and his friends.

Behind them, in the cage, the white blanket moved aside as if by magic. A baby floated out—and promptly vanished. Then a roasted leg of boar appeared, and dropped quietly into the crib. The white blanket covered it.

A baby's arm appeared for a moment, and then a flash of chubby leg. Then they were gone, mysteriously vanishing into thin air. The baby chose that moment to start wailing, but the harpies paid no attention. Why should they? Of *course* the baby was crying—it wanted its mother! The fact that the crying now came from *outside* the cage went unnoticed.

"Well?" the queen screamed. "Answer me! Where's our food?"

Lauren glanced at Hal, then back at the greasy, angry creature. "Things have changed. The people of the village have turned. The majority has voted, and from now on carts of food will *not* be brought up here in exchange for stolen babies."

The queen quivered with rage. "What?"

"You heard me. It's a shame about the baby. I'm sure the mother will be very upset. But the people of the village have hired us to take care of the problem, and we intend to take care of it."

"She's going to sacrifice one of us!" the harpies on the cart began screaming again. "They said so, down at the village!"

"You misunderstood," Lauren said loudly, her gaze not once leaving the queen. "Yes, there will be a sacrifice today. But it won't be a harpy. Killing one of you wouldn't make the slightest difference."

Hal tensed. Lauren turned to him, and gave a nod.

Hal changed into a dragon, and there was a sudden flurry of activity. Harpies scattered in all directions, and the queen fell back, her eyes blazing and her teeth bared. Screeches came from all around.

"Go ahead, take the annoying little brat!" the queen screamed. "See if I care! We'll just get another when you're gone!"

"That's why we're not taking it," Lauren said. She raised her voice. "The people of the village are sacrificing one of their own for the greater good. The people will not be bullied into giving away food, and they will not spend their lives fearing attacks from the likes of you." She turned to Hal. "Burn it!"

Hal roared and hurried deeper into the harpy nest. With his sensitive dragon nostrils, the smell almost knocked him out. He tried to ignore it, and concentrated on the task at hand. The cage stood before him and he stamped toward it. Harpies jumped out of his way.

Smashing through the flimsy wooden framework, Hal breathed fire all around, burning all the cribs until they were black, and paying particular attention to the one with the leg of roast boar inside. The white blanket blackened immediately, became a roaring inferno, and the crib burst alight and collapsed. The meat sizzled and blackened too. It split open and popped.

Seconds later it was unidentifiable.

Chapter Eleven
The burning

The joint of meat, now a smoking charred lump nestled within a burnt blanket, continued to shrink and dry amid the brittle remains of the crib. A painfully thin harpy ventured closer, her mouth open. She poked at the lump with a dirty foot, watching it rock back and forth.

His job done, Hal turned and hurried back to Lauren.

The harpy queen stood aghast. She stared in disbelief at what was left of the cage, and the burning cribs within.

"What—what have you *done?*" she whispered. "You burned that baby!"

"Now you have nothing to bargain with," Lauren said, her voice trembling. Her small chin jutted out as she drew herself up. "A sacrifice has been made. The mother will be upset—" *Upset!* Hal thought. *No kidding!* "—but the people of the village recognize that this is for the best. Take their children if you must—but you won't get a single grain of corn in return. Your efforts will be wasted."

As the cribs burned, and flustered harpies returned to the ground, a silence fell. Hal looked around. Good—Dewey and Emily had slipped away, gone to join Darcy and the baby. He listened carefully, and thought he heard the galloping of hoofs receding down the hill.

"That's the sacrifice done," Lauren said. "It's time for your punishment."

The queen's eyes widened. She backed away, eyeing Hal warily. She almost backed into Robbie, and jumped clear as he lazily reached for her.

Lauren marched deeper into the harpy nest, and Hal fell in step. Abigail buzzed alongside, and Robbie took up the rear. Fenton remained on the cart, guarding the trussed harpies.

"Where are you going?" the queen screamed. "Everyone—attack!"

But the harpies ignored her. Hal could feel every pair of yellow eyes following him as he stamped through the nest after Lauren.

Lauren marched with purpose. She ignored the filth and didn't even flinch when some of the braver winged creatures flew down to intercept her. Hal gave a short burst of fire and sent them flapping again.

It would have been easy to breathe fire around the place, Hal thought to himself. But what would that achieve? Charlie had been right. No amount of damage to the nest would rile the harpies, because there was nothing but trash here. They'd probably enjoy seeing the place go up in flames!

The queen flew overhead and leapt in front of a curious gap in the rocks near the back of the nest, under the cliff. "Turn around now," she growled, "and I'll forget this ever happened."

Lauren never missed a step, because Robbie was there with her. He jumped forward and scooped the harpy sideways with a powerful arm. She sailed in an arc and collapsed in a heap. But she shook herself and got up immediately, screaming at her minions to attack. Some came swooping in, but Hal breathed fire in their direction, and Robbie lashed out with flailing arms. Harpies dropped out of the air, either smoking or bruised. The rest backed off once more, uncertain.

Then the queen made a motion with her hands, some secret signal. Dozens of harpies scurried around and came up with little green shoots, which they stuffed into their mouths and chewed quickly. As they chewed, they frowned in concentration and dust storms sprang up. The queen broke into a grin as the harpies narrowed their eyes and, somehow, caused the dust storms to move toward Hal and his friends.

The wind was sudden and violent, and the dust vicious. Abigail shot up into the air, while Lauren jammed her eyes shut and stood still, shielding her face. Robbie—whose head stuck up above the miniature storms—turned and lunged for the queen.

The dust stung Hal's dragon eyes, but through constant blinking he saw the ogre's massive fingers clamp around the queen's throat. The harpy's wings beat frantically, but she wasn't going anywhere. Robbie reached out with his other hand and grasped one of those fluttering wings.

"Don't!" the harpies screamed from the back of the cart. "The queen! Don't let the monster pull her wings off!"

Suddenly aware of the danger, the shoot-chewing harpies lost focus and crouched low, wings shivering, eyes darting toward Robbie. The dust storms dissipated and small stones fell to the ground.

Lauren moved on, and Hal followed. Abigail dropped out of the sky and landed lightly, staying close to Hal's side.

Once past the narrow gap in the rocks, the pathway led through a crack in the cliff, rather like an archway, about ten feet high and four feet wide. Surprisingly, daylight lay beyond. Stepping through, Hal and Lauren came upon a bowl-shaped depression surrounded on all sides by smooth, towering rock walls. It was a secret place on the edge of mountain, accessible only through this archway or from the sky above. The enclosure was blanketed with vegetation—the beloved green shoots. *Harpy catnip.*

Ignoring the screeching queen, Hal stepped into the middle of the lush green plants. Abigail buzzed in the air as Robbie squeezed through the archway. He tossed the queen aside and towered protectively over Lauren.

"I could have my friend burn it all," Lauren told the battered, dazed queen. "But I'm feeling lenient. Hal—burn a quarter of it."

Hal did so, breathing a long, unbroken jet of fire across a full quarter of the planted area. Green shoots blackened, withered and died, while harpies screamed in anguish. Hal made sure that the shoots were thoroughly burnt out.

The queen clapped her hands to her head. Her wings sagged. "No, no, NO! Do you have *any idea* what—"

"I know exactly what this plant means to you," Lauren said evenly. "That's why I ordered only a quarter of it to burn. I'm merciful, you see."

And cunning, Hal thought. *Burn it all and we'd have nothing left to bargain with, and the harpies, with nothing to lose, would turn to revenge. Leave most of it alone and they'll feel grateful, relieved, and more willing to listen.*

Lauren stepped closer to the harpy, and knelt to stare into her eyes. "If you attack the village again and steal babies, they will be worthless to you. *You will no longer be given food in return.* And the villagers won't want the babies back, either. Once taken, they're tainted, see?" Hal was amazed at the depths of Lauren's fibs! "You'll have to feed them yourself, nurse them, change their diapers, and raise them as your own. Do you understand? Once you take a baby, it's *yours*—unless you kill it. Can you do that? Can you kill a baby?"

The harpy queen looked uncertain, perhaps even troubled. Then she scowled. "I've killed 'em before. Anyway, why the sudden change of heart? I don't believe you. Humans wouldn't just give up their own like that."

Lauren spread her hands. "They have no choice. When you take so much food for yourselves, you're forcing families to starve—including their young. Everyone suffers. That's why they called us. Sometimes it takes outsiders to see the situation objectively. And the solution is simple: no more bargaining with babies. Sacrifices have to be made for the greater good. It's a tough decision, but it's the only way."

Hal had to admire Lauren. She was lying through her teeth, making it up as she went along, and doing a great job.

"Who *are* you kids?" the queen snapped.

"Paid mercenaries," Lauren said. "We go around the land solving problems."

"But you're so *young*."

"Yet wise beyond our years," Lauren said lightly. Her voice hardened. "Just to be clear: the villagers are unanimous. They will not be blackmailed anymore. And the next time you attack the village—the next time you mess with the clouds and give the villagers reason to *think* you're going to attack—my dragon friend here will return to burn every last plant in this place, along with as many harpies as he can catch. You may escape with your lives, but your precious plant will be gone and you'll have to suffer your miserable lives stone-cold sober."

95

The queen's mouth dropped open. "How do you know about—about the—"

"What, the effect the shoots have on you?" Lauren shrugged. "I know all sorts of things. I also know that, with the help of the plant to heighten your senses, you harpies can manipulate the wind. Creating cute little dust storms is a neat party trick, but forcing clouds to gather over the village to mask your approach . . ."

"You can't *possibly* know about this! It's a closely guarded secret."

Lauren shook her head. "Not anymore. Although why you kept that a secret, I don't know. With power like that, you could do so much good."

"Who cares about doing good?" the queen cried, pulling at her straggly hair. "Life as a harpy is *hard*. This plant makes our filthy, depressing nest bearable." She glared at Lauren. "You're just a girl. You wouldn't understand how we feel. We used to be beautiful! But the humans *shun* us. We're outcasts. They won't *give* us food, so we have to *take* it."

"Oh, *please!*" Lauren snapped, and suddenly transformed into a harpy. The queen fell back, her eyes wide. Compared to her, Lauren was like an angel—pure, dazzling white. "Why should the villagers just *give* you food?" Lauren demanded. "What have you done to earn it? Look at yourself! You're disgusting!"

The grimy creature looked down at herself, then studied Lauren with an expression of envy. She seemed to sag at the shoulders, and her wings went limp. "Life is hard," she repeated quietly.

Abigail buzzed closer. "Perhaps if you worked with the humans, helped them in some way, did some manual labor instead of lazing around up here in this disgusting place, created a bit of rain when there's a drought . . . well, who knows, maybe you could *bargain* for food in a decent, civilized way, where nobody gets hurt. Maybe, over time, the people of the village will start to treat you as people, instead of vicious, nasty, smelly creatures." Abigail pinched her nose. "And let's face it—you *stink*."

Hal, Lauren, Abigail and Robbie left the harpy queen gazing forlornly at her precious plants. The harpies offered no resistance—they appeared too shocked to even think straight. They just watched, silent and resentful, as the foursome left the nest.

Back at the cart, Robbie waited until Fenton had climbed down and then tipped the whole contraption up on end. The thirteen trussed harpies slid out in a heap, yelling and complaining.

Hal changed back into his human form, and climbed aboard. He helped Lauren up, and Fenton once more slithered on board. Abigail buzzed down and took a seat. "Homeward, Robbie!" she called cheerfully.

* * *

It was a slow but pleasurable journey back to the village. People cheered as they trundled along the streets. Word had obviously gotten around quickly! Then, out of the crowds stepped redheaded Charlie Duggan, with Darcy, Emily and Dewey at his side, all waving happily. With them stood a woman and her baby, her eyes red from crying, but her smile broad.

"You got back okay, then," Hal said, jumping down.

Darcy nodded. "Switching the baby for a leg of boar was easy, but I thought the game was up when she started crying. Once you changed into a dragon though, all those harpies flew up in the air and I just slipped out unnoticed. Dewey and Emily soon caught up with me."

"It was nice riding on Dewey's back again," Emily said, patting the boy on the shoulder, "although this time I had to share with Darcy and *this* sweet little thing." She leaned closer to the woman's squirming bundle and smiled. "You liked the ride, didn't you? Yes, you did! You went right off to sleep, didn't you?"

"I'm just glad you stuck to the plan and left when you did," Hal said. "It was a little dicey for a while, and I kept expecting harpies to swoop in and take Lauren or Abigail prisoners."

"I wish they'd tried," Abigail said fiercely, her fists balled.

The woman stepped closer so that Hal and his friends could see the baby. Lauren started cooing immediately, and Abigail grinned, but Hal just stared. He had never seen a real live infant human up close before. Even the one he had rescued during the harpy attack had been covered. People actually started out this small? He studied the little girl's chubby cheeks and clear blue eyes, and watched as she clenched her tiny fingers around Lauren's thumb.

He shuddered inwardly. Even though Lauren's idea had been nothing but a ruse, the very idea of burning a—

He ended the thought right there. It didn't even bear thinking about.

They spent the rest of the day enjoying the village. The mood had changed. It wasn't that the villagers took for granted that the harpy attacks had ended, but now there was some small degree of hope. Some insisted that the attacks would continue, and even suggested they'd be worse next time—but the general response was, "We'll see." The vigilance would not end; the goblin sentries would remain in the towers and the people would always keep one ear open for the sirens and an eye on the nearest doorway.

But Hal knew that the most difficult task lay ahead. Part of the hope the villagers felt was that he, Hal, would come up with some clever way to stop the dragons from attacking. If Lauren could give the harpies pause for thought, perhaps Hal would be just as successful.

Still, Hal was doubtful. In fact, he was terrified. As he joined his friends for dinner that evening in the friendly inn, he knew he wouldn't be able to eat much, or sleep that night. His friends were relaxed and happy, chatting idly—except for Fenton, who remained stuck in his lizard form. He had gone off somewhere to lie low, probably wishing he could change at will instead of having to fall asleep. What a handicap that was!

"I wonder if he's hungry," Darcy mused, watching steam rise from her bowl of rich lamb and vegetable stew. "If he eats while in his lizard form, would he need more food to fill up than if he ate in human form?"

"What do gargoyles eat anyway?" Robbie demanded.

According to Miss Simone, Fenton's particular species of lizard monster was so rare it had no name. But since the boy had been seen clinging to the sides of buildings and spitting jets of water, 'gargoyle' seemed pretty apt.

Darcy pointed her spoon at Robbie. "What if *you* ate a dinner now, here at this table, as a human . . . and then changed into an ogre? Would you feel hungry again? Would you need more food to fill your bigger belly? And what if you filled up as an ogre and then turned human again? Would all that food still be inside you, bursting to explode out of your smaller stomach?"

Lauren laughed. "More to the point, if Robbie was an ogre, would he want to eat sticky insect eggs like the rest of them?"

While the others joined in with the laughter, Robbie grimaced. "All I know is, when I saw the ogres eating those eggs, I felt sick. So I guess not. I'm still human even when I'm an ogre."

"Hmm," Emily said. "Look at poor Thomas, though. He's obviously lost some of his humanity. Why else would he try and eat Hal and Abigail for dinner?"

The reminder of Thomas the manticore attacking them in Black Woods on the island brought back the memory of Hal changing into a dragon for the first time. He had felt powerful and strong then, almost invincible. But that was against a *manticore*. As dangerous as manticores were, other dragons were likely to be much worse.

"You're very quiet, Hal," Darcy said.

Abigail, sitting to Hal's side, nudged him gently. "Fretting about tomorrow?"

Hal blanched. *Tomorrow!* The subject had not even been discussed fully, but somehow he knew it was *tomorrow* that he would have to face the dragons.

"You'll be fine," Emily said brightly. "I have complete faith in you."

"Really?" Hal shook his head. "I can't think why. I'm a young, small, inexperienced dragon. And I can't fly. How am I supposed to be a match for all those hundreds of dragons down in the labyrinth?"

"You've got us," Robbie offered, his mouth full.

Hal gave a wry grin. "Thanks. But . . . not to be rude, how does an ogre, or a centaur, stand up to a fire-breathing dragon? Can harpies fly as fast, or as high? And Fenton . . . I mean, he's pretty scary, but he's basically a slow-moving oversized lizard that spits water." Hal looked around at the circle of faces. "I'm not trying to be big-headed here, but dragons are probably the most feared creatures in this land. So how can I . . . how can I do anything that . . ."

"We have a secret weapon," Abigail said.

Hal turned to her, and found a familiar gleam in her eye. "Like what?"

"Well, my brains, for starters." Everyone laughed, and Hal felt the knots in his stomach loosen a fraction. "Look, we're a team. We might not be a match for dragons, but we just have to use our brains to come up with a way to trick them or persuade them. And don't forget, we have armies on our side."

"Armies?"

Abigail nodded. "Emily could call on the naga and all the snakes. Robbie could gather hundreds of ogres. Dewey could round up his centaur friends." She shrugged. "What I'm saying is, it's not all on *your* shoulders, Hal. You're really just a translator and advisor. You can guide us, but the problem belongs to *everyone*, and we're all involved. We just need to figure out what we're going to do, discuss it with Charlie and the villagers, and work up a solution."

"Right," Emily said. "Lauren was able to get into the minds of the harpies and come up with a plan that ordinary people might not have thought about—because they knew nothing about harpy catnip and would never have considered a pretend baby sacrifice."

Hal winced.

"So all you need to do," she continued, "is get into the minds of the dragons, perhaps see where they live . . . and come up with a solution."

"Easy," Hal muttered.

"The question is," Robbie said, still chewing, "do we make bold demands, or trick them, or blackmail them, or persuade them, or beg them—or what?"

Hal didn't know—yet. When he was a dragon, he felt invincible. A mere human standing in front of him making demands would annoy him. A human trying to blackmail him would be instant grounds for a roasting, as would trickery if the ruse was uncovered. Begging? Hal suspected he would find that kind of behavior pathetic and contemptible; he would probably turn his back and walk away in disgust, and flatten the beggar with his tail as an afterthought.

Surprised, Hal realized he was already thinking like a dragon to some extent. What approach would work best, then, from his point of view as a dragon? If he enjoyed eating humans, what would make him change his mind?

"Hal?" Abigail asked.

"Thinking," Hal murmured, staring into his stew.

Bold and honest, he decided. Then he corrected himself: bold, honest, and *respectful*. But no groveling!

Hal chewed on a hunk of bread, vaguely aware that his friends were staring at him in silence. "Bold, honest and respectful," he said, after he had chewed for a while and swallowed. "That's what Miss Simone said too. I think that's got to be the first approach. Just ask them outright to stop eating humans." He grimaced. "They'll laugh. I can tell you now, they'll laugh."

"But you do have to ask first," Abigail said. "That makes sense. Give them the respect they deserve, right? If they spit on that respect, then we can try another approach."

Hal took a first sip of his drink, then looked at it in surprise. It was like nothing he had ever tasted before.

"Carrot juice," Emily said. "Mixed with avocado. I already asked about it. Charlie said it's good for you."

"Helps you see in the dark," Darcy added.

And so the conversation shifted again. As Lauren questioned whether carrot juice actually did help you see in the dark, and Emily insisted that it did, Hal looked around for Charlie. The innkeeper was seeing to other guests at another table, but as he headed back to the kitchen, Hal waved and ushered him over.

"What can I get you, young man?" Charlie said cheerily.

"Uh, nothing, thanks," Hal said. "I just had a question. Have there been any other shapeshifter dragons before me?"

The chitchat around the table ceased. "Ooh," Emily said. "Good question."

Charlie frowned, then circled the table and sat heavily in Fenton's vacant chair between Darcy and Robbie. "There have been a few. There really isn't much in the way of records about shapeshifters from more than a hundred or so years ago. The whole science of shapeshifting was kind of hit and miss back then—and they were used for nefarious purposes rather than for good. In the old days, kings used certain fearsome shapeshifters like dragons as personal bodyguards, and the fast or winged shapeshifters for transport. But sometimes they were used as weapons. How easy it was to send an innocent child into an enemy camp, posing as a messenger . . . and for that child to turn into a dragon and burn them all."

Hal sucked in his breath.

"But those days are over," Charlie said, looking apologetic. "We don't even have kings or queens anymore. Shapeshifters are our royalty now."

"You mean we get to live in castles?" Abigail said, grinning.

Charlie burst into laughter. "If you like, yes. You certainly don't need to work for a living, nor your parents. Shapeshifters owe nothing—especially when we're putting our lives on the line. Take Lauren, for instance." He reached across and patted her hand. "If what she did today works, and the harpies stop bothering us, think how many carts of food that'll save us, not to mention injuries, damages and occasional deaths. The entire village is instantly in your debt." He jabbed a finger at Hal. "You too, of course. And Robbie. *All* of you."

Charlie's helper, Mirabelle, came over and whispered in Charlie's ear. He listened, then nodded. "Sure thing, you get off home. See you in the morning." As Mirabelle hurried away, Charlie grinned and lowered his voice. "Got a date, bless her. Anyway, where was I?"

"Dragon shapeshifters," Hal prompted.

"Ah." Charlie sat back in his chair, and it creaked alarmingly. He thought for a moment. "As you get older, you'll probably yearn for something else to do besides your shapeshifting job. You'll open an inn, or become a teacher, or whatever. But that's all on the side. See, people pay me for a room and meal here, but outside of that, they owe me in a much bigger way for the amount of times I've tangled with griffins or warned off passing troublemakers—you know, put myself in danger on behalf of the village."

"Who's actually in charge of the village?" Darcy asked.

"Ah, good question," Charlie said eagerly. Hal got the distinct impression the man was trying to avoid talking about dragon shapeshifters. "Every village is different. Most have a small committee of leaders, and a spokesperson. In Louis we have ten wise old codgers who make decisions about everyday trivial stuff. I'm the go-to man when there's trouble from outside. Simone is the spokesperson for Carter, but she practically runs the place in all respects. A very important lady, she is, our Lady Simone. But she doesn't care about titles. She'd be happier if people just left her alone to do her *real* job instead of pestering her with petty things . . ."

"What about dragon shapeshifters?" Hal asked again.

Charlie sighed. "All right, all right, I suppose I should tell you. There *was* one in recent years. One of my generation."

Hal's mouth dropped open. "You went to school with him?"

"Yes. There were twelve of us. One was a dragon, but he disappeared a few months ago. He, uh . . . he didn't make it."

Chapter Twelve
Into the chasm

Blacknail looked grumpier than ever the next morning when he started the engine of the six-wheeled iron buggy. It hadn't moved since being parked in the alley a couple of nights earlier, but a team of bartering kids had done a good job cleaning it up in return for a promised ride around the village.

Those kids looked on with envy as Hal and his friends climbed the ladder and took their seats, ready for the journey to the chasm where the network of lava tubes formed the Labyrinth of Fire.

Hal felt rested. The inn was extremely comfortable. Despite his worries about the dragons, and what Charlie had told him of the previous dragon shapeshifter, Hal had eventually managed to enjoy a hearty dinner and a good night's sleep. That morning they had all met once more for breakfast, including Fenton, who had finally managed to sleep off his transformation.

Freshly scrubbed and cleaned, Hal was as ready as he ever would be to meet the dragons. He was pleased—or perhaps relieved—to see that both Robbie and Fenton had also had a good wash! He wasn't certain, but he thought Lauren was hanging a little closer to Robbie today.

"Kids," Blacknail complained, as he backed the buggy out of the alley. "Washed every seat 'cept mine. Typical."

The morning was already hot, and Hal longed for a respite. A spot of rain, perhaps—or even a patch of fog! He leaned into the shadows of the overhanging roofs as the buggy inched down the street, and then sighed with disappointment as they left the buildings behind. Out in the open once more, the sun was relentless.

Blacknail steered the buggy up a slowly curving road that led in the opposite direction to Harpy Hill (as Abigail called it). They passed a number of steaming pools, from which thick pipes and machinery sucked greedily. As they left the village behind, short metal towers came into view, where workers—men and goblins—used wheelbarrows to move glowing orange rocks from the entrance of a mine to waiting horse-drawn carts.

The huge iron wheels dug into the dry landscape and threw up plumes of dust. As they crested a hill, a new landscape opened up before them, and Hal gasped.

On the way to Louis they had seen some pretty substantial chasms. But all paled in comparison to this one. It stretched across the entire eastern horizon from one end to the other. The earth had split open, leaving a gaping wound. The air was filled with the dark smudge of steam or smoke. Hal couldn't see the lava itself, but he knew it was there, deep in the chasm. And just beyond the chasm, almost lost in smog, was the mound of a volcano. Hal was pretty sure he didn't want to go anywhere near the place.

Only . . . part of him was drawn to it. Some dragon part of his brain welcomed the idea of intense heat and tunnels below the ground.

The journey to the labyrinth, Blacknail snarled rudely, would take about two hours. It was farther than it looked. The landscape was flat and barren.

The passengers said little. Anxiety had settled over them all now.

Hal considered what Charlie had said about the previous dragon shapeshifter. Upon arrival in Elsewhere with his friends, Felipe was eager to establish a good human-dragon relationship. It was dangerous at first, because the dragons didn't quite know what to make of him. He *looked* like a dragon, but acted like a human. In the end they tolerated his presence, but there was no escaping the fact that Felipe would always be a nobody in their kingdom. While he could safely mingle with the dragons, they remained cold toward him. In the end Felipe gave up. He would never be in a position to lead or even influence them, so he left them alone. Many years passed and the dragons in the labyrinth eventually forgot he existed.

When the news came, six months ago, that the dragons had started attacking the village and eating people, Felipe set off immediately for the chasm, grim and determined. He was never seen again. The fact that the dragons continued to attack the village suggested that Felipe had failed miserably.

All in all, it didn't bode well for Hal.

Abigail fished in the secret pocket of her mottled green dress and carefully pulled out the tiny glass ball the faeries had given her. She hunched over it, holding it so close to her nose that she appeared cross-eyed.

Hal didn't like to interrupt, so he watched her a while, casting her sideways glances. After a minute, he became convinced that she was dozing off, even though her eyes remained open. "Abi?" he said.

She blinked, and looked up. "What?" She frowned. "Oh. I think I almost fell asleep there. It's hypnotic. There's something inside, like a colorful inky substance that pulses . . . If you watch it long enough, you kind of get drawn in."

Hal borrowed it from her. It was no bigger than his smallest fingernail and he could hardly make out anything inside. And yet . . . he *did* see something, a pinprick movement from the center of the miniature sphere . . .

"We need a magnifying glass," Abigail said, taking it gently from his fingers and restoring it to her pocket. "It's for faeries to look into, but faeries are the size of my hand so this ball is actually pretty large from their point of view."

Emily turned around in her seat and raised her voice above the noise of the engine. "So did Charlie say *why* he wasn't coming with us?"

For some reason, everyone looked to Hal.

He shrugged. "Only what he said this morning at breakfast—that this is something I need to do on my own. Well, with your help, of course."

"Yes, but that doesn't make sense," Emily argued. "Surely it would be better to have him along with us? And any other shapeshifters too, for that matter."

"There aren't any others in Louis," Darcy said. "Charlie said that in these parts you'll find dragons, harpies, a few ogres, a whole army of griffins, trolls—"

"Trolls!" Dewey exclaimed. Then he looked sheepish. "Sorry. I used to have nightmares about trolls."

Emily giggled. "You mean from the *Billy Goats Gruff* story, with the troll under the bridge?"

"Anyway," Darcy said, "my point is that most of the shapeshifters are needed down south, near Carter."

Conversation eventually fizzled out as the chasm loomed ahead. The air shimmered in the heat, filled with a strange burning odor. Beyond the chasm, a veil of smog parted to reveal the rounded hump of the volcano, which now seemed gigantic. A massive column of pure white smoke rose slowly from its vent. The surface of the volcano was dark gray and smooth.

Blacknail was driving cautiously now. He hunkered in his seat, eyes darting around. His speed had dropped. He steered toward an enormous boulder, parked next to it, and switched off the engine.

Silence reigned. Now Hal could hear sounds in the distance, coming from within the chasm and the volcano beyond: bubbling, spitting sounds, deep rumbles, screeches, roars . . .

He shuddered. *What are we doing here?*

Blacknail turned to face them. "We don't drive no more," he rasped. "We walk from here. Grab the food, and be on the lookout for dragons."

As a couple of sacks were tossed out, Hal clambered down from the buggy thinking it was a little ironic that they should be wary of dragons when their sole reason for being there was to talk to them! But he understood. He didn't want any accidental, chance meetings; he wanted to talk to whoever was in charge.

Whoever was in charge. All of a sudden, the idea sounded ludicrous.

Blacknail led the way across the tortured landscape. Where it had once been dry and dusty, now it was solid rock. They approached the edge of the chasm. Now Hal could see the other side, two hundred feet away but partially obscured behind a veil of drifting smoke. As they stepped closer, the lower parts of the walls on the opposite side came into view, deeper and deeper until at last the chasm floor was visible.

It was mostly black or dark gray, curiously shiny and metallic in places. It looked solid enough, long since cooled, but farther along the chasm nearer the volcano Hal saw a huge pool of bright orange lava covered with a thick crusty surface that bobbed and moved. In the middle it churned and frothed and boiled.

And there were dragons. Hal saw three together, soaring low across the base of the chasm, dangerously close to the bubbling lava. He saw another emerging from a tunnel in the side of the chasm wall, flexing its wings and tipping forward off the ledge. It plummeted straight down, then swooped low and flat across the chasm bed, its wings not beating once. The dragons were too far away to see in detail, but they were there.

"It's safer in the daytime," Blacknail said. The children turned to him, listening intently. "Most of these dragons are nocturnal." He gestured through the smoke to the volcano. "That's active. It can erupt any time. It churns a lot, sends up smoke, oozes lava, but sometimes it gets clogged up. Pressure builds and it blows its top. Then it rains rocks." He pointed at the bubbling lava. "The lava pours into the chasm one way or another, usually down through tunnels on the other side. Careful what you stand on down there. Even if the ground looks solid and dark, it might not be. It might just be cooling lava. When the air gets to it, it skins over quickly, turns dark. But if you poke at it, put a hole in it, stand on it . . . well, you'll soon find out how hot it still is inside. So watch where you walk. Don't let it spatter you."

Yeah, right, Hal thought, rolling his eyes. *I'll try and remember that. Don't be spattered by lava. Good advice.*

Blacknail sniffed the air. "Smell that? That's sulfur. It's okay, but if you start feeling sick, go find some fresh air. The closer you get to running lava, the more poisonous the air. The really runny stuff fresh from an eruption—that's lava with gas inside. As the gas escapes, the lava slows and cools. Good rule of thumb: stay away from lava when it's bright orange and runny."

A distant roar caused Hal to prick up his ears. Oddly, he thought he knew what that roar meant: *Stay away!* Hal assumed the dragon was talking to others that were venturing near.

Blacknail pointed across the chasm. "The labyrinth is on the other side, right under the volcano. The place is riddled with lava tubes, old and new. Don't get caught in one if the volcano erupts."

"What *are* lava tubes?" Emily whispered.

The goblin scowled. "Tunnels."

"Yes, but, why are they called—"

"They're caused when lava flows out of the volcano," Blacknail interrupted impatiently. "You know how water finds its own path and winds down the hill? Well, so does lava. Sometimes, if it runs for long enough, it crusts over on top and on the sides, forms a sort of channel with a lid on it. But the lava keeps flowing underneath."

"In a tube," Robbie said, nodding. "Cool."

"No, *not* cool," Blacknail snapped. "Anything *but* cool." He shook his head and sighed. "Eventually the lava runs out and leaves an empty tube. Next time there's an eruption, some lava will flow back down the tube, but more will pour over the top and turn to rock. So the ground level gets higher, see?"

"And the tube gets lower," Hal said. "Soon there's a whole labyrinth of them."

Blacknail grunted. "Some of these tubes are too small to crawl through, others wide and tall enough to fit a—well, an ogre." He shook his head. "For some reason the dragons love these tunnels."

"I guess they're hot," Hal said.

"How are we supposed to get to the other side of the chasm?" Darcy asked, peering through the drifting smoke. "Isn't that where the dragons live?"

Blacknail waved them closer to the edge. They all shuffled forward, half expecting the ground to crumble away. But it was solid here, long cooled.

"See?" the goblin said, pointing directly downward. "There's kind of a path."

Kind of a path was pretty apt, Hal thought, horrified by the narrow ridges he saw. The face of the cliff on this side was not as steep as he expected, but still incredibly dangerous, falling away sharply at the top and becoming more shallow as it neared the bottom a few hundred feet below. The ridges were random outcrops of varying sizes—and in places non-existent. But Hal saw, with some reluctance, that Blacknail was right: there really was *kind of a path.*

"Once you're at the bottom, just walk over the lava," Blacknail said. "It's cool enough here. Most of it, anyway. But watch out for hot spots. Lava keeps on leaking down from under that volcano. You'll run across some fresh stuff if you're not careful."

"Why not just wait here?" Abigail asked. "Surely a dragon or two will pass by? Hal can wave to it and get its attention."

"Well, whatever," Blacknail said. "If you think that'll work. Right, I'm off. When you need a ride back to the village, I'll be waiting yonder." He pointed into the distance, well beyond where the buggy stood. "See that rocky mound? I'm gonna drive over there and shelter behind it, out of sight."

The mound was probably a mile or two away. Hal nodded. "Well, thanks for the ride. I guess we'll take it from here."

Without another word, Blacknail ambled away. The children watched in silence as he returned to the buggy and started the engine. Steam shot out from underneath, gears clanked, and the great wheels began to turn, rolling forward on one side and backward on the other, scraping on the smooth rocky ground as the vehicle spun around. Once pointed in the right direction, gears clanked again and the buggy kicked forward. Soon it was trundling off into the distance, back on more familiar terrain, kicking up dust and stones, heading for the rocky mound he'd pointed out earlier.

Silence fell again, only this time with a terrible loneliness and sense of doom. Hal stared around at his friends. Despite the heat, all four girls stood stiffly, arms folded, as if cold.

"So . . . I guess I'll try and get the attention of a dragon," Hal said, uneasily. "But I'll go off somewhere on my own. You can all hide."

"We're in this together," Robbie said firmly.

Hal shook his head. "Thanks, but ogres burn just as easily as faeries and harpies and centaurs. I should go alone."

"I'll go with you," Fenton said. Everyone turned to face him in surprise, and he scowled. "What? You think I'm chicken?"

"No," Darcy said, smiling. "Not at all."

"Well, then."

"That's great, really," Hal said. "But you can still burn." He looked at Emily. "And you, Emily. And you too, Darcy. I just can't risk it. Let me do this part on my own—just to see how it goes. Didn't we agree that the first step should be a respectful, bold and honest request? Well, that's what it'll be. If they don't want to play ball, then . . ." He shrugged. "Then I'll come back and we can think about how to gang up on them."

Hal grabbed a bottle of water out of the sack and took a few swigs. Then he returned the bottle, gave a mock salute, and turned to go.

Abigail grabbed his arm. "You'd *better* come back uncooked, buster."

"I'll do my best," Hal said.

He walked along the top of the chasm, heading north, leaving his friends behind. After a while he decided to try the path down to the bottom.

The ridges down the chasm wall were easy to navigate at first, with just a few leaps and bounds to get down past the difficult bits. Then came a sheer drop, with the nearest suitable ledge over ten feet away. He stared at it, wishing he could fly.

Hal retraced his steps and found a longer, but safer route. He had to let himself down carefully onto a ledge just a foot wide, which was terrifying—one slip and he'd go bouncing down the cliff. But once on that narrow ledge, it quickly opened onto a large flat surface that, in turn, led to a dusty, winding path. Well, not exactly a *path*, he corrected himself as he lost his footing and slipped about five feet. *Kind* of a path.

Rubbing his sore backside, he stopped for a moment and looked around. The trouble with climbing down cliffs, he realized, was that he couldn't afford to pay attention to passing dragons. There was one now, coming along the chasm, wings spread and beating once, twice, lazy but powerful. It was at least twice the size of Hal at full stretch—about forty feet from its snout to the tip of its clubbed tail. The wingspan was about the same. Fascinated, Hal watched how the long, jointed wing-fingers flexed, and how the thin, leathery webbed skin bulged upward like a sail, with the air trapped underneath. The dragon's flight was soundless except for an odd creaking noise as it beat its wings. The slightest twitch of its wings, the tiniest tilt, altered the monster's direction, and yet it did so without even seeming to think about it.

Hal was envious. *He* should be able to do that!

As it approached, unaware of Hal's presence, he wondered: should he call it? The whole point of being there was to speak to the dragons . . . only now that he had the chance, he just wanted to curl up into a ball and hide.

The dragon's scaly hide was blackened in places. It had seen some action, either with other dragons or with the lava. It was the same dark green shade as Hal's own scaly skin, only it was rougher, worn down, like it had spent a lot of time scraping around upside down on the rocks.

As Hal fought to make a decision, the dragon rushed past maybe fifty feet away. In seconds it was receding into the distance.

Hal sighed. A lost opportunity. But, he told himself, now would have been a bad time to make contact. He was high on a cliff, and he couldn't fly. He'd be better off lower down, in case he was forced to run and hide—or worse, knocked off the ledge.

He continued his descent. The heat wasn't so bad now. It seemed that most of the heat emanated from farther along the chasm, toward where the volcano loomed on the opposite side. Lower down, the air seemed cooler and less toxic.

He reached a broad flat surface and knew he was finally out of danger from falling. It had taken him twenty minutes, but now he stood on a floor of smooth, dark gray rock. It had curious ripples and wrinkles in it. Hal imagined lava cooling quickly, skinning over and moving slowly like thick paint pouring into a tray . . .

He walked carefully. The ground here was solid and cool. Far along the length of the chasm the ground was sliding ever so slowly, and a great orange patch in the center bubbled up once in a while.

Now what?

Hal stood alone and vulnerable. Perched in the middle of a rounded hump of rock, he at least had an elevated position from which he could see up and down the chasm. Behind him, to the south, the chasm petered out. But looking north it stretched for miles. Not too far north, on the east side, was where the volcano stood, and where the labyrinth riddled the rock. Hal hated to head that way, but he saw no dragons in these parts. He would have to get a little closer.

With trepidation he headed north along the chasm. As he walked he started to see tiny openings in the wall on the right side—tunnels. And in these tunnels, he saw movement. Watching closely, Hal glimpsed a head poke out and disappear, then another. A dragon shot out and soared into the sky, then circled around and headed east beyond the volcano. What did these dragons do all day long? Blacknail had said they were mostly nocturnal, but Hal had seen ten or more so far. He dreaded to think what it would be like when the rest woke.

The heat was rising again, and Hal stopped, flapping his shirt open. Directly ahead he saw a strange thing: a huge rounded lump of rock opened an eye and stared at him. But quickly he realized the rock was still molten; some movement from within had caused the skin to burst, and now it peeled back and intense heat glowed from inside, smoke pouring from the wound. The rock began to move, ponderously, spreading and flattening, until it stopped five feet later.

Hal could go no farther. If he stood on that molten rock, he'd put his foot through and burn himself. But the labyrinth was right over his head. The holes pockmarked the high rock face all the way down the chasm, past the volcano and beyond.

He waited.

Then he steeled himself and called out. "Hello!"

His voice echoed.

Dragons peered out from the tunnels, seeking the source of the voice—two of them, three, now six . . . Hal swallowed, his heart hammering.

Then they saw him.

Chapter Thirteen
Hal the dragon

With a throaty, indignant roar, a dragon burst out of its lair and launched itself off the ledge, wings immediately snapping open as it cleared the confines of the tunnel. It soared toward Hal.

Three more followed.

Hal waited. As the dragon tilted and came out of its dive, its hind legs lowered and claws stretched. Hal recognized the maneuver; it was exactly what birds did when coming in to land.

Or when snatching up prey.

When he could see the yellows of the monster's eyes, Hal changed. He'd fought off the instinct to change as long as possible and his chest was heaving, but now, letting go, he almost exploded into dragon form. He staggered, adjusting to the shift in balance.

The approaching dragon's eyes widened and the creature veered away with a bellow. It circled around, but by now the other three were upon him.

Hal held his breath.

They didn't attack. Somehow, Hal hadn't expected them to. He'd remained human as long as possible to get their attention before showing them that he was also a dragon. Now the four adult dragons landed heavily before him, their great wings causing such powerful downdrafts that Hal felt as though a storm had just blown up.

Up close and personal, no more than ten feet away, the adults towered over him, each twice his size and probably three times older. Perhaps they wouldn't be so inclined to eat him since he was a mere youngster.

Hal tried to stand tall and proud, but knew he was cowering. It was hard not to. The sheer size of these monsters . . . the yellow eyes, the fangs, the flaring nostrils that shot out puffs of steam with every breath, the immense wings, spread so wide that light filtered through the taut webbing . . . Hal noticed that these dragons put all their weight on their bulky, muscular hind legs, holding their smaller front legs off the ground for much of the time. *A show of strength*, he realized immediately. Standing taller made them look more fearsome. He would have to try that sometime. So far, most of his efforts to stand on his hind legs had resulted in falling flat on his face! He had so much to learn.

Who are you, boy?

The voice startled Hal so much that he took a step backward. There were no words—it was just a grunt with certain inflections. But, impossibly, Hal knew exactly what the grunt meant.

"Uh—my name's Hal Franklin," he said. As usual, his words came out as a growling rumble, which to his friends was terrifying but in the presence of these adult dragons sounded like a child's whine. "I'm, uh, a shapeshifter."

Two more dragons thumped down, their wings creaking. Both were slender in snout and body, less muscular—but more vividly colored, and with cream underbellies. *Females.*

The dragon that had spoken, the one who had been first on the scene, had a curious lump on the side of its head, as though its skull had been smashed at some point, and had healed badly. *Lumphead*, Hal dubbed him. Another had blackened scales along its flank—it was the one that had flown by earlier. *Burnflank, then.* Hal guessed that Lumphead was more dominant than the others.

Lumphead swung around to face the others and grunted. In return, two of the three males let loose with deep rumbling sounds.

Hal fought the urge to run. He wouldn't get far anyway. These dragons were discussing whether he had a right to be here. The translation was a little more awkward this time, but the message was fairly clear.

A human in our midst? Or dragon? Lumphead asked.

He was human moments ago. Has a name too.

Just a runt. Use him for sport.

Lumphead swung back to face Hal and studied him. But before he could say anything, Burnflank crept closer until he was just a foot away. The enormous nostrils twitched and flared, and then he grunted a single word:

Talk.

Hal had his audience. Six fearsome dragons crowded him, and several more watched from the tunnel entrances above. Nearby, a sizzling sound reminded him just how close they all were to only partially cooled lava.

"I'm here to . . . to respectfully ask that you stop eating humans from the nearby village," Hal said, hearing the words come out as a low moan. All right, that was the respectful part. Now to add a bold statement. "People are not as weak as you think. They'll only stand for so long, and soon they're likely to send armies to fight." Finally, he tried the humble, honest approach. "The people are hoping to become better acquainted with you. As a shapeshifter, I can translate. So if you need anything that the humans can help you with, I can—"

Why are you here? Lumphead growled, dropping to all fours and leaning closer. Like Burnflank, he sniffed at Hal, looking him up and down suspiciously.

Hal was confused. "I just told you. I'm here to ask that you stop eating humans from the nearby village."

There was a long silence. Six perplexed faces stared at him. Then one of the females made a sound that Hal translated into something like, *Is he for real?*—although he couldn't imagine a dragon saying those exact words.

The snickering was unmistakable, though. It came out as odd whistles through their noses. All but Burnflank enjoyed a moment of merriment, which Hal bore patiently. His heart sank. Although expected, laughter was a bad sign.

Burnflank continued to stare, his nostrils twitching. His expression and manner—ears pricked, head tilted slightly to one side, eyes narrowed and reptilian brow slightly furrowed—suggested that he was puzzled or curious rather than hostile. Of them all, Burnflank seemed the most approachable.

Or perhaps he was a cold-blooded killer, more dangerous than all the rest put together. There was no way to tell for sure.

Lumphead suddenly thumped his front feet on the rock, his claws clicking noisily. He vented steam from his nostrils and bared his teeth.

Choose. Human or dragon.

A silence fell again, but now Hal sensed an excitement within the small group. Burnflank remained still, but the other two males, along with the two females, hunkered down as if ready to pounce, their mouths open a fraction. If dragons could grin, that was what they would be doing right now.

Choose between human and dragon? Hal turned the question over in his mind. He assumed it meant to pick a side. If he chose human, then he'd likely be ripped to shreds or burned. But if he chose dragon . . . well, then what? Would he have to prove himself somehow?

"I'm a dragon," he said. "But I'm human too. I'm both."

Savage roars told him that this was not an acceptable answer. Lumphead pounded the rock once more.

Choose!

Hal wished the ground would open up and swallow him. Then he thought better of it: he wished the ground would open up and swallow *them.*

He made a choice. "Dragon," he rumbled from deep within his throat.

Burnflank tipped his head in the slightest of movements. Was that a sign of approval?

Most of the other dragons seemed a little disappointed, but Lumphead was waiting for this answer. With a triumphant cry, he reared up, spread his wings, and blew fire into the air. Then he thumped back down, lifted a front foot—and pointed at Hal with a claw.

Hal jumped in surprise. A simple, everyday human mannerism like pointing a finger stood out a mile when a dragon did it.

Are you willing to prove it? the lump-headed dragon snapped.

Sighing heavily, Hal wished and wished he were somewhere else. He had guessed correctly—this monster was going to test him. But what choice did he have, except to nod glumly?

Lumphead roared. He spread his wings and launched into the air, soaring off over Hal's head. Where was he off to? Hal started to turn, but one of the female dragons snuffled closer and began sniffing his neck. Disturbed, Hal backed away, but the dragon made a strange whining sound and quickly matched his step, then curled her tail around him. At first Hal thought the female was attracted to him, but then he figured out that she was a highly maternal mother dragon, apparently keen on adopting him as her own.

Hal squirmed out of her grip and backed up. He swung around, looking for Lumphead. There—he was just reaching the top of the chasm. The dragon roared triumphantly, and Hal heard a sharp cry of terror.

A chill went through him. Surely—no, they couldn't be—

He craned his neck, but could see nothing. Lumphead was up there, out of sight, and there were several screams and yells. His friends! *What were they doing here?* Hal had walked some distance north along the chasm, and all the while had thought he was leaving his friends behind, safe and sound out of sight. But no, they had *followed* him, keeping track of him, probably watching his every move. And now they'd been spotted.

Hal beat his wings. He was desperate now. He had to fly. He rose up on his legs, fighting for balance, planting his tail firmly so it acted like a third leg. His wings pumped, faster and faster.

But nothing happened. He let loose with a cry of frustration, uncaring that the watching dragons were huffing with mirth.

Horrified, he watched anxiously. All was silent high up above the chasm. Then Lumphead reappeared—and he carried something. *Someone.*

Abigail.

Hal moaned, and watched as the adult dragon plummeted toward them, then sailed into a graceful arc and came to rest on the rocks. Gripped in one huge front paw was Abigail, pale and terrified. The dragon's claws easily circled her waist, and her legs dangled beneath, her arms pinned to her sides.

"Let her go," Hal snarled, his heart hammering with rage.

Dragons eat humans, Lumphead snapped back. *Eat!*

The dragon thrust Abigail forward, causing her head to jerk and her hair to fall over her face. Her scrunchy had gone missing somewhere along the way. She peered out from behind her hair, her eyes wide and teary.

Hal thought hard, quickly weighing his limited options. He couldn't fight a single dragon, never mind all six. He couldn't grab Abigail and escape, because he couldn't fly, and even if he could, there were still six of them—more if he counted the numerous heads poking out of the labyrinth high in the cliff face.

What about reasoning?

Yeah, right. Fat chance, he thought bitterly.

Threats? They'd be empty.

Trickery? He couldn't think of a single ruse that might help.

Begging? They'd just laugh at him.

For a second he wondered about his friends high on top of the chasm. Could *they* help? But the moment he considered the idea, he rejected it—and hoped they wouldn't be so foolish as to come anywhere near.

Eat! the dragon roared, and thrust Abigail toward him again. Now her face was inches from his. Her lips trembled and tears rolled down her face.

He hated to see her this way, so helpless. Where was her cheeky grin, that wicked gleam in her eye? Hal *needed* her right now.

The words tumbled out of his mouth before he could stop them. "This one has something of mine," he blurted, in what sounded to his ears like a muffled grunt. "I can't kill her yet, not until I get it back."

Lumphead looked scornful, while Burnflank's eyes narrowed again.

Hal blundered on. "But I really want to prove to you that I'm worthy to be a dragon. Is there some other way? Perhaps a fight?"

He kicked himself—but the words were out. Most of the dragons just burst into laughter, a cacophony of grunts and huffs.

One of the males came forward and circled Hal on all fours. *Think you can fight?* he snarled. *Ever been burned before?*

Hal ducked to avoid a sudden wash of fiery heat and red-hot flames as the dragon breathed hard in his direction. But he was too late; the fire licked his head and one of his ears and he felt a horrible burning sensation even through his scales. He yelled and pulled away, but he was in pain. He could feel scales melting on his forehead, his ear on fire . . .

Whether it was pure instinct or a brilliant idea at the back of his mind, Hal changed into a human and danced around on the rocks, yelling and clutching his head. He was hurting terribly, but when he changed into a dragon again, the pain eased a little. He changed once more, becoming human and slapping at his face and head with puny pink hands, grateful that the pain was healing with every transformation. He changed again and again, from human to dragon and back to human, until at last he stood shakily on the rocks on two feet, gingerly feeling his ear and prodding at his scalp.

He seemed to be fine. Repeated transformations had fixed him up good. Worried, he tugged carefully at his hair. Some had come loose in his hands, but whatever hair had burnt away seemed to have grown back.

Suddenly aware that six dragons and a human girl were staring at him, he changed back into his dragon form and turned on the one who had burned him. He leaned in close and roared for all he was worth, and a gigantic sheet of flame burst forth, right into the dragon's face.

Now it was the dragon's turn to scream and dance around. It was a pretty funny sight, Hal thought grimly, all that twisting and thrashing and grunting . . .

The dragon had no way to alleviate the pain, and he stumbled away, wings beating hard. He launched into the air, but he was blind and hurting, and his flight was uncertain. For a second it looked as though the dragon would fall straight into the nearby lava, but at the last second he corrected his course and flew upward. But to where? Blind, he was unable to return to his tunnel, so he soared high into the sky and disappeared.

Lumphead was staring at Hal. So was Abigail. Hal wasn't sure whose eyes were rounder.

Useful trick, the dragon grunted reluctantly. *Not a mark on you.*

Worth keeping alive, Burnflank agreed.

We have no use for him, Lumphead said shortly.

Better he's on our side than the side of the humans.

Burnflank was no fool, Hal realized. For some reason this particular dragon was watching out for him.

But Lumphead wasn't convinced. *He's not the first half-breed to come here. We had no use for the other one either.* The dragon glared at Hal. *Despite your age, youngster, you've proved you can fight. Now prove you have no affiliation with humans. Eat!* Again he thrust Abigail forward.

Hal glanced at Abigail and saw a mask of fear and anxiety. Luckily the poor girl had no idea what was being said. All she heard were grunts, roars and growls. She seemed to be in some discomfort from being squeezed so tightly around the waist. Lumphead stood on three legs, holding Abigail a couple of feet above the rocks so she dangled helplessly. He held her almost absently as though she were a plaything that he'd momentarily forgotten.

"I need her alive," Hal said firmly. "She took something valuable from me."

What can she possibly have of yours? Lumphead said with a sneer.

"A . . . a diamond," Hal said tentatively.

The dragon cocked his head, but said nothing. Somehow Hal had a feeling that of all the things in the world a dragon might want to possess, a large shiny diamond was high on the list. The way it sparkled in the sunlight . . . The idea of glittering objects appealed to his dragon senses.

"I can find other humans to eat," Hal promised. "I'll bring them to you, and we'll share them."

Lumphead glanced up at the cliff.

"No, not those ones," Hal said hurriedly. "I mean *real* humans, from the village—not shapeshifters." He gestured toward Abigail. "Let her go and I'll bring you five in exchange for this one." In case dragons couldn't count, he added, "That's one human for each of you."

How quickly his plight had changed. He had started out trying to save people from the dragons. Now he was offering to capture some himself!

Lumphead said nothing for a moment. Behind him, Burnflank, the two females, and the other male waited silently, ears pricked up. Hal waited, holding his breath.

Then Lumphead grunted, *Deal.*

Hal started to breathe a sigh of relief.

But double the amount of humans, Lumphead continued. *By sundown.*

The dragon reared up again, clearly aiming to take Abigail with him. Hal thought desperately. He *had* to delay things, somehow talk the dragon out of taking her.

Lumphead gave Hal one last look. *The human stays with me until you return.*

And he leapt into the air, wings thumping. Abigail screamed.

Hal changed back into his human form and yelled after her. "Don't worry— he's just holding you hostage! I have until sundown—I'll come for you!"

Whether Abigail heard what he said, Hal wasn't sure. He thought she had. He *hoped* she had. He watched in despair as the dragon soared across the chasm and disappeared into a tunnel. Hal made a very careful mental note of the entrance so he could find it again later. At the moment he had no idea how he was going to get to her, only that he had to somehow—or die trying.

The females gave him a final once-over before leaving. The males remained, but Burnflank was quick to turn on the other and send him off with a savage snap of jaws. Finally, Hal was alone with Burnflank.

The older dragon sighed, and glanced over his shoulder at the terrible burns along his flank. *When I came here six months ago and got into a fight, I could have healed myself as you did . . . but then I would have given myself away as a shapeshifter. So I remained in dragon form and suffered the pain.*

Hal's mouth dropped open. "Felipe?"

The dragon cocked his head. *Charlie told you about me?*

"He said you were dead!"

It's better he thinks that. I can't go home to my village now. Not after—

"After what?"

The dragon sounded sad. *It takes time to rise to a dominant position in the fleet. You can't just come along and hope to change things in one brief encounter, especially if you're only half a dragon. A half-breed has no chance of power here. So I came here six months ago as a full dragon. They accepted me easily enough, and I worked my way up the ranks the dragon way, ingratiating myself with the Old One. Not there yet, but getting close.*

Hal felt his hopes soar. "Can you . . . can you stop the attacks on the village?"

Burnflank heaved a sigh. *I've seen many people die. Dragons last a couple of* *weeks without food, and then they go hunting. Some attack the village, bring* *people here to the labyrinth, keep them alive until they're needed . . . I can't bear* *it, but have no way to stop them, at least not yet. One day, maybe soon, I'll be able* *to overthrow or outwit the dominant bull. Then . . . then I can stop the attacks.*

"That was the dominant bull?" Hal said, wanting to be sure. "The one with the lump on his head?"

Actually his daddy is the dominant bull—very old and wise, but weak. He *bends to his son's will much of the time. If it weren't for him . . .*

Burnflank turned to look up at the tunnel entrances.

I have to go. They'll get suspicious.

"Wait!" Hal urged. "Can you help me—"

I can't get involved. This is one girl you're talking about. I'm sorry for you, *but my mission is far greater than the life of one girl. You have to understand.*

The dragon let out a roar as if rudely ending an argument, then abruptly turned and sprang into the air, wings pumping. Hal watched him go, and felt as though his only hope was slipping through his claws.

Hal stood alone on the rocks. He was no longer afraid for himself. Somehow he had bargained for his life. However rudely the dragons had treated him, he felt they had accepted him. Until sundown, that is. If he failed to deliver ten humans by that time, then Abigail would die a horrible death, and probably Hal too if he showed his snout around here again.

Yet he would never dream of bringing ten humans to the dragons' dinner table! And even if he did, why on earth would Lumphead allow Abigail to go free afterward? For that matter, what if, right now, the dragon was—

Shuddering, and ashamed, Hal fought back tears and looked for the nearest route back up the cliff.

Chapter Fourteen
Rescue plans

Hal's friends were huddled behind some rocks. At first he was afraid to show his face, so he paused and waited, listening to Emily and Lauren sobbing onto each other's shoulders. The others sat staring into space.

Fenton was in his lizard form. He must have heard Hal coming because he turned and stared right at him. Having been spotted, Hal nervously approached. Then Robbie made an exclamation and jumped up. "Hal!"

As everyone rushed toward him, Hal held up his hands and backed away. "I'm sorry, I'm sorry—I'll get her back, I promise—"

He was nearly knocked off his feet when Darcy flung her arms around him and Robbie pounded him on the back. Through her sudden wash of tears, Darcy actually looked happy to see him. As Hal looked from one face to another, he realized that they *all* were.

"You're not mad at me?" he said, hopefully. "I . . . I messed up bad."

"You did not," Robbie said firmly. "*We* messed up. We should have stayed out of sight. Now Abigail—"

"It was awful!" Emily cried. "The dragon—"

Everyone started talking at once, and Hal raised his hands for quiet. "One at a time. Tell me what happened up here."

Robbie started to talk, but Hal gently stopped him and asked Darcy instead. Robbie had a habit of exaggerating. So Darcy took a breath and told, fairly briefly, what had happened.

They had been crouched at the top of the chasm, watching Hal trying to talk sense into the dragons. "You were *so* brave!" Emily broke in. Then the big bully dragon (as Darcy called him) launched into the air and soared up the cliff toward them. They had scattered in a panic, trying to find a place to hide, but the dragon was upon them all too soon.

"Then we all changed," Darcy said.

As Darcy spoke, Hal imagined the scene from the dragon's point of view, and all became clear. The dragon had hovered high above the ground, wings beating furiously, looking down at seven children scattering this way and that. As they scattered, they *changed*. One became a harpy and flew off. Another simply vanished. A third turned into a centaur and galloped away, and a fourth became a giant shaggy monster.

A nice, big, juicy plump boy became the dragon's primary target—but even he changed, becoming a giant black lizard that the dragon had no interest in whatsoever. He focused his attention on the remaining children—two girls running toward some rocks. One was screaming, being pulled along by the other. They would do. Maybe the dragon could snatch up both together. He swooped in, stretching his forearms, his claws ready . . .

But the screamer changed suddenly into a repulsive wriggling snake, although her head remained human.

The dragon was already committed to his descent, so he simply ignored the snake-girl and snatched up the other instead. For a second he thought he saw wings appear out of the girl's back, but they retracted quickly as his claws closed around her waist and yanked her into the air.

Hal knew the rest. He snapped out of his reverie as Darcy finished talking, and took a deep breath. "We need a plan."

* * *

"So, what you're saying," Robbie said slowly, "is that Darcy is going to walk into the dragon's lair for a look-see."

The children sat cross-legged on the floor in a small circle, behind a clump of rocks. Fenton, still in his lizard form, lay behind Emily, Lauren and Darcy, and his long, long tail wrapped all the way around the entire group.

"When she's invisible," Hal explained, "she's *really* invisible. And she doesn't smell, either, like she normally does."

Darcy looked indignant. "What do you mean by that?"

Hal rolled his eyes. "I don't mean you *smell*. I just mean—well, dragons smell better than humans."

"They do not!" Emily said, holding her nose to demonstrate her distaste. "When *you're* a dragon, you let loose with some really nasty—"

"No, I mean dragons *smell* better." Hal pointed to his nose. "We have a better sense of smell than humans. I can smell Darcy from ten feet away." He caught her glare and hurried on. "Not that she smells *bad*. She smells *good*. That's the problem—she stands out as smelling good, so is easy to pick up. But when she's invisible, one of those wood nymph creatures, well, her smell is kind of hidden."

"Just to be sure," Robbie said, "we can roll her in the dirt."

"You will not!" Darcy exclaimed.

"Actually, that makes sense," Lauren said. "The dirt will mask your very *nice* smell, making it even more difficult for the dragons to pick you up."

"Just make sure you don't bump into any of them," Dewey said quietly.

Darcy sighed. "I can't believe we're doing this. It wasn't so long ago we were at school on the island, with fog outside, and Mrs. Hunter giving us boring math tests . . . and now we're sneaking around a nest of dragons near a volcano."

"Brute strength won't get us anywhere," Hal said, glancing at Robbie. "So we have to use our brains and talents. Darcy, it's dangerous, I know. If there was any other way . . ."

Darcy shuddered. "I don't even know how to *get* to the tunnel that Abigail was taken into. I'd have to climb down into the chasm and walk across the rocks, and climb back up the other side to what you think is the right tunnel—assuming I can climb up that side at all. There's lava below that part of the wall! And dragons everywhere! And *even* if I get into the tunnel, how do I find Abigail? She could be anywhere. I might get lost."

"I have an idea," Lauren said. She shuddered visibly, as though the idea she'd thought of terrified her. She took a deep breath. "Being with the harpies yesterday, and seeing how filthy they are . . . Somehow I understood that part of the reason they allow themselves to get so disgustingly grimy and greasy is because they know dragons and other monsters don't like the taste. I think that a harpy could fly near dragons without being eaten alive."

"But you could still be roasted," Robbie protested. "And *then* eaten alive."

"No, dragons don't like cooked meat," Hal said. He blinked, wondering where *that* information had just popped into his mind from.

"She could still be roasted," Emily pointed out. "Just out of spite."

"Maybe," Lauren said, "but I'm going to have to risk it. Darcy can hang on to my feet, invisible, while I kind of sweep by. I'll pretend to be nosy, drop Darcy off, and get out of there."

There was a long silence.

This is nuts, Hal thought. "Good plan," he said, nodding.

"And how does Darcy get back out again?" Emily demanded.

There was another long silence. Then Robbie had an idea. "What if Darcy comes back to the tunnel entrance and lobs a few rocks out? The dragons won't think much of it, but we'll see it as a signal. Then Lauren could go fetch her."

That's a terrible, ridiculous idea, Hal thought. "Yeah, that'll work."

Emily frowned. "Thinking ahead," she said slowly, "all Darcy can do is find out *where* Abigail is. She probably can't get her out safely."

"I know that," Hal agreed, "but once we know where she is and how she's guarded . . ." He shrugged, wishing he'd thought out this part of the plan already.

Emily leaned forward, and Hal saw something in her eyes, a brightness that he recognized from the good old days on the island. She was *organizing*, planning ahead, doing what she did best.

"I'm going to find a snake," she said. "Darcy can take the snake with her, inside her dress so it's invisible too."

Darcy exclaimed loudly with some surprisingly crude swear words.

"It'll be in a pouch or something," Emily said, holding up her hands. "When you find Abigail, let the snake go. It'll find its own way out. I'll be waiting for it, somewhere on the surface on the other side of the chasm. It can lead me—or one of us—back into the tunnel to where Abigail is."

Crazier than a loon, Hal's mind screamed. This time he couldn't even bring himself to agree with the idea out loud.

"And you're going to talk to this snake?" Darcy asked suspiciously. "You're going to give it instructions? And it's going to understand you?"

"Not in the way you're thinking," Emily said. "I can talk to all snakes, large and small—including the sea serpent, remember? It's not really like talking to them with words, more like giving them ideas, pictures in their minds. Like giving them an urge to do something instinctively."

"Brainwashing?" Lauren asked.

Emily shrugged, and climbed to her feet. "I'll be back in a moment."

She stood still, facing away, arms outstretched. Hal had a brief flashback of watching Abigail change that first time, in his dad's garage. She'd stood in exactly the same pose. But instead of wings sprouting, Emily's dress started to melt into her skin, became scaly and hard. At the same time, below the hem of her dress, her lower legs and feet fused together and became a scaly snake-body, thick and round. Coils of the new body spread across the rocks, growing longer and longer.

Hal had seen all his friends transform before, but it was still fascinating to watch—when he wasn't being chased by some monster or other. Emily's change was slower this time, perhaps deliberately.

Emily turned, grinning. "Notice anything different?"

It took a second to register. "You have arms!" Robbie exclaimed. "But you didn't the last time you changed."

"I was underwater the first time," she said. "Arms are pretty useless there. Easier to swim without them. Above ground, though . . ." She shrugged, her bare shoulders a little scaly but otherwise human. "That night we arrived in Elsewhere, when you were all sound asleep, Miss Simone told me the naga people are actually two different species—those who live on land, and a more primitive type that lives underwater. She said I was a mix of both types. A 'slight adjustment in the creation process,' she called it."

As before, her translucent dress clung to her torso and shoulders like a second skin. She slithered away, bobbing from side to side.

Darcy rubbed her eyes. "This is turning out to be the craziest day of my life."

Robbie climbed to his feet. "The chasm ends over that way," he said, pointing to the south. "Once Darcy is safely delivered, I guess we'll all take a long walk around the chasm to the other side—right?"

Hal nodded. "We could go and find Blacknail, but I'm afraid the dragons will hear or see the buggy now that they know we're around somewhere. Especially as the day goes on and more dragons wake up."

It was some time before Emily returned carefully holding a shiny black snake in her hand. It was coiled neatly around her wrist and arm, its head resting on the palm of her hand. Darcy shuddered.

Robbie, fascinated, stroked its head, while Lauren drank the last few drops of water from a pouch and handed it to Emily. After whispering to the snake, and stroking its head, Emily eased the wriggling serpent into the pouch and carefully tied the top, making sure to leave it loose so air could circulate.

She handed the pouch to Darcy. "There. Stuff that down your dress, girl."

"Stuff *you*," Darcy said rudely. She tentatively took the pouch, cringed at its weight, shuddered when she saw it move, and hung it around her neck. Then she tucked it inside the top of her dress.

"Now I have my hands free," she said, sounding disgusted. "But if this thing bites me, Emily, I'll slap you *so* hard."

Emily smiled. "You'll be fine."

A loud *whump!* sound caused Hal to jump and swing around—but it was only Lauren, in her harpy form. Having met so many filthy, greasy harpies in their nest on the hill, he now appreciated how clean and lovely she was in comparison, with pure white feathers under her snug, feather-patterned dress.

"Ready?" she asked Darcy.

"Oh, wait—we need to throw dirt on you," Robbie said, looking around. But there was nothing but solid rock this close to the chasm. "We could walk over that way, where it starts getting dusty—"

"Forget it," Darcy said. "I have a snake hung around my neck and I'm about to be flung into the dragons' lair. I am *not* going to roll around in dirt just because Hal says I smell bad. Let's go."

They cautiously approached the chasm with heads low. Darcy looked over the edge, then closed her eyes. "I can't do this," she whispered. "I thought the *buggy* was high off the ground. This is . . . this is crazy."

"Lauren won't drop you," Hal said, hoping that were true. He knew adult harpies could carry fairly substantial weight; he had stopped a male harpy from snatching Abigail during the village attack. But could Lauren?

Lauren put her feathered arm around Darcy's shoulders. "Trust me, okay? I won't drop you. You won't even need to hold on."

"We'll head on round to the other side, Lauren," Robbie said quietly. "You'll wait here for Darcy's signal, right?"

Lauren nodded. She turned, took a few bounds, and launched into the air, her snow-white feathered wings flapping hard. She circled around and returned, hovering over Darcy's head. Hal thought she was waiting for Darcy to open her eyes and reach up to grab her ankles, but Lauren's bird-like feet flexed and opened wide. Her talons, which Hal had not really studied before now, were long and powerful. Her clawed toes—three at the front and one at the back—wrapped around Darcy's shoulders and up under her armpits for a secure grip.

Lauren lifted, and Darcy stifled a scream, her eyes snapping open for a moment as her feet left the ground. Then she closed them again and reached up to grab Lauren's ankles, holding on for dear life.

"Change!" Dewey called urgently.

Darcy became an almost invisible blur, a smudge in the air. Now it seemed strange that Lauren labored under the weight, because it looked as though she was carrying nothing at all. But as Lauren picked up speed and headed out across the chasm, her flight appeared natural, especially when she soared around in large circles like a vulture.

Hal and his friends lay on their bellies right on the chasm edge, and watched anxiously. There were a few dragons around, a couple of them hunkered on the rocks by a slow-moving pool of lava that was oozing from a split in a mound of rock, like a huge fiery pimple that had burst open.

More dragons were lounging in their tunnels, high up the cliff wall, their heads poking out. They looked like dogs in kennels on a lazy, hot afternoon.

Let's hope they stay put, Hal thought.

He had explained very carefully to his friends which tunnel Lumphead had taken Abigail into. He hoped Lauren remembered correctly.

Dragons were following the harpy's slow descent. They didn't appear excited in any way, just curious. Hal could almost imagine what they were thinking:

What's that harpy doing? Is it lost?

It needs to bug off. This is dragon territory.

Keep on flying, greasy bird. Don't make me come after you.

It was only when Lauren made a sudden dive for a tunnel that a couple of dragons raised their heads. One, some distance along the chasm in another tunnel, stirred and leaned out to see what the harpy was doing.

The tunnel entrance that Lauren headed toward was empty—for now. She flapped so close that her wingtips brushed the chasm wall. She hovered there a moment, just above the tunnel floor, a puzzling sight for watchful dragons.

Down in the chasm, a dragon roared. This brought a few more heads out of their tunnels—but Lauren was already flying away, briskly, as if she had just doubled her strength and power. In seconds she was a dot in the sky.

Hal released a huge sigh. Robbie closed his eyes for a moment, then turned to Hal. "That's my girlfriend," he whispered proudly.

"*Girlfriend?*" Hal repeated. "Since when?"

"You know—since the harpy attack."

Hal had to think about that. He didn't remember Robbie and Lauren holding hands or kissing or anything of that nature—not then, and certainly not since. But then light dawned. "Wait a minute. Are you talking about when she was crying and you put your arm around her?"

Robbie grinned and looked up into the sky, trying to find the harpy.

Oh boy, Hal thought. *I wonder if Lauren knows about this.*

"We'd better get going," he said. "We have a long walk around the chasm."

* * *

They gave the chasm a wide berth, venturing out onto the dusty plains. To speed up the journey, Robbie turned into an ogre and trotted along. Dewey carried Emily on his centaur back. Hal, as a dragon, had the unfortunate task of offering a ride to Fenton, who was stuck in his lizard form and couldn't travel very fast at all.

"You're useless," Hal grumbled. Fenton was perched awkwardly across Hal's broad back, his long black tail lashed around Hal's belly. It was embarrassing. He would much rather carry Emily; at least she was a *girl*. "Why can't you make an effort to change back? It's annoying, waiting until you fall asleep every time."

Of course he spoke in grunts and Fenton ignored him.

Maybe Hal could *drag* Fenton, the way he had dragged Thomas the manticore through the tunnels back on the island. Ha! How ironic *that* would be, dragging Fenton through the dirt . . . exactly as the big bully had done to Hal and Robbie on many occasions in the past.

In the far distance, Hal saw the collection of flat boulders that Blacknail said he was snoozing under. He resented the goblin for that. But he also knew that an additional person wouldn't help matters in any way. Hal's friends were probably the best allies he could have hoped for. Even Charlie, a powerful griffin, couldn't achieve much against fire-breathing dragons. Brute force would accomplish nothing; they were far outnumbered. A more subtle approach was needed, and what could be more subtle than an invisible wood nymph?

Leaving the surly goblin to nap in the shade, Hal and his friends hurried on to the end of the chasm. How was Darcy doing, on her own in the labyrinth? Hal hardly dared to think about her. She was one very, very brave girl. And Abigail—

Pushing thoughts of chewed-up faeries to the back of his mind, Hal glanced around, looking for dragons that might be lurking nearby. He saw none.

He thought of Lauren. After she'd dropped Darcy into the tunnel on the other side of the chasm, Lauren had flown high into the sky to escape the attention of the dragons and to make them think she had gone for good. Five minutes after Hal and his friends had set off around the chasm, she had returned and disappeared behind some rocks by the chasm's edge. There she awaited Darcy's signal. The problem was, nobody knew how long Darcy would be in there, and if she released the snake, and the snake found a way out, then Emily wanted to be there on the other side waiting for it. And Hal wanted to be there too, in case Emily's crazy idea actually proved useful.

The chasm narrowed to about twenty feet, then abruptly to five, and then finally petered out. Looking north along the length of the chasm was an incredible experience—a dead straight crack in the earth, partially shrouded in smoke and haze, with a volcano standing not too far away on the eastern side. Beyond the volcano, much farther to the east, steam rose off the mirrored surface of a lake.

The group quickly moved on. Hal was amazed how far he could trot in dragon form with nothing more than a slight burn in his calf muscles, even with Fenton sprawled across his back. His lungs coped easily, although he panted like a dog. Robbie seemed to have no problems either, lumbering on and on with great arms swinging. And Dewey was in his element, clip-clopping through the dust with his back straight and chin up, Emily sitting behind and gripping his waist.

Small rocks the size of soccer balls littered the terrain. They had a spongy texture, and were paler than other rocks, a yellow-white color. Hal imagined these rocks blasting from the top of the volcano and raining down in all directions. He hoped the volcano didn't erupt any time soon!

On this side of the chasm were enormous mounds of that dark rock, much of it smooth and flat. The taller, more jagged rocks provided a natural barrier to hide behind. They were now directly over the labyrinth.

Hal spotted a hole in the ground, ten feet in diameter, just off to his left. He paused to peer in, wondering if it was part of the labyrinth. It was old and crumbly with pale gray walls, dropping away into blackness. There could be holes like this all over the place, he realized—topside tunnel entrances.

He urged the others to be careful as they headed on toward the volcano. It was so wide and round, and so shallow near the bottom, that it was hard to pinpoint exactly where the volcano ended and the ground started. It was a pimple on the face of the earth, and lava had erupted from it many, many times—and was doing so now. Smoke poured from its blunt peak and from numerous orange rivers flowing down its side. But the lava didn't pour over the edge of the nearby chasm; instead it found its way into tunnels and down through the labyrinth.

Hal had to wonder why dragons chose to live here. He could understand and appreciate the heat; as a human he found the afternoon sun far too warm, but as a dragon he hardly felt the warmth at all. No doubt the volcano was a luxurious setting, for all the heat it generated. But Hal was also acutely aware that fire, and obviously lava, could burn and kill even dragons. And the dragons lived *in* the labyrinth, where all the lava was pouring!

He thought of Abigail again, presumably being held prisoner. Did dragons have any concept of how little tolerance humans had to heat? Did they even care?

They arrived in the vicinity of the tunnel where Abigail had been taken. Hal shook Fenton off his back and motioned for the others to wait while he shuffled across the smooth rock between huge, jagged boulders. At the chasm's edge, he peered down to get his bearings.

Finally he figured out where he was. Just a little farther and they'd be right over the tunnel where Abigail was being held. Hal scanned the opposite chasm wall two hundred feet away and eventually spotted Lauren hiding there. He gave a wave, and she waved back.

So Darcy was not through with her search yet. Or she had run into trouble.

Hal returned to the others and ushered them onward. He led the way, spotting more and more tunnel entrances leading down into the ground. They were all huge, some twenty or thirty feet across. Most were pale gray, the color of ash, but Hal came across one that was clearly fresh, with a redness to the smooth, solid walls. A wave of heat emanated from this hole. Naturally lava couldn't find its way down *every* hole, through *every* tunnel—it just poured into the nearest. So only certain tunnels in the labyrinth were dangerous. As long as he stuck to the old, pale gray tunnels—the ones that had cooled long ago—and avoided the ones that looked fresh and new, he guessed it would be all right to explore.

Once again he checked his position at the chasm edge. Then, satisfied, he found a decent hiding place for them all, close to the edge between a clump of tall, rounded boulders, where they would be able to keep an eye on Lauren.

Then they waited.

Chapter Fifteen
A way into the labyrinth

Fenton basked on a large, smooth rock out in the open, in full view of passing dragons. The flying beasts paid him no attention.

Robbie was thoroughly bored after just twenty minutes. He glanced around, then crept out from behind the rocks and crawled over to a large sponge-like boulder. It was so big he was unable to stretch his arms all the way around, and yet he lifted it easily off the ground, even in human form. "Pumice," Robbie said triumphantly. "Filled with air bubbles. Not dense at all."

"Unlike you," Hal retorted.

Robbie held his sides and mimed laughter.

Then Emily jerked upright and pointed. They all stared across the chasm. In the distance they saw Lauren, in harpy form, standing there with her wings spread.

"The signal," Emily whispered. "She must have had the signal."

They watched as Lauren tipped herself off the cliff and soared into the chasm. She was gone from view immediately, and the children scrambled across the rock to the edge so they could look down and watch.

Lauren wasted no time. Unlike before, she dove straight down to the tunnel, spanning the chasm and reaching her target in seconds. A dragon bellowed somewhere, then another. Directly below, Hal saw the tunnel entrance in the sheer cliff face, and a blur or smudge poking out. Darcy! Lauren came in so fast she had to use her legs as buffers against the cliff; her knees buckled and her wings brushed the rock, sending a few feathers fluttering into the air. But her wings continued to beat hard. She positioned herself over the tunnel entrance and reached down with her talons . . . and then she was away, this time heading straight up toward Hal and his friends.

They scurried back to the cover of the rocks. Then Lauren shot up over the cliff and flew low over their heads. There came the thud of feet on rock and Hal was bumped roughly by something that wasn't there—and then Darcy materialized next to him, hunkering down next to Emily. Lauren landed and hurried under cover too, changing back into her human form as she did so.

Two dragons soared over the cliff, then a third. Hal and his friends pressed together, hidden behind the rocks. The dragons would spot them if they came around the exposed southern side of their hiding place, or directly above, but they spread out and flapped around the sky in large circles, looking perplexed. Once more they ignored the huge black lizard basking on the rocks; they were busy looking for a nosy harpy. A fourth dragon appeared, but by this time the others had given up the search. They all disappeared into the chasm.

The children sighed with relief, and the three girls hugged each other tight. Robbie looked like he wanted to hug Lauren, but he simply grinned and told her, "Good job."

"That was terrifying," Darcy said, her face white. "Lauren dropped me at the tunnel entrance and I nearly lost my balance and fell off the cliff. Did I tell you I don't like heights? But once inside, it was so dark and smelly that I just wanted to run back out again." She shuddered. "I never even thought about the darkness before I went in there. It was pitch-black. But it went uphill pretty sharply and after a while there were holes in the ceiling—little skylights that let daylight in. Not *much* light, but enough to see by. The tunnels got really confusing then—lots of forks and splits, some in the ceiling, some in the floor . . . I knew I was going to get completely lost."

She grabbed a pouch of water and gulped noisily from it.

"Did you find Abigail?" Hal asked. He couldn't wait for the entire story.

Darcy nodded, still drinking. Finally she wiped her mouth. "I had to hide a few times. I kept hearing dragons, grunting or roaring, some in the distance and others really close. Their noises echo up and down the tunnels. One time, a dragon came around the bend, hurrying along, breathing hard . . . I nearly screamed. I had to run fast back down the tunnel until I found a little niche in the side. I stood there and this dragon passed me by." Darcy held up her hands so they were a foot apart. "*This* close. I could have touched it."

"And where was Abigail?" Hal asked.

"I had to be careful to remember my way," Darcy went on. "You can't even count left, left, right, left, and so on, because sometimes the tunnels become like intersections with three or four tunnels leading off. In one place it was a big cave with a huge hole in the middle of the floor. And I didn't have any chalk or anything. So I just had to remember my way, really carefully, doubling back a few times to make sure I had it straight."

She finished the pouch of water and tossed it aside.

"There was one tunnel that felt warmer than the others. Most of the tunnels are cool, but this one . . . it was really warm. And I could hear a dragon. I was going to turn and go the other way, but then I heard a voice—Abigail."

Hal sucked in his breath, his heart thumping.

"She was complaining about something. I couldn't make out what she was saying, because her voice echoed so much, but I knew it was her. So I went up the tunnel. Around the bend there's this cavern, and in the cavern . . ." Darcy paused. "Well, it was like a nest. The tunnels link them all together. Anyway, this nest had *stuff* in it. Clothing. Shoes. Huge piles of stuff, all jumbled together and rammed into a corner. I think . . ."

She swallowed, and her eyes filled with tears.

While Emily gently stroked her shoulder, Hal urged her to continue.

"Well," Darcy said, "I think those clothes belonged to all the poor people who were . . . who were eaten."

Horrible images filled Hal's head. "Dragons are fussy eaters," he whispered. "They don't eat harpies because they're filthy. They don't cook their food. And I doubt they'd enjoy clothing either. I guess . . ."

He broke off, not wanting to voice his thoughts. Did dragons eat people and then spit out the clothes afterward? Or did they somehow tear the clothes off their victims first?

"And that was just *one* cave," Darcy said. "There were a few dragons there—I guess a male and female, and a younger one too. A family. There was a vent in the top—quite a narrow one, but letting a lot of daylight in. And there was a smaller cave at the back. That's where Abigail is."

"She's not hurt?" Hal asked eagerly.

"No, she's fine," Darcy said.

Relief washed over Hal.

"But she can't escape?" Lauren asked.

Darcy shook her head. "No. The female dragon was lying right across the front of the little cave where Abigail was sitting, and the male was there too. Even if he wasn't there, the small dragon seemed very interested in Abigail. I say small, but even a baby is the size of a cow, or a donkey. The mother kept pushing it back, like it was saying, 'No, not yet.' I guess the dragons are keeping Abigail alive and well, just as they said they would."

Hal felt a bizarre, almost ridiculous moment of pride then, that his kind would honor an agreement. He shook it off. He had nothing to feel proud about.

"Keeping her alive *for now*," he muttered. "We need to get her out of there."

"Did you release the snake?" Emily asked eagerly.

Darcy shuddered. "Yeah. Horrible thing. I opened the bag and dropped it, and the snake came out and slithered off."

"Fat lot of good *that* is," Robbie blurted rudely. Then he looked ashamed. "Sorry, Emily, but . . . I just can't see how . . ."

Emily rolled her eyes and climbed to her feet. "I'll be back in a while."

As she went off, Hal looked around at his friends. Fenton glared at him from the nearby mound of rock. "Okay. Darcy, you said there was a vent over the dragon's cave. That's got to be our way in. Somehow we'll have to climb down."

Darcy snorted. "Climb down? Are you nuts? Right onto the dragons' heads? How does that help?"

"Why can't Abigail just fly *up* the vent?" Robbie asked.

Darcy shook her head. "I told you, it's too narrow. It's only two or three feet wide. Bit of a squeeze to *crawl* up, never mind fly up."

"If only we had some rope," Dewey said. "We never thought to bring any. Blacknail might have some in his buggy."

Hal considered it, then sighed. "He's so far away, though. And that's *if* he has some rope. I just want to do something right *now*."

"Like what?" Darcy said.

They all stared with great concentration at the ground, silent. It was during this silence that Fenton climbed off his rock and crawled over to them. He had been listening as usual. He maneuvered into the middle of the group and turned, bumping them as he did so.

"Sit *still*, Fenton," Darcy said crossly, slapping him gently on his back.

But Fenton was trying to tell them something. He coiled his long tail around the entire circle of friends, bumping against them enough that they all got irritated.

"Fenton, if you want to say something, you'll have to change so you can talk to us like a normal person," Lauren said.

"It's really not that hard," Robbie grumbled. "You just focus your mind—"

"His tail," Hal said suddenly. "Wait a second. Is he trying to suggest we can use his tail as rope?"

They all stared at the black lizard creature. Fenton was around nine or ten feet long from the tip of his elongated snout to the rear end where his tail started. But the tail itself was a further ten feet or more, quickly thinning to the girth of Hal's forearm, and thinning even more at the tip, where it was like a point. Overall the creature was at least twenty feet long, with a ridged crest running the entire length.

"He's pretty long," Darcy said thoughtfully.

"He can cling to walls," Robbie added.

Fenton gave a nod.

"So you're saying that you'll dangle down the hole backward?" Hal said. "And let Abigail climb up your tail?"

Fenton was motionless.

Dewey shook his head. "The tunnel's not wide enough for that. But she *could* hang on to his tail and then Fenton could *pull* her up."

Fenton nodded again.

Hal pursed his lips. "This is assuming she can even get to the vent. We'd have to distract the dragons somehow. Maybe cause a noise in the other tunnels . . ."

The plan was only half formed, but it was a start. Once more, Hal was filled with the idea that all these ideas were just plain silly, impossible, dangerous. And yet, so was the idea of Lauren dropping an invisible Darcy into the tunnels, and that had worked out fine.

Emily returned. She was in her naga form, and she slid silently across the rocks. As before, she had arms. In one hand she held a wriggling snake.

Hal's mouth dropped open. "You found it?"

"Wasn't hard," she said. "I just called, and it came."

Everyone stared at her in amazement. Hal began to regret doubting his friend. After all, he knew nothing about naga creatures. "How?" he gasped.

Emily let her tongue slide out. It was long and forked, and it quivered silently. She looked at her friends and shrugged. "Somehow, I can hear other snakes and creatures with my tongue."

Darcy snorted. "You have ears on your tongue?"

"No," Robbie said. "She means that her tongue kind of translates vibrations into sound, like hearing through the jaw bones."

Emily looked surprised. "Is that how it works? Well, anyway, I can feel vibrations through my body, and almost taste vibrations and smells using my tongue. It's amazing. I had no trouble finding my friend here."

She held up the snake, which seemed perfectly content in her hands. Darcy made a noise and shuddered.

"Want to show me where you came from?" Emily whispered. She placed the snake gently on the rock, and it slithered away. Emily went after it, her huge coils pushing her along.

Hal jumped to his feet and hurried after her, and the others followed. The little black snake was wriggling fast, but Emily's huge coils easily matched its speed a few feet behind. Glancing back, Hal saw that Fenton was following too, his sinewy legs shoving his bulk along. What a strange group they were!

Moving away from the chasm's edge, they passed several cave-like openings and narrow vents. The ground was riddled with them. Perhaps they all joined up, or crossed paths . . . or perhaps many led to dead ends. There was no way to know without exploring them all.

The snake vanished. Emily slowed and peered down into another of those large craters, where an ashen gray tunnel disappeared into blackness. It dipped away at a shallow angle.

Hal stared, somehow knowing that this was indeed the tunnel that led to Abigail. Unbelievably, Emily's idea had worked. "Emily—you're a genius."

She went red. "Shut up."

Darcy touched her gingerly on the back. "I have to say, you're pretty cool. I mean, you're scaly and all, kind of creepy . . . but, I mean, *wow*."

"If this leads to Abigail, the vent Darcy mentioned must be close," Hal said. "Trouble is, this tunnel could twist and turn all over the place." He looked at Darcy. "Um . . ."

Darcy sighed heavily. "You want me to come in with you," she said flatly.

"The rest of you can wait here," Hal said. "But listen out for Abigail. Darcy said there's a vent in the ceiling of her cave. If I can get her to yell or scream, you'll hear her and maybe figure out which of these holes in the ground is the right one. If so, Fenton can do his thing and act like a rope."

Hal and Darcy headed into the tunnel entrance. But then a deafening boom shook the ground and echoed like thunder throughout the chasm. Darcy stifled a scream and dropped to her knees. "What's happening?" she cried.

Hal hunkered down with her, looking out of the tunnel to where the others crouched with their hands over their heads. "I guess the volcano burped," Hal muttered. "Let's go."

He changed into a dragon, his tail nearly knocking Darcy flying. He tried to apologize but growled at her by mistake. *Never mind*, he thought. *Apologize later.*

Darcy changed too, and became invisible. But now Hal couldn't see or smell her, especially in the darkness of the tunnel. How could he follow her? As he pondered the problem, he felt Darcy struggling to climb up onto his back. He lay down and waited until she was comfortable. She pulled on his reins; as usual his smart clothes had bunched up into a thin strap around his neck.

He headed into the low tunnel, hoping she had the sense to keep her head down. It was dark, but somehow that didn't bother him. He used his nose, trying to pick up Abigail's scent. He could smell dragons, but no humans, at least not yet. In total darkness he blundered on, downhill, feeling the walls of the tunnel scrape his sides from time to time as he veered off course. He heard Darcy wince as her foot got caught. Then, on a hunch, he spread his wings carefully. There were small claws on the tips of his wing-fingers, and he used these to touch the walls. Instantly he felt more secure. His wings acted like feelers, or like the whiskers of a cat; he was able to stay absolutely central and know exactly how narrow or wide the tunnel was at all times.

For a moment the wall on his left disappeared and he knew he'd just passed a tunnel leading off to the side. But he continued straight. He saw light ahead.

The tunnel leveled off and he heard the grunting of dragons. Here, tunnels led off in all directions. As Darcy had said, it would be easy to get lost. He wished he could find the snake again, but it was long gone—or he'd passed it along the way. But still, he felt he was getting close.

Warmth. The tunnel split, and Hal was faced with a choice. Heat radiated from the right-hand fork, but so did a pool of deep red light. *Worth a try?* He waited for direction from Darcy, but none came. She didn't recognize this area.

He proceeded into the tunnel. It descended sharply, and after just forty or fifty feet became a sharp slope that dropped into the top of another tunnel running at right angles. Darcy started yanking at his reins and kicking his sides. She whispered, "No—back up, back up!" But before he did so, Hal peered down into the tunnel and gasped. Steaming lava flowed there, a moving sludge of bright orange molten rock that sizzled and popped.

The heat rising from the tunnel was becoming unbearable, even for a dragon. Hal backed up, suddenly thinking of Darcy and how hot *she* must be! This was a tunnel to avoid.

He retraced his steps and took the left-hand fork instead, which also wound downhill, but not so steeply. This tunnel was dark and cool. The distinctive sounds of dragons rose in volume somewhere up ahead.

The tips of his wings told him that the tunnel was widening. Then, suddenly, he arrived at a cavern. It was enormous, with a huge domed ceiling and two more tunnels leading off into darkness. Two wide vents in the roof allowed daylight and fresh air to flood in. Against one smooth wall, surrounded by dozens of thick, knobby stalagmites of cooled lava, three dragons grunted noisily at each other, while around the perimeter at least ten more lazed or snoozed soundly. The smell in the cavern was pungent, even with fresh air wafting down the vents.

Hal immediately recognized two of the grunting dragons: Lumphead and Burnflank. But the third . . . the third was *old*. Hal had not met many dragons, only enough to know that male adults were large and females more slender. But this particular dragon was *ancient*. Whereas Lumphead and Burnflank had tough, vibrant hides, the old dragon was faded and gray, and some of the larger scales on its back were cracked and brittle. It had folds and wrinkles all over, and its claws were yellowed with age. It rested on a huge pile of clothes—something Hal chose not to think about too much.

Lumphead was growling and grunting urgently, and Hal strained to hear. After a moment Burnflank interjected. *What about the young half-breed? There will be no need to attack if he brings ten of the—*

Lumphead rounded on him with a snarl. *Quiet! We attack tonight no matter what. The young one has made me hungry.*

So feast on wildebeest, Burnflank urged. *Why risk retaliation from humans?*

This angered Lumphead. He tensed all over, his muscles bulging and flexing, and his tail swinging back and forth. *There is no honor in going after wildebeest. My father requires humans. A human heart is filled with anger and nobility, a meal fit for our leader—unlike the docile, flighty wildebeest you forever speak of!*

Burnflank grunted something that Hal couldn't hear.

Lumphead bared his fangs. *Our leader—MY FATHER—will feast on the courage and tenacity of humans, not the cowardice of wildebeest.*

The old dragon feebly lifted a paw. *My son, perhaps our wise friend is right. At my age, any old meat will do—*

No, father, it will not, Lumphead growled. He glared at Burnflank. *And sometimes I wonder where our wise friend's loyalties lie.*

As Burnflank once again began to argue in a low rumbling tone, Hal was filled with dread. He had to warn the others. He had to get word back to the village immediately.

But first . . .

He crept through the cavern, weaving between the snoozing dragons and staying close to the wall wherever possible. He headed for one of the tunnels on the opposite side. The one at the lower end of the dome seemed the most likely; it led downhill, surely in the direction of the chasm. Hal waited for a blast of recognition from Lumphead, but none came—he was facing the ancient monster, whose eyes were half closed.

But Burnflank saw him. His eyes widened, but he remained motionless.

Reaching the tunnel, Hal hurried on into darkness. He heard Darcy panting with fear, felt her trembling even through his thick scales.

They came to an intersection where three more tunnels led in all directions. One of the tunnels was brightly lit; it appeared to have no roof at all, just two very smooth, flat walls a foot apart. Above was a sliver of daylight. This tunnel was nothing more than a giant crack in the ground.

But Darcy whispered in his ear. "To the right. See the red glow?"

The middle tunnel was black, but the right-hand tunnel had a strange red glow at the far end, a pool of light that shone through a crack in the wall. Hal hurried toward it. As he reached the red glow, he felt its heat. A slab of rock had broken free to reveal a peephole into an adjacent tunnel. That tunnel was an almost blinding orange, and although Hal couldn't quite see it, he knew that lava flowed just beyond the thin wall.

"I saw this before," Darcy whispered. "I came this way by mistake from the other direction, and knew I'd gone wrong. Keep going."

The tunnel plunged into darkness once more, and the temperature dropped. Hal's wing-fingers gently traced the walls and he walked dead center of a passage four feet wide. Then he bumped hard into a dead end and bruised his snout.

"Go left," Darcy urged.

Hal felt to his left. His wings told him there was nothing but walls—*Oh.* He found a fairly small opening, probably quite a squeeze for an adult dragon. The tunnel beyond was wide though, and up ahead he saw more light.

"We're here," Darcy whispered.

They reached another intersection of tunnels, but one was only ten feet long and led straight into a cavern, much smaller than the last, and with just a single vent in the ceiling. An enormous female dragon lay there, facing away, with a hatchling the size of a cow snuggled up to her side. Hal guessed that these were Lumphead's mate and offspring. On the opposite side of the cavern, directly in front of the mother's snout, was a small alcove. *Abigail!*

Hal sighed with relief when he saw her. The vent in the ceiling of the cavern let in a faint pool of light, just enough for Hal to see that she was alive and well, sitting up with her back to the wall, staring at something in her hands.

There was no way she could simply walk out. The hatchling dragon alone was more than a match for Abigail, as Darcy had said—except that it was now sound asleep. However, the mother dragon was wide awake and watching Abigail very closely, *staring* at her. The vent in the ceiling was directly over her back.

Hal glanced with distaste at the pile of clothing stuffed against one side of the cavern. It was flattened down, as if it had been used for bedding.

He stood for a while, deep in thought. Abigail hadn't seen him yet—but then, how would she recognize him anyway? Yet another dragon in a labyrinth of dragons! He needed to get a message to her.

He backed out of the cave. In the tunnel just outside, he changed into his human form and was aware of Darcy collapsing on the floor with a gasp. At the same time he felt a wave of uncomfortable heat. It was hot underground!

He looked for Darcy, but she was totally invisible in the subdued light. But then she grasped his arm and he knew she was standing right beside him. "Get a message to Abigail," he whispered. "Tell her to scream and shout as much as she can, so the others can hear and figure out where we are." He paused. "And tell her to get ready to climb up Fenton's tail—but not until I create a distraction and get the mother dragon away."

He felt rather than saw Darcy's nod.

Then Hal remembered Lumphead's words. "The dragons plan to attack the village tonight. No matter what happens, some of us *must* get back to warn them."

"Okay," she said.

Darcy released his arm and stepped into the cavern. As she moved into the light, Hal saw her blurred image creeping over the flat, rock floor. She had to cross right in front of the dragon's snout. The monster's scaly nostrils twitched and flared. Then the great head lifted.

Hal transformed and stepped noisily into the cavern, his claws scrabbling on rock. The mother dragon turned her head and stared at him.

In the alcove, Abigail was focused intently on what she held in her hands: the tiny glass sphere. Hal returned his attention to the dragon. "Um," he said, suddenly at a loss for words.

The hatchling's eyes snapped open. Immediately it saw Hal and gave an indignant roar. The mother slowly got to her feet and turned around, her tail nearly squashing Abigail into her cave.

What's the meaning of this? the dragon snarled. *You dare enter my lair?*

Hal dipped his head and cowered, somehow understanding that this was a sign of submission. "I'm sorry," he grunted. "I got lost."

A second later, Abigail started yelling, "Let me out of here! I don't want to be here anymore! Let me go!" and then started screaming and wailing.

While the mother dragon turned and glared at her prisoner, the hatchling approached Hal and growled like a dog. The nerve of the thing! Hal could probably knock it flying if it came too near . . . but then again, he wasn't certain he wanted to risk its mother's wrath.

When Abigail had been screaming for over half a minute, the irritated mother dragon roared inches from her face and Abigail tumbled back and fell silent. Hal glimpsed a smudge cowering on the floor nearby.

The dragon swung her head back to Hal. *You're new here?*

Thankfully this particular dragon had not seen him before. She was not one of the females he'd met out in the chasm; she'd most likely been in her lair all the time, protecting her young.

Hal glanced up at the vent in the ceiling, wondering if his friends had heard Abigail's screams. If so, was Fenton likely to appear any time soon? Behind the dragon, in the small cave, Abigail and Darcy were pressed against the wall, no doubt looking for an opportunity to escape. Abigail's round eyes darted from one side to the other, but at the moment the large female dragon was blocking the way with her ample backside and tail.

What's that around your neck?

Hal was confused by the question, until he remembered his reins. "I was being used by the humans as a riding dragon," he lied. "I escaped and came here."

The dragon looked disgusted. *This is not your lair. Go, before my mate returns. He'll kill you for stepping foot in here.*

Hal bowed and hurried out of the cavern. But once in the tunnel, he stopped and waited. After a moment he snuck back to the cavern and craned his neck to peer around the corner. The mother had settled again, in the same position, facing her prisoner . . . but now the hatchling was sitting there too. Oops!

Minutes passed. Hal kept an eye on the vent above the mother dragon's back. Was it growing darker? Hal stared, wondering if he was imagining things . . .

Then, very slowly, a thin black tail appeared, hanging down the vent. Hal's eyes widened. Although he had been hoping for this, he still found it an amazing sight—and decidedly creepy. The tail inched down until it was dangling clear of the vent by a couple of feet, right above the dragon's arched back.

Hal knew that now was the time. Abigail's eyes had grown round again. She didn't react, but she had seen the tail. She and Darcy were ready to escape.

Chapter Sixteen
Escape

Hal rushed into the cavern and skidded to a halt on the smooth rock floor. "Come quick! The king—the leader—the old one—he's dying! Your—your mate said to come immediately!"

The mother dragon sprang to her feet and took three steps toward Hal before pausing and narrowing her eyes. She was huge in the confines of the cavern. It was a wonder a family could live in such close quarters. But it was close to the old dragon's chamber, so perhaps that was reason enough.

Why didn't he just call? she growled.

Hal was confused. Then he realized that a dragon's roar, from one mate to another, could probably be heard for some distance echoing through the tunnels. "Uh . . . he didn't like to make too much noise with his father dying in his arms."

Hal kicked himself. Dying in his arms indeed!

The mother dragon remained motionless, staring at him, and her hatchling stared too. Behind them, Abigail was tiptoeing out of the alcove, edging along the wall. Ahead of her was a blurred figure.

Why would you lie to me? the dragon said softly, with a deep, throaty rumble. *What do you want? You wish to lead me into danger?* She cocked her head as a distant crack sounded, followed by a muffled boom. Seconds later the ground shook and she planted her paws wide.

Abigail reached for Fenton's tail, but it hung too high, just out of her grasp.

Now that he thought about it, Hal could have used the volcano as a more plausible diversion. He could have said, *The place is falling apart! We must get out of here!* But it was too late now. He blundered on, stalling for time. He needed to distract the dragon for a couple of minutes. Since only one girl would fit in the tunnel at a time, Fenton would have to pull her all the way to the top and return for the other. On the other hand, if necessary, Darcy could simply walk out the same way she had walked in. If only Abigail would hurry up . . .

"I'm not lying!" Hal roared, trying to sound indignant. He stamped his feet and swung his tail, making a spectacle of himself, as Abigail sprouted wings and hovered by the hanging tail. *Go, Abigail! Go now!*

But instead she came down and reached for Darcy. With her hands locked around an invisible weight, Abigail rose to the ceiling, her face reddening with the effort. Hal saw the black tail twitch as invisible hands grasped it.

Whether it was the sound of Abigail's wings, or a draft in the air, the mother dragon caught on. She whipped her head around and stared in confusion as a snake-like object disappeared up the vent with something strange attached—something that made her squint and blink. She gave a roar and blew a sheet of flame up the vent.

Then she turned her attention to Abigail, who was buzzing around the cave toward Hal, her head nearly hitting the ceiling. The hatchling immediately jumped toward her with jaws snapping.

"No!" Hal shouted, his roar echoing around the cavern. He pounced and shoved the young dragon aside as Abigail zipped into the safety of the tunnels.

But the furious parent jumped on Hal and sank her teeth into his neck.

The pain was terrible. With jaws locked tight, she climbed onto his back and pinned him down so that she could tear into him. Hal had never felt such a colossal weight. His right wing bent painfully to the side and he squirmed, trying to roll. He was aware of Abigail screaming, but he wished she'd just get away while she could instead of hanging around.

The hatchling snapped at his tail like an excited dog and he lashed out, trying to whack it, but it kept dancing away. He felt something tear on the back of his neck and he cried out as hot blood poured out, splashing down on the rock in front of his face.

He felt the dragon loosen her grip and knew she was about to take an even deeper bite. In that moment he changed, becoming human—and the mother dragon lost her balance and staggered.

Hal was spread-eagled on the rock, face down, his right arm squashed under the dragon's weight. That was bad enough, but when she shifted, getting to her feet, he felt a bone break below the elbow. The pain was sharp and hurt so much it took his breath away and he couldn't yell out. Meanwhile, he felt more blood oozing out of his torn neck.

He changed again, twisting around as he did so, blasting fire from his throat and lashing out with his left arm. He felt his claws skim off the underbelly of the mother, but also heard her gasp as his fire singed her powerful right shoulder. She bellowed and her jaws opened wide, right in front of Hal's face.

He became human again, and wriggled sideways as a sheet of fire scorched the rock floor. He cried out as he bumped his broken arm. He gripped her hind legs and pulled himself out from under her body, sliding easily. He got to his feet, gasping. When the mother swung around to face him, Hal changed into a dragon and blew fire at her, then changed yet again and darted around to her rear side.

With each change his neck and arm felt a little better, but he was a long way from feeling perfect. He felt sick and giddy, and his clothes were drenched in blood. *His* blood. He slipped in a wet patch on the floor.

But at least he seemed to have stopped bleeding.

Hal spun, changed, blew fire, bit and clawed, changed again, dove for cover as fire blasted over his head, changed again, leapt onto the mother's back, tried but failed to sink his teeth into her neck, slid off as she bucked under him, changed again . . .

The hatchling was howling. At some point it had decided—or been told by its mother—to stay out of the fight. Sweating and gasping, Hal performed several more maneuvers and then, in human form, rushed out of the cavern into the tunnel, almost knocking Abigail over as he roughly ushered her away. Behind them, the mother dragon gave a grunt of surprise and Hal imagined her standing there looking around, checking under her feet, turning her head this way and that, wondering where the shapeshifter was hiding.

"Run," Hal whispered hoarsely, his arm clamped around Abigail's shoulders. He guided her across the intersection and up the tunnel he and Darcy had come in through. But almost immediately he knew that wasn't going to work. He heard the panting of an enormous bull dragon heading his way *down* the tunnel. Lumphead was answering the call of his hatchling, or perhaps the frustrated, angry bellows of his mate. Either way Hal and Abigail weren't leaving this way.

Dragging Abigail back down the tunnel to the intersection, he watched with horror as the mother appeared in the entrance of her lair, just ten feet away. A split second later Hal was shoving Abigail into a random tunnel, heading downhill. Was this the one Darcy had come up earlier, from the direction of the chasm?

Hal groaned inwardly. Even if they emerged at the chasm's edge—then what? He couldn't fly! But Abigail could, once she got clear of the tunnels, so at least she'd be safe. Then Hal could lose himself in the tunnels, perhaps fight his way out somehow . . .

There was a sudden cacophony of overlapping, echoing bellows. Somehow the noise reminded Hal of the siren the goblin sentries had sounded back at the village during the harpy attack. *Red alert! Action stations!* Dragons were rushing in from everywhere, answering the distress calls of their esteemed second-in-command and his mate.

Hal had not only stolen Lumphead's meal, he had attacked his family. There would be no talking his way out of this now.

Running blindly down an almost-black tunnel, hand in hand, Hal and Abigail breathlessly came to a fork. One way was lit up red and emanated heat, so Hal chose the other tunnel without pause. This tunnel was pitch-black. *Surely* it led to the chasm? They stumbled with hands outstretched—but then the blackness illuminated briefly ahead. Fire from an approaching dragon! Hal and Abigail silently swung around and returned to the fork, then headed down the glowing red tunnel.

Heat washed over them. Hal was already sweating from exertion and panic, but now he felt as though he were standing too close to the fireplace in his kitchen at home. He wanted to back off, turn away, but he couldn't.

They hurried on around the bend, slower now, watching with increasing horror as the tunnel brightened. It was headed downhill, so Hal was certain he wasn't likely to find lava rushing toward him—but the tunnel might very well lead into active lava tubes.

Somewhere behind, dragons came snout to snout at the fork and bellowed at each other. Then Hal heard scrabbling claws, pounding feet, and panting breath. They were following.

The tunnel curved around until Hal guessed it was running parallel to the chasm, no longer sloping. "Hal," Abigail gasped, tugging on his arm and giving him a savage jab of pain. His bone wasn't yet fully healed. "We can't go this way."

"We *have* to," Hal urged, knowing that she was right. He untangled her fingers from his arm, wincing with pain. "Let's see where it leads."

They hurried on, hearing angry roars echoing down the tunnel behind them. Hal looked back once, but the curvature of the tunnel offered no clue as to how close the dragons were. They would come into view shortly though, now that the tunnel ran straight.

The heat ahead was so intense that Hal felt as though his skin was about to blister off his face. He heard Abigail moaning, and she slowed, but he reached back with his good arm and took her hand again, pulling her along. Then the tunnel dipped suddenly, and widened. They stumbled down the slope and came upon a giant crack in the ground, an abyss that spanned five feet. Beyond the abyss, a much narrower tunnel wound on into darkness, wide enough for Hal and Abigail to duck through, but too narrow for dragons. Safety!

Far down in the abyss flowed a river of lava.

If it weren't for Abigail, Hal would not have hesitated. He would have leapt across the abyss and continued on into darkness. But Abigail screamed and planted her feet like brakes, yanking him to a standstill. Sweat poured down her face, and she looked faint. "I can't," she gasped.

Behind her, a blast of fire shot around the curve of the tunnel. The massive bulk of a bull dragon appeared. It was Lumphead.

"We're going *now*," Hal said evenly.

Abigail was shaking her head, staring wide-eyed at the abyss.

Hal took her face in his hands, a little more roughly than intended. Her eyes focused on his. There was a silence. Then he spoke calmly, ignoring the dragon fast approaching over her shoulder, sixty feet away, fifty-five feet, fifty . . .

"Grow your wings, and fly across. It's easy."

"I can't," Abigail said weakly. "It's too hot. They'd melt."

"You don't know that—"

"I *do*!" she yelled.

"Then jump," Hal said. "It's just a short jump. Then we're away to safety."

"I can't," Abigail said, shaking her head.

"Look behind you."

Abigail wrenched out of Hal's grip and looked over her shoulder. She screamed again, then pushed past Hal and ran at the abyss. She jumped, and came down heavily on the other side, slipping on the rock and landing flat on her back.

Lumphead bore down on them, blowing fire and stinging Hal's back as he took his turn at jumping the abyss. For a horrible second he was certain he'd misplaced his feet and jumped too early. Five feet wasn't much of a jump when playing games in a field or jumping across a stream . . . but it stretched into infinity when lava boiled and bubbled below. Time slowed as his feet and legs started cooking halfway across the gap. Then he saw Abigail sprawled on the floor ahead, trying to get up, and he knew he was going to land on her.

He somehow skidded, tripped, bumped her roughly, but shoved her in front of him at the same time. He heard the bull dragon's heavy panting, then a deep intake of breath—and Hal changed into a dragon, blocking the small tunnel, and took the full brunt of the fire as Abigail staggered safely into the darkness ahead.

Once more in pain, Hal changed back into his smaller human form and hurried into the tunnel as the dragon took another deep breath. The fire came again, licking at Hal's feet as he ran.

Then, unbelievably, they were away, with nothing but lovely cool blackness ahead, and a tunnel far too narrow for even a hatchling dragon to enter.

They gasped and panted and staggered a little farther, then collapsed. Behind them lay the abyss, now just a red glow; ahead they saw nothing at all. The tunnel was such a tight squeeze that they couldn't even sit with their backs to the wall and stretch out their legs; their knees were forced up into a cramped position. So they turned back to back and leaned on each other, with Abigail facing the unknown tunnel ahead and Hal facing the known terrors behind.

But Hal couldn't sit in that position for long. "My arm," he groaned, squirming and trying to get comfortable. "My back. My *neck*."

"That'll teach you to mess with females," Abigail said weakly.

"Not just *any* female. A *mother*."

"Dearie me. Beaten up by a girl. You'll never live it down."

Hal would have laughed if he wasn't hurting so much.

"Great rescue, by the way," she added.

"Are you being funny?"

Abigail gave a short, trembling laugh.

"That should have been *you* climbing up Fenton's tail," Hal grumbled.

Abigail was silent for a moment. Then she sighed. "I guess you're right. It's just that Darcy was petrified of that dragon. I'd grown used to it, so it seemed sensible to let her climb up to safety first."

"She could have walked right out of these tunnels unseen, once you'd gotten safely away," Hal said wearily. "Me too, maybe."

There was another long silence. "I'm sorry," Abigail said softly.

Hal twisted around, wincing. "Hey—*ow!*—it's okay. You just did what you thought was right. It would have been fine if that dragon had given you more time. Or if Fenton had lowered his tail just a little farther so you didn't have to fly up to it. It was a crazy plan in the first place."

"I'm glad you came," Abigail said. "I knew you would. But . . . I'm sorry you got hurt."

"It's okay," Hal said, gritting his teeth. "My neck's still sore, but I think it's stopped bleeding. That dragon tore a chunk right out of me. Well, it *felt* like it did, anyway. I'm just glad that transforming heals us, otherwise I'd be toast by now."

He became aware that Abigail was shaking. "You're not cold, are you?" he asked, incredulous. When he received no answer, he twisted around again and felt for her shoulder. Then he heard a sob. "You're crying."

He heard her take a great suck of breath. "I'm fine," she said, and sniffed loudly. "Just . . . just thinking about the island."

"The island?"

"Yeah. Life was much simpler on the island. No dragons, for a start."

"Except for me."

Abigail patted his hand in the darkness. "I could have coped with one."

A dragon bellowed. Hal wasn't sure from which direction it came.

He sighed. "I guess we'd better get out of here." Groaning, he climbed to his feet. The bone in his right arm throbbed. He reached up to touch the back of his neck, terrified of what he'd find—and grimaced as his fingers brushed lightly over a huge swollen mound. In the center he felt an open wound about five inches long. It was wet and gooey, but there were also signs of hardened scabs where it had begun to heal. It didn't appear to be leaking much.

His upper shoulders felt as though they were still on fire. With a shock he realized his shirt was burned away around the back. He said nothing, but stayed close to Abigail as she led the way forward into blackness. He wished he could change repeatedly and heal himself, but it was impossible in this narrow tunnel. He shuddered at what would happen if he tried to transform in the confines of a passage like this!

They walked for several minutes, hearing occasional dragon roars and one or two rumbles from deep below the earth. Then light showed ahead. The tunnel

142

widened and became a large, irregular cave with two or three passages leading off. All was quiet, but Hal didn't trust the silence. For all he knew, Lumphead had already hurried around to cut him off. These dragons probably knew every inch of the labyrinth—at least the tunnels they could fit into.

Water dripped somewhere, with a steady echoing *dwoip*.

Hal took the opportunity to transform before Abigail could get a good look at his injuries. He didn't want her fussing. Still, her eyes widened just before he changed. Immediately he changed back, then switched forms again and again. After numerous transformations he started to feel tired.

"I wonder if there's a limit to how many times a day we can do that," he said.

"You're looking better," Abigail said, stepping around behind him. She gingerly touched the lump on the back of his neck, which was now a neatly closed wound with a dry scab. "Does that hurt?"

"It's just like a bruise."

"What about your skin?"

Hal shrugged. "Can't feel it."

Abigail was silent for a moment. She prodded his bare back between the shoulder blades. "You can't feel your skin?"

"No, I mean I can't feel anything *bad*. It doesn't hurt anymore."

"Good," she said. "It looks okay, anyway. How's your arm?"

Hal flexed his fingers. "Good enough."

They walked around the cave, peering into passages.

"Let's try this way," Abigail said, pointing to one that was faintly illuminated.

"That's downhill," Hal warned. "It leads to the chasm. We can't get out that way." Then he frowned. "But *you* could, maybe. Let's go see."

They followed the tunnel. It curved around sharply, but was short, and before they knew it they were standing in an opening on the edge of the chasm, blinded by the bright daylight. Below, fresh lava flowed freely from somewhere lower down the chasm to their left. Hal stared at it. *That's the lava from the abyss.*

The sun was beginning its steady descent in the far west. A few more hours and it would be dark. Hal hoped Darcy had heeded his warning about the dragons' planned attack. It would be forty minutes around the chasm back to Blacknail, and then a further two hours back to the village. By then it would be dusk.

"You could fly to safety," Hal said, leaning out and looking up. "It's just a short flight to the top, and then—"

"I'm not leaving you here," Abigail said firmly.

Hal considered. "What if I told you that it would make it easier for me? I could just walk out and most dragons wouldn't look at me twice. But with you around—"

"You can't just leap and kind of glide away?"

Hal peered down. "No," he moaned. The fresh, steaming, bubbling lava pool directly below assured him that he wasn't ready to experiment.

They ducked back inside as two dragons came flying along the chasm, wings stretched wide. "Okay, let's try another tunnel," Abigail whispered.

There were only two others. They picked one at random and followed it in silence. In the darkness they felt their way with hands outstretched before them. They quickly reached a dead end and groped in the dark, sure that there must be a small, hidden passage leading onward. But after a few minutes they gave up and returned to the cave.

"Last chance," Abigail whispered. They took the remaining tunnel. It led uphill and veered in the direction of the lava abyss. Hal kept imagining Lumphead appearing, out of breath, after hurrying the long way around.

Once more in darkness, they stretched out their hands and walked blindly. Hal wondered if he should become a dragon again. That way he could feel his way along the tunnel with his wing-fingers and not worry so much about scraping himself on the rock walls.

Something was bothering him. Why was it so quiet? Occasionally he'd hear a deep, ominous rumble, some kind of volcanic murmur, but he'd expected to hear more angry roaring from dozens of dragons. Hadn't Lumphead raised the alarm and sent out the posse? He must know *roughly* where the narrow abyss tunnel emerged; wouldn't he come tearing around to meet him?

The more Hal thought about it, the more he sensed he was running into trouble. If *he* were a dragon . . . too big to fit down that narrow abyss tunnel . . . he would not want to scare his quarries back *into* that tunnel, so would wait and hide to make sure they were clear of it. There were only two possible ways out—the chasm, where dragons would surely be waiting . . . or up the tunnel he and Abigail were now stumbling.

Hal slowed and reached for Abigail. He squeezed her arm silently in the darkness, hoping she'd get the message and say nothing. He wasn't sure what was worse—the chasm in broad daylight, or the unknown trap ahead.

He gently pulled Abigail back the way they had come, downhill toward the cave. All he could think about was the safety of the narrow passage that the dragons couldn't venture into. They would be trapped there, but *safe*.

The cave ahead was bathed in light. Hal and Abigail hurried toward it. But then a shadow fell, and the light was blocked for a second. They halted, alarmed. A dragon had just flown in, and was waiting for them.

Now they had no choice. Once more they headed up the tunnel.

"Climb on my back," Hal whispered. He transformed, feeling a tingle as the wound on the back of his neck healed a little more. He hunkered down, and waited while Abigail clambered aboard. He waited a little longer until she found his reins—or what was left of them. He imagined they'd be a little thinner now that the back portion of his shirt was missing!

When he felt a tug around his throat he moved onward up the tunnel. It was a gentle slope but the tunnel floor became uneven and slippery with moisture. Water trickled down from the rock ceiling.

A sudden bellow from behind made him hurry. He didn't look back, but in the corner of his eye caught a momentary flicker of yellow, and heard Abigail's gasp. The dragon was back there, breathing fire to light the way.

Hal breathed fire of his own. He figured it wouldn't make any difference now, since they clearly knew where he was. As a jet of flame lit up the darkness and shadows danced, he realized that this wasn't so much a tunnel as a cavern—with a deep pit just a few feet ahead. The cavern's walls leaned inward, meeting high above. The air was moist here, almost humid. In the brief illumination, Hal thought he saw puffs of mist, but decided he was imagining things.

Abigail leaned forward and whispered in his ear. "The ground runs out."

I know, Hal thought.

He edged forward, aware of the approaching dragon behind. It was panting now, its claws clicking on the rock. It would be on them in no time.

The ground ended.

Chapter Seventeen
Trapped

With a heavy heart, Hal knew they had come as far as they could. He lit the darkness again with a burst of flame, taking in everything at a glance before he ran out of breath and his flame petered out.

There were no paths or ledges around the pit. The walls were flat and smooth. High on the opposite side of the cavern another tunnel led into darkness, but the pit was at least fifty feet across. Abigail could fly . . . but Hal was sure he saw movement in that elevated tunnel. A dragon was waiting for them.

He stared down into the pit. Had he glimpsed water? His nose told him there was definitely a lot of water somewhere; the air was humid, filled with a fine mist that tickled his nostrils. He leaned over.

"No," Abigail whispered urgently. "You can't."

The tunnel lit up again as the dragon at their rear breathed fire not more than thirty feet away. Hal prepared to jump. He would rather risk drowning than stand here and be roasted.

"No," Abigail said again, louder this time. "I think it's a hot pool down there. There's steam coming off it. It could boil us alive."

Hal hesitated. *Boiled alive . . . or roasted?*

Another burst of fire lit the tunnel—but this one was from the tunnel on the opposite side of the pit. In the brief dancing light Hal recognized Lumphead, and heard his odd, huffing laughter. He was leaning out over the pit, watching intently.

Hal swung around to face the dragon at his rear. A long growl echoed off the walls and another sheet of flame told him it was almost upon them.

"Change," Abigail cried, quickly sliding off his back. All sense of secrecy had been abandoned now.

Trusting her, although feeling he was making a huge mistake, Hal changed into his feeble human form. Vulnerable, he and Abigail backed up to the pit and faced the dragon. It had been approaching slowly. Now it bellowed triumphantly and launched itself at them, panting noisily.

Abigail, standing behind Hal, slipped her arms under his, locked her hands together across his chest, and squeezed tight. For a moment he thought she was just giving him one last hug—but then she pulled him backward into the pit.

They fell just as a blast of fire roared over their heads. Hal awaited the plunge into the boiling water below. Maybe he would be safer if he changed into a dragon again; then the boiling water wouldn't scald so badly. Abigail would be all right; she could just hover in the air while he thrashed around looking for a way out . . .

He felt a sudden upward tug, heard the buzzing of wings, and knew that they were hovering above the spitting, bubbling water. He felt hot splashes on his toes and pulled his legs up in horror. If Abigail could just fly around and—

But he remembered back on the island when he had lost his shoes and she had carried him across the jagged rocks. She had quickly run out of breath. Faeries were not designed to carry people.

Already Abigail was struggling. He could hear her panting, could feel her straining to keep them in the air. How long could she keep this up?

"Let me go," he said calmly.

She said nothing, but buzzed around carefully in the darkness. The water gurgled just below his feet, and the hot steam made Hal sweat like a pig.

A blast of fire from above—and then a second from the opposite side—lit up the pit. In those few seconds Hal glimpsed the steaming, churning water stretching from wall to wall, an oval-shaped pool thirty feet across and fifty feet in length, with sheer rock walls all around. There was no way out—no tunnels, no secret caves, not even a ledge to rest on. And Abigail was tiring fast.

"Let me go," he said again. "I'll change. Let me go."

"No way," Abigail said through gritted teeth.

But Hal could tell she was giving out. His foot touched the water again and he yanked it up with a cry. *Yep—it's boiling.*

If only he could fly. The cavern was small but *just* large enough to—

"I see something," Abigail gasped. Hal couldn't understand how she could see *anything* in the total darkness, but then remembered that she had faerie eyes. She gave a low moan, shuddering with exertion.

As twin jets of flame from above once more lit up the pit of boiling water, Hal looked to where Abigail was headed. He saw nothing but a smooth rock wall, dark and glistening like all the other walls.

Except . . .

The fire went out and they were plunged into darkness again. But then he felt rushing movement as Abigail flew at the wall. He braced himself.

But there was no impact. Instead they crashed roughly to the floor.

The floor!

Hal sat up, stunned. He patted the solid, unusually flat floor all around and shivered in the sudden cool air. He reached out blindly. "Abi?"

"Here," she replied, breathing hard. "Give me . . . a second . . ."

Hal climbed to his feet. "Where are we? I didn't see a tunnel. How—?"

Abigail was still gasping for breath, so Hal moved around slowly, trying to get his bearings. The floor felt different. He bent and touched it. It wasn't rock, but *stone*—flat stone tiles. Man-made. He crossed the floor, one foot in front of the other, groping in the dark. He crashed into something. It was a table or bench, and it made a horrendous screeching sound as it scraped on the floor. He reached out, feeling glass bottles . . . *dusty* glass bottles . . . and books . . . and a lamp.

He fumbled with the lamp, but it had a cord and switch and he couldn't make it come on. Hardly surprising—there wouldn't be any electricity here.

"This is nuts," he said finally, as he bumped into a shelf that was fixed to a wall. He felt his way along and found some steps leading up. "A room inside a labyrinth. Underground. With dragons everywhere. And a volcano nearby."

"I don't think we're in the labyrinth anymore," Abigail said faintly. "Or anywhere near the chasm."

Hal climbed the steps. They were metal, and clanged under his heavy feet. The pitch-blackness was so complete that for a crazy moment he wondered if someone had thrown a thick blanket over his head. At the top of the steps he paused at what he assumed was a door. Yes—there was the handle. He turned the knob, expecting it to be locked.

It was.

With a frustrated yell, he switched to his dragon form and felt the staircase groan. The steps under his feet bent slowly downward, and the railing buckled as he pressed against it.

He launched himself at the door and felt it give a little. He tried again, and something splintered. Ordinarily he would have knocked the door down in one go, but it was a little more difficult at the top of a staircase.

On the third try the doorframe broke and the door burst open.

Daylight blinded him. Blinking, he squeezed through the doorframe. He took some of the frame with him as he stumbled into a musty room. He knocked over a table and spilled old plates onto the floor, where they smashed into small pieces. He tipped chairs over and they broke under his weight. He was in a kitchen, long vacated, dust blowing up in clouds as he stamped around the small, dim room. Floorboards cracked under his weight.

The daylight came from two filthy windows, one over the kitchen sink and another in the top half of an external door. Hal crashed through the door without stopping, catching his wings painfully as he went. Choking in a cloud of dust, he stopped outside in knee-length grass. The sun was shining but there was a cool breeze. The air smelled fresh and clean.

The house sat at the foot of a grassy hill. The terrain was pleasant—rolling and green, thousands of yellow daffodils bending in the breeze . . . and absolutely no sign of the chasm or the volcano or the dragons.

Hal turned to look back at the house. It was a small, single-story building with gray, badly weathered wood siding and a roof that looked like it was about to cave in. Falling apart, obviously empty for years. The grass was long, and weeds covered what was once a pathway leading to—a road? It might have been a wide, hard-packed dirt track at some point, but it was mostly grass now. Nearby stood a rusted pickup truck with flat tires and weeds growing up through gaps around the hood. A small shed stood around the back, with an old bicycle leaning up against it, almost completely smothered with ivy.

Abigail appeared in the ruined doorway of the cottage, blinking. "You're like a bull in a china shop," she complained.

"Sorry," Hal said. He gestured behind her to the busted basement door. "I guess we went through a hole, then."

Abigail grinned. "Yeah. I saw it over the hot pool—just a dark smudge. It was all black and smoky, like the one underwater by the lighthouse."

Hal shook his head. "How lucky was that?"

Abigail raised her eyebrows. "Lucky? You mean the part where I was held prisoner by dragons and nearly served up for dinner? The part where you were half killed by an angry mother? Or the part where we were chased through the labyrinth and nearly boiled alive?"

Hal smiled. "Put like that, I guess we've been pretty lucky all day long."

Abigail rolled her eyes and sighed. "Well, I'm glad we—"

There was a sudden, tremendous racket from the basement. Things flew around the room down there, smashing, scraping, rattling, and bouncing, while a familiar furious bellowing threatened to shake the cottage apart. Abigail's eyes went round. "No! It came through *after* us!"

They stared in horror through the open door, looking into the dusty kitchen. In the wall opposite, the busted doorway led down to the pitch-black basement. A second later, that blackness illuminated in a fiery glow as the dragon roared.

"We'd better go," Abigail said.

They took off, heading up the grassy hill. Behind them came muffled angry bellows and crashing sounds. There was a wrenching of metal, noisy clangs, and Hal knew the dragon had found the stairs. Not that it could use them; adult dragons were far bigger and heavier than Hal. It would also have trouble getting out of the basement through that narrow doorway, but it wouldn't be long before it tore out of there in an explosion of wood and drywall.

They crested the steep hill, panting. Immediately they saw dozens of other homes dotted around the countryside, much larger than the one they had just emerged from. There were paved roads, all cracked and overgrown with weeds, but paved roads all the same. "Pick a house," Hal shouted, tearing down the hill toward the nearest street. Any hiding place would do. They didn't need to fight the monster, just *hide* from it. They just had to get to the nearest house and stay quiet for a while.

As they tore down the hill, almost tripping in the long grass, the crashing sounds grew more violent. There was a brief pause before they started again.

"It's out of the basement," Hal panted. "It'll be out of the cottage soon."

The nearest house suddenly seemed miles away. They'd never reach it in time. If the dragon flew up into the air and *saw* them, then the cover of a house wouldn't do much good for long.

"Change of plan," Hal yelled, and steered Abigail to the left where a huge truck and trailer stood abandoned in the road. The cab was bright red under the grime, with chrome fenders and side mirrors. The long rectangular trailer was a dirty pale gray color with COSCO written on the corrugated metal sides.

He yanked on the cab's passenger door and it squealed open. Abigail climbed up and Hal followed her in, then pulled the door closed, hinges protesting.

It smelled old in the cab, but it was surprisingly clean. Hal and Abigail sank below the dash and peered out of the filthy windshield as the dragon rose into the air over the hill. It was Lumphead, as Hal had feared. The ornery beast soared high, screeching, then circled around, bent on spotting its prey.

The nearest house was still fifty or more yards away. Hal and Abigail would never have made it in time. Still, Lumphead apparently assumed they had. He swooped down to the house and started tearing into it, clinging to the side with one huge forefoot through a broken window and his hind feet digging into the siding, scrabbling for a hold. His wings beat once in a while, more for balance than lift, while his tail thrashed around. With his free front paw he started ripping at the wall, pulling off first siding, then some papery material, then sheets of silver-coated insulation and plywood, before punching through to bundles of pink fluffy insulation and finally the powdery drywall of the bedroom beyond. In half a minute the dragon had made a hole big enough to squeeze through—and when he was inside, bellowing like crazy, he started punching windows out. The house was shaking and groaning. Then fire blew and the building started to smoke.

"I think he's mad at you," Abigail whispered.

Hal noticed something farther down the road. People! He stared, amazed, as a small group appeared—four adults dressed in strange bright yellow one-piece hooded suits with black boots and canisters strapped to their backs. Each face was hidden behind a glass visor, with a black tube running from the mouthpiece to the canister. *Biochemical suits.*

Hal nudged Abigail and pointed.

The people were staring at the house at the end of the old, ruined, overgrown street. Hal didn't think they had seen the dragon go in; they had emerged because of the commotion. Now they stood and watched with obvious amazement as the house began to burn.

A crash from the house made Hal jump. A large bulge had appeared in the pitched roof. Another crash, and the bulge burst open. Then the dragon flew out in a shower of debris and a cloud of smoke.

The yellow-suited men stood motionless, staring into the sky as the dragon came around. Beneath their masks Hal imagined their mouths hanging wide open.

Then Lumphead spotted the men, and bellowed. He pulled his wings back, straightened his body, and dove.

The men scattered, yelling. Three of them made it into various buildings, where they disappeared in fright. The fourth man was not so lucky. Lumphead landed in front of him, bent low, and clamped his jaws around him. Then the dragon threw back his head. Legs kicked from between his fangs. Then the legs slipped inside his mouth. The dragon crunched once. He stood there with all four feet planted on the ground, tilting his head from side to side as if working the meal around his mouth. Half a minute later the dragon spat once, then again. A huge glob of something landed in the road—mostly bright yellow, with a black boot, and a mass of—

Hal ducked low and closed his eyes. Abigail was crying.

It was a while before Hal looked outside again. There was nothing left but a mess on the road. The dragon was in the sky once more, screaming and blowing fire, circling the houses.

Abigail was shaking uncontrollably, hands over her face. Hal tried to comfort her but she seemed to have lost all control. He held her grimly and waited.

By the time her sobs became sniffles, the dragon had moved on to another street. The yellow-suited men—the remaining three—had gathered together once more, talking urgently. Then they hurried off together out of sight.

"Look," Hal said peering through the windshield. A large dark green vehicle rumbled into view. It had endless wheels within gigantic metal tracks. The vehicle was shapeless, just a large heavy lump with a smaller section on top that swiveled around as it drove. "That's . . . that's a *tank*."

The dragon heard the rumbling tank and came to investigate. It flew in with a roar, eager to tear this strange beast apart, knowing there were people inside.

The turret turned, and the long gun barrel raised. The dragon swooped down.

Hal saw the flash a split second before he heard the boom. The entire tank rocked backward, and the dragon blew apart in the air, showering the road with limbs and wings and gory lumps.

* * *

Hal and Abigail decided not to approach the people and their tank. The scientists or soldiers might detain them, keep them from seeking a way home—or worse. "But they're *people*," Hal had insisted at first. "They won't hurt us. They're obviously not crazy; they're wearing chemical suits. We could speak to them, find out what—"

"Not today," Abigail said firmly. "It's getting late. We need to figure out how to get home and warn the village. *Maybe* Darcy and the others made it away from the chasm okay and are heading home as we speak—but we still need to find our way home sometime this century."

In the end Hal agreed, even though he secretly thought the men in the biosuits might be able to help in some way. But perhaps Abigail was right. The men could just as easily take them away to some secret underground bunker and do experiments on them to find out how they had survived the virus without suits.

So, when it was safe, they left the truck and headed back to the cottage over the hill. The place was a mess, half fallen on one side, with bits of furniture and debris all across the grass.

"I don't relish going back in there," Hal said, as they stared down into the pitch-black basement. The staircase was gone.

"Nor do I," Abigail agreed. "There are probably dragons waiting for us."

"How did Lumphead get through the hole?" Hal marveled. "He must have watched us disappear. I bet that riled him up! He must have flown around in that confined space above the boiling pool, probably scalded his tail trying to come through the hole. No wonder he was angry."

Abigail sighed. "So . . . what should we do then? Risk it?"

Hal thought it over. "There are other holes," he said at last. "If we could find our way back to the island, we could—"

"That's *ages* away! We could maybe find the coast and follow it south—we'd probably find the island okay, I guess. But it would take *days* of walking, maybe a week, and that's just to get back to the lake we arrived in!"

"If only I could fly," Hal groaned.

Abigail narrowed her eyes. "Hold on. What did Charlie say about that hole on the top floor of the building he took us to?"

"I'd forgotten about that. It leads through to a gigantic lake." Hal looked around, squinting at the sun. "The village is about two hours west of the chasm, so the lake in *this* world must be about two hours west too."

The sun was descending over the distant mountains. That was the direction they needed to head toward. Hal wished he had grabbed Blacknail's compass, but he never could have guessed that he'd need it. He went into the cottage to see if he could find one. His dad had always kept a compass in the "bits and pieces" drawer in the kitchen, which also contained keys and other useful gadgets.

But he couldn't find a compass anywhere, and Abigail was getting impatient. "Come *on*," she griped. "Let's just head toward the sun."

"But," Hal said, frowning, "it would be safer to have a map or something."

He spotted something on the floor by a small overturned table. A book lay there, along with a broken mug . . . and something else.

"Did you find a compass?" Abigail asked, sounding surprised, as Hal went to pick it up.

"No. It's a magnifying glass." Hal handed it to her. It was dirty but intact, with a long, smooth wooden handle and a circular glass piece three inches across. "You wanted a magnifying glass to see into your little faerie crystal ball."

"Oh yeah," Abigail said, her face breaking into a smile. She slipped the magnifying glass into her pocket. "Okay, let's *go*."

They set off, heading west. After leaving Louis it had taken around two hours in the buggy to reach the chasm, traveling at the pace of a horse's canter. Two hours . . . which, on foot, would be . . . at least half a day's walk at a fairly fast pace, probably closer to a full day! "Surely not," Abigail said, wrinkling her nose as though the realization was a bad smell. But it was true. The prospect of walking for so long did not appeal to either of them, but they had no choice. And even if they chose the other route and managed to get back through the hole into the labyrinth, and avoided all the dragons, they still might find that Blacknail had already left with the others. They'd *still* have to walk back, no matter what.

As the afternoon began to cool, they walked steadily across fields of long grass until they reached a silent, empty town, which they navigated with a mixture of fascination and dread. Cars lay abandoned, buildings stood empty, weeds grew everywhere. It was a ghost town, with trash all over. They tried to stay on a roughly straight route, but had to detour down side streets. They kicked at squashed soda cans and rolled an old shopping cart filled with junk until it tipped over with a crash. They stopped dead when they saw people standing in a shop window, absolutely still, but then realized they were mannequins.

"Where are all . . . you know, the dead people?" Abigail wondered aloud. "If people died from the virus all those years ago, where are their bones?"

Hal didn't want to think about it. He liked to believe that small groups of survivors took the time to bury all the dead—or at least burn the rotting bodies. Still, it was hard to believe they got to *all* the bodies. Maybe the streets were cleared, but what about all the houses?

He shuddered.

Eventually they reached the other side of town and headed away from the buildings, back out into the countryside. They followed a railroad track, since it was headed their way; it was easier than cutting through fields.

The sun was rapidly sinking. In an hour it would be dark.

Tired, Hal and Abigail sat for a while near a clear stream running under the railroad tracks. They were hungry but had no food. The water in the stream tasted funny, but it quenched their thirst. It was peaceful, sitting there in the waning light, under an oak tree by the side of a field. But they felt very, very alone too, and worried for their friends and the people in the village.

"Hand me that glass ball," Hal said. "And the magnifying glass."

Abigail dug in her pockets and, with a moment's hesitation, handed both items to Hal.

Hal looked at the tiny ball through the magnifying glass. It showed up much bigger, filling the three-inch convex glass. Abigail leaned closer to look.

"Oh!" she said, delighted. "That's *so* much better! Now I can actually see what's inside."

"There's *nothing* inside," Hal said, puzzled. "Just a sort of misty stuff. Is that what you've been . . . what you've been looking . . ."

He trailed off. He felt strangely mesmerized by the swirling misty cloud within the ball. It changed colors very slowly, from pale gray to yellow, then to green, then to blue, then violet . . . and all the while it pulsed in and out, rhythmically, in tune with his heartbeat.

After what seemed an age he stopped seeing pretty colors and instead saw other images within the mist—images of himself, somehow trapped or stored in the ball. He saw himself as a small boy, hurrying to school with an equally small Robbie, huge grins on their faces as they joked about something Hal had long forgotten. He saw himself munching a sandwich, sitting on the jetty down by the docks, staring out at the foggy sea. He saw himself opening gifts at Christmas; he clearly remembered the year his dad had given him that watch, when he was old enough to wear it. How sad that the very same watch had been pulverized on the rocks just recently, back on the island, when he had transformed into a dragon and nearly scared Darcy to death.

The images flickered in the glass ball, speeding up. The misty substance seemed to grow until it filled his vision, and the images were bright and colorful as if he were actually *there*, back on the island all those years ago, like a ghost standing to one side watching his every move . . .

Chapter Eighteen
Memories

Hal watched, intrigued, as a younger version of himself in the glass ball took down a painting from his bedroom wall. He remembered that painting—it had bothered him for months, ever since his mom had put it up. It was of a large dog chasing a boy through the boy's own back yard, while at the edge of the picture the boy's dad was leaping out of his car and waving frantically to ward off the dog. It was a scary picture and Hal hated it. Why had his mom supposed he would like such a horrible thing? He'd taken it down and hidden it, and his mom *must* have noticed but never questioned him about it. But now, looking at the painting again, Hal realized that the dog wasn't chasing the boy at all. The boy's dad was grinning, as if he had just arrived home from work. The boy was simply rushing to greet him, with the dog in tow. It was a *nice* painting.

He saw himself talking to Darcy. She looked as cute as a button in her red dress and her blond hair tied up in pigtails. She couldn't have been more than five or six. Her lips were moving; she was asking an equally young Hal something. Hal somehow remembered this. She was asking whether he would like to come around to her house and play. Hal told her no, he was going to Abigail's instead. Darcy's face screwed up and tears started to roll. She stuck out her tongue and ran off, leaving a perplexed Hal wondering what had gotten into her. He remembered Darcy being mean to Abigail the next day, but not to *him*, which was odd at the time. There were other incidents like this too, when Darcy had acted funny around him. Older, wiser Hal suddenly realized that she had *liked* him, and he'd snubbed her. Still, he'd been just five or six years old; how could he have known?

Thomas Patten filled the picture and Hal held his breath. In his lifetime he had seen many, many photographs . . . but all of them were from the time before the virus, photos his parents had saved from their previous lives Out There. Robbie's dad was once interested in photography and had an old 35mm camera, but he had no expertise in developing the pictures in chemicals. Therefore Hal had never seen pictures of himself or his friends. Thomas was nothing but a distant memory.

So to see Thomas again now, six years old, running around as he used to, with short red hair and freckles . . . Hal stared and stared, fascinated to see these moving pictures of his classmate in the weeks before he had fallen off the cliff, apparently gone forever.

Just as he thought about the cliff, adult faces swam into view—horrified, saddened faces. Hal knew he was revisiting, in perfect detail, the afternoon that Thomas had chased a groundhog through the undergrowth and, after getting caught up in the bushes, snagging his clothes and grazing his skin, he had transformed into a red-furred, lion-like beast with a scorpion tail and a face full of teeth. His mother, trying to catch up with him in the woods, had come across Thomas the manticore moments after he had changed, and she'd screamed in horror. That scream had sent her terrified son stumbling away, and . . .

Of course, Hal had heard a different version of the story at the time. As he huddled with his friends in the living room at Mr. and Mrs. Patten's house, the adults moved slowly through the house and back yard, comforting one another and talking in low voices. Hal's dad came over to explain everything to the children. "Thomas was playing near the cliffs. He fell and was killed on the rocks." The children were so shocked that they said nothing, just sat in silence.

Looking back on the scene, Hal saw something more in the way Mrs. Patten told her story. He could see her sitting in a rocking chair out on the back porch, with her husband on his knees beside her. She was shaking uncontrollably, and using her hands to describe something. Now that he knew the whole story, Hal could almost put words to her motions: "He had claws *this* long, and a huge scorpion tail with . . . with *quills*, and so many teeth . . ."

Later that evening, someone had knocked on the door of Hal's house. His dad answered, and Hal heard low voices. When he looked out the window he saw someone shrouded in darkness, someone with long hair, wearing a cloak. At the time he had assumed she was one of the moms, but now he saw her clearly as Miss Simone, here to explain that Thomas was *not* dead, that she had in fact rescued him from the sea, that he was safe and sound but on the loose somewhere in Elsewhere. She must have warned all the parents to keep up the pretense, to let the children go on thinking they were normal for a couple more years. After she left, Hal's dad haltingly explained to Hal that Mr. and Mrs. Patten had gone away somewhere, but he didn't say where. Hal's mom finally said, "They've just gone, Hal. Left the island. There's nothing here for them now that their son is dead."

For the next few years Hal and his friends firmly believed Thomas was dead. If his parents had confessed that the red-haired boy was, in fact, still alive, they would have had to explain *everything*—which made Hal wonder how he would have coped, at age six, knowing that he might turn into a monster sometime in the future. Perhaps all the secrecy really was for the best, that it was better to reveal everything to the children *after* they started to change.

Years flew by. Hal turned eight, then nine, and his parents questioned him continually. "How do you feel?" his dad asked cheerfully every morning. "Feeling strong? Different in any way?" Hal was bored silly with the routine. Apparently all his friends were questioned in this way too. Mrs. Porter, the island doctor, had often mentioned that the children had amazing immune systems, so Hal assumed his parents were worried he was somehow in danger of losing that quality, that he might one day grow sick. Looking back, it was obvious that his parents were simply waiting for the transformations to begin.

Fenton started being mean. He had grown more plump, and was taller than the other kids, so he threw his weight around. Hal heard some news that Fenton's parents, Mr. and Mrs. Bridges, were arguing a lot these days—probably about Fenton being fat and mean, Hal thought at the time. He wished they would keep him at home so the rest of them could enjoy school without fear of being bullied. Robbie in particular was scared of the big boy; he was so thin and puny, and had such a geeky fascination with bugs, that Fenton just couldn't seem to help picking on him. One late evening, Mr. and Mrs. Bridges were heard shouting and screaming at each other. Mrs. Bridges had stayed at the Morgans' that night; Hal asked Dewey about it the next day and Dewey said that Fenton's mom had had enough, she was leaving her husband.

It never happened, though. The next day Mrs. Bridges returned home and all was quiet again—for the most part. *It's that Fenton causing trouble again*, Hal had assumed. *He really stirs it up!* But now, looking into the glass ball, Hal wondered . . . Perhaps the boy was just reacting to his parents' arguments? How would *he* react if his parents argued all the time? How could he go to school and be cheerful and friendly with that kind of thing gnawing away at his heart? For the first time, Hal began to realize that perhaps Fenton's constant bullying was a *symptom*—a reaction to his parents' arguing rather than the other way around.

He turned ten. He had always liked his friends (except Fenton) and enjoyed their company, even the girls, but lately he had started thinking that girls were kind of silly. They seemed to spend a lot of time messing with their hair and commenting on pretty dresses and shoes. It was all so *pointless*. Hal started hanging out with Robbie more than any of the others—not because he liked bugs, but because the only other boy was Dewey, and Dewey was so timid and quiet that he was boring. Robbie could be a pain sometimes, but at least he was always ready for adventure. Together they climbed trees and went to the docks and sometimes even snuck into the forbidden Black Woods. And the girls . . . well, they liked picnics, but they couldn't just grab a sandwich and eat up a tree somewhere, they had to bring hampers and blankets and do everything in a *civilized* way. Especially Emily, who had always been bossy and was getting steadily bossier by the day. Darcy and Lauren were okay, although they tended to whisper and giggle a lot.

Abigail was a funny one. Hal had liked her at one point; she was a little annoying but a good sport, always ready to play boys' games. But she went through a boring girly phase and Hal didn't want to be around her anymore. For some reason this made Abigail more annoying. She kept pestering him all the time, giggling like a loon and getting on his nerves. This phase eased off after a while and Abigail left him alone, hanging out with the other girls more.

Hal had been relieved. But now, looking back through the glass ball, he plainly saw that she had . . . she had *liked* him. She had liked him more than any of the others, and he had snubbed her, just as he had snubbed Darcy years before.

He felt like a heel. This glass ball was stirring up too many memories. He didn't like it. He blinked, trying to draw himself out, to end the slideshow.

He was partially successful. He saw the images shrinking as he pulled away, and felt a strange tug as though he were tethered to the glass ball with a length of elastic. But he knew he could pull free if he wanted to.

Only . . . suddenly he was twelve and scratching a curious itch on his arm. He allowed himself to be tugged back into the scene, and watched himself pull up his sleeve and study the slightly reddened skin. There was nothing to see, but it sure did itch.

The itch persisted for the next week. He watched as he went to school or lounged in his bedroom, absently scratching his arm, occasionally looking to see what kind of bug bite he had, but finding nothing at all. After school one day, Robbie told him he had "something amazing" to show him in Black Woods. Hal knew it was just some boring new bug, but Robbie was insistent and off they went. That was when Hal first saw the fog-hole.

Then the itch turned into a green, scaly rash. That was frightening enough, but Robbie began experiencing sudden bursts of strength, and it turned out that Abigail could grow wings! Hal's rash, she said, was merely the start of something, but he refused to see it that way. It seemed obvious, looking back on it, that his rash was something special. He had an excellent immune system, had never had a cold or illness in his life, and even when he had been bitten or stung by bugs the wound had healed very quickly. Darcy had broken her ankle once, and Mrs. Porter had applied some healing paste . . . although, now that he thought of it, Hal realized it was more likely Darcy's own immune system, and her extraordinary healing powers, that fixed her ankle quickly—not some strange gunk that Mrs. Porter had concocted in her potion workshop.

Fascinated, Hal watched himself transform into a dragon. Now he appreciated how fearsome he looked to others! He saw himself flapping his wings feebly, and he snorted with derision. Yeah, right, as if *that* would get him off the ground. Dragons don't just flap their wings and launch into the air. Flying takes strength as well as skill. Even as he watched himself crossing the plains in Blacknail's buggy, on the way to the village of Louis, he realized how pathetic he'd been in his attempts to fly. It was like throwing a chick out of a nest and expecting it to fly on its first attempt. Even with all the skill in the world, a dragon needs to build up the strength in his wings before launching from the ground.

Hal really needed to jump off a cliff. He didn't need much strength to glide; for that he simply needed the correct skills, and of course he had the skills already—all that information was right there in his brain. Yet he had been right not to jump from the labyrinth tunnel into the chasm. He would have plummeted to his death. He saw very clearly, now, how far off the mark his attempts to fly had been so far. There was no guesswork involved—he couldn't just flap his wings and expect to fly! He had to flap them in the *exact right way*, angle them just so, compensate for shifts in weight and the direction of the wind, and—

Hal shook his head, amazed at how silly he'd been. How had he not seen this before? The mysterious glass ball was practically shoving all his mistakes and misunderstandings in his face, shaming him. He struggled to draw himself out, fought against the elasticity, and tore his eyes away from the misty substance.

The pictures faded, and he blinked.

Sitting next to him, Abigail blinked too. She frowned and rubbed her eyes, then looked at Hal with a quizzical expression.

"Some trip," Hal said, wondering exactly what she had seen.

"I saw my whole life," Abigail said. "It was like . . . it was like I was there, looking at myself, seeing things in a different way."

"Clearer," Hal agreed. "I saw myself too. And you . . ." His face heated up. "I, uh . . . I never realized that . . . I mean, I guess I was sort of rude to you back when we were younger . . ."

Abigail stared at him, and a smile tugged at the corners of her mouth. "You were just a boy. Girls mature faster than boys."

"They do not!"

"Do too." Abigail looked around. "How long have we been sitting here?"

The sun appeared to be in exactly the same position as before, even though it felt like Hal had been staring dreamily into the glass ball for hours. "Half an hour?" he guessed. "Ten minutes? I don't know. But we should get going."

They continued along the railroad, both deep in thought. The sky began to develop tinges of orange and a faint moon appeared opposite the sun.

"Hold on," Abigail said at last. "I just want to try something."

She sprouted wings and buzzed into the air. Hal noticed that her ears were slightly pointed, and was about to comment on it when there was a small popping sound and Abigail shrank to the size of a sparrow.

Hal stopped dead, staring in amazement. Her tiny mouth moved, but all he heard was a distant squeak. He shook his head and cupped a hand around his ear.

The faerie moved closer. She was about six inches tall and no longer buzzed like a large dragonfly; now she zipped with the sound of a mosquito, a high-pitched whine. She hovered near Hal's ear and the whining sound gave Hal goose bumps. "I can shrink!" Abigail yelled in his ear, still sounding as though she were far away.

"I see that," Hal said quietly, nodding. He grinned. "You're a regular faerie now, pointed ears and all. You did it!"

And I can do it too, he realized with absolute certainty. *I can fly.*

It wasn't that he thought he could *probably* do it, or that he was *fairly certain*. There was no doubt in his mind—he knew for a *fact* that he could fly. But he also knew he wouldn't be able to launch from the ground. Not yet, anyway. He needed an elevated position, maybe a cliff, or . . .

He spotted a gigantic metal-framed tower looming over the trees, high above the ground. Hal had seen lots of these towers throughout their journey, all lined up across the horizon, spaced fields apart. They seem to do nothing more than carry lengths of cable for miles across the landscape.

"I want to climb that tower," he said, pointing. "I can use it as a launch pad."

Without waiting for an answer he hurried across the railroad tracks and struggled through the hedge into the field beyond. The tower was gigantic, much bigger than it looked from a distance. How tall was it? Two hundred feet? In any case it was plenty tall enough for what he had in mind. But it didn't look easy to climb. Higher up he could see a simple ladder, but it was far out of his reach.

Abigail zipped by his ear, then suddenly appeared with a popping sound, human-sized. She looked down at herself and grinned. "This is *so* cool. How come I couldn't do this before?"

Hal was beginning to get impatient. They needed to get back to Louis urgently, and here they were messing around in a field in the middle of nowhere— and in the wrong world! "Can you lift me up to that ladder?"

Abigail looked, and made a face. "Maybe. I guess, if we're quick. But when you start flying, I expect you to give me a ride."

"Deal," Hal said.

Abigail came around behind him and reached under his arms. She gripped him tight. For a second Hal felt awkward, and he wondered if Abigail felt it too. Something between them had changed when they had gazed into the glass faerie ball; feelings had been brought into the open. He now knew that Abigail *liked* him . . . and he supposed he liked her too. Maybe she was his *girlfriend* now, the way Robbie imagined Lauren was his—only more real than that.

Then Abigail lifted off, and Hal's feet left the grass. He reached for the ladder, grabbed a rung, scrambled to put a foot on another—and Abigail released him with a gasp.

High off the ground, Hal began to climb. The only sound was his breathing and the muffled clangs of his smart-soled feet fumbling for the rungs. He climbed without stopping, never once looking down, seeing only a ladder stretching into the darkening sky.

Some way up, the structure of the tower changed and angled outward. Hal swung around to the other side of the ladder and kept climbing. The cables stretched off into the distance. Hal saw tower after tower, perfectly aligned, the farthest just a speck on the horizon.

Abigail buzzed noisily nearby, a worried look on her face. "Don't fall."

"I'll try not to," Hal grunted, his arms starting to grow tired. He almost looked down, but forced his gaze upward. *Just watch my hands*, he thought fiercely. Sweat soaked his palms. He felt as though he might slip at any moment.

He arrived at the huge cross-section at the top, the part of the structure from which all the cables hung. He clambered onto the topmost horizontal beam and sat gasping, trembling all over. He dared not look down, but was staggered by the view around. It made him feel dizzy.

Hal moved out along the beam to the end, so that he was clear of the vertical framework. Abigail hovered nearby.

Now that Hal was in position, he had no idea how to proceed. He was terrified. Earlier he had been sure he could fly, but up here, miles above the earth, he wasn't so certain. What if he messed up? He only had one shot at this. He doubted Abigail could arrest his fall if he plummeted like a stone.

He stared down. The railroad below was like a toy. The town they had passed through earlier seemed just a short hop away, although they had walked miles. In the distance he saw tiny houses nestled in the hills, where the dragon had been blasted from the sky. The world was huge, and yet everything in it was tiny and insignificant.

"You don't have to do this," Abigail said from where she hovered nearby.

Tense all over, Hal carefully shifted around until both his legs hung on one side of the beam. He was ready to jump.

"Hal—"

He looked at Abigail. "I'll be fine," he told her, thinking the exact opposite. "I can fly. And if I can't, I can at least glide to the ground. Don't worry."

Glide to the ground. Somehow that made him feel better. Yes, one step at a time. He knew how to flex his wings, knew how to angle them to catch the air in just the right way. He *knew* this stuff. So he would simply *glide* down to the ground, and if he happened to fly, well, even better.

"Keep up with me," he said weakly, leaning forward. Before he could change his mind, he tipped himself off the tower and fell like a stone.

His heart stopped.

The sudden rush of air in his ears was louder than he expected. His hair whipped back and his eyes dried in an instant. It was like tearing along the road on his bike, only worse, *much* faster. The ground sped toward him at a frightening rate. He had only a second.

He changed into a dragon. *That* part worked easily. But the ground was already upon him. He panicked, flexed his wings, angled them *just so*, felt a colossal weight straining at the thin membrane of his wings—

The long grass tickled his belly as he swooped low to the ground, hurtling away from the tower and across the field. The toes of his hind feet dragged in the dirt. Hal adjusted his wings just a fraction, and he rose, then soared upward.

A moment later he was high off the ground again—and beginning to fall back to earth. He tumbled, straightened, swooped again, leveled off, felt the grass tickling his belly . . .

Once more he rose into the air, although not so steeply this time. He flapped his wings, once, twice. With each beat he felt a little lift. It didn't take much now that he was already in flight, but he knew it would be extremely difficult to launch directly from the ground. *Like pedaling my bike, but starting off in the highest gear*, he thought. That was it—dragons had no low gears. It took immense strength to launch from the ground.

He beat his wings again, over and over, stretching his snout and neck, streamlining his body.

His fear began to dissipate, and excitement set in. He was flying! He circled around and around the field, soaring and swooping, trying different things—a slight adjustment here, a flex there. He found that his tail played a part too. If he let it dangle low, it increased drag and acted like an air brake. If he followed through with his body, bringing his hind legs down, and then his belly, but continuing to flap hard, he ended up in slow descent. But rather than land, he quickly straightened up and gained speed once more. He didn't relish the idea of climbing the tower again.

He lost track of time, but eventually remembered his mission—and Abigail. She was standing in the field, arms crossed, patiently waiting. He swooped lower and shouted, "Climb on!" But of course that came out as a roar. Abigail probably thought he was just showing off.

Still, she buzzed into the air and attempted to catch him up. He tried to slow, but hovering was difficult. So he climbed into the sky, and Abigail followed. High above the ground he approached her rapidly, then switched into what he considered landing mode, with tail down and legs akimbo. His wings angled and snapped into position like a sail, and his body swung downward. With his speed greatly reduced, Abigail whipped around and grabbed his reins. As she settled on his back, Hal dove, picked up speed, and soared into the sky.

"*Wheeeeee!*" Abigail screamed, clinging tightly to his neck and back.

Now Hal wanted to show off. He beat with all his might, straightening his entire body from snout to tail, and shot through the air. The ground rushed by—trees, fields, a few houses, more fields, a river, a hill with a monument on top, more trees, *lots* of trees . . .

Just to experiment, Hal let loose a blast of fire. He immediately regretted it. At this speed it just blew back in his face, stinging his eyes. He also heard Abigail yelp. "Sorry!" he yelled.

Finally, *finally*, he was flying. And all because of the little glass ball that the faeries had given Abigail. It had revealed his own mind to him—to both of them. Everything he needed to know to fly was there in the back of his head. Hal's lack of flight was never a physical limitation, just a mental block. Somehow, crossing to Miss Simone's world too early had fuzzed his brain, locked away certain bits of information before he had had a chance to study them. The glass ball had simply reopened his mind.

There was hope for Orson after all. And if Fenton glanced into the ball, he would learn to change back to his human self *at will* instead of waiting for sleep.

All Hal and Abigail had to do now was get home.

Chapter Nineteen
The hole over the lake

Hal and Abigail lost track of the distance they traveled, but came across more and more lakes as they headed west. They knew that the hole leading back to the village of Louis lay over a large lake—but which one?

"Go higher," Abigail urged. "Up as far as you can go."

So Hal rose high into the sky, wings beating steadily. The curvature of the earth grew more pronounced, and the landscape seemed to lose all its bumps and dips, becoming more like the smooth surface of a soccer ball. The horizon to the west was as bright as day, yet an ever-darkening shadow cast the east into night.

As he ascended, the air thinned and he found it more and more difficult to catch his breath. He decided to glide instead, descending slowly while he studied all the lakes in the area.

There were a few possible contenders. One or two seemed way too far south; another in the north was nestled in the mountains. There were a number of small bodies of water dotted around the countryside, but they were more like ponds.

"How about there?" Abigail called.

He couldn't see where she was pointing, but he looked carefully and finally spotted a large flat area farther west. It was quite a way north of the direction they had been traveling, but their westward route had been guesswork anyway. It looked like this lake might be the one. It was certainly large—so large that it probably seemed like an ocean from the ground.

He angled toward it and tilted his wings so that he began a long, steady descent, picking up speed as he went.

What else had Charlie said about the hole? Just that it hovered high above an enormous lake—but how high above? It was hard to judge since the terrains in the two worlds differed so much. The research laboratory in Louis had been built *around* the hole, so the hole over the lake *might* be roughly four floors above the water—more when you took into account the ground level itself. Then again, nothing about the holes seemed logical, and it was a big lake. It was going to be like looking for a needle in a haystack.

Hal pondered as he flew around. Charlie had used the hole many times. As a griffin he could probably launch himself through the hole on the fourth floor of that building in Louis, and pop through into the sky above the lake here in this world. But wouldn't it be dangerous returning the same way? Hal imagined a huge griffin soaring through the hole and emerging into a small fourth floor laboratory, knocking over tables and equipment . . .

Abigail patted his back. "I see a pier. Didn't Charlie say he built one?"

Hal nodded, spotting a pier on the south side of the lake. But then he spotted several more. Which one was Charlie's? And why build one anyway?

Then Hal remembered that the scientists also used the hole. Since they weren't shapeshifters and couldn't fly, that probably meant a boat was needed to get to the hole. That would explain the need for a pier!

Hal flew around studying all the docks and piers, including small jetties half covered by unkempt bushes and overhanging trees. In the thirteen years since the virus, any remaining boats floating in the water without a cover would have been rained on many times over by now, and sunk without a trace. Or they would have been swept away by storms, or dashed to pieces against the banks.

Yet there, moored to a small, modest pier to the west side of the lake, bobbing gently in the water, was a solitary boat covered with a tarpaulin. Hal gambled that his hunch was right and came in for a landing on the solid ground near the pier. It was a heavy landing and his feet skidded and threw up clods of dirt and grass. Abigail clung tight and screamed.

When Hal changed into his human form, Abigail stumbled against him, lost her balance, and fell. She climbed to her feet, brushed herself down, and glared at Hal. "You landed. Are you going to be able to take off again?"

"Hopefully I won't need to. Look."

He walked along the pier to the waiting boat. It had a small motor on the back and was big enough for four people. Hal reached down, tugged the tarpaulin off one corner, and climbed in. It rocked alarmingly until he sat down. He cleared a space for Abigail, who climbed in with a look of bewilderment on her face.

"Charlie said the hole was high above the lake," she said.

"I think we reach it using this boat," Hal said. "Somehow."

Abigail looked even more bewildered. Then she sighed. "Okay, so how do we know which direction to go? The lake is huge. The hole could be anywhere. And it's getting really dark."

Hal shrugged. "I don't know. But this is Charlie's boat."

"How do you know?"

"It's the only boat on the lake. And it's been used on a regular basis. See, our seats are much cleaner than the ones at the front end. Passengers always sit here, at the back, and take a ride out to the lake. Wait . . ." His fingers had found something tucked into a pouch under his seat. He drew it out. "What's this?"

Abigail stared, then gently lifted it from Hal's hand. It was a long, ivory-colored horn with a spiral pattern running up its length. It was hollow and fairly light, roughly eighteen inches long. "My mom has one of these."

Hal studied the motor. It wasn't likely to start; boats like this needed fuel. But he flipped open a little panel anyway—and gasped. Inside was a geo-rock, glowing orange from within, with two rods sticking out and wires running off into the inner workings of the engine.

Hal triumphantly raised his eyebrows at Abigail.

She nodded, rolling her eyes. "Okay, I admit it. You're on to something."

Hal flicked a switch, and the engine roared into life—just like that. After clearing its throat with a small belch of black smoke, it rumbled smoothly and the boat began to move. Hal quickly glanced around for a rope to untie, but there wasn't one. The boat left the pier and took a dead straight route across the lake.

Hal and Abigail waited with bated breath, not moving a muscle in case the magic spell somehow broke. Hal understood how the boat was powered, but not how it was guided. Their course couldn't just be random, and he noticed that the bow jigged from side to side like a dog on a leash, held on course by some unseen force. Intrigued, he awkwardly clambered to the front of the boat and peered down into the water. There he found a chain attached to the bow, dangling in the water but straining toward the stern as if the boat were dragging something heavy. Hal puzzled over it until the journey ended five minutes later. There was an odd clunk deep below the surface and the boat suddenly dipped at the front end as if the chain had snagged on something. The rumbling engine eased to a gentle idle, and the boat gradually became still in the water.

"Oh!" Hal said, light dawning. He was watching the chain at the bow, which had now slackened. "There must be some kind of guide deep below the lake—like a long cable or something, stretching from the pier to here. The boat powers itself, but it can only go in one direction because this chain runs along the guide cable." He clambered past Abigail to the back of the boat and peered down. "Yeah—see, there's another chain. One at each end. I guess that stops the boat from turning and spinning around . . ."

"Look!" Abigail said, amazed.

To their right side, just out of reach, a four-foot-square wooden platform rose silently out of the water until it was as high as the boat.

When Hal got over his shock, he leaned into the water and splashed around with his hands, trying to bring the boat closer.

"Would you like a paddle?" Abigail asked, holding one up.

"No, we're there now." Hal grasped the platform and dragged the boat closer. Finally it thumped against the side of the platform and he was able to climb out.

"Help me," Abigail said, discarding the unused paddle. In her other hand she still clutched the horn. She stood up gingerly, and Hal gave her a hand. Then they stood on the platform together and wondered what was coming next. The boat's motor continued to idle.

"There's the hole," Hal said, awed.

It hovered in the darkening sky directly above, a faint smoky substance, pulsing eerily. But it was way out of their reach, more than a hundred feet up.

"Is this platform supposed to lift us up there?" Hal wondered aloud.

"Maybe something is supposed to trigger it," Abigail said. "But I don't see any switches or anything."

Just then the boat revved and backed away, quickly and smoothly. Hal felt a tinge of worry as it stranded them there on the platform. It reversed slowly across the lake, traveling in a dead straight line toward the pier. Now he understood why the boat hadn't been lashed to the pier with a rope—it didn't need one when it was already tethered below the surface.

After a moment, Abigail lifted the narrow end of the horn to her mouth and blew. No sound came out, and nothing immediate appeared to happen.

"Now what?" she asked, staring up at the hole. "I could easily fly up there, but you'd think there would be a way to—Oh!"

Hal gasped. Far above, a rope had appeared. It dangled from the hole and descended toward them, with a triangular-shaped foothold on the end. It lowered slowly and steadily until it reached the platform. Then it stopped.

Abigail laughed and reached for the rope. "I don't believe it." She tucked the horn under her arm, stepped onto the foothold, and held on tight. "Coming?"

Hal hesitated, but then the rope started ascending and he jumped on quickly. There was only room for one of his feet alongside Abigail's—the rope was designed for just one passenger—so he hung awkwardly, face to face with Abigail as they rose into the darkening sky.

"This day gets weirder and weirder," she said softly.

Craning his neck, Hal looked up. The rope disappeared into the hole above, cranked by some unseen winch like a bucket being pulled up a well.

Hal studied the curious pulsing hole to Elsewhere. It was small, no more than four or five feet across. He wondered if he could enter the hole from any direction. Would it make a difference? Then he wondered if it had some sort of edge or definable boundary. What if a large creature, like a dragon or a griffin, tried to fit through? What would happen to its wings as it flew in?

As he and Abigail ascended, he reached out with probing fingers and found a strange resistance at the hole's far edge, a thickening in the air where the pulsing blackness began to fade. It sent eerie tingles up his arm. For one alarming moment he felt his fingers *snag* on something. He snatched his hand back.

There was a brief moment of blackness, and then they were in a room—the fourth floor of the research building. The winch above their heads was suddenly noisy and clanking, but it rattled to a stop as soon as their feet were clear of the hole. Five adults stood around a low fence, staring at them in surprise.

Hal looked down. Yes, it was just like hanging over a well, only instead of a solid circular stone wall it was a lightweight fence, and instead of a shaft leading down into the ground it was a pulsing black cloud just above the floor. A short set of stairs to one side allowed them to step easily into the cluttered room.

There were two women and three men, all dressed in pale gray smocks. One of the men had small round glasses sitting askew on his nose. All five adults looked puzzled. Behind them, in a large glass tank, a strange and hideous creature the size and shape of a rat swam back and forth, bloated, furless and gray, with long, trailing tentacles and a spiky tail. It seemed to be spraying some kind of inky substance, which Hal found oddly mesmerizing.

Finally, one of the women broke into a smile. "Welcome back! Your friends are worried about you—well, we all were. Charlie's organizing a small army out there, preparing to stand off against the dragons."

"Our friends are back?" Abigail said, sounding relieved.

"They returned about an hour ago," one of the men said. "What I don't understand is—how on earth did *you* end up *here*?"

"We'll explain later," Hal said. He rushed to the window and found empty streets. "Where is everybody?"

"Just follow the noise," the woman said.

Hal and Abigail had no time to marvel at the endless tables full of glass bottles and test tubes and small mechanical contraptions—the room was clearly a scientist's delight. Abigail handed the horn to the woman and followed Hal from the room. As they left, the man with the glasses asked, "Hey—the horn was supposed to be left in the boat. Did you put the tarpaulin back on?"

"Uh, no, sorry!" Hal shouted as he and Abigail tore down the stairs. He heard the scientist mutter with annoyance.

Outside, the air was cool and stars were beginning to sparkle. Hal and Abigail tuned in to the sounds of yelling crowds, and hurried along the empty streets. They received several surprised looks as they ran, and one man said, "Hey, aren't you—?" before they left him well behind.

They eventually found their way, gasping, to a large crowd near the outskirts of town. Charlie Duggan's booming voice carried over the heads of dozens of men armed with pitchforks and a variety of gardening tools.

"What are they going to do with those?" Abigail whispered. "Hoe the dragons to death?"

". . . cannot be allowed," Charlie was shouting. "We may not be a match for dragons one on one, but as a team—and with a concerted effort—we can stand our ground and defend our territory. Tonight we won't run. Tonight we will bring down some dragons!"

A cheer went up, and makeshift weapons were brandished.

"No more running and hiding, scattering in all directions," Charlie went on. "From now on, when the dragons attack, we'll stand together and—"

"No!" a young voice shouted. *Darcy!* "You have to hide! I keep telling you, the dragons are on their way here *right now*, so hide where they can never find you, in the hills or down in the mines. You can't fight the dragons with shovels and picks—they're too strong. There are too many!"

Charlie turned to her. "If they don't find us tonight, they'll return tomorrow night, and the night after that, until they do. Enough is enough. Your friends died to help us, and they failed. Now our dragon shapeshifter is gone—the second in six months. We have no hope of communicating with these creatures. Fighting is our only option."

Hal scanned the crowds, looking for the rest of his friends. There was Emily, tearful and white-faced, and Robbie, holding Lauren's hand, and Dewey, in his centaur form. No sign of Fenton, but hopefully the slithery serpent was around somewhere, hanging from a building or loitering behind a shed.

"Time to say something," Abigail said, nudging him.

Hal nodded. He pushed his way through the crowds with Abigail a couple of steps behind. Charlie was just about to open his mouth and speak when somebody gasped and pointed. "Hey! Aren't they—?"

Heads turned as Hal and Abigail approached Charlie. A silence fell.

Then Darcy squealed and ran at them. She threw her arms around both Hal and Abigail together. Emily and Lauren came rushing over, equally noisy, and for a moment Hal was unable to breathe, see, or even hear himself think. As he gently eased his way free, Robbie bounded up, grinning all over his face. "We thought you were dead!" he yelled.

Dewey came clopping up, and Hal feared the boy was about to forget he was in centaur form. But he didn't; the boy was beaming, but proved to be the most restrained of the group. "It's *really* good to see you both."

"You too, Dewey," Hal said, grinning. Abigail, pulling free of the other girls, gave Robbie a punch on the arm and Dewey a gentle pat on the side.

Charlie's huge hands came to rest on Hal's shoulders. "Son," he rumbled, "you had us all worried. How did you get back?"

"We used your boat," Hal said. "Forgot to put the tarpaulin back on, though. I hope it doesn't rain any time soon."

Charlie looked bewildered. "How could—" Then his face slowly cleared. "You found another hole. Where? In the labyrinth?"

"In the labyrinth," Abigail said. "We were pretty lucky."

"And we remembered what you said about the lake and the pier," Hal added.

"What happened to your shirt?" Emily asked, tugging at Hal's tattered collar. "It's missing from the back. Is that blood? And are those . . . burn marks?"

The crowds pressed in close all around, but there was an odd silence.

Hal nodded. "Yeah. I got toasted once or twice."

"What's that lump?" Lauren asked, prodding at the back of his neck.

Hal winced, and brushed her hand away. "Do you mind? That's still healing. A dragon bit me."

Abigail snorted. "*Bit* you? It nearly tore your head off." She touched Hal's right arm, and spoke to the crowds. "And he had a broken arm too. That was where a dragon fell on him."

There were several low murmurs.

"Uh, well," Hal said, feeling a million pairs of eyes staring at him, "no big deal. I heal easily. Look, we need to be prepared. Darcy's right—the dragons are planning to attack. Tonight."

The crowd murmured again. One man piped up, "So nothing's changed? After all you went through, they're still going to eat us?"

Charlie held up his hands, shaking his head. "Now, now, folks. Nobody expected things to change overnight. Hal has initiated communications. No matter what he went through, at least—"

"Are we going to fight or what?" someone shouted, wielding a pitchfork.

"Yeah, let's show 'em who's boss," another agreed.

The crowd suddenly grew restless and noisy. Irritated, Hal transformed into a dragon and rounded on the villagers. He gave a roar and blew fire into the air. Everyone fell back, startled.

Hal stood there a moment, his wings spread. He realized he was up on his hind feet, balanced on his tail. This allowed him to hold up his front paws in a menacing way, claws extended. He bared his teeth and growled long and slow.

Abigail buzzed into the air and hovered near Hal, looking down on the crowd. "What my scaly friend is saying, is that you're no match for even one small dragon. He can roast the lot of you in one go. You think that pitchfork is going to help?" She waited for an answer, but none came. "The adult dragons are much bigger and a lot more vicious than Hal ever will be. You really want to stand out in the open and wait to be eaten? Darcy's plan is much better—since we know they're coming tonight, let's all go and hide in the mines."

There was a long, long silence, and slowly pitchforks were lowered.

Hal changed back and found himself standing alone in a very large space. "Maybe they won't attack at all. The big dragon leader is very old, but the one who was *really* running the place—the one who seemed to be leading the attacks on the village—well, he's dead. Maybe . . ." He shrugged, thinking of Burnflank but not wanting to mention him here in this crowd. "Maybe they won't be so eager to attack now."

Not entirely convinced, the crowd mumbled and grumbled for a while.

Finally Charlie called for silence. He turned to Darcy, but made sure everyone could hear.

"Darcy, the idea of hiding in the mines may seem like a simple solution, but it just isn't practical. The half-hour walk to the mines outside the village is not so bad, and we can take blankets and even some food and water—but the real problem is safety. With so many people traipsing down into the mines . . ." He shook his head. "We considered this idea months ago and eventually abandoned it. Usually we have no idea when the dragons are coming, except that it's roughly every couple of weeks. What do we do, spend several nights in the mines, just in case? And the mines are dangerous. There's always a risk of the roof falling in, killing more than the dragons ever could in one night, not to mention the fact that many of the tunnels are so tight you have to crawl through them."

Darcy nodded glumly. "Okay. But what about the hills? *Anywhere* but here."

Charlie spread his hands. "There are nearly two thousand people in this village. Where do you hide two thousand people?"

"We have to stand and fight!" a man yelled. Immediately a chant went up, and it was a minute or two before order was restored.

"I suggest we stand guard as always," Charlie said loudly, "only tonight the men will be ready and waiting, and our centaur friends have offered to help as well. Tonight we have advance warning, and we're going to make it hard for the dragons. Tonight we take a few down."

The villagers agreed, and the chant started up again. Hal looked on in horror as hundreds of pathetic weapons danced above the crowd.

Then he felt something. He frowned and put a hand to his chest. What *was* this? It was like a buzzing, or a tingling. Goose bumps were rising on his arms and the back of his neck was beginning to crawl. He felt an urge to transform again, become a dragon and join the—

That was when he knew.

He pushed through the crowd and tugged on Charlie's arm. "They're coming," he said urgently. "The dragons—they're coming."

Charlie's eyes widened, and he yelled for quiet. When the noise died, he stared long and hard at Hal. "The dragons are coming? When? Now?"

"They're already here," Hal said quietly.

As if on cue, sirens started blaring. It was a different sound to the harpy alarm, and the result was more dramatic. Instead of a silent dash for nearby homes, people began screaming and tearing down the streets, bent on returning to their families. It was pandemonium, and Hal found himself being shoved aside as villagers hurried this way and that. He stood still, frightened to get in anybody's way, and saw his friends standing motionless too, like the mannequins he and Abigail had seen in the deserted shop windows of the ghost town.

Over their heads to the east, the dusky sky was filled with black shapes and the steady, rhythmic beating of leathery, creaking wings. Flashes of orange fire pockmarked the night like giant lightning bugs.

Awed, Hal could only guess at the number of dragons—a hundred, maybe a hundred and fifty. They flew directly over the village, close enough that he could count the claws on their feet and distinguish between the brutish males and more slender females. The males far outnumbered the females—but no doubt there were many more females back at the chasm, waiting with their young for mealtime.

Hal looked for Burnflank, but there were just too many dragons. There was no definite leader in this fleet, just a mass of monsters vying for the lead, eager to be the first to swoop down on its prey.

The streets were clearing, and weapons had been abandoned and left lying in the dust. So much for standing and fighting! But Charlie and a handful of others remained with the children. Among them, an old woman said, in a quavering voice, "They're not stopping."

Half a minute passed, and the last of the dragons passed by. They had flown right over the village—and not attacked. Charlie swept a hand through his red hair, and turned to stare at Hal in amazement.

"Whatever you did, son—whatever you said—worked. They've ignored us, gone on to the plains where the wildebeest roam. *They're leaving us alone.*"

Chapter Twenty
Geo-rocks

Dinner at the DOG & BONE INN that evening was a happy, joyous occasion. Hal was so hungry he ate two platefuls of Charlie's evening dinner without saying a word. It was fish tonight, and truly excellent. After he washed down his last mouthful with a drink, he sat back with a sigh and belched rudely.

The dragons had flown by without stopping—and returned twenty minutes later carrying countless dead wildebeest from the nearby plains. Stunned, the villagers had watched the dragons fly by, even daring to stand out in the open on the streets. When the last of the dragons had receded into the distance, a great cheer had gone up. The celebrations were still going on an hour later when Hal and his friends had finally returned to the inn to get washed and changed.

Abigail filled in the details of the events in the labyrinth. Charlie pulled up a chair so he could listen in. Fenton, although still in lizard form, refused to be left out this time and lounged on the floor near the crackling fire. Seeing him, the rest of the inn guests had fled the room.

"So you saw the bull dragon blown to bits by a *tank?*" Charlie said, amazed. "We always guessed the military was still around, along with scientists and so on, but I've never seen head nor tail of them. There are survivors, but they're mostly in underground bunkers. The streets are clear, towns are empty. I guess you came across a bunch of scientists taking samples or doing tests. That's promising."

"Why?" Emily asked.

"Well, just to know that there's still civilized life," Charlie said. "Maybe one day someone will find a way to inoculate people against the virus." He grinned suddenly, and turned to Abigail. "So how on earth did you find my boat? And how did you get to the lake so quickly without transport?"

Abigail smiled and winked at Hal. "You tell them."

Emily was quick to get excited. "Tell us what?"

"Yeah," Robbie muttered, looking distinctly annoyed that he wasn't already in on Hal's secret. "What's the big news?"

"I can fly," Hal said quietly.

Charlie pounded the table and barked a laugh. "Fantastic! You flew! That explains how you got here so quickly. How did you find the boat?"

Hal shrugged. "We just remembered what you'd said, that the hole was above a huge lake. We found the lake, and then the boat, and figured it must be yours."

Charlie grinned. "Did you like it? Clever, eh? I designed it myself." He turned to the others. "It's fully automated—you just switch it on and it goes out across the lake, following a cable guide below the water. It returns to the dock about two minutes later. A completely innocent boat, and nobody suspects a thing. Not that subterfuge has been necessary for the last thirteen years, and I even leave the key in the box these days. But when I first moved to Louis, I made it one of my jobs to design the boat and platform system, and keep the hole's location secret. Can't have just *anyone* coming through the hole, you know." He looked at Hal, then Abigail. "And you used the horn?"

"My mom had one," Abigail said. "It brought Miss Simone running, so we figured this one might bring *you* running."

"Ha! Yes, it sent a signal to lower the rope. Mermaids can hear these horns for miles around, even across the boundary between worlds, yet nobody else can hear a thing. It's primitive, but perhaps the only means of communication between worlds. But we can't have mermaids waiting around for signals, so Simone found the answer. There are a few other water-dwelling creatures that can hear the horn, and they tend to go a little crazy when it sounds. The rat-squid can hear it. When the rat-squid squirts, that's the signal to send down the rope." Charlie beamed, obviously proud. "Putting weight on the rope sends it back up. Clever?"

Everyone agreed that it was indeed clever. But now Hal wondered about the *other* hole, the one in the old basement of the destroyed cottage. Had the owner of the house discovered it? Perhaps so—and been boiled alive in the hot pool, or roasted by a dragon. Or perhaps the owner had left the hole well alone. Or perhaps the hole was relatively new, appearing in the last few years when the owner was already long dead.

When Hal mentioned this, everyone hoped that the owner had died from the virus rather than a boiling or roasting. "Not that the virus is much better," Darcy added after a pause.

"Where do they come from?" Dewey asked. Everyone turned to look at him, and he was suddenly bashful. "I mean . . . the centaurs think that mining for geo-rocks causes earthquakes, but maybe the mining causes holes too."

Charlie frowned. "There is a theory that these rocks, left alone, condense and implode, becoming tiny black holes or something like that. All that energy has to go *somewhere*. But we don't have any experts to answer these questions. If we could have brought a few physicists across into our world . . ." He sighed. "Anyway, it's interesting you thought about that, young Dewey. Maybe you're right. Maybe these geo-rocks somehow develop into holes between worlds."

"Yeah, but how does one end up floating above a lake?" Robbie demanded.

Charlie shrugged. "Good point. But listen—eat up, and then we'll go and send a message back to Carter. I'm sure they're anxious for some news."

After dinner, Charlie took Hal and his friends to the four-story laboratory. Although it was late and the building stood empty, there was an on-duty communications operator on the lowest floor.

"There's always someone here," Charlie explained, "in case Carter or one of the other villages sends us a message. There'll be someone on duty at the other end, too. Fire her up," he added cheerfully, patting the operator hard on the shoulder. The small, wiry, bald-headed man winced and frowned, and turned to the transmitter.

It was a bizarre contraption involving four glowing geo-rocks and a strange collection of rods and wires attached to a round bowl of blue-tinted water. It was illuminated somehow—the water glowed brightly, and when the operator flipped a switch, four small dots of light appeared at the base of the bowl, creating a faint haze of white.

The operator motioned for Charlie to stand in a certain spot on the floor, clearly marked with a red painted circle. Charlie stood there and waited. Around him, four cylindrical contraptions hung from the ceiling, pointing inward directly at Charlie's head. They were like telescopes with the smooth outer casings removed, exposing a complex set of lenses and mirrors within.

When the operator gave a thumbs-up, Charlie spoke. "Greetings, village of Carter. Charlie Duggan here, from Louis. This is a message for Lady Simone Dupont to say that all is well—the harpy *and* dragon situations have been resolved. The young shapeshifters were successful. They are unharmed and will be returning home tomorrow."

Charlie stepped away from the red circle and folded his arms, watching while the operator flipped a couple of switches. Then they waited. After thirty seconds, the blue water developed a white cloud in the center, and then a man appeared, head and shoulders only, blurry and flickering. The operator twisted a dial and the man's features cleared. "Thank you, Mr. Duggan," a faint, warbled voice said. "I will relay the message to Lady Simone. And . . . congratulations."

The image faded.

"Now," Charlie said, rubbing his hands. "Let's go for a stroll. It's a wonderful evening, cool and clear. Come on, I'll take you to the park."

"Lady Simone *Dupont*?" Emily whispered as they filed out of the room.

Twenty minutes later, Hal sat with Charlie on one of many curved wooden benches overlooking a hot pool lit with perimeter lamps. Steam rose into the night sky. The picturesque park on the outskirts of Louis was surrounded by enormous rocks and neatly trimmed hedges, a peaceful getaway frequented by many of the residents. Hal's friends had taken over three more benches on the other side of the pool; Charlie had wanted a quiet word with Hal, alone.

"I wanted to ask you about Felipe," he said quietly. "I wanted to know if . . ."

Hal debated whether or not to tell Charlie about Burnflank. The dragon had indicated that he would prefer to be dead to the world. Still . . .

Hal sighed and leaned forward to stare at his feet. "He's alive and well."

Charlie slapped the seat next to him. "I knew it! Whenever the village was attacked, a lone dragon always came along ahead of the pack, shooting fire and swooping low. The rest of the pack followed a minute later. The villagers always thought that the first dragon was sent ahead as a sign of terror, to get everyone riled up and panicking. Everyone knows dragons love to hunt. Given a choice between a man that's hiding in a house and a man that's standing in plain view waiting to be eaten, they'll tear up the house just for the thrill of the hunt."

Hal nodded. "That's why Lumphead liked to eat humans."

"Lumphead?"

"The dominant male. I gave a couple of them names. Felipe has a burn on his side, so I called him Burnflank. I didn't know who he was at first."

"You *called* these dragons by these names?"

"Not out loud," Hal said hastily. "Just in my head. Dragons don't have names. At least, not names that translate. I can translate most dragon talk into words, but when it comes to names . . . well, they're sort of weird. I couldn't sit here and repeat dragon names if I tried, unless I was a dragon myself."

"Ah, yes," Charlie said. "Griffins are like that too."

"Anyway," Hal went on, "Lumphead said humans are—" He struggled to remember what the dragon had said. "—*tenacious*, that was it. He said that eating human hearts give dragons strength and courage."

Charlie snorted. "What a load of superstitious nonsense. Anyway, the point is, I always wondered if that lead dragon was actually flying ahead to *warn* us. Reckon it was Felipe?"

"He couldn't stop the attacks," Hal agreed, "so he did the next best thing. He's ashamed. I think he'd prefer it if the village thought he was long dead, rather than living with the dragons. People might think . . . well, you know."

"What?" Charlie looked confused. "That he was *joining in* with the attacks? Eating his fellow humans? Eating his *friends*?" Charlie shook his head. But then he frowned and pursed his lips. "Hmm. Maybe he has a point."

"It's not like he never *tried* to stop them," Hal said. "He's been trying to work his way up through the ranks. He's done well in the last six months."

Charlie stared at him with interest. "And?"

"Well, he and Lumphead were arguing in front of the big old chief. I guess Burnflank—I mean, Felipe—was pretty well respected, but he could never outrank the chief's own son. But the chief's son is dead now, so I guess Felipe has taken over as the chief's advisor." Hal gave a wry grin. "The chief is probably relieved. He seemed tired."

"Why didn't Felipe just kill this Lumphead fellow earlier?" Charlie asked. "Maybe things would have been—"

"It doesn't work like that," Hal said, annoyed. Didn't *anyone* understand dragons? "It might work that way with other big animals, but dragons are smart. It's not the biggest, toughest dragon that gets to be leader, it's the smartest and wisest. Any dragon who tries to muscle in by force will be torn apart by the rest. These dragons work as a group, *for* the group. They have certain rules. They all seem to understand that a pack without a leader is like a classroom of kids without a teacher: nothing gets done." *Well, unless Emily is in the class*, he thought. "And you just don't come along, join the pack, and announce that you're smarter than everyone else. You have to *prove* it, and that takes time. I bet Felipe has a few tales to tell about how he went from a nobody to the chief's third-in-command."

Charlie nodded slowly. "I see. A steady rising, earning respect, establishing himself as a potential leader. But he couldn't rise high enough."

Hal imagined he would feel like a failure if he rose easily through the ranks and was then balked by a stubborn, human-hungry monster whose dad was the ancient chief. If Lumphead had met with an accident of some kind, then Burnflank could have moved up a step and been second-in-command . . . but how does one dragon arrange a fatal accident for another without arousing suspicion? From what Hal had experienced, killing a dragon was a noisy, messy affair.

"I think Lumphead was so angry with me that he risked everything to follow me through that hole," Hal mused. "He must have hit that water and scalded himself. It might have looked like he misjudged things and boiled himself alive. Either way, dragons watching from above saw him disappear for good. Felipe was nowhere near at the time, so never would have been suspected of anything."

Charlie smiled. "So you paved the way for Felipe to step in." He stared hard at Hal, then patted him heavily on the shoulder. "All's well that ends well, then."

"Except for Felipe," Hal murmured, staring at the steaming pool. "He has to live the life of a dragon just to keep them away from the village."

"Maybe not forever, though," Charlie said. "Once things have settled into a new routine, and those who once feasted on humans have forgotten they liked the taste . . . well, maybe then Felipe can come home from time to time."

"Maybe," Hal agreed doubtfully.

Across the other side of the pool, Abigail was holding the magnifying glass and ball so that Fenton could stare into it. The huge black lizard remained absolutely still for about a minute. Then he shook his head and looked around.

Fenton's four sinewy black limbs suddenly changed and became human legs and arms. At the same time his black, scaly skin rippled and pulsed like bubbling fluid, and became pale and smooth. His torso contracted, and his smart clothes, which were draped like a second skin over his back, somehow reformed and solidified. Finally his snout shortened and hair grew from his head quickly and untidily. The boy was human once more, kneeling on the rocky path.

He stared at his hands, then looked up and grinned broadly. Everyone clapped and cheered, and just for once Fenton was as good-natured as the rest, joining in with the conversation, laughing and joking.

Charlie had been watching with surprise, and Hal explained how the glass ball had given him the ability—or rather, the *knowledge*—to fly. "Abigail can shrink to the size of a real faerie too," he added. "She couldn't before."

"Simone will be ecstatic," Charlie boomed, grinning. "Not just for you and Abigail, but for Orson too. And for any others who haven't fully developed their abilities. I always maintained that there are probably things we shapeshifters can do that we don't even *realize* we can do. Maybe that tiny glass ball will help us truly discover ourselves."

Charlie turned and studied Hal closely. "Speaking of Simone . . . When you return, I want you to tell her, privately, that her brother is alive and well. Tell her everything you told me. Felipe is a hero. She needs to know that."

Her brother?

The big man got up and called the others, saying it was time to head back. Hal sat glued to the bench until Robbie and Abigail came over, looking puzzled.

"You look like you've seen a ghost," Robbie said.

Hal shook himself and climbed wearily to his feet. His transformations healed injuries, but they seemed to do nothing for aching muscles. All that walking, and especially flying, had worn him down. At least he could relax the next day, sitting in the buggy while Blacknail drove them home to Carter. Hal couldn't wait to see his parents again.

"I'm ready for bed," he said, yawning.

* * *

Hal slept well and woke late the next morning. The streets outside were already bustling. Feet stamped up and down the hallway outside his room, and doors banged. He knew he was late getting up, but lay there anyway, staring at the ceiling and enjoying the soft, plump pillow and cool sheets for as long as he could. Finally Abigail pounded on the door. "Are you *ever* getting up?"

Sighing, Hal washed and dressed. Ready for the day ahead, he and his friends tucked into breakfast and ate heartily. Charlie joined them briefly before hurrying back to the kitchen to help poor, flustered Mirabelle serve guests. The dining room was full—a clamor of happy faces and excited conversation. The main topic of the morning was how the dragons had sailed right over their heads the night before and not bothered attacking. It was a very good sign indeed.

178

"First the harpies," one lady said brightly to her friend at the next table, "and now the dragons. I'm telling you, things are on the up. And it's thanks to those kids over there."

The children were inundated with grateful smiles and pats on the back that morning. They felt like heroes, and spent the entire breakfast beaming. Even Fenton was happy, and for the first time in ages seemed content—and normal! No dribbling on his shirt, no unusual fangs . . . It seemed that Fenton was in full control of his transformations now.

Abigail allowed Emily to look into her little glass ball, using the magnifying glass. Entire life histories were viewed in a matter of minutes, and with interesting results. Emily realized that there were in fact three forms of naga.

"There are those who live in the forest," she explained, her eyes shining. "They're the most human-like, and live in small villages. Then there are the ones who live underwater. That was the kind I first changed into, back on the island. They don't need arms because they're more like serpents and don't really have a civilized culture. They're more free and . . . well, primitive, I guess." She frowned. "But there's also a third kind, a very rare species that lives in the mountains. They like the cold. They're the least human-like, and not particularly nice." Emily shuddered. "But how do I *know* all this?"

"I was wondering that too," Hal said. "How do you even know how to talk the language of snakes? Is it instinctive? Human language isn't; we grew up learning it. So how is it I can understand dragon grunts and growls without learning that?"

Abigail passed the glass ball and magnifying glass to Dewey. "The ball only shows us what we already know, or what we've already got locked away in our heads but are having trouble getting at. So what we know—languages, customs, skills, and so on—must have been added when we were . . . you know, *created*."

Robbie snapped his fingers. "We were cloned! I bet that's it. The scientists took some cells or whatever from a dragon, and an ogre, and a centaur, and somehow their memories were stored in those cells."

Abigail pursed her lips. "Cloning doesn't work that way. You've read too many science fiction novels."

"Well," Darcy argued, "I read one time that a man lost his arm, so the doctors gave him a new one that they took off a recently dead person, and then this man started killing people with his new arm because he couldn't control it, because the arm had memories of its own, and it turned out that the previous owner was a serial killer who was always—"

"Was that a novel too?" Abigail asked, smiling sweetly.

Darcy sat back. "Might have been," she mumbled.

Dewey looked up from the glass ball, wide-eyed. "Hey."

Everyone fell silent as the small boy struggled to form his thoughts.

"Now I know why the centaurs want the mining to stop." Dewey carefully put the magnifying glass on the table, but held the glass ball between finger and thumb. "Geo-rocks are the cause of the holes between our worlds. If left alone, they implode harmlessly. They condense and shrink and finally vanish in a little bright speck of light, as Charlie said. But if they're interfered with, and are broken open . . . well, then they explode and tear holes between the two worlds." He put the glass ball down, sat back, and stared around with big round eyes. "Sometimes it's a clean hole, punching right through in an instant. So if a hole is five feet underwater in one world, then it's five feet underwater in the other."

"Like the one we first came through, near the lighthouse," Hal said.

"But they're not always clean," Dewey said.

"And what does *that* mean?" Robbie demanded.

Dewey shrugged. "It means the holes don't line up exactly."

"Like the hole in the laboratory," Hal said. "It's four floors up in this world, but at least a hundred feet above the lake in the other."

"Yeah, but don't forget to take into account the ground itself, which is always going to be higher than the water," Robbie argued.

"Not necessarily," Hal said. "That would be true if we were talking about *sea* level, but we're not—we're talking about a lake."

"And what about the hole in that puddle back at the goblin settlement?" Darcy said. "Miss Simone told us it leads through to a hole a hundred feet *below* the water, under the cliff on the island, where Thomas fell."

There was a long silence. Lauren rolled her eyes, folded her arms, and sat back. "My head hurts. Wake me up when you're finished."

A gleam appeared in Dewey's eyes. He looked around the table and lowered his voice, even though the rest of the room was empty. "When a geo-rock is cracked open, there's an explosion of energy. It's very dangerous. But that explosion is just a small, insignificant part of what really happens. The part you *don't* see is a hole being ripped between the worlds, often miles from where the rock was cracked open in the first place. There's often a slight delay between the moment the geo-rock is cracked open and when the hole forms. Earth moves through space at eighteen miles per second, so it *moves on* while all that energy is temporarily outside our plane of existence. You see?"

Everyone stared at Dewey in silence. He was sounding disturbingly like Miss Simone at the moment.

"Thousands of years ago," Dewey went on, "humans used to have rock-cracking ceremonies. They believed that the energy trapped in the rocks needed to be released. So whenever they found a glowing rock, they would set it down, perform some ancient ritual, and a man would sacrifice himself by bashing the rock open on a boulder. The explosion was big—instant death for the man but a small price to pay for the greater good."

"That's madness!" Emily exclaimed.

Dewey shrugged. "No worse than the Aztecs sacrificing humans to the sun gods in *your* old world."

"What do you mean, *my* old world?" Emily demanded.

But Dewey ignored her. "We centaurs realized what was happening. As more rituals took place, more holes opened up between the worlds. Holes last for decades, a hundred years, sometimes even longer before closing, so you can imagine that our twin worlds were riddled with the things. Even when human sacrifices stopped, the rock-bashing rituals went on—until a few hundred years ago when humans finally became *civilized*." Dewey looked intensely scornful at this point, and he glared around the table. "Eventually the rocks were forgotten, and the holes began to heal. Now there are just a handful of holes left."

"Only now we've started mining for the rocks," Hal said quietly, "and sticking rods in them."

Dewey scowled. Short fangs appeared as his lips peeled back. "And no doubt more holes will be created as time goes on. New ones have already appeared through clumsy handling of the geo-rocks. Insert those rods too far, and . . ."

"We just crack open a rock and *wham!*, there's a new hole through to our old world?" Fenton asked incredulously. "I've gotta try that!"

Dewey grew red in the face. His brow was more pronounced than usual, and hair was sprouting from his chest, just visible below his collar. "No," he growled in a tone quite unlike his normal self, "you must *not*. This is exactly why humans must never find out about this, and why the mining should stop."

Startled, everyone sat in silence. Fenton and Robbie, seated on either side of Dewey, quietly shifted their chairs away from him.

Abigail, who had not said a word throughout Dewey's speech, now said sternly, "Dewey, remember who you are. You're one of us, remember? You seem to be slipping a little."

Dewey stared at her, his top lip curled into a sneer. Then a puzzled expression came over his face and he stared in wonder at the thick hair on the backs of his hands. "Oh."

"Are you back with us?" Abigail asked.

Dewey looked sheepish. In an instant the thick hair was gone, his ears returned to their normal round shape, his fangs vanished, and the wicked gleam left his eyes. "I . . . I don't know how that happened."

"Looks like you saw a little more of your centaur self than normal," Hal said. "Funny how you know all that stuff about holes, though. Maybe Robbie's right, and memories come with the cloned cells."

"I want to find out more about that sometime," Abigail said. "But right now I think we should get going. We have a long journey ahead."

They helped Mirabelle clear away the breakfast things and found Charlie busy in the kitchen, frying eggs, red-faced but happy. "We're off," Emily said.

Charlie raised a finger as if to say, "Hold on a second," and deftly slipped the eggs onto a plate along with bacon, a large dollop of hash browns, and a tomato. When Mirabelle took the plate from him and hurried into the dining room, Charlie wiped his hands and came over to say goodbye.

"You've done us proud," he boomed. "Go home and relax. We'll keep our fingers crossed that the harpies will change their ways and the dragons will stick to wildebeest." He winked at Dewey. "And you'll go home and tell the centaurs how important the geo-rocks are to us, right? They give us efficient, portable power, and that's all. We're not interested in all that superstitious mumbo-jumbo the centaurs spout. Make sure you tell 'em, son."

Hal thought he saw a wicked gleam returning to Dewey's eyes, so he hurriedly said, "I'm sure he'll do the right thing. We'd better get going. Thanks for letting us stay here."

"Come back any time," Charlie said. "Give my love to Simone." He then whispered to Hal, "And don't forget to tell her you-know-what."

Chapter Twenty-One
The return home

The journey home was uneventful. Blacknail took a slightly different route this time, through the same forest as before only farther to the east, right past a small village of elves. As the buggy rumbled by, many of the petite, blue-skinned pointy-eared people stood defiantly outside the perimeter gate wielding spears and swords. More perched in the trees with bows and arrows at the ready. The reception was stern and unwelcoming, but they made no move to attack.

"Nice," Hal said as they left the village behind.

Whether Blacknail heard him or not, the goblin shouted over his shoulder, "They're all right as long as we leave 'em alone."

But what Blacknail really wanted to show them lay south of the forest. A never-ending plain of lush grass stretched before them, with occasional hilly islands full of trees and bushes, and a pond or two. It was here that Hal and his friends experienced the thrill of seeing real, live unicorns in the far distance, just a small herd of ten or eleven, each gleaming white. It was impossible to tell from so far away, but Blacknail told them that unicorns were larger than horses, and almost twice as fast. Their distinctive, perfectly straight horns were shorter than Hal had expected, and a sort of pale yellow color. The goblin explained how nobody ever got close enough to unicorns to study them properly. They had extraordinary senses and could smell or hear a man from miles away.

Still, it was nice to see the unicorns even if they did nothing but graze.

Robbie and Lauren each used the glass ball for a few minutes, but neither said much afterward. Either there was nothing to say, or they were embarrassed by what they had found out. Hal suspected that Lauren was ashamed.

Then Darcy tried it. After she handed the ball back to Abigail, she turned into a wood nymph and sat there, barely perceptible, causing everyone to blink rapidly as they tried to focus on her. Then she reappeared—and everyone gasped.

Her eyes were huge, her face long and thin, and her normally blond hair was now short and hard like tree bark. Her skin was also the color and texture of wood. Though her shoulders were wide and knobbed, her body was oddly thin at the waist, with legs and arms that seemed abnormally long. Her dress remained intact but had pinched up around the waist and widened at the shoulders. It was the color of silver bark.

"*This* is what dryads look like," Darcy said.

Emily, wide-eyed, tentatively reached across her seat and touched Darcy's face. "Ooh, your skin is rough."

"This is my natural dryad form," Darcy said, looking pleased with herself. "I can blend in too. That's how you normally see me—or not! I just hadn't realized that I could be, you know, *solid* too. I've never seen a dryad before, but the glass ball showed me a few things about myself."

"Are you always like that when you change?" Hal asked. "I mean, with the big eyes and . . ." He began to feel flustered. "Not that you're—I mean—well, I just assumed you were an ordinary *human*. Invisible, but human."

"I usually am," Darcy admitted. "This is the first time I've tried this form."

"But Miss Simone didn't say anything about your transformation not being complete," Hal said, confused.

"Darcy's always invisible," Abigail said. "How would Miss Simone know a full transformation from a partial one?"

"Did you ever get to shrink, Abi?" Emily asked. "That was something Miss Simone was concerned about, wasn't it?"

Abigail smiled. "I guess I forgot to show you." She stood, then immediately shrank down to the size of a small bird, her wings sprouting as she did so. She zipped around the buggy and made everyone duck and weave to avoid her high-pitched buzzing. Then she returned to her seat next to Hal.

It was funny how things had changed, Hal thought as they all settled back to continue the journey home. He looked across the aisle at Robbie, seated with Dewey. Just a couple of weeks ago he and Robbie had been best friends, and Abigail nothing but a pest. Now he felt as though Abigail was his closest friend. Did Robbie mind? Maybe he was a little fed up with the situation . . . but then again, he had his eye on Lauren most of the time, his so-called *girlfriend*, although she probably knew nothing about that.

"Penny for your thoughts?" Abigail said, nudging him.

Hal blinked. "Sorry. Miles away."

"You can go sit with Robbie if you want," she said with a sigh. "I'm sure you boys have a lot to talk about without us boring girls around." She laughed. "Don't look so shocked. I saw you looking at me, then across at Robbie. Would you rather I sat somewhere else?"

She leaned forward as if to get up and move, looking at him quizzically.

Hal shook his head. "No, Robbie's busy talking to Dewey."

"So you'd *rather* sit with Robbie, but I'll do since he's busy?"

"Uh—no, I meant—" Hal frowned. "Are you messing with me?"

Abigail laughed again, and sat back. "Hal Franklin, you can't get rid of me that easily. I'll just keep on being a pest and teasing you until you admit that you actually like me quite a lot."

Hal stared into space, wondering exactly what she meant by that. Of *course* he liked her. They were friends. They'd grown up together! Or did she mean something a little more than that?

"I *do* like you," he said with a shrug. "We're *all* friends, right?"

Abigail shook her head slightly, a faint smile on her lips. "Did you know that Darcy once had a crush on you?"

Hal snorted. "Yeah, like six years ago! We were just kids."

"Kids have feelings. She was upset when you told her you liked me better."

"I never said that!"

There was a long pause. Then Abigail spoke slowly, with a look of intense concentration. "So you *don't* like me better?"

Hal sighed heavily. Why were girls so difficult? "Look, you're great, you're wonderful," he said in a flat monotone. "You're amazing, you're funny, you're pretty, you're brave and strong, you're smart, you're . . ." He thought for a moment, then gave up. He'd run out of compliments.

Abigail grinned. "You think I'm pretty?"

"I—did I say that?"

"You did." Now she had a defiant look that dared him to deny it.

"Well, okay, then. I guess you must be."

A little embarrassed, Hal looked away in case his face turned red. She'd rib him to death if she thought she'd got him all flustered.

"So," Abigail said slowly, "what is it about me that's pretty? My cute nose? My big brown eyes? My adorable little chin?"

"Well, I *really* like your mouth," Hal said seriously. "At least, when it's not flapping up and down." He leaned back in his seat, closed his eyes, and began to snore loudly. "Wake me up when we get there."

He heard Abigail stifle a laugh before she replied. "Fine, be like that." Then all was quiet, and the sun was warm, and after a while Hal fell asleep for real.

* * *

The village of Carter finally came into sight in the moonlight. Someone poked Hal in the ribs and he woke with a start.

"Are we there yet?" he murmured. "How long have I been asleep?"

"Hours," Abigail said. "We've all eaten. Blacknail wanted to keep moving so we ate on the move. I didn't want to wake you so I gently stuffed a sandwich in your mouth and washed it down with water while you snored."

"I don't snore," he muttered.

Even though they'd only spent one night in Carter, the small village already felt like home because that was where his parents were waiting.

And waiting they were. As the buggy rumbled at a moderate pace down a dirt track on the side of a hill, the passengers saw crowds beginning to gather, and numerous lamps bobbing in the darkness. Hal strained his eyes and finally spotted his mom and dad along with his friends' parents. Miss Simone was with them too. By the time the buggy eased to a stop close to the perimeter fence, people were spilling out of the gateway and surrounding them.

The engine died and the children tumbled down the ladder, rushing to meet their folks. Hal's dad squeezed him so tightly that he could hardly breathe, and his mom's tears soaked his shoulder. Hal lost track of the amount of times she told him she'd been worried sick, but it was only when he got a good look at her face that he realized how drawn she looked, somehow older. Was there more gray in her hair, or was he imagining it?

"We're proud of you, son," his dad said several times, his bushy beard tickling Hal's face every time he snatched another hug.

Meanwhile the people of the village were smiling and congratulating them, and Hal became aware of complete strangers patting him on the back. Looking around, he spotted Robbie and Dewey surfacing from the crowd before they were swallowed up again. There, briefly, was Abigail—and then she was gone.

Eventually, villagers drifted away. When it became possible to move around unimpeded by jostling bodies, Miss Simone appeared again. "Okay, children, listen up. Go home, get some sleep, and meet in the village hall in the morning at ten. I'm eager to hear all the details, but I guess I can wait." She smiled, looking happier than Hal had ever seen her, and turned to go.

"Oh," Hal said, remembering something. "Miss Simone, wait." He turned to his parents and lowered his voice. "I'll be along in a minute. I just need to tell Miss Simone something important. Something private."

He left his bemused parents, tried to ignore Abigail's questioning look, and took Miss Simone aside.

"Hal?" the woman said, once they were out of earshot.

"Um . . . it's about your brother."

Miss Simone closed her eyes for a moment. "I should have told you about him, but—well, you were worried enough without learning what happened to the *last* shapeshifter dragon." She looked away. "He went missing months ago. When the dragons started attacking the village, it was his duty to go to them, to somehow reason with them. I guessed he failed. He never came back."

"Well, that's just it," Hal said. "He's alive and well."

Miss Simone said nothing for a long moment. Then: "What?"

Hal took a deep breath and explained his meeting with the dragons, focusing on Felipe's presence and how the dragon had watched out for Hal as best he could. "He couldn't do much," Hal said, "because that might have given him away or made him seem disloyal. He had a much bigger mission than saving my skin. But he helped some."

Miss Simone nodded, her bright blue eyes wide, as Hal briefly mentioned the heated conversation between Felipe, Lumphead and the ancient chief dragon, and how Felipe had tried to talk them out of an attack on the village. Hal left it there, saying only that Lumphead was now dead and Felipe was second-in-command . . . a position powerful enough to steer the pack away from a human diet.

"He did it," Miss Simone murmured. Her trembling hands had risen to cover her mouth. "He really did it."

"He might never be able to come home though," Hal warned.

"Never say never," Miss Simone whispered, tears welling up. "My brother is alive. He succeeded in his mission. Not only that, but . . . A human in charge of an entire fleet of dragons . . . Do you realize how important that is?"

"He's a hero," Hal said, agreeing. "He's given his life to this. All I did was tip the scales in his favor. But do you want people to know the whole truth? If people find out, they *might* think he's a hero too . . . but some people won't understand. They'll just say, 'What took so long? People died while he did *nothing*.'"

"I'll *make* them understand," Miss Simone said fiercely.

"Well," Hal said, "before you say anything, just think about it for a while."

Miss Simone reached out and touched his face lightly. "You're a very brave and mature young man. You're *all* brave and mature. I couldn't be more proud."

Hal grinned. "We have some more news, but that can wait until tomorrow. Maybe you can ask Orson to come along."

"Orson? Why?"

But Hal shook his head. It was only right that Abigail be the one to reveal the news about the glass ball. He turned to go. "See you tomorrow, Miss Simone."

"All right. And . . . Hal?"

He turned back, and she smiled.

"Thank you. For the news about Felipe. It's funny; he's my twin, and yet we never had that . . . that *connection* twins are supposed to have. You know? I feel like I should have known he was still alive, but I had no idea. All these months I've believed him to be dead."

She turned to stare at the moon, lost in thought.

Hal snuck away.

* * *

They all met at the village hall the next morning. Once again Gristletooth the goblin was there, slouched in his seat, saying nothing, a deep grimace on his face as Hal walked in. Goblins were a moody lot, he decided.

Hal wasn't the first to arrive, but by no means the last either. He avoided the goblin in the third row and sat up front in the first row with Robbie, Darcy and Lauren. They waited.

Miss Simone came in with Orson. Today the bearded teacher wore a baggy shirt and loose-fitting pants. They were smart clothes, but he managed to make them look old and scruffy. With his straggly beard and long hair, he looked like an old hermit—and yet he and Miss Simone were the same age. He slouched as he walked, eyes lowered, hands in pockets.

In contrast, Miss Simone walked with her head held high and her shoulders squared, golden hair and silky green cloak flowing behind. The hall was not well lit, but in the gloom her eyes shone bright and blue.

Dewey and Fenton entered together, and then Emily and Abigail. All eight children sat in the front row. Even though Abigail was the last to take a seat, for some reason a space had been left for her next to Hal. This amazed him; *he* hadn't saved her a seat, and hadn't noticed anyone else doing so—it just seemed to happen on its own, as though there was an unspoken rule that a seat should be left next to Hal for Abigail, his *girlfriend*. The very idea! He felt mildly embarrassed when Abigail smiled and sat down. He felt like saying, "Look, it wasn't *me* that saved this seat," just to let her know that he wasn't going soft.

Miss Simone and Orson dragged spare chairs out of the first row and turned them to face the children. "Now," Miss Simone said, crossing her legs and draping her cloak on the back of the chair. She smiled. "Tell me everything that happened. Every detail. We have all day, so don't leave anything out."

And so, tentatively at first, Emily began the story, starting from when they left Carter in Blacknail's buggy. For a while they had enjoyed the ride, but then they had grown restless and a few of them had run or flown while Blacknail continued on. When Emily mentioned how Fenton had nearly fallen from the vehicle and instantly grown a tail to hold on, Miss Simone pressed Fenton on the matter. "You were stuck like that for the rest of the day?" she asked, shaking her head. "That's not exactly practical."

Then Abigail told of her visit to the fae folk at the edge of the forest. She held up the little glass ball and explained that, at the time, she hadn't known what it was for. Miss Simone and Orson glanced at the ball but made no comment. They didn't appear overly interested. *But they will be*, Hal thought.

Robbie mentioned his less-than-proud moment with the ogres. "They were eating *insect eggs*!" Emily exclaimed, unable to contain her revulsion. Annoyed, Robbie told her that insect eggs were full of protein and something of a treat in the big wide-open landscape.

Miss Simone broke into a smile when they arrived in Louis and met Charlie Duggan. "He's a character, isn't he?" she said. Orson shook his head gently, a smile on his lips. Hal decided that one day he'd have to hear all about this older generation of shapeshifters. Miss Simone, Orson and Charlie—and Felipe for that matter—had grown up together. A mermaid, an almost-flying horse, a griffin, and a dragon. Who else was in their group? Hal remembered something about a gorgon, and felt a sudden, intense fascination. He vowed to meet the others in the group someday to find out who—and *what*—they were.

Robbie started to talk about the harpy attack, but Darcy gently interrupted and gave a less embellished version. Miss Simone nodded soberly, then froze when she heard that a baby had been taken. "But Lauren came up with a plan," Emily said proudly. She nudged Lauren. "Go ahead."

Lauren launched into her tale. She had been quiet up until now, but spoke clearly and in detail about her thoughts during the attack and afterward. She took out a small, withered shoot from her pocket and held it up. "It's like harpy catnip or something," she said. "I've only had a tiny nibble myself, but immediately I felt a reaction—like a slight dizziness, and then a feeling of being relaxed. It didn't last long, but harpies walk around with these things, chewing on them and giggling like idiots."

"Narcotics," Miss Simone said, fascinated. "But they don't affect us?"

"Not that I'm aware," Lauren said.

"Still, worth looking into," Miss Simone said, taking the shoot from Lauren's outstretched hand. "Thank you. We use various types of plants for painkillers and all sorts of other medical reasons. I've never seen this kind before, though."

When Lauren explained how she and her friends had marched up the hill and tricked the harpies into believing they'd actually *burned the baby*, Orson burst into laughter, but Miss Simone looked shocked. She said nothing, though, and Lauren continued to the end, when they had burned a quarter of the harpy catnip as a way to demonstrate their power. "Or harpynip," she added.

Miss Simone stared long and hard at her, then sighed. "It's impossible to predict what other species will believe. Humans would never have bought that trickery. Burning the baby indeed! But most humans never would have considered stealing babies in the first place. Harpies are bad to the core so I guess it didn't surprise or shock them so much when you pulled your ruse."

When Miss Simone asked whether Lauren was able to conjure windstorms as the other harpies had, Lauren looked surprised. "I don't know," she said, staring at the small green shoot. Then she nodded. "Yes, I can."

"Well, show me later," Miss Simone said, looking doubtful.

They moved on to the matter of the dragons. For this Miss Simone leaned forward and stared at Hal intensely as he revealed how he had met with the dragons down in the chasm—and nearly got himself roasted by one of them. Hal told how he had changed over and over in succession to rid himself of the pain and heal his blistering skin, and how he had returned fire and sent that dragon scuttling. Orson laughed loudly again.

"One of those dragons was the old leader's son," Hal said. "And another was the third-in-command, who actually turned out to be—" He stopped, remembering that his friends knew nothing of this. He raised his eyebrows at Miss Simone.

She nodded, and Hal continued, talking more to his friends now than Miss Simone, since this was all new to them. He explained how one of the dragons was Felipe, the dragon shapeshifter from Miss Simone's generation. He didn't mention that Felipe was Miss Simone's brother, feeling that to be a little personal . . . but Miss Simone filled in that detail anyway, looking extremely proud.

Hal and Darcy's attempt to rescue Abigail didn't go quite as planned, but Miss Simone seemed thrilled at the way they had all worked together, using all their individual skills. "You flew right into the dragons' nest and delivered Darcy into a tunnel?" she exclaimed to Lauren. She looked at Darcy. "And you walked into the labyrinth?" She shook her head and glanced at Orson. "These kids . . ."

She said Emily's use of the snake to find a way in from above was 'inspired,' and Fenton's idea to hang backward down a vent and dangle his tail . . . "How on earth did you come up with this stuff?"

But the plan went wrong, as Hal went on to explain. Abigail was supposed to get out that way first, because Darcy could easily have walked out without being seen. But Abigail ushered Darcy up the vent instead.

"I was trying to be brave and selfless," Abigail said with a sigh. "Instead I nearly got Hal killed."

Hal turned to Darcy. "Tell your story next. What happened to you?"

"Well," Darcy said, "I climbed out in a blast of heat as that dragon tried to fry me. Once outside, we were all panicking and wondering what to do. Fenton started to climb back down. We all told him not to, but he went anyway. He hung down that hole, waiting for Abigail to climb up."

"You *did*?" Abigail said, leaning forward to peer along the row at Fenton. "You might have been roasted, hanging in that vent like that. It's a good job for you that the dragon was occupied with Hal."

"I heard a lot of noise," Fenton said. "But I was facing upward and couldn't see anything. After a while you all disappeared off somewhere. I waited, but . . . you never came back."

There was a silence. Then Abigail sighed. "Fenton—thank you."

Fenton scowled. "Don't get all mushy."

"She's been getting mushy a lot lately," Hal agreed.

Robbie grinned. "We think Hal and Abigail are—"

"*Any*way," Hal said loudly, his face heating up, "what happened next, Darcy? How long did you stick around?"

"Oh, not too long. Not there, anyway. There were dragons everywhere after that. They seemed pretty excited about something. We decided to head back to the buggy and wait as long as we could for you. We knew that we had to get back to the village and warn them of an attack."

"Good for you," Hal said. "We hoped you would."

Hal then began to explain what had happened under the tunnels. He wanted to skip the seriousness of his injuries, but Abigail wouldn't have it. She told them all how the back of his neck was torn open and his shoulders and back were blistered, not to mention his broken right arm.

"All okay now, though," Hal said, shrugging.

"You see?" Abigail said crossly. "He plays it down like we're talking about a couple of bruises. Anyone else might have died with injuries like that."

"This is why Charlie and I were a little less concerned for your safety than we might otherwise have been," Miss Simone said. "I know it sounds like we just sent you off into extreme danger—and we *did*—but most other people can't regenerate and heal the way you can. With those injuries you described . . . anyone else would have been in serious pain for weeks or months afterward. But we shapeshifters can heal. The power to heal wears off as you get older, though. Being young, you're able to heal much more efficiently than us adults." She leaned forward and wagged her finger at them as if they were in school. "But don't get it into your heads that you're indestructible. You can die just like everyone else. You can heal, but only if you're alive to do so. And if you're unconscious from a serious wound, you could conceivably bleed to death."

"Charming," Abigail whispered.

"It's just that there are pros and cons to our jobs. When we're young we never get sick and we heal quickly. As we grow older we don't heal as well, and one day we'll catch our first cold. And when we're over forty . . ." She shrugged. "One day we won't be able to transform at all."

After these sobering comments, Hal continued with the story. Everyone gasped when he and Abigail jumped the abyss of lava and then ended up trapped in a pit of boiling water. But Miss Simone was most interested in the hole leading through to the other world, where they came across a group of scientists or soldiers—or both. Hal's friends cheered when the tank blew the evil dragon into a million pieces.

"Oh dear," Miss Simone said quietly. "The military blew up a dragon. That's not good."

"Not good?" Robbie demanded. "In what way is that not good?"

Miss Simone glared at him. "If the military saw a real live dragon, they will undoubtedly track where it came from. They'll find that cottage, they'll go down into the basement, and they'll find the hole. Then they'll go through the hole and find the boiling water in a pit, and will eventually realize they're *in a different world*." She got to her feet and began to pace slowly. "It's a matter of time before they figure out there's a whole world here that they never knew about, a world with breathable air."

Hal's mouth dropped open. "You mean . . . you mean they'll start bringing people through? To live here?"

"But that's a *good* thing, isn't it?" Emily said, frowning.

"Is it?" Miss Simone said sharply. She looked around at them all, one by one. "You'll have to give that one some serious thought, children. Because trust me, it's been on my mind for the last thirteen years, ever since the virus struck."

Orson cleared his throat. "Let's stay on topic. Hal, what happened next? How did you find your way back to Louis so quickly, on foot?"

Hal returned to the story and told how he and Abigail headed west to find the hole over the lake—the one that came through to the fourth floor of the science building. But it was here that he had to stop. "We sat down for a rest, and that's when we took another look at Abigail's little glass ball. Only we used the magnifying glass." He looked at Abigail and gave a nod.

Instead of trying to explain it, she handed the glass ball and magnifying glass to Orson. "Look at the ball through that. Just . . . stare into it."

Puzzled, Orson did as he was told. His perplexed frown remained for a second or two more. Then his face cleared. His eyes widened and his mouth dropped open. He looked closer . . .

Chapter Twenty-Two
Revelations

Orson looked up from the glass ball, his face a mask of pure astonishment. He started to say something, then stopped. He looked at Miss Simone and held up the glass ball between forefinger and thumb. Again he tried to say something, but gave up. Shaking, he handed the ball carefully back to Abigail, closed her hand around it, and squeezed gently. Then he hurried outside.

"*What* is going on?" Miss Simone demanded, getting up. She grabbed her cloak, threw it around her shoulders, and rushed from the hall.

The excited children, and a bemused Gristletooth, followed.

Outside, they found Miss Simone pleading Orson to tell her what was wrong. Orson stood in the small courtyard, in the middle of the lawn, with his hands out as if to tell Miss Simone to stand back. "I can't explain it," Orson said, his eyes shining. "Ever since we moved here I've been unable to fly. I've tried all sorts, even jumping off the cliff—remember?"

"I remember," Miss Simone said dryly. "A classic example of how useful it is for us shapeshifters to be able to heal. Your legs were—"

"Never mind that," Orson said impatiently. He noticed the children standing to the side of the lawn, and grinned. "Ask the kids. *They* understand. I have to go."

"Go where?" Miss Simone said weakly.

Orson changed. Like Dewey, his transformation was fast and explosive, and he reared up on hind legs. His black feathered wings spread wide, and he cantered to the far edge of the courtyard. Then he turned and galloped across the lawn, straight toward the backs of cottages on the far side. It wasn't a long journey for a speeding horse—no more than a few seconds—but he accelerated fast and launched himself into the air.

Miss Simone cried out, fully expecting him to crash straight into the cottage wall and break his neck.

But Orson somehow turned in mid-air, wings tilting, and he ended up *running sideways* along the cottage wall with bits of stone and mortar chipping off under his flashing hoofs. And just when it seemed he would fall onto his side and crush his left wing, he leveled out and soared upward. His breath came in short, steaming pants. He whinnied and grunted, and his lips peeled back to reveal a comical horse's grin as he flew dangerously low over the heads of the crowd on the lawn. Hal ducked to avoid a flailing hoof.

193

Then Orson was off into the sky, legs kicking as though he were galloping through the air, wings beating steadily.

Miss Simone stared in astonishment, her mouth hanging open, as her once-flightless friend disappeared over the rooftops. Then she spun to face the children and stood speechless a while longer.

Abigail smiled sweetly. "My little magical faerie ball reveals things about yourself that you never knew. When they gave it to me, I assumed they meant it for my eyes only. But—" She waved at Hal. "—when Hal looked into it, he suddenly realized he knew how to fly."

"I had the technique all wrong," Hal agreed. "Plus, it takes a while to build up strength in the wing muscles. I flew back to Louis, but only because I climbed a tower and jumped off. Gliding is easier, and once you're up, it's easy to stay up. It's launching straight up from the ground that's hard."

"You can fly," Miss Simone repeated.

"And I can shrink," Abigail said.

"And I can grow arms or *not* grow arms," Emily added.

"And I can change at will now," Fenton chimed in.

"And I know how to turn into a proper wood nymph," Darcy finished.

A huge smile spread across Miss Simone's face, and tears welled in her eyes. This was the second time Hal had seen her cry in the space of twelve hours!

"I have nothing left to teach you," she said, and gave a long, exaggerated bow complete with sweeping arms. "You've been here just a few days and have already proved yourselves more than capable. Not only that, but you've brought a wonderful gift. Abigail, that little glass ball—may I borrow it?"

"Of course," Abigail said, handing it to her. "You'll need this magnifying glass too."

* * *

That afternoon, Miss Simone went to see Thomas. She had an idea that the little glass ball might help with his *taming*, as she called it. The children tagged along.

Thomas Patten was locked away in a cage within a secluded barn that stood just outside the village. He stalked his cage exactly as a lion would—which was hardly surprising since he was a manticore: mostly lion but part human, with a scorpion tail. His blood-red fur was clean and shiny after a much-needed but very-much-unwanted hose-down and vigorous scrubbing with long-handled brooms. His long, segmented tail arched freely over his back like a cobra, but the ball of poison-tipped quills on the end, including the deadly stinger, had been covered with a thick bag. Thomas still had his claws free, so great care was taken when venturing near the cage.

194

Thomas's human-like red-furred face was as eerie as the first day Hal had laid eyes on it in the middle of Black Woods, back on the island. The bright blue eyes were particularly strange and out of place in such a creature.

The manticore had three permanent helpers. One was a very fat man with thick black curly hair, who was calm and patient in nature, and very good at working through psychological problems. His name was Eric and he sat in a stout but protesting rocking chair that creaked every time he moved. He talked quietly, and Thomas answered occasionally in a very bored voice.

A woman by the name of Winifred fed Thomas several times a day—normal meals meant for humans, not scraps of meat normally thrown to the dogs. Since Thomas wouldn't, or couldn't, transform into his human self, knives and forks were out of the question, so he snaffled it right off the plate, getting gravy all over his red fur. Still, eating a cooked meal of venison, potatoes and carrots instead of a slab of raw animal was a step in the right direction.

The third helper was Winifred's daughter, Rebecca, and she helped prepare food as well as clean out the cage after Thomas had answered the call of nature. He refused to go in a bucket, though, which was rather unpleasant.

The manticore's eyes widened when Miss Simone and the children walked in. He got up and pressed his face to the cage bars.

The girl smiled. "Hi. Be careful—don't get too close to the bars. We can't trust Thomas yet."

Eric chuckled softly. "I know there's a good little boy in there somewhere. I just need to draw him out of this monster."

Miss Simone stepped forward and held out the glass ball and magnifying glass for Thomas to see. "I thought you'd be interested in this, young Thomas," she said pleasantly. "Would you like to see?"

The manticore glared suspiciously at the objects, but didn't look *into* them. His blue eyes flicked back and forth from one person to another.

Winifred pulled her daughter back from the cage a little. "Careful, Rebecca."

"He can't reach me, Ma," the girl said.

"Thomas," Miss Simone said, moving closer. "Take a look at this."

"Why should I?" the manticore snapped. Most of the time his voice was unusually high-pitched and fluty, but sometimes it was accompanied by a deep, rumbling growl as if there were two creatures in one body. "Take it away and let me out of here." He appealed to the watching children. "Please—you've got to release me. I belong in a forest. I'm not human."

"You're one of us," Hal said.

Abigail stepped forward and held out her hand for the glass ball. "Let me have that back, please, Miss Simone. Thomas is being rude and ungrateful and doesn't deserve this gift. I don't want him to see it—please let me have it back."

Miss Simone glared at her and was about to say something when Hal interrupted. "She's right. Why should he get to enjoy it like the rest of us? He hasn't earned the right. Don't let him see it—quick, take it away!"

But Thomas was suddenly interested in this strange, precious gift. He stared into the glass ball, straining to see. Miss Simone, finally catching on to the ploy, stepped a little closer.

"Reverse psychology," Eric murmured, a smile on his lips.

"Careful," Winifred whispered urgently. "Lady Simone, you're too close."

She was—but Thomas had gone into a trance. A moment later he snapped out of it and blinked. Then he frowned.

Everyone was silent, watching him.

Thomas turned and looked around his cage. He seemed deep in thought. Then he turned back and cocked his head. "I remember everything so clearly now," he whispered. "I remember the island, the classroom, Mrs. Hunter, and all of *you*. I remember chasing a groundhog and changing into . . . into *this*." He looked down at himself. Then he looked up again and grinned. His mouth was filled with razor-sharp teeth, like three rows of needles. "I remember everything!"

He turned away, hunkered down, and concentrated. Then he changed. His great bushy red mane and red fur was sucked into his skin, leaving bare human flesh. The enormous scorpion tail thrashed and shrank, leaving the safety bag behind, while his body and limbs reshaped in a rippling, pulsing liquid manner. Quickly, dramatically, Thomas became a puny, bony, redheaded, and completely naked boy curled tightly on his knees, hunched over as if sick to the stomach.

"Oh dear," Emily said loudly, and looked away.

"Get him a blanket," Winifred told her daughter.

Amazed, Hal studied Thomas's face. He appeared confused, or perhaps ill. Or maybe just embarrassed. When Rebecca returned, Miss Simone absently handed the glass ball and magnifying glass to Dewey, who happened to be the nearest. As he backed away, gingerly holding the precious objects, Miss Simone unlocked the cage door and stepped inside to cover the boy with the blanket.

Now that only his red hair was showing, everyone stepped closer.

"Thomas?" Miss Simone said, tapping him on the shoulder. "Are you okay?"

The boy slowly sat up, pulling the blanket tight around his shoulders. His bright blue eyes were piercing, and his face thin. Freckled all over, Thomas looked just as Hal remembered him—except six years older. He looked tired.

"Is this what you want to see?" he said quietly. "You really want *me* back?"

"Of course we do, Thomas," Miss Simone said. "Your parents have been desperate to see you."

The boy climbed unsteadily to his feet. "My parents," he muttered. "Where are they, then? Why aren't they here?"

"They're in the village," Miss Simone assured him. "They've seen *you*. But I advised them not to talk to you yet. It was when your mom screamed at the sight of you that you turned away in the first place. I didn't think a reunion at this stage was a good idea, in case you felt . . . resentful."

"Indeed not," Eric agreed. "A meeting while you're still filled with hate and frustration? No. But a meeting when you're calm and ready to communicate in a civilized way, certainly."

Thomas said nothing for a moment. Then: "I didn't remember you before," he said, turning to look at Miss Simone. "But now I do. The glass ball . . . it showed me who you are. What you did."

"What *I* did?"

Hal sensed something bad in the air. He took a few steps closer to the cage.

"Yes, what *you* did," Thomas said. He scowled. "Pulled me under the water. That was you, wasn't it? Pulled me deep down underwater to drown me. I was lucky to get away."

Miss Simone looked confused. "No, I *saved* you. That was the only way—"

Thomas moved fast. He transformed and pounced on her, the blanket falling away and his tail rearing up. There was a terrible roar and Miss Simone went down under the manticore's weight, claws digging into her shoulders. The tail came swinging down, deadly black stinger oozing venom.

But amid the screams and yells and roaring, Hal and his friends were acting. It all happened very quickly, with no more than a split second between each event. First, Fenton spat a jet of water through the bars and drenched Thomas's face. Then Hal blasted the cage with flames, setting the manticore's fur alight. Then the bars exploded and the entire cage disintegrated as Robbie's huge ogre arms smashed their way through. In less than two seconds, Hal, in dragon form, was on top of the manticore, grappling with it, while an ogre was grabbing for the stinger and shoving the rest of the cage aside. Fenton's black lizard was right there too, breathing hard on Thomas's wet face so that the liquid set and turned gummy. Thomas began struggling for breath and all the fight went out of him.

But Miss Simone had been stung. The stinger had come down and jabbed her on the cheek. Already a large black bruise was spreading, and the small open wound rose into a mound. It looked like a tiny volcano about to blow. Her eyelids fluttered. Her lips moved, but no sound came out.

In the commotion, somewhere between screams, Hal heard Eric yelling at someone to go get the goblins. But rather than wait for them to come to her, Robbie scooped Miss Simone into his enormous arms and stood, shrugging off bits of broken cage. Everyone stepped back as he bounded to the barn doors and shoved his way outside. The barn doors buckled and fell in a shower of dust, and a bolt zinged past Hal's ear.

Hal changed back into human form and joined the rest of them as they rushed to follow the ogre. In the corner of his eye he saw Fenton standing over the manticore and wondered if he should stay behind to keep watch. But Thomas wasn't moving much, and Fenton looked suitably big and mean.

Villagers hopped aside in fright as Robbie stamped onto the village streets. Ahead of him flew Abigail, shouting for help, calling for goblins, asking which way to go. Several people pointed, and one or two joined in the rush, hurrying ahead and leading the way. Meanwhile Miss Simone lolled in the ogre's arms.

"Change!" Hal yelled, running alongside the lumbering ogre. "Miss Simone, you have to change! Turn into a mermaid!"

But the woman was barely conscious. Darcy suddenly screamed something, and Hal looked to where she was pointing. A horse's water trough? What—

Then it dawned on him. He joined in, yelling at the muddled ogre to drop Miss Simone in the water trough. The ogre, not very sharp, was at least obedient. He tossed her in with a huge splash.

The moment dirty water sloshed over her face and in her mouth, Miss Simone's legs came together and turned into one big fishtail. As the water settled, she came up gasping. She was conscious, but the welt on her cheek seemed unchanged.

"Again!" Hal urged her. "Change! Turn human again."

Miss Simone blinked and tried to focus. Then she struggled to stand, saw the large fishtail where her feet should be, and changed instinctively. She staggered, climbed out, and stood for a moment. Water instantly began to dry on her skin. Then Emily rushed forward and gave her a shove.

Miss Simone toppled backward into the trough once more. Her fishtail appeared again. She choked, gurgled, and sat up. This time Hal saw the tiniest improvement in her wound. He guessed—*hoped*—that it was healing on the inside first; that nasty external wound was only superficial. Perhaps with enough changes she'd repair herself nicely.

"Stop that!" she spluttered.

As she transformed once more and climbed back out of the trough, she glared at Emily and held up a finger as if to warn her away.

"Change again!" Abigail shouted. "If you don't, we'll keep dunking you."

"Don't you dare," Miss Simone gasped. "I'm perfectly capable of—"

But she swayed and almost collapsed, and it was lucky Darcy and Lauren were right there to catch her. Instead of standing her upright, they laid her down nice and flat—in the water trough.

Miss Simone was really angry now, but at the same time struggling to remain alert and conscious. She was like a drunkard outside the inn in Louis. Still, she was more lively than she had been just a minute or two before.

Goblins came stamping up, heavy chain vests jingling. They wasted no time. They pulled Miss Simone out of the water trough and dumped her on the dusty street. Out of the water again, she transformed. Her fishtail folded and vanished, and legs formed once more. Her dress was sodden and twisted, but faithfully changed along with her form. Her cloak had gotten lost somewhere along the way.

As if by magic, water quickly ran off her skin and out of her hair, pooling in the dirt. Suddenly she was dry.

The welt on her face was closed now, but her entire left cheek was black and swollen. She had slipped into unconsciousness and her breathing was shallow. Still, the three goblins who leaned over her seemed unconcerned after a careful check of her vital signs. "She'll be all right," one said roughly. It looked like he was scowling, but Hal realized the goblin was actually grinning happily.

When he took stock, Hal was amazed at the amount of people crowding the streets. Everyone looked concerned for their Lady Simone as she was wrapped in blankets and lifted carefully onto a stretcher.

"Where are they taking her?" Emily asked a man.

"Doctor's house. Down this street, turn right. Big sign out front."

Emily nodded. "I'm going too."

Lauren and Darcy immediately followed. Trailing along behind were Winifred and Rebecca. Eric, who had just arrived, was completely out of breath and looked like he might be next to fall into the water trough. Robbie turned human and watched them go.

Abigail buzzed down from the air and landed neatly. "I don't think *that* was supposed to happen," she said. "Thomas definitely saw something in that glass ball—but it made him worse!"

"He has some serious issues," Robbie agreed.

Dewey nudged into view. He was in his centaur form. Hal hadn't even been aware of him in the confusion. "What's up?" he asked, seeing Dewey's wide eyes.

"I need to talk to you," he whispered. He looked at Robbie and Abigail. "All of you."

"Then let's talk," Hal said. He led the way through the remaining spectators, ignoring their curious stares, and found himself at the large pond in the center of the village. They found a bench and sat, while Dewey clip-clopped restlessly in a circle.

"If you're going to talk to us," Abigail said, "you're going to have to stand still. You look like you need the toilet."

There wasn't an ounce of humor on Dewey's face. Something was really bothering him.

"What is it?" Hal asked.

Robbie added, "Yeah, spit it out."

Dewey swallowed and surveyed the little park nervously. Then he leaned closer. "I was worried about the geo-rocks. You know I told you how they cause holes, and how the centaurs don't want the humans to find out. That's why they want to stop the mining. That's why they're opposed to all this modern technology. It's not because of the technology itself; it's because they want to stop the geo-rocks being accidentally cracked open, to prevent more holes appearing."

"We know this, Dewey," Abigail said softly. "What else is on your mind?"

Dewey surveyed the park again. "We were wondering how we know all this stuff. How do you, Hal, know how to fly when nobody taught you? Is it natural instinct, or something dragons learn?"

"A bit of both, maybe?" Hal ventured.

"Not for me," Dewey said. He tapped his head. "I *know* things. I know things I shouldn't know. Things I can't *possibly* know. My head is filled with a strange language—the language of centaurs. But if we had to learn English in school, how can I just *know* an entirely different language? When did I learn to speak in the language of centaurs?"

He held up the little faerie ball and magnifying glass. Hal blinked, surprised to see the objects. But then he remembered that Miss Simone had passed them to Dewey back at the barn.

"Ever since I looked into this thing," Dewey said, sounding distraught, "I've been having visions of . . . of numbers. Strange markings, symbols, that sort of thing. Little equations on endless piles of paper. Experiments. It's like a memory, but it's not *my* memory."

Hal was fascinated, but increasingly alarmed at Dewey's manner. The boy was on the verge of panic.

Dewey's hands trembled. "I saw something in Louis, when I looked into the glass ball. It was just a flash, like a photo, but it made me wonder. So when Miss Simone handed this to me back at the barn just now . . . while she was going into the cage with Thomas . . . I had another look in the glass ball."

Abigail leaned forward. "And?"

Dewey's voice turned into a hoarse whisper. "I saw how far the centaurs are willing to go to protect their land. They suffer human neighbors only because they have no choice. They pretend to get along because humans outnumber them. Things have been okay for a long time, but then the mining started twenty years ago and the centaurs got worried. Mining for rocks, sticking those rods in them to draw out the energy . . . there was bound to be some accidental rock-cracking going on, which meant—"

"Yes, yes, more holes, I get it," Robbie snapped. "So what?"

"The more holes there are, the greater the chance of humans finding a way through from the other world. And nobody wants that."

"But if humans knew that geo-rocks *caused* the holes," Abigail argued, "they'd stop mining for them . . . wouldn't they?"

"Is that what you think?" Dewey retorted. He shook his head. "You can't stop progress. No matter what, the rocks will continue to be mined and used, and accidents will happen, and new holes will appear . . . Think about how things were *before* the virus—millions of humans with advanced technology. Think what it would be like if those people *found this world*! When the mining started twenty years ago, the discovery of a hole became the single biggest threat to centaurs in their history. Imagine modern humans pouring through holes into *this* world. Imagine tanks and fighter planes, men with guns—"

Dewey broke off.

Hal fought back an urge to cover his ears. An awful nagging thought had just entered the back of his mind. "So what did the centaurs do?" he asked quietly.

"They vowed amongst themselves to stop the mining," Dewey said. "They started campaigning against it. But in case that failed, they wanted a back-up plan. In case thousands or millions of humans poured through and started taking over the land, shooting everything that might be a threat, the centaurs developed something that would wipe out the human race for good. Something that would kill the humans *only*, and not the centaurs or anything else."

He waited, clearly feeling that he'd said enough.

"The virus," Hal whispered.

"What?" Robbie said. "No! You're not—but—"

Abigail said nothing, just stared and stared.

Dewey looked down at himself, then abruptly changed into his human form. He shakily handed her the ball and magnifying glass, and stood awkwardly, wringing his hands. "I don't think I want to be a centaur anymore."

Hal was having trouble believing it. "What *happened*?"

"The centaur I'm cloned from—or however it's done—was one of the centaurs working on the project. That's how I know all this. I guess Miss Simone wanted a volunteer and this one offered, being a scientist and all. He obviously had no idea some of his memories would carry over to me." Dewey shrugged. "I don't know exactly what happened, except that I have a feeling of fear and worry and disaster, like something went wrong. Maybe it was an accident. Maybe they tested the virus and it got out of control. Or maybe a rogue centaur released it on purpose. I don't know, but I have a strong feeling that it wasn't supposed to happen."

"Only it did," Robbie said grimly.

"Yes," Dewey said. "And of course they covered it up, pretending to work on an antivirus. Maybe they *have* an antivirus already." He gave a sudden, bitter laugh. "Imagine that. They release a virus by mistake, killing millions, and then hurry to Miss Simone's aid and act horrified and supportive, working around the clock to create an antivirus. Then, as time passes and they realize they actually *got away with it*, that nobody suspects them . . . well, then they decide to hold off on the antivirus after all. They just *pretend* to work on it, hoping that—"

Dewey broke off, and Abigail got up to put an arm around him. She stood a couple of inches taller, so his head fit nicely on her shoulder as he struggled to fight back tears.

As the village of Carter went about its business, and Miss Simone recovered from her nasty sting, Hal, Robbie, Abigail, and Dewey stood there in the park with the weight of the world on their shoulders. The weight of *two* worlds. They needed to tell Miss Simone, of course . . . but then what? Would this be the start of a war against centaurs? Could they be made to help deliver an antivirus and put things right, or would they stand firm and refuse?

And what about the hole in the labyrinth? What if those soldiers traced the dragon back to the basement of that demolished house? Hal and Abigail may have inadvertently led them to this world, just as the centaurs had feared.

Hal closed his eyes. It had seemed that his troubles were over and he could spend a few days relaxing, enjoying his new home with his friends. Now it looked as though the *real* trouble was about to start.